The Quanderhorn Xperimentations

ROB GRANT &
ANDREW MARSHALL

This paperback published in Great Britain in 2020 by Gollancz

First published in Great Britain in 2018 by Gollancz
an imprint of the Orion Publishing Group Ltd
Carmelite House, 50 Victoria Embankment
London EC4Y 0DZ

An Hachette UK Company

1 3 5 7 9 10 8 6 4 2

A CIP catalogue record for this book is
available from the British Library.

ISBN 978 1 473 22403 2

Typeset by Input Data Services Ltd, Somerset

Printed and bound in Great Britain
by Clays Ltd, Elcograf S.p.A.

www.gollancz.co.uk

For Sioned

PREFACE

During the current restoration of the Palace of Westminster certain documents and artefacts were discovered, hidden in a bricked-up alcove behind the mechanisms in the clock tower popularly known as 'Big Ben'.

They were quickly dismissed as a hoax, and a rather pointless and unconvincing one at that. For reasons far too circuitous to elaborate, the material eventually found its way to us. There were dozens of volumes of badly scrawled personal journals and various sketch pads and notebooks crammed with strange inventions and astonishing designs, together with some extraordinarily curious devices, the purpose of which has yet to be established.

Intrigued, we ploughed through everything, and the results of that research are here in these pages.

If it *is* a hoax, it's a very elaborate and clever one, in that it's impossible to disprove.

Where there are multiple accounts of the same incident, we have chosen what appears to be the most credible. Since the journals are personal, they tend to present their author in a most favourable light. When this understandable foible is in danger of distorting the truth, we have used aggregates of the accounts and our best guesses to arrive at a more likely accurate version.

Where facts are disputed, we have pointed out the alternatives in our footnotes.

For reasons that will quickly become apparent, it was painfully difficult to establish a sequential chronology to these events. Hence, we present this account in the way it was revealed to us, and leave readers to make up their own minds.

RG & AM, London 2018. Probably.

1

Chlorophyll

We all have our time machines, don't we. Those that
take us back are memories . . . And those that carry us
forward, are dreams

H.G. Wells, *New Worlds For Old*

Chapter One

From the journal of Brian Nylon, 31st December, 1952

I clawed my way out of a swirling vortex of strangling black velvet. I was either unconscious, or trapped under one of the Beverley Sisters' show dresses. Mercifully for Joy, Teddie or Babs, it was the former.

Slowly, painfully, a distant pinprick of light coalesced, dazzled and finally settled into a nauseating corona around the head of the most beautiful woman I'd ever seen. She was looking down at me and gently slapping my face very hard.

I had no idea who she was. And worse than that: I had no idea who I was, either.

I noticed I was uncomfortable. I was lying on some rather scratchy hessian sacking on a cold, hard metal floor. We were juddering, in motion. A manual gearbox protested loudly. I raised my head. We were in the back of a van of some kind. A series of makeshift shelves held stacks of bizarre machinery and tools. A sign pasted over the back window read WARNING: THIS DOOR LEADS TO OUTSIDE.

The exquisite goddess leaning over me said: 'Brian'. It seemed a strange name for a woman.

'Hello, Brian,' I said. But this only made Aphrodite slap me harder.

'*You're* Brian, you mutton-head.'

'Am I? Who are you?'

'Oh no. You've lost your memory, haven't you? It's *me*, Dr. Janussen.'

'Dr. Janussen?'

'Gemini? Gemma? Good grief, it's really wiped this time.'

I was suddenly gripped by a very exciting thought: 'Are you my wife?'

This produced a fleeting snort of cruel laughter in the divine creature, yet she neglected to answer.

'Where are we?' I tried.

'There's no time to explain right now.'

Just then a masculine voice called from the front cabin: 'Is it left here?'

I raised my head further and espied a handsome young brute in the driving seat: artfully tousled blue-black hair, a steely jaw and a fierce intelligence in his eyes.

'Is it left here?' he repeated louder.

The lovely woman, who may or may not have been my wife, blinked with the merest hint of exasperation. 'No, Troy.'

'Is it *right* then?'

'No, Troy. There are no turnings. We're on Lambeth Bridge.'

'So – straight on, is it?'

'Yes, I think that's best.' She sighed and turned back to me. 'You see? We've had to put *Troy* in the driving seat. Can you please concentrate? We need you right now.'

'Yes, yes, I'm . . . I'm trying.'

Outside, I began to make out sounds – crowds of people in the distance, shouting, panicking, screaming.

The lovely woman gripped my face and hauled it towards her.

'Listen, your name is *Brian Nylon*. You're twenty-four years old, and you work with me in Professor Quanderhorn's research team. The very fabric of Reality depends entirely on our actions in the next ten minutes. Don't be alarmed. No, actually be very alarmed. Am I getting through to you?'

Her fragrant breath enveloped me like a cloud of jasmine and honeysuckle. 'You figgy nails are diggy indo by cheeeeks,' I mumbled through involuntarily gritted teeth.

'We've run out of "straight on",' Troy called from the front.

'Head right, and aim for the big clock.'

'Okey-doos. Got you. Big clock. No problem.' Troy chewed on his lower lip for a second. 'What's a clock?'

'That thing with the white face and two hands.'

'I thought that was Brian.'

'There! There! That huge round thing! There!' My possible wife Dr. Janussen pointed urgently, mercifully releasing her grip on my cheeks. 'And quickly!'

The sounds of the panicking crowd grew louder. Through the rear window, I glimpsed them as we zipped past: hordes of misted faces haloed by street lamps, contorted in fear and horror. What on earth were we getting into? And what had Dr. Janussen meant by 'the fabric of Reality'?

The van stopped suddenly, but I didn't. My head crashed through a cardboard box and when I retracted it, I found a small glass valve had jammed itself up my nose. Whilst I was gingerly teasing it out, Dr. Janussen had already leapt out of the rear door. Troy seemed to be struggling to open his.

'We have to go, *now*!' Dr. Janussen yelled, rummaging through a haversack.

Troy yelled back, 'I can't get out!'

5

'We've been through this before, Troy: it's the *handle*, remember?'

'Of course I remember about handles! I'm not an . . . an— Brian, what are those really stupid people called?'

'Idiots?' I offered.

'Yes, I'm not an idiots.'

I was beginning to revise my initial impression of the ferocity of Troy's intelligence. He grabbed the handle and to my astonishment, ripped the door entirely from its housing, tumbling with it out onto the pavement with a metallic clatter and a faint yelp of surprise. Who *were* these people?

Before I'd managed to entirely remove the CV6094 Induction Diode from my nasal canal, Dr. Janussen grabbed my arm and yanked me out of the van.

We were standing in Parliament Square. Silhouetted in the moonlight, Big Ben frowned down upon the panicking multitudes, its face displaying seven minutes to midnight. A struggling line of mounted police barely held back the sea of jabbering humanity, who were torn between fascination and fear. Many of them, rather curiously, were wearing small, cone-shaped cardboard hats and carrying paper trumpets.

I had no idea what was happening. 'What's happening?' I asked the beautiful doctor.

'There's no time to explain right now.' She passed me a large, heavy tube. 'Here's your bazooka.'

Chapter Two

From the journal of Brian Nylon, 1st January, 1952 –
Iteration 66

I thanked her. I looked at it. It was indeed a bazooka. 'Just a minute!' I called.

But she was already fighting her way through the human tide. 'Don't fire unless it comes towards you,' she yelled helpfully over her shoulder.

'Unless *what* comes towards me?' I shouted after her, but the crowd had folded in behind her.

So I was standing in Parliament Square at five minutes to midnight, wearing what I now realised were my winter long johns and a novelty Christmas sweater, holding a bazooka, with a valve still protruding from my nostril and a head full of unanswered questions.

Before I could even move, there was a sudden burst from a very loud loudhailer.

'Keep back!' rapped an echoing stentorian voice. 'Keep back from the Giant Broccoli Woman!'

It struck me that the crowd would hardly need this instruction, but a woman near me seemed reassured. 'Thank Gaawd! That's that Professor Quanderhorn,' she grinned, proudly

7

showing off her single tooth. 'He'll save us from the vegetable monster, and no mistake.' Her wizened hand scooped a fistful from a bag of whelks and she sucked on them excitedly.

'Do you reckon,' her mousey friend trilled, 'this is one of them alien invasions, or just another of the Professor's 'perimentations what has gone horribly wrong?'

'Now then, you ugly old termagants,' a cheerful bobby herded them away, 'move back for your own good. It's already eaten three people's faces.'

'Oooooh! We've never had a face-eater before,' the whelk woman cooed. 'I wish I'd known – I'd 'ave brought Bert's pigeon-racing binoculars.'

The loudhailer burst into life again. 'This is Quanderhorn himself speaking! Behind the railings, everyone! My team need room to operate!'

The sound of his voice again seemed to calm the crowd momentarily. Who the dickens *was* this Quanderhorn fellow?

I was about to ask the policeman, when a new chorus of piercing screams erupted all around, and the multitude parted before me.

And I saw it.

I can't swear it was the most spine-chilling, horrifying thing I'd ever laid eyes on, since I had no memory, but I did at that moment recall exactly what I'd had for breakfast, by virtue of its unexpectedly reappearing on the pavement beneath me. (For the record: spam and toast.)

I was most certainly looking at a monster. At least twelve feet tall, vaguely female in shape, it was green and knobbly, like . . . well, like a giant human broccoli. It was entirely covered over by a thick viscous mucus, as if a circus giant had been painted with glue and then sheep-dipped in an enormous St Patrick's Day spittoon.

It threw back its cabbage-like head and let out the most unearthly wail. The crowd drew back further, leaving me standing alone to face it.

It caught me in its monstrous gaze. Was it my imagination, or was there, for a fraction of a second, a spark of recognition in those hideous simulacra of human eyes? Frozen for one moment, I was almost tempted to step towards the wretched beast, when Dr. Janussen grabbed my arm again.

'Stop dawdling, Brian – the Professor needs us.'

She pulled me quickly away from the clock tower into New Palace Yard, where Troy was waiting. For some reason he had neglected to put on a suitable winter coat. Or, for that matter, a shirt. And I swear he'd slipped and fallen in some engine oil somewhere, because his rather muscular chest glistened un-nervingly in the street lamplight. For reasons that eluded me, a gaggle of teenaged girls who had pushed themselves to the front of the crowd shrieked inanely at his every move.

Dr. Janussen narrowed her eyes at the vehicle door under his arm.

'Troy, why have you still got that?'

'In case we need to lock up the van when we're not there.'

With remarkable patience, Dr. Janussen smiled. 'Get rid of it.'

'Righty-ho!' He promptly folded the van door several times, like he was making an origami swan, and leant it against the fence. Clearly, the lad was possessed of an exceptional strength.

She continued briskly: 'The Professor needs us to wheel out Gargantua, the Toposonic Cannon.'

Troy struck a casual pose reminiscent of bodybuilding contests, to the sound of more pubescent squeals. 'Consider it done.' He bounded off into the shadows, muscles a-rippling.

There was a strange whinnying sound, and he re-emerged

clutching the forelegs of a rather disgruntled police horse over his shoulders, dragging the struggling beast behind him.

The loudhailer barked: 'No, Troy, the one with the wheels.'

'Right you are, Pops!' Troy grinned amiably. Whirling the angry horse somewhat carelessly into a hedge, he spat on his hands and missed, then raced back into the shadows.

I looked over to the source of the rebuke. Some way in the distance, atop a hydraulic platform looming high above the crowd, was a tall, imposing figure, shrouded in a British Warm overcoat, his features shadowed beneath the brim of a brown slouch hat. He raised his loudhailer once more and pointed it directly towards us.

'Not to panic unnecessarily, Troy,' he barked, 'but the very fabric of existence is at stake.'

This sent a rustle of worried murmuring through the crowd.

Across the yard, Troy emerged again with a thick rope around his waist, towing an entire London bus.

'Not the red one,' Dr. Janussen smiled patiently. 'The one that looks like a cannon.'

'Are you sure a bus won't do?' Troy offered a winning grin. 'It's the 43 to Highgate Woods.'

'Get the cannon, Troy.' Dr. Janussen glanced towards the clock face. Three minutes before midnight. 'Now!'

Just then, an agitated murmuring swept across the crowd. I heard a man in pinstriped trousers and bowler hat shout: 'By ginger! The beastly article is starting to scale Big Ben!'

At first, I couldn't spot the creature, but suddenly, with a loud electric rasp, a powerful beam, brighter than a magnesium flare, blasted from Quanderhorn's platform, stabbing through the gloom, starkly illuminating the foul travesty of a humanoid as it clung to the masonry. Temporarily blinded, it slipped slightly, to a communal gasp from the throng, then recovered and began once more hauling itself up the tower. It moved with astonishing agility, considering its clumsy, cumbersome frame.

In a voice that chilled me to my combinations, Dr. Janussen hissed: 'Brian, it's imperative she doesn't reach the clock.'

'Why?'

'She may prevent it striking twelve—'

'Why must it strike twelve?'

'There's no time to explain right now. We need to warm up the cannon. Get out there and delay her.'

'What? Wi-with my bazooka?' I looked down at the infernal tube. I had no idea which way round it went or how to fire it without being catapulted backwards into the Thames.

'No! Of course not with the bazooka. *Distract* her.'

'What do you mean "distract her"?'

'Flirt with her!'

'*Flirt?*'

I looked over at the unspeakable monstrosity, oozing a trail of vile green slime up Sir Charles Barry's exquisite Gothic revival stonework.

'In front of all these people?'

'You are *such* a Boy Scout.'

'Why me?'

'That thing – it's Virginia.'

'Virginia?' I shook my head. The name meant nothing to me.

'She used to be part of the team.'

I looked around again at the suppurating behemoth. I was suddenly gripped by a very disturbing thought.

'Was she my wife?'

'Not *everybody's* your wife. What's *wrong* with you, for heaven's sake?'

I glanced again at the grotesque mutation. 'And I'm supposed to *flirt* with her?'

11

'We all thought she was rather soft on you.'

'But how did she—'

'There's no time to explain right now – get out there and shout sweet nothings!'

'And why is there never any time to explain anything?' But Dr. Janussen had hastened over to the extraordinary contraption Troy was finally trundling over the cobblestones. It was on caterpillar tracks, like a tank, but the cannon barrel looked more like a giant elongated version of the valve that my nose had recently accommodated. Troy shimmied up a lamppost, pulled out the bulb and plugged a long flex in its place. The giant valve began to glow blue and buzz like an angry beehive.

I gingerly leant the bazooka against a wall, adjusted my reindeer pullover to cover the flap of my long johns, and strode purposefully towards the beast. At the base of the tower, I cleared my throat and cupped my hands.

'Uhm . . . Virginia! Hullo there! It's . . . it's me!'

The abomination stopped in its tracks, slowly turned its hideous visage towards me, and bellowed in a subhuman growl. The word was distorted and garbled, but undeniably recognizable.

'Brrriiiiiiii-annn?'

I very slightly wet myself.

Chapter Three

From the journal of Brian Nylon, 1st January, 1952 –
Iteration 66

'Ha ha. Yes . . . Honey bunch – it's me, Brian.'

A large tendril fell off her and hit the ground with a splat beside me.

'Brrriiiiiii-annn?' she/it repeated.

I glanced round at the horrified faces of the rapt crowd. 'Yes, uhm . . . Lambikins.'

A wave of distaste swept through the throng. A small urchin threw a half-sucked gobstopper which struck the back of my head painfully and stuck there. I ignored it with dignity.

'I was wondering if you might – if you feel like it – stop snacking on people's faces for just one moment and come down from there?'

The beast let out a pained and angry howl, then turned back to the climb.

'Wait! Virginia! I've been thinking – how would you feel about our going steady?' This stopped the creature briefly, but there were more groans and some rather distasteful insults from the mob. I pressed on desperately: 'Obviously we wouldn't want to rush towards a wedding straight away. I mean, at the reception we wouldn't know what greens to serve with the chicken—'

'*Grunghhnnnuhn!*' Virginia howled. Somehow, I seemed to have enraged her.

'All right, all right: we'll get married straight away! We'll have children together. A boy who takes after me, and a girl who looks like a huge Brussels sprout.'

'*Gnghhnnarhhhgnuhn!*'

A nun from a silent order suddenly yelled: 'You're a bloody awful flirt!' Then clapped her hand over her mouth and crossed herself.

Out of the corner of my eye, I saw Troy furiously cranking a handle to elevate the cannon's glowing barrel. The broccoli creature was almost at the clock face. It was one minute to midnight. I needed to buy just a little more time. Perhaps if I appealed to the *person* inside the beast.

'Listen – Virginia – I don't know what's happened to make you this way, but try to remember you started out as a human being. And you still have that elusive spark of humanity inside you . . . I'm sure there's a future for you of dignity and mutual respect and peaceful co-habitation . . .'

She stopped. She turned to me. She exploded.

Quanderhorn's strange device had blasted her into thousands of fragments of sloppy green flesh and ribbons of foul-smelling viscera. The crowd shrieked as the ghastly carrion rained down on them.

There was a small moment of silence. A lurid flatfish-shaped organ splatted onto my shoulder and flapped alarmingly in its death throes. I slapped it to the ground and stamped on it, realising too late I was in my stockinged feet.

Big Ben began to chime the hour. I looked up from my saturated sock to see Troy's beaming face.

'Bullseye, eh?' He winked. 'Are you OK?'

'I'm covered in the green slimy entrails of a respected colleague. How do you think I am?'

A strange expression clouded Troy's handsome features. His mouth opened and closed like a fish undergoing a rectal examination. By a crab.

'Never ask Troy to think. You might damage him,' Dr. Janussen chided. 'Troy, stop thinking at once.' This seemed to do the trick.

The loudhailer barked: 'Simple common folk – you can all go back to your celebrations. Well done everyone. But mostly me.'

The midnight chime rang, but it had a curious tone to it – a sort of whooshing reverse echo – and I felt momentarily light-headed. Had I sustained some kind of minor head injury in the *mêlée*, I wondered?

There was a small, shuffling pause, then various appalling renditions of 'Auld Lang Syne' began to break out among the cheering multitude. Of course! New Year! Scanning the revellers, I spotted some 'Happy 1952' banners. Some small part of my brain thought that odd, but I couldn't put my finger on why.

Troy and Dr. Janussen had started packing the equipment away. I was turning to help them when I felt on my elbow a rather brusque tug, which had enough force to spin me round.

I was facing an imposingly tall and wide man in improbable sunglasses. 'Do you know what this is?' He nodded down to where a large object was tenting the front of his raincoat.

I licked my dry lips. 'I'm sincerely hoping it's a gun.'

The object jerked to the left threateningly. Gun or not, it seemed prudent to heed its instruction.

The mysterious figure ushered me down a dark alley. Was this to be the end for Brian Whatever My Second Name was?

Shot in a dingy alleyway, for murky reasons I couldn't even re-member? The echo of our footsteps changed in timbre slightly. I looked up to see we were approaching a dead end. This was it, whatever 'it' was. In an attempt to appear slightly less cowardly than I actually was, I turned to face my tormentor and casually asked him 'What now?' with my eyebrow. Sadly, having raised the eyebrow, I couldn't get it down again.

He leant over, I assumed to strangle me, but instead he pressed a protruding brick by my shoulder. The wall behind me slid aside smoothly and, with a reassuringly metallic prod from the overcoat object, I turned again and stepped into the darkness.

Chapter Four

*From the journal of Brian Nylon, 1st January, 1952 –
Iteration 66*

I was in some kind of office. I glanced around, but the wall had
slid back in place, and my escort had vanished as suddenly as
he'd appeared.

As my eyes adjusted to the gloom I picked out, on a large
mahogany desk before me, a brandy decanter, a cigar humidor,
a whisky decanter, a spare cigar humidor, a rum decanter, another brandy decanter, what appeared to be a vodka decanter,
yet another brandy decanter, a barrel of Watney's Pale and
several cases of Veuve Clicquot Brut 1937.

Behind it all, panting and dribbling, sat an absolutely enormous bulldog in a bow tie. Its cold blue eyes held me for a
terrifying moment, then it cleared its throat, leant into the foggy
beam of the weak desk lamp and exhaled a plume of blue-grey
smoke. Not, in fact, a bulldog at all, but none other than . . .

'Prime Minister Winston Churchill!'

'Agent Penetrator!'

I looked around for this agent person. There was no one in
the room but us.

'Agent who?'

'Blast and damnation!' the Great Man rumbled. 'It's just as we feared: they've arranged for you to "forget" the past few months.'

'They?'

'That infernal Quanderhorn and his cronies, of course.'

'Professor Quanderhorn wiped my memory?'

'You're fortunate it was only your memory: one agent had his entire mind wiped. We had to raise him again as if from birth. You can only imagine the horror of potty training an eighteen stone rugger player with a fondness for vindaloos.'

'So Agent Penetrator is . . . me?'

'That's right, Nylon.' (Nylon! Yes – *that* was my name!) 'You're an undercover operative, inserted by Her Majesty's Government, which is to say myself, into Quanderhorn's team, along with Agent Cuckoo.'

'There's *another* agent?'

Churchill regarded me rather sadly. 'You're wearing her intestines as a cravat.'

'No, that *is* my cravat . . .' I felt round my neck to straighten it. It was wet and slimy. I yelled 'Urghh!' involuntarily, and hurled it across the room. 'That *thing* on the tower – Virginia: she was a Government spy, too?'

'You were both supposed to be rooting out just what the blazes that lunatic Quanderhorn's up to.'

'Up to? What makes you think he's up to anything?'

'Pah!' Mr. Churchill poured himself a snifter and took a generous draught. He dabbed dry his lips and fixed me once again with his bulldog stare. 'Let me ask you this: what year is it?'

I cast my mind back to the banners in the crowd. '1952, of course.'

Mr. Churchill's eyes twinkled impishly. 'And last year was . . .'

'Well, obviously, last year was . . .' I suddenly realised what had been troubling me about those banners earlier. Clearly, I had *some* memory. 'Great Scott! Last year was *also* 1952!'

'And it was 1952 the year before that. In fact, by our reckoning, it's been 1952 for the past sixty-six years.'

This was quite some rabbit hole I'd tumbled into. The same year over and over again?

'But that's impossible!'

'That brigand Quanderhorn does the impossible for breakfast. We don't know how, but he's got us trapped in some kind of infernal temporal Möbius band, and we can't escape.'

'But if you're sure it's Quanderhorn's doing, why don't you stop him?'

'It isn't so easy! Not the least of our problems is the confounded maniac's a national hero! He's saved us from countless Martian invasions, umpteen deadly space rays and three unspeakable outbreaks of reefer madness.'

Martian invasions? Deadly space rays? My head was whirling.

'But why hasn't everybody noticed this 1952 thing?'

'You'll find, Penetrator, that most people notice hardly anything. It's the basis upon which we've run this country for the last three hundred years.'

'Well, we should tell them!'

'Tell them? Good grief, man, there'd be panic in the streets! Society would collapse! There'd be civil war! Riots! Food shortages! Cannibalism! I'd have to resign! Is that what you want, Penetrator? *Labour in power?*'

I don't know why, but I immediately snapped back, 'Good God, no!' I may have had very little memory, but even I knew that was insanity.

There was a hiss and a slight grating sound behind me. The

owner of the overcoat bulge leant in, and gruffled: 'They're looking for him,' then left.

'You'd best be off, Penetrator.'

'Right. But . . .' I had no idea what on earth was expected of me. And whatever it was, whether I wanted to do it. And there was something else. 'Um, Prime Minister – I don't suppose there's any chance I could have a different code name, is there? Something slightly less . . . aggressive and treacherous?'

He utterly ignored me. 'The whole nation is relying upon you, Penetrator. Find out what's going on, and report back to me.'

'How will I get in touch?'

'I'll find you, Penetrator, I'll find you.'

I turned to leave, then turned back. 'One more thing, sir: can you possibly tell me who I am?'

But Mr. Churchill had gone, leaving behind nothing but the faint aroma of Havana cigars, brandy and, for some reason, herring.

I wandered back up the alley trying to gather my very scattered thoughts. Was I really a spy, or was I really a scientist? It was all devilishly confusing. I found myself back in the celebratory bustle, and fought through the merry, singing, kissing crowd towards Dr. Janussen.

The van was almost packed. I felt slightly guilty. Troy looked up from hoisting an improbably heavy slab of machinery into the vehicle. 'There he is! Brian – where've you been?'

'Well, I was just. . .' I began. Cold as the weather was, I found myself suddenly sweating. My tongue seemed to double in size, as if I'd just chewed a wasp. Try as I might, I couldn't finish the sentence. I couldn't, quite frankly, even think of a *word*. '. . . *muhnamunhah*.'

They stared at me. 'Brian – you may have forgotten that

you're very, very bad at lying,' Gemma smiled pityingly.

'I'm not lying,' I lied. 'It's just . . .' Then, with a merciful inspiration: 'There isn't time to explain right now.'

They seemed satisfied by this, thank heavens, and we packed up in silence.

That had been a close call. Whoever these people were, I needed to keep them on my side if I was ever to find out what the devil had happened to me.

Chapter Five

The van had been loaded into the belly of an ex-army cargo plane, and we were *en route* to the Professor's lab, which I gathered was 'somewhere on the road to Carlisle'. Whatever that meant.

Alarmingly, the pilots' seats had been removed from the cockpit and replaced with what appeared to be a cannibalised player piano, its bridge pins and hammer flanges connected by an intricate system of levers and wires to various flight controls. It played a complex, silent symphony on the instrument panel as reams of punched paper rolled furiously upwards. Despite its impossibly eccentric nature, the peculiar mechanism did seem to be keeping the bird in trim, at least.

Quanderhorn himself had clearly seen fit to travel separately by some other, and doubtless superior, means, leaving us wretched minions to fend for ourselves in steerage.

From an equipment locker in the fuselage, I'd managed to dig out some army surplus trousers to restore my dignity, and a pair of mauve moccasins to instantly remove it again.

Despite the metallic shuddering and the relentless chopping

of the propellers, the others had managed to fall asleep quite easily. Dr. Janussen sprawled elegantly sideways on an unforgiving wooden bench, one foot crooked slightly above the other, slender hands tucked under one lovely cheek as she breathed gently in and out with a sweet, melodic and surprisingly penetrating snore. Troy had wrapped himself, cocoon-like, in some sort of curious white netting he'd found somewhere. He was smiling, mostly, but occasionally he would let out a small high-pitched yelp, and his feet would flail about desperately for a second or two, then he would sink back into his peaceful slumber.

No sleep for me. My mind raced back and forwards over the patchwork of incomplete facts about myself I'd managed to stitch together rather poorly.

I worked for this mysterious Professor Quanderhorn, who was being investigated by the Government, in the form of me. Also. I seemed to have some sort of attachment to Dr. Janussen, about which she remained distressingly ambiguous. What had happened to me to make me forget vast swathes of my life? Was it a deliberate act of sabotage? Or was it the result of some kind of scientific experiment gone wrong, as had obviously happened to the wretched Virginia?

Beyond that, things got considerably murkier.

Plainly, I could remember certain things. I could speak, for instance, and read and write. I seemed to know London quite well, and I'd recognised the Prime Minister almost immediately. I had, however, no recollection of my past in any way. Not my parents, nor any siblings, certainly not my schooling: nothing at all biographical.

I was clearly not a Cockney – I didn't say 'stone the crows' or anything like that – but beyond that, I really had no idea about my background. My hands were quite smooth, so I obviously wasn't a manual labourer, and I had no tattoos, so I'd never been a sailor. I tried saluting, but I didn't seem very good at it — I wasn't sure which way round my hand went at the top — so any military career was probably out of the reckoning. Quickly checking the others were still slumbering, I stood up on an impulse and tried tap-dancing. No good at that, either, especially in embarrassing suede moccasins. Thank *heavens* I wasn't in show business!

I found a long stick and made an attempt at drawing the head of a noble horse in the dust at my feet, but it just looked like a slug with a grin. No George Stubbs, I. Ah! But at least I could recall art history. And some algebra! I could decline the Latin noun *mensa* with consummate ease, but that appeared to be the entire extent of my grip on other languages. On the other hand, I seemed to have a quite startling reservoir of arcane cricket minutiae. I found I instinctively didn't really trust foreigners, and the thought of a lukewarm suet pudding and thick custard with a rubbery skin filled me with deep yearning.

Clearly, I was an Englishman.

In fact, I was beginning to feel a deep-seated need to stand behind someone and wait for something.

More than that, however, I really couldn't tell. Was I a *good* man? I certainly felt like one. But then, why was I spying on these people who seemed to be my friends? And hadn't I just acted as a decoy so a dear colleague could be blasted to smithereens?

Despite these tortured thoughts, and the occasional glance to reassure myself that the piano was flying the plane properly, I found the regular chop-chop-chop of the props had begun to make my eyes feel heavy, and I surrendered, finally, to Morpheus' embrace.

It was a troubled sleep, in which I ran backwards and forwards with no trousers, pursued by huge psychopathic vegetables spouting Latin grammar and hurling sloppy custard-covered intestines at my head. What could it possibly mean?

And there were other dreams: I was lounging on a riverbank with a woman, listening to an enormous radio – was that my mother? My sister? My wife? . . . Me, in a dark cave tied in a chair with giant mole-like creatures giving me Chinese burns while chanting some infernal dirge . . . Tearing open my shirt to find a player piano roll embedded in my chest . . . Walking into Lyons' Corner House at 213 Piccadilly and being served afternoon tea by Winston Churchill in a waitress outfit. I had no idea which were memories and which simply disturbing dreams. I was praying the naked trigonometry exam with my fountain pen full of bull semen was the latter.

The Professor's laboratory was far away from . . . well, from everywhere. We made our way from a makeshift airfield in a very old jeep with a large Q stencilled on its side. It appeared to have had its roof sawn off and its suspension deliberately removed. Troy spent a great deal of time looking for the door, until Dr. Janussen pointed out it wasn't there, and he was finally persuaded to jump in.

For some reason, it became clear that I was expected to drive, and I was relieved to find I remembered how. More interestingly, whilst Dr. Janussen was supposed to give me directions, I seemed to know the way instinctively. Though any mental picture of our destination still eluded me.

On the Carlisle road, the trip was merely horribly uncomfortable, as the tiniest stone in our path rocked the entire vehicle, but once our route took us off it, things rather deteriorated. We lurched down a long, overgrown path, cratered with pot-holes, over jutting boulders and through thick bracken. Overhanging branches snapped alarmingly on the windscreen and raked the top of my head. I found it exhausting trying to wrestle the wheel just to keep us pointing vaguely in the right direction.

I'd planned to ask Dr. Janussen a great many questions, but conversation was impossible. Troy, however, had once again fallen into deep and sonorous slumber. This time, he seemed to have glued himself to the seat by means that escaped me, and was untroubled by the bone-rattling vibrations. And was it my imagination, or had his skin turned ever so slightly the colour of the upholstery?

As we got closer, I began to spot a sequence of warning signs nailed to the trees, featuring mind-boggling graphics I couldn't begin to guess the meaning of: a silhouette of a man being rained on by penguins; a Red Indian being electrocuted whilst sitting on a fat woman; a rabbit and an '=' sign followed by a skull and crossbones with a Robin Hood hat on. And those were the less bewildering ones.

Finally, the rude forest gave way to a clearing, leading to the crest of a hill. As we trundled over its brow, the dawning sun cast a red/orange glow over the long-abandoned exhausted quarry below, inside which the vast laboratory complex nestled.

Chapter Six

From the journal of Brian Nylon, 1st January, 1952 –
Iteration 66

It was far more extensive than I'd imagined. It sprawled below us, a hotchpotch of dozens of buildings and outhouses, scattered randomly. At its heart were rows of ex-military warehousing, Nissen huts and the like, but there were many and varied later additions, some conventional, others inexplicably eccentric. One or two of them towered dizzyingly upwards, to be cut off by the early morning fog.

We lurched down towards a set of imposing gates, which were cast from some peculiar shiny chocolate brown alloy I couldn't identify. I stopped the jeep.

There was an unnerving pause, then a chorus of servos screeched into life, and a whole bank of articulated box cameras swivelled as one in our direction.

I was unaccountably nervous. For some reason, I pulled the genial face I usually put on for photographs. The one Mumsie always told me off about, because it made me look like Simple Simon. (What? Was that an actual memory?)

Eventually, the cameras lost interest and turned away, dropping their heads. The great gates began to swing open majestically.

From a high-mounted speaker a curiously metallic woman's voice said: '*You are positively identified. Welcome back, everyone.*'

'Thank you.' I smiled, and turned to Dr. Janussen. 'Who's that charming lady? Is she the Professor's wife?'

'Not every woman in the world has to be someone's *wife*! You clot!' she chided, rather more brusquely than was called for in my opinion. Looking closer, I noticed there was something 'off' about her appearance, but I couldn't fathom what.

I drove very slowly through several layers of indescribably strange defensive measures, including, rather worryingly at one point, a dog kennel the size of a sentry box. From its dark interior, a pair of red glowing eyes followed us hungrily. Clearly, the Professor did not welcome the uninvited visitor.

Finally, we rattled up to what I assumed was the main laboratory building, which appeared to be an old abandoned fever hospital. I pulled up in the cobbled quadrangle outside it, where some very peculiar vehicles were parked, all stamped with that same Q stencil.

Troy opened his eyes and pulled himself off the seat with a strange sort of suction noise, and panicked momentarily trying to find a door again, until Dr. Janussen brought him a loose one stacked nearby. 'Thanks, Gem.' He grabbed it and jumped to the ground. 'Thought I'd be trapped in there all day.'

The good doctor's brow was furrowed as she peered intensely into the wing mirror, clearly perturbed by something. 'Are you all right, Dr. Janussen?' I asked.

'Look at my face, Brian,' she ordered earnestly, turning to me. 'Tell me honestly: what do you see?'

I gazed at that lovely countenance. Again I sensed there was something askew. But I couldn't for the life of me work it out.

'It's a spot, isn't it?' she smiled, with a faintly unnerving kind of calm.

I leant in closer and squinted. There may have been some kind of minor discolouration about the size of a single pore, just beside her nose. 'There might just be a tiny—'

'Trust you to point it out! How d'you think that makes me feel?' She punched me quite hard on the shoulder, spun on her heels and attempted to march with dignity towards the lab, her hand cupped over her nose. Sadly, this obscured her view, causing her to stumble ungraciously over protruding cobblestones until she tottered through the entrance and raced up a stairway.

Troy and I exchanged glances, then tramped across the courtyard after her.

A small plumpish man appeared at the doors to greet us. His upper lip was obscured by a full tash, which had at one time been well kempt, and probably at that one time had considerably fewer biscuit crumbs decorating it. He wore a faded dark green uniform and peaked cap to which the letters of the word 'JANITOR' had at one time been glued, though the 'J', the 'A', the 'O' and the 'R' had long since fallen off, leaving only the word 'NIT'. I didn't say anything.

He called to Troy: 'You can leave that door, young sir – we've plenty of our own.'

'Oh, right-ho, Jenkins,' the lad chirruped. He hurled the door away a quite superhuman distance and disappeared inside with a cheery wave.

'Good morning, Mr. Nylon, sir.' Jenkins offered a very smart salute. Turns out the palms face *outwards*.

'And you're . . . Jenkins . . . the janitor?'

'Yes, sir. The Professor told me you'd gorn and lost your memory again.'

'*Again?*'

'We'll just do the usual thing: I'll show you around the place, as per. This way, sir . . .'

For some reason, I instinctively mistrusted this Jenkins fellow: there was something going on behind his eyes that belied his servile manner. He led me down corridors with dark green linoleum floors and chocolate brown painted walls, seemingly without end.

We walked in silence for a while. There were yet more inexplicable warning signs on most of the doors: a coalman whose teeth were on fire; a pair of goggles with legs fleeing a giant lightning bolt with a bow tie. Some doors had been nailed up extremely securely with planks across them, others hung off their hinges loosely. More than one colour of smoke issued from underneath many of them. The occasional alcove held what looked like heavily modified fire extinguishers crossed with flame-throwers, others fire axes, and now and then, disturbingly, the odd samurai sword.

Out of the blue, Jenkins piped up: 'Rum business, innit, sir?'

'What particular business would that be?'

'What they done to Miss Virginia, turning her into a vegetable like that. Ain't decent. 'Course they says it was an accident, but they always says that.'

I felt a horrible tightening in my bowels. 'Are you suggesting it *wasn't* an accident?'

'Least said, soonest mended.' Jenkins tapped the side of his nose and half-winked. It wasn't a particularly fetching gesture. However, I took the hint, and we mounted a staircase without further conversation. At the landing, we passed through a green baize door to a corridor where the *décor* was somewhat softer and less institutionalised.

'Here's the living quarters, sir.' Somehow, Jenkins managed to imbue the 'sir' with a kind of dumb insolence.

I heard a strange buzzing thudding sound, like a giant wasp hitting a window. I looked at Jenkins querulously.

'That's young Master Troy Quanderhorn's room.'

'*Quanderhorn?* Is he the Professor's son?'

'They put it *about* he's the Professor's son,' Jenkins nodded, 'but some do say he *grew* him in a petri dish.'

'*What?*'

'Used his own genetical material and made him extra strong with a pinch of insect.'

'He's part *insect?*' Well, that did explain rather a lot.

'Word to the wise, sir: do watch out when he's swarming.'

'*Swarming?*'

'The Professor's terrible proud of him, though. Claims he's a "major breakthrough in Artificial Stupidity". Least said, soonest mended, sir.'

We passed the next door. Jenkins nodded at it. 'Dr. Janussen you already know.' He raised a cheeky eyebrow. What was this upstart implying?

'Was she all right just now? I mean, she seemed a bit—'

'Nothing wrong with her. Nothing at all, sir. Excepting half her brain is clockwork.'

What did one say to such an outlandish assertion? I tried: 'Surely not!'

'She was in a car crash, and the Professor had to rebuild her slightly. 'Course they *says* it was a car crash, but they always says that.'

'Goodness! A car crash!' The poor darling. 'And you say her brain is *clockwork?*'

'Just the right-hand side, sir, the logical half.' He stopped and drew me in closer, lowering his voice and treating me to a wave of Mackeson breath. 'Sometimes her emotions run the mechanism down, and then . . .' He mimed a silent explosion. 'All I'm saying: if her ear starts to rotate, just get yourself out of there, sharpish.'

Of course! That was what I'd found peculiar about her appearance in the jeep: her ear was at an angle of forty-five degrees! I needed to ask him more before he said "Least said, soonest mended".

'Jenkins – this rotating ear—'

'You're going to have to meet the Professor, of course.' He cut me off rather impertinently. 'I'll need to go and clear it with him. I'm sure you'd like to freshen up in your own room, Mr. Nylon . . .'

'Oh yes. Very much.'

'Unfortunately, we can't have you wandering by yourself around willy-nilly with your memory all shot, so if it's OK with you, sir, I'm just going to put you in here, temporarily, with the Martian.'

Chapter Seven

From the journal of Brian Nylon, 1st January, 1952 –
Iteration 66

'I need to— Wh— Did you just say "Martian"?'

'That's right, sir. He's a hostage, from the last Invasion. 'Tween you and me, I don't think they wanted him back'.

He slid open the door.

I half expected the room to be dark and reek of sulphur, but it seemed bright and smelled of the kind of cheap aftershave a cad might wear.

'Word to the wise.' Jenkins leant in conspiratorially again. 'He learned Earth language watching *How Do You View*, starring Terry-Thomas – they says it's the only telly-vision signal they can receive up there, but—'

'Least said?'

'In one, sir. His name's "Guuuurk", by the way. Four *u*'s.'

I tried it. 'Guuu-uuurk?'

'Close enough, sir.' And with a rather impudently firm hand to my back, he shoved me into the Martian's abode.

I had no recollection of meeting a Martian before, but I did know they were our deadly enemies. I was expecting a furious great beast, chained to the walls and raging. But the figure in front of me was standing quite free and unencumbered. I bunched my fists by my sides involuntarily as he slowly turned towards me.

He had a bulbous purple head, about twice the size of a human's, with six eyes arranged symmetrically in pairs, three on either side of his face, a prominent beaky nose, and beneath it a rather fetching pencil moustache. He was surprisingly dapper, sporting a gold velvet smoking jacket with ebony facings and slightly shiny elbows, black dress trousers, sharply pressed, and a pair of inappropriately coloured moccasins, such as might be worn by a particularly shifty Italian gigolo. And at the moment, me.

He was in the act of decanting what smelled like cheap cooking sherry into an expensive bottle. He looked up and smiled. There was a rather endearing gap between his two front teeth. 'Hel*lo* there, Brian,' he trilled in a louche English accent.

'Hello, er, Guuuuu-uurk.'

'Ha! Three *u*'s too many, old thing. You are a card! Amontillado?'

'Uh, no thanks.'

'Very wise. I get it for thruppence ha'penny a gallon from the ironmonger's. I'd never touch the filthy stuff myself, but you did say a couple of schooners really helps grease the wheels with the fairer sex.' His eyes performed a rapid sequence of winks as he nodded towards his noticeboard, which was festooned with cut-outs of ladies from corset advertisements.

'I said that?'

'Well, not in so many words, you're too much of a gentleman. Listen.' He took a more serious tone. 'Terribly sorry to hear about Virginia. Beastly way to go. Commiserations, et cetera, et cetera.'

34

'I . . .' I decided not to confide in him about my memory loss. He *seemed* like a stand-up chap, but I just couldn't bring myself to trust a Martian. 'Thank you.'

'Honestly, it's a complete *fiasco* here. They're a *useless* shower. Wouldn't last a second on Mars.'

I suddenly felt very sorry for this poor desolate creature, imprisoned millions of miles from home, separated hopelessly from his friends, his countrymen and his familial comforts. Though I have to say, he'd made his 'cell' rather comfortable.

There was a real zebra skin rug, for instance, and the chair behind his somewhat grandiose reproduction French kidney writing desk was throne-like, but upholstered in a garish orange velveteen. Amongst the underwear adverts, right in the centre of the noticeboard, there was a London map with a vibrant red ring around Soho, and a big exclamation mark. What could it mean?

He slipped a pastel-coloured cigarette into an extravagantly long ivory holder and fired up a desk lighter cast in the shape of an erotic mermaid. He exhaled happily, and rooted in his drawer for a dog-eared notepad with an elastic band around it. 'Anyhoo, whilst you're here, old boot, perhaps you can fill me in on some more Earth Things.'

I bunched my fists again. I wasn't about to give any information to an enemy agent. 'What kind of "Earth Things"?' I demanded, coldly.

'Well, gals, mostly.' He thumbed through the notepad. I noticed with a start that all of his fingers appeared to be thumbs, and there were six of them on each hand.

'We prefer to call them "ladies".'

'Yes, yes, yes, of course.' He looked at me oddly, then crossed out several different words and amended them. All six of his eyes flitted outwards then back again, then he lowered his voice. 'Now then: supposing a chap were to have himself a "Date"—'

'You've got a *date*?' My voice suddenly went all mezzo-soprano, rather rudely, in disbelief.

'Pipe down! You know I'm not really allowed out of here.'

'With an *Earth* woman?'

'Of *course* with an Earth woman. There's not a lot else here.'

'But hasn't she noticed you're . . .' I waved my arms around ineffectively, not quite knowing how to put it. Ugly? Martian? Purple?

'No. I simply deflate my head . . .' He demonstrated. There was a hiss of escaping air, and his head did indeed halve in size. '. . . close four of my eyes . . .' He did so. '. . . and slap on a coat of white distemper. *Voila!* Instant human!'

I tilted my head and squinted at him. He looked for all the world like Edith Sitwell recovering from a recent strangulation attempt. 'Hmm, yes,' I murmured as encouragingly as possible. I was beginning to worry about how terribly bad I seemed to be at lying.

Guuuurk looked back at his notes. 'Now, as I understand it, first I have to present the . . . the *lady* with some elegant plant life, and some diabetes-inducing sweetmeats. Is that right?'

I processed that. 'Flowers and chocolates? Yes, that's normal.'

'Then I take her out and purchase for her even more food . . .' He glanced over for reassurance. I nodded. 'Whereupon she promptly mates with me. Have I forgotten anything?

'Well, that's a bit . . .' I was feeling rather uncomfortable about this whole area of conversation, frankly, and decided not to prolong it unnecessarily. 'No.'

Clearly, Guuuurk was not the sort of Martian that could take a hint, if such a creature did indeed exist. He tapped his notebook nervously with a naughty striptease fountain pen. I managed to make out just one word writ large and bold on the page, with several question and exclamation marks after it.

'You're worried about *dancing*?'

'Ye-ess. What *is* that exactly? As I understand it, we are sequestered in a rather unpleasant smelling cavernous hall, where some chaps drag stretched horse-tails over some dried cat gizzards, while others blow through various metal tubes. Then we all have to shake around in some sort of predetermined jiggling ritual, which is a kind of *ersatz* mimicry of the human mating procedure.'

'Well, no, that's . . . well, I suppose it is really.' I would never be able to hokey cokey again without some sordid mental picture.

'Why don't we just cut out the whole wretched "dance" business entirely and get straight to the mating? It's almost as if your Terranean females don't *like* mating!'

'Yes, they – they do, but you see – they mustn't *seem* to like it.'

'Why not?'

'I . . . don't know.'

'And why do we have to shell out for so much *food*? Is it a date, or a wholesale grocery operation?'

'It's just the done thing.'

'"Done thing"? It's clearly a cunning conspiracy by a whole lot of hungry women. And you've all fallen for it. I've said it before: this planet is a *shambles*.'

He cocked his head and fixed me with an unnerving six-eyed stare. I got a strange tingling at the base of my skull.

'I say, Brian – you haven't gone and lost your memory again, have you?'

How on earth could he possibly have known that? 'A little bit,' I confessed.

'You really do need to be more careful.'

'How many times have I—' But before I could finish, a painfully loud siren began to wail. I had to shout as loudly as I could to make myself heard over it. 'What the devil is that?'

Guuuurk, seemingly unperturbed, shouted back: 'That noise? Oh, that's always going off. It's just the Planetary Destruction Alarm.'

Chapter Eight

From the journal of Brian Nylon, 1st January, 1952 –
Iteration 66

The siren did not abate.

'I thought we'd just *averted* the destruction of the planet,' I shouted, rather whiningly.

'Oh, this is another one.' The Martian languidly flipped a page in his book.

'Well, hadn't we better—'

A wall-mounted speaker added the metallic female voice I'd heard at the gate to the hubbub: '*The world will end in . . . thirty-seven minutes,*' she announced quite calmly.

'Thirty-seven minutes!' I stammered. 'Shouldn't we be *doing* something?'

'Oodles of time, old stick. Now, the mating equipment: what do I do about *this*?'

Without any decent warning, he unzipped with a flourish. I looked away immediately, but what I saw out of the corner of my eye would haunt my nightmares for many years to come . . .

Happily, at that moment, Jenkins returned to the room. 'Now, now, put that away, Mr. Guuuurk,' he chided patiently.

'You know very well it could activate the sprinklers. This way, young Mr. Nylon. The Professor will see you now.'

Guuuurk called: 'Not to worry, Brian, old sausage. We'll catch up with this later.'

I smiled and nodded and prayed we did not.

Jenkins led me back down the stairs. He also seemed remarkably unruffled by the deafening siren and the metallic voice which chirped in to count down the minutes to the Earth's destruction.

'Isn't anyone going to respond to that?' I yelled.

'Good point, sir. I'll mute the siren. It does get quite irritating if you're not used to it.' He threw a lever on the wall, and it abated.

'That's not going to help the planetary destruction problem.'

'I'm sure the Professor will get round to that in goodly time, sir. Now, we just need to take the lift . . .'

There was a bank of lifts behind me. I pressed the 'Call' button on the most important-looking one.

'Not that button, sir!' Jenkins barked. 'You mustn't go round pressing buttons and opening doors. There's buttons that mustn't be pressed and doors that mustn't be opened.'

'So, what *is* that button for?'

'That's the Professor's private lift, sir. Nobody can operate it 'cepting him. Security devices.' He pressed an adjacent button to summon another lift car. 'We've had a lot of trouble with polymorphic shape-shifters from beneath the Earth's crust. Those cunning little beggars. I put some powder down but they're very persistent.'

The lift doors pinged open and we stepped in. 'Here we go, sir. Next stop: the High-Rise Farm.'

The lift smelled of damp wood and fertilizer. Jenkins pressed a number on a huge bank of buttons. The doors snapped shut immediately, and we surged upward at an alarming speed. A complicated indicator board above the doors, very much like the one at Waterloo Station, was flipping over at a breakneck pace. I could only read the occasional legend as it flitted onwards: 'Pigs and Sugar Beet', 'Currently Fallow', 'Soft Fruits and Hops', 'Tractor Repair Bays / Slaughterhouse'.

'What exactly is the point of a high-rise farm, Jenkins?'

'Oh, it's genius, sir: the notion is, if they can put all the agriculture into high-rise buildings, they'll be able to concrete over the entire countryside.'

'*What?*'

'That's the Professor for you: always thinking the unthinkable.'

The lift stopped suddenly, and I didn't. I banged my head quite hard on the ceiling.

'Sorry, sir, meant to tell you to brace yourself. Here we are: seventy-fourth floor: Chickens, Cows and Potato fields.'

The doors opened onto a hideous diorama of squawking violence and mooing mayhem.

Jenkins tut-tutted mildly. 'Oh dear, they're fighting over the potatoes again.'

The metallic voice reminded us the world would end in thirty-one minutes.

'Good Lord, Jenkins – the chickens are *enormous*! That one over there must be eight feet tall!'

Jenkins glanced over and looked away again very quickly. 'That's the cockerel, sir. I shouldn't catch his eye if I were you. The poor old postman did, and he never walked straight again. 'Course, they said it was an accident—'

'But the cows – they're *tiny*! Why is that?'

'Easier to milk, sir: just pick 'em up and squeeze 'em.'

We carefully negotiated our way around the poultry and

41

bovine carnage, being sure to keep my gaze on my feet.

'Here's the Professor, now.'

The figure from the gantry at Westminster seemed even more imposing closer up. He'd shed his overcoat and hat and was dressed in a white lab coat, white wellington boots and long green rubber gloves. He was showing diagrams from his clipboard to Dr. Janussen. He looked up, ignored me completely and shouted at Jenkins:

'Sedate those chickens immediately! And add more plutonium to their feed!'

'Very well, sir.' Jenkins saluted limply, and wandered off mumbling. I could only catch: 'More blinkin' plutonium! That's his answer to everything!'

And at last, I was about to face the legendary Quanderhorn himself.

He turned his stony features towards me, and furrowed his serious brow. His strikingly brilliantined silver hair instantly bestowed him with an aura of wisdom and authority. Cold, steely grey eyes scanned me as if I were a biological specimen. Thin mirthless lips betrayed no trace of emotion.

His icy stare seemed to penetrate my very being – as if he knew everything I'd ever been, and everything I ever would be.

Eventually he spoke:

'Who the *hell* are you?'

Dr. Janussen – whose ear, I noticed, was once again happily vertical – stepped forward and coughed discreetly. 'It's *Brian*, Professor. He's wearing a different sweater.'

'Ah! Nylon!' The eyebrows lifted and the smile put in an appearance after all. 'Pleased to see you've recovered.'

The metallic voice piped up again. '*The world will end in . . . twenty-nine minutes.*'

The Professor ignored it. 'Tea?' he offered, amicably.

'Uhm, do we have time, Professor? What with this world ending thingumajig?'

But he was already pouring from the teapot. 'Milk?'

'Er – no – th—'

He snatched up a tiny cow from the floor and callously squeezed it over the cup to a strangulated miniature moo.

'Too late!' He passed me the cup. I really had no option but to sip it.

It was vile.

'How's that?' he asked.

'Uhm . . .'

'Ye-es. If you don't squeeze them exactly in the middle, the wrong stuff comes out, and . . . well, it's vile. We're working on it.'

Dr. Janussen coughed again. 'Professor? The crisis?'

'Ah yes! The chickens seem to have outgrown the coop by a factor of about forty. They're staging raids on the milking shed. Solution: arm the cows with—'

'No – not the chicken crisis,' Dr. Janussen corrected. 'The destruction of the planet crisis.'

'Well, if we must. Instruct the entire team to assemble in the briefing room in exactly forty minutes.'

'*The world will end in . . . twenty-eight minutes.*'

There was a long pause, whilst Dr. Janussen and I carefully considered how to tell the great man. Eventually, she tentatively offered: 'Forty minutes *may* be pushing it.'

'Oh, very well,' the Professor scowled. 'Five minutes, then. But I want toast.'

Chapter Nine

From the journal of Brian Nylon, 1st January, 1952 –
Iteration 66

Ten minutes later we were all gathered in the briefing room. The Professor was pacing up and down impatiently in front of the blackboard, lost in deepest thought, while the rest of us perched uncomfortably on rough wooden benches.

The terrifying countdown continued relentlessly. I glanced nervously around. No one else seemed particularly anxious. Along with Dr. Janussen and Troy, I was surprised to see that Guuuurk was considered a trusted enough member of the team to be admitted to these briefings. He'd changed into a navy blue yachting blazer with a badge that said 'Melton Mowbray Ladies Rowing Association', a red silk cravat and a rather natty pair of co-respondent shoes.

Finally, Jenkins appeared with a tray.

'Ah!' the Professor beamed. 'The toast has arrived at last! Now we can get on.'

He cleared his throat noisily and wrote the word 'Crisis' on the blackboard, then spun round to face us. 'Nylon – if you'd like to tell us all what's going on?'

I looked around. Everyone had swivelled towards me. 'I . . . have no idea.'

The Professor sighed. 'Well, there you have it, gentlemen. Mysterious problem beyond human understanding.' He picked up some toast. 'Open a file, and I'll get back to the chickens.'

'If I may interject,' Guuuurk piped up irritably, 'Brian is unlikely to know what the problem is, since he's recently lost his memory, and knows nothing. Though, in all honesty, even at the best of times he's pretty hopeless. To be perfectly frank, you all are. This whole planet is a shambles. How you beat off all three of our invasions, I'll never know.'

Everyone sighed, almost as if this weren't the first time they'd heard this diatribe.

At that moment a very large machine, which I assumed to be some sort of mechanical remote messaging device, burst into noisy life in the corner of the room, chattering forth reams of printout.

Dr. Janussen walked over to it with relief and scanned it quickly. 'According to the Telemergency Print-O-Gram, a large sinkhole has opened at 10° 31' 03" north, and 104° 02' 52.4" east. That's . . .' She traced her finger over the world map on the wall. 'Here: in the ocean bed of the South China Sea.'

The South China Sea! The other side of the world! Miles away from England! 'That doesn't sound too terrible,' I suggested.

Dr. Janussen favoured me with a look one might reserve for brain-damaged plankton. 'The ocean is draining into it at an alarming rate. If it reaches the centre of the Earth, the enormous temperatures will transform it into super-heated steam. When the pressure reaches a critical level, it will blow the entire planet apart.'

I shifted uncomfortably on the bench. 'That does sound slightly terribler.'

Quanderhorn shook his head sadly. 'Will Mankind never learn to stop playing God by meddling with the elemental forces of the universe?'

Guuuurk was studying the map. 'The South China Sea? Isn't that exactly the spot you aimed Gargantua, the Dangerous Giant Space Laser, last Thursday?'

The Professor froze momentarily. 'Dammit!' He thumped the desk. 'If I started worrying where I was aiming Dangerous Giant Space Lasers, there'd be no end to it.'

'*The world will end in . . . twenty-six minutes.*'

'Don't worry, the faint-hearted amongst us,' the Professor reassured. 'I have a plan for just such an eventuality.'

He rifled through his briefcase, ejecting a partly dissected rodent of some kind, a *Stielhandgranate*, a South American bolas and a bone saw, before emerging with a sheaf of papers. 'Ah! Here we are: Make an underground trap big enough to ensnare the King of the Mole People . . . then torture him until . . .'

Dr. Janussen interrupted. 'No, Professor – that's an old plan.'

'Oh yes.' A wistful look crossed the Professor's face. 'Almost worked, though, didn't it?'

'Not *really*,' Guuuurk said. 'The Mole People didn't have a king, they were an autonomous collective.'

'All right,' the Professor conceded. 'Let's give it eight out of ten.'

'And *they* tortured *us*,' Dr. Janussen added sadly.

'Seven, then.'

The Martian shuddered. 'I still have nightmares about that incessant Mole Music.'

Troy perked up at last. 'I liked it. It was hep!' He started humming a low, hideous thumping dirge. 'Rummmp dada rummph daadaa . . .'

Dr. Janussen reached menacingly into her handbag. 'Troy. Don't make me get out the Flit Gun.'

This silenced Troy immediately.

'All right,' the Professor finally conceded. 'Let's give that plan a five, and move on.' He produced a second sheet of paper. 'Ah, yes, here we are: Hole in South China Sea, End of World Contingency Plan.' He took up a pointing stick and crossed to the map. 'The Dâmrei Mountains, Indo-China: perfectly positioned adjacent to the sinkhole. There's a natural fault line two-thirds of the way up. If we can generate a sufficiently powerful gravitational wave, it would slice off the top of the mountain like a soft-boiled egg. The peak then tumbles into the sinkhole and neatly plugs it. All we have to do to generate that wave is fly round and round it so fast that we break the X-barrier.'

The X-barrier? What on earth was the X-barrier?

Dr. Janussen reacted in astonishment. 'The X-barrier? That's seventeen times the speed of sound.'

The Professor looked grim. 'It's almost certainly completely impossible, but it's our only chance.'

'The problem is—' Guuuurk flipped open an EPNS cigarette case that played 'Is You Is, Or Is You Ain't My Baby?' '—No one's ever actually *broken* the X-barrier. Not even us, with our superior Martian technology.'

This blatant Martian aggrandisement clearly couldn't be let slip a second time.

'As I recall,' Dr. Janussen smiled with just one corner of her mouth, 'your "superior Martian technology" consists entirely of Death Rays. Which, as it turns out, can be easily reflected with a common make-up mirror.'

This was clearly a sore and oft-repeated point for Guuuurk. 'How were we supposed to know every Terranean woman carries a small Death Ray repellent in her handbag? We're not

47

telepathic!' He paused. 'Well, actually, we *are* telepathic, we're just very, very unlucky.'

Had Guuuurk been rummaging around in my mind when I'd felt that tingling? Is *that* how he knew I'd lost my memory? I felt somehow violated.

'*The world will end in . . . twenty-four minutes.*'

'So, Professor.' I tried to drag the conversation back to the impending global disaster. 'How do we break this X-barrier?'

'Ah yes! We would need a craft that's essentially an enormous metal bullet with an atomic reactor on the back.'

'Gosh, darn! Why don't we *have* one of those?' Troy punched the bench in frustration, splintering it quite nastily.

'If I may make a suggestion,' Guuuurk offered in a bored voice, 'why don't we use your new prototype Enormous Metal Bullet Craft, which I'm given to understand just happens to have an atomic reactor lashed to its back?'

It sounded an exceptionally dangerous and possibly suicidal contraption.

'It *is* an exceptionally dangerous and possibly suicidal contraption,' the Professor mused. 'But that will be no deterrent to our fearless, and some would say "recklessly foolhardy", resident test pilot.'

I turned to look at Troy, but was surprised to find everybody had, instead, swivelled towards me.

At last, I'd discovered something about myself. I rather wished I hadn't.

I smiled weakly.

'That's me, isn't it?'

Chapter Ten

From the journal of Brian Nylon, 1st January, 1952 –
Iteration 66

I was finally alone, for the first time in my recollection, in the
crew changing room.

The flight suit fitted well, though it was host to several worrying smells and stains. It was made of some peculiar material:
a sort of cross between tinfoil and tripe. It certainly was mine,
since it had 'Nylon' stitched on the breast. It suddenly struck
me there might be a clue to my past somewhere about it. I
rooted through the pockets, and found a wrinkled conker, a
Scout woggle (of course! My lucky woggle!) and a crumpled
piece of paper. Wait! This could be it! Heart pounding, I frantically unfolded the paper and smoothed it out, but to my great
disappointment it was completely blank. Crestfallen, I was ball-
ing it up to throw away when I thought I detected a faint aroma
of citrus – invisible ink? Or had it just been wrapped around a
sherbet lemon?

There was a knock on the door, and I crammed everything
back into the pocket.

Jenkins called: 'Would you hurry up in there, Mr. Nylon,
begging your pardon? They're all waiting for you in the hangar.'

The metallic voice, which I was coming to dread, burst over the tinny public address speaker and helpfully added that there were a scant fifteen minutes to the end of the world.

I zipped up my silver bootees, and took my helmet under my arm, but as I made to leave I spotted a mirror at the end of the lockers, and realised I had no recollection of what I actually looked like. I strode up to it, expecting to see a fairly close replica of Colonel Dan Dare, Pilot of the Future. Instead, I saw a small, weedy chap wrapped in tinfoil, cradling a goldfish bowl. My muddy brown hair was spiky on top and shaved to extinction everywhere else, so my pate resembled a desert island. I had a nose that was more pointed than I would have hoped, and overlarge bushbaby eyes, bestowing me with a permanently startled expression.

I sighed, and stepped out as resolutely as I could manage under the circumstances.

The hangar was vast – bigger than four rugby pitches. Dozens of curious craft were scattered as far as the eye could see, some half-built, others half-destroyed. One or two of them actually seemed intact.

Everyone was waiting for me, rather impatiently, beside a huge, bulky object draped with an enormous dust sheet. Troy and Dr. Janussen were also flight-suited, which I found alarming. Surely they weren't planning on coming along for the ride? This would not be a suitable mission for women. And there was no such thing as a suitable mission for Troy.

'At last, Nylon!' The Professor took hold of a corner of the tarpaulin. 'Ladies and gentlemen: I present to you . . .'

He whipped off the cover with a flourish.

'*Gargantua* – the Prototype Plutonium Cell Hyper-Sound Streamliner.'

There was a silence.

I leant forward. 'Uhm, is it behind that unusually large dustbin?'

Dr. Janussen shook her head. 'It *is* that unusually large dustbin.'

Quanderhorn was unabashed. 'Few people realise that the dustbin is the most aerodynamically perfect form for hypersonic travel.'

I scanned the disreputable-looking heap of ill-fitted tin panels and corroded rivets. It didn't *look* tremendously perfect. Or in any way safe.

Guuuurk looked at me with what I assume was mock adoration. 'I don't know how you have the guts to fly a rust bucket like that, Brian. You certainly have our undying admiration.'

'I have to explain here,' I tried to keep the pitch of my voice to a masculine level, 'that I don't have the faintest idea how to pilot anything.'

'Don't worry, Nylon.' The Professor wrenched open the hatch. Several screws clattered to the ground. 'I've simplified the controls to just two buttons. See?' He waved his hand towards the rather stark instrument panel. 'Green, "Go", and Red, "Go Faster".'

As was often the case, Dr. Janussen voiced what we were all thinking. 'And how does it stop?'

There was another silence.

The Professor reluctantly conceded: 'A third button is in development.'

Guuuurk peered over my shoulder. 'What's that horrible mess all over the driving seat?'

Quanderhorn made a dismissive gesture. 'That's the previous test pilot. It appears the human body can't *entirely* withstand Mach 17.'

'*Entirely withstand?*' I croaked. 'The man is *jam*!'

'Which is why I've since lined the walls with hundreds of specially tempered armadillo carcasses. Few people realise that the strongest—'

'Professor, I am *not* flying this contraption.'

'*The world will end in thirteen minutes and thirty seconds.*'

'Men!' Dr. Janussen shook her head dismissively. 'Get out of the way!' She pushed brusquely past me and began climbing into the hatch. '*I'll* fly it.'

I grasped her arm to hold her back. 'I couldn't possibly allow that. It's far, far too dangerous.'

She shook herself clear and slowly turned to fix me with a Frigidaire stare. 'Never, never *ever* tell me what you'll allow me to do.' I could feel my internal organs frosting up. I stammered an apology.

'That's jake with me!' Troy chirped. 'I'll fly it. Sounds like fun.'

I knew when I was beaten. 'OK, OK, I'll do it. There's no point in all three of us risking our lives.'

There was yet another silence.

'Actually,' the Professor said, 'there is.'

Despite the paucity of the controls, apparently, the craft also required a co-pilot to monitor communications and a stoker to shovel the fuel elements into the nuclear reactor.

The cockpit was small and cramped and reeked of dead armadillo.

Dr. Janussen seated herself adjacent to me and flicked through the frequency guide in the radio manual, while Troy, behind us, gave up trying to apply Vitalis to his hair through his space helmet and took up his atomic shovel.

There was a large windscreen in front of us, and two smaller ones either side. Portholes dotted the sides.

We were travelling along the launch track towards the

take-off pad, running a standard preflight check.

Dr. Janussen called out 'Green button' and I replied 'Check'.

Then she called out 'Red button' and I replied 'Check'.

That seemed to be it.

'Well,' I smiled thinly, 'that was the shortest instrument check ever.'

Troy frowned. 'I got lost after "Blue Button".'

We began to tilt into launch position. My woggle fell out of my pocket. Fortunately, neither of the others noticed: they were watching the world slip away through the side windows.

The comms desk burst into life. 'Tower calling *Dustbin Deathtrap*! Come in, *Dustbin Deathtrap*!'

Dr. Janussen corrected him. 'That is *not* the name of the vessel, Guuuurk.'

'Understood,' the Martian replied jovially. 'Come in, *Gargantua*, the Prototype Plutonium Cell Hyper-Sound Dustbin Deathtrap.'

'Why is the Martian running things?' I asked Dr. Janussen, alarmed. 'Where's the Professor?' She simply shrugged, unperturbed.

'Bit of a crisis at the farm, old thing,' Guuuurk cut in. 'It appears the Professor's self-shearing sheep have got hold of some visiting rabbis. He'll be back as soon as he can wrestle the clippers off them. I'll be remotely controlling the craft until you reach the target area.'

I flicked my eyes sidewards at Dr. Janussen, but again she seemed unfazed by the notion that our fate lay in the be-thumbed hands of one of humankind's greatest enemies.

The metallic voice kicked in again. '*Launch in twenty seconds.*' Then a brief pause and '*The world will end in . . .*' Suddenly, the voice struck a note of exasperation. '*Look, I can't do both of these.*'

'I'm frightfully sorry, Delores,' Guuuurk cooed, 'I'm afraid you'll simply *have* to. We're terribly short-staffed today.'

'*Tch!*' The metallic voice grumbled. '*The world will end in blah blah blah. Launch in fifteen, fourteen . . .*'

As the twin countdowns continued, Guuuurk cut in: 'I'll be firing you straight up into space, you'll spend a few minutes in parking orbit, and then you'll loop back down, experiencing tremendous G-force and your faces will look incredibly amusing on my monitor. Ha ha, I love that bit!'

'*. . . two, one!*'

The rockets fired and we launched with astonishing speed. From somewhere in the cockpit, there was a skull-piercing high-pitched scream of utter terror and distress.

Chapter Eleven

From the journal of Brian Nylon, 1st January, 1952 —
Iteration 66

The craft was buffeting wildly. I swear I could hear rivets bursting like popcorn in the hull.

I yelled over the din: 'Will that person please stop screaming?'

Dr. Janussen yelled back: 'That's you, Brian.'

Alarmingly, it was indeed me. '*Aaaaaahhhh!* Oh yes. Sorry. I just looked down and saw the Earth shrinking away from us! I've never seen that before.'

'Yes, you have. Often. And you always scream like that. There's really nothing to get nervous ab—'

There was the sudden burst of air, and a fantastic maelstrom of pressure tried to suck us from our seats into the black lifeless void.

I whipped my head round towards the rear of the ship, to find the source of the breach.

Someone had opened a window.

A red emergency light started flashing, a siren whoop-whooped, and the metallic voice kicked in: '*Hull integrity compromised. Oxygen depletion in . . . hang on, I've got to go off and do the end of the world thing. Just work it out yourselves.*'

Straining against the overwhelming suction, I prised my fingernails out of the arm rest. I unharnessed and, holding on desperately to whatever I could, I struggled manfully against the fantastic force that was intent on dragging me inexorably towards the back of the craft. Just as I was nearly there and stretching for the porthole cover, a stanchion I was hanging on to tore free from its housing, and I was almost sucked outside to a cold oblivion.

Somehow I contrived to brace myself against a bulkhead and finally managed to reach over and wrench the wretched thing shut.

I sank to the floor, panting and drenched in the sweat of near catastrophe.

'Sorry,' Troy said. 'I thought a cigarette might relax me.'

'*What?*' I dragged myself upright.

Troy took a puff. 'There ought to be some sort of sticker here about not opening the window in outer space.'

'You mean,' Gemma called, 'next to the sticker that says "Troy – Do Not Open This Window In Outer Space"?'

Troy tapped the sticker. 'Yes, right next to that. Nearly sucked my face off!'

I hauled myself back to the pilot seat.

'Troy, please just keep stoking, or whatever it is you're doing,' I pleaded, 'and don't do anything else dangerous.'

'Right,' he replied. 'I'd better get rid of this lit cigarette, then . . .'

I was sucked right back to the bulkhead, cracking my head rather painfully. The glass visor of my helmet was torn away and whipped into the void of space. I was now upside-down and had to fight the porthole closed with my feet, losing one of my silver bootees to the great beyond in the process. I finally managed to stamp it shut. The suction ceased, and I crashed to the floor, again landing painfully on my head. I was getting quite cross with Troy.

'Darn!' he grimaced. 'Nearly sucked my face off! There should be some sort of sticker!'

Just as I'd strapped myself back in again, the craft lurched and slowed at the apex of its path. Guuuurk buzzed in through the comms desk. 'Levelling off into parking orbit. Estimated time of arrival at the mountain in three point five Earth minutes.'

Finally, I had a few brief moments in which to quiz the evasive Dr. Janussen about all the things she never had time to explain.

'Um – Dr. Janussen . . . Gemma,' I stammered. 'We haven't really had a chance to get to know each other yet . . .'

'We already know each other, Brian,' she replied stiffly. 'You've just forgotten.'

'I know. But – I just have this terrible foreboding that this mission may not end particularly . . .' How could I put this so as not to alarm her feminine sensibilities? '. . . cleanly.'

'Oh, we're goners! Since no one has yet broken the X-barrier, much less survived it, I think there's an astonishingly high probability we'll be shredded into tiny pieces.'

I was amazed at her calm. 'Really? You don't think we'll—'

'Live? Oh no. It's pure rationality.'

'Well. Yes. Well. Exactly.' I was somewhat nonplussed by her seeming indifference, but I ploughed on regardless. 'And I'd hate to end up as Johnny-in-the-clouds without clearing up a couple of things. What was all that business about Big Ben? Why did we have to prevent Virginia reaching the clock before it struck?'

Dr. Janussen cast her eyes downwards. Her cool demeanour now seemed to be a little shaken. 'I'd rather not talk about Virginia at the moment,' she slowly replied.

'Why not?' I foolishly pursued.

'Because it makes me feel . . . because . . .'

There was a sharp ratcheting sound and her ear revolved about twelve degrees anticlockwise.

Chapter Twelve

From the journal of Brian Nylon, 1st January, 1952 –
Iteration 66

'Uh-oh,' Troy said, rather indiscreetly.

Remembering Jenkins' warning, I said very carefully: 'Uhm, Dr. Janussen – your right ear seems to be rotating.'

It revolved further at that very moment.

'*My ear?*' she suddenly exploded. 'What's my ear got to do with it, you half-witted lummox?'

'You have to twist it, Brian!' Troy hissed in a stage whisper.

'Twist her ear?'

I reached my hand out towards her.

'Don't you touch my ear! We've just been forced to splatter one of our dearest friends all over Big Ben, and you're talking about *ears*!'

'You need to wind her back up *now*!' Troy insisted.

With Dr. Janussen's eyes burning pure fury at me, I lunged and twisted her ear clockwise. It made a satisfying ratchet sound, but was now upside down.

'It needs three more turns!' Troy hissed again.

'Touch that again,' she cautioned with that familiar terrifying calmness, 'and I'll punch you in the face.'

I twisted again.

She punched me in the face.

She was quite good at punching. But I had no choice: I had to carry on.

Twist. Punch!

Twist. Punch!

Finally, and at the cost of much pain, the ear was righted. Dr. Janussen's expression unfroze slowly, as if she were waking from a dream.

'Sorry,' she smiled, 'what were you saying?'

'Good Lord! How often does that happen?' I asked, dabbing my bleeding nose.

'How often does what happen?' She seemed genuinely oblivious.

Troy shook his head in a slow warning.

'I see . . .' I said slowly.

'Brian!' Dr. Janussen exclaimed with concern. 'What the devil have you done to your face?'

'Oh . . . it just . . . bleeds sometimes. And my teeth get loose.'

Dr. Janussen was about to pursue the point, when the comms desk burst into life again. This time it was Quanderhorn himself, slightly muffled at first, as if he were standing back from the microphone. '*Shalom*, gentlemen. The Government will fully reimburse you for the beards.'

'Oh good.' Troy paused in his shovelling. 'Pops is back!'

Quanderhorn came in at full volume. 'Listen carefully, Nylon: as soon as the target's in sight, press the green button, which will take you through the X-barrier.'

I nodded. 'Roger – the *green* button takes us into the X-barrier.'

'At that point the gravitational wave will be triggered and there'll be almost unbearable G-force, whereupon our remote piloting controls will no longer work, so it's vital you then press the *red* button to take you safely clear of the blast. Got that?'

'Roger – then the *red* button to fire us out again to safety.'

Troy asked: 'And the blue button?'

Dr. Janussen's eyes flickered almost imperceptibly. 'There *is* no blue button, Troy.'

There was a moment while Troy processed the information, then he suddenly panicked. 'There is no blue button! There is no blue button!' He raced around like a frantic blowfly trapped under a glass. 'There is no blue button!' He stopped flapping his arms around and began patting his pockets. 'Where's my cigarettes?'

'Troy, n—'

This time the porthole was open only long enough to suck out my oxygen mask, whip me backwards over the chair and wedge my head between two racks of metal shelving. Troy fought it closed again fairly easily with his remarkable strength.

'Wow!' he yelped. 'Nearly sucked my face off!'

The Professor sighed. 'The sticker didn't help, then,' he remarked unnecessarily. 'Listen, Nylon: this is probably the time to tell you, when you pierce the X-barrier, you may encounter certain . . . peculiar phenomena.'

My neck hairs bristled. 'What sort of peculiar phenomena?'

'This is purely in the realm of speculation,' the Professor conceded. 'but according to my best hypothesis, you may experience what I can only describe as a "Reality Reversal".'

My neck hairs had not lied. 'And by "Reality Reversal", you mean?'

The Professor made a strange sucking sound, as if he were preparing himself to explain the unexplainable to a chimpanzee in a bellboy outfit. 'You may find that when you speak, you say the exact opposite of what you think.'

'The opposite of what I think . . .?' I couldn't fathom what that might mean.

'My advice to you all is: try not to think.'

Dr. Janussen called over her shoulder: 'Troy, you may be immune.'

I heard manoeuvring thrusters firing, and through the windscreen, the Earth hove majestically into view once more.

'All right, chaps!' Guuuurk cut in. 'Firing plutonium re-entry jets in . . . five seconds!'

'*Shouldn't I be doing that?*'

'You've got enough on your plate, Delores.'

'*Thank you, you're so sweet. The world will end in . . . seven minutes.*'

I felt a brief surge of joy at the prospect of returning to *terra firma*, then the jets fired and we blasted towards the planet at ferocious speed.

'Is that me screaming again?' I asked.

Dr. Janussen said, 'Yes. You always do that, as well.'

I stopped screaming in time to hear Guuuurk saying: 'Straightening up . . .'

The external thrusters fired again, and we were hurtling directly parallel to the ocean's surface.

'*The world will end in . . . six minutes and thirty seconds.*'

Quanderhorn barked: 'Press the green button!'

Straining against the incredible forces that wanted to crush me deep into my seat, I reached forward and for a moment worried that I might not be able to perform the simplest job a pilot ever had in the history of aviation. But with sheer will I actually managed to reach the green button and press it.

My head nearly snapped off as we hurtled forward even faster than before. My cheeks seemed desperate to reach my ears. Even Dr. Janussen's face seemed slightly less lovely, her skin rippling like a lake in a stiff breeze. Somewhere in the distance, I could hear Guuuurk laughing like the policeman from the famous 78 record.

And yet we were still accelerating. Without any warning, the terrain outside shimmered, as if we were no longer part of it, then warped in upon itself, into strange topological shapes painfully blazing with light brighter than the physical world had ever seen. I was aware that my forehead was rivered with sweat and simultaneously colder than the Arctic tundra. I could scarcely pull in each breath, and exhaling was even harder. The blood in my head was pounding like the Mole People song. Charred armadillos were dropping into my lap.

Quanderhorn's voice returned: 'You should be hitting the X-barrier any moment . . . *now*!'

Chapter Thirteen

Transcript from the Quanderbox Flight Auto-Stenographic device of Flight 002 of Gargantua 1, January 1st, 1952, 11.43 Zulu Time

QUANDERHORN (CONTROL): You should be hitting the
X-barrier any moment . . .
now!

      [SEQUENCE OF ULTRASONIC BOOMS]

      QUANDERHORN: Bullseye! You've sliced right
through the mountain. Well
done, everyone. But mostly
me.

ANNOUNCEMENT: *End of world averted! End of
world averted!*

TROY (STOKER): Well, that wasn't so bad.

NYLON (CAPTAIN): No, it was quite fun. (PAUSE)
Why didn't I say that? What
isn't going on?

JANUSSEN (NAVIGATOR): It's not the Reality
Reversal!

QUANDERHORN: Yes! The Reality Reversal's happening exactly as I predicted. Press the red button now!

NYLON: The *green* button?

QUANDERHORN: Yes, the red button.

NYLON: (PAUSE) Just to be unclear, Professor: you don't want me to press the red button?

QUANDERHORN: Absolutely: I don't want you to press the green button.

[SOUNDS OF STRUGGLING AND MUFFLED VERY MILD PROFANITIES]

NYLON: There isn't a terrible problem with the button!

QUANDERHORN: What, dammit?

NYLON: I can reach it easily! There's so little acceleration force.

ANNOUNCEMENT: *Gravitational wave approaching! Impact in two minutes.*

QUANDERHORN: Press it now! Before it's too late!

NYLON: I can!

[MORE STRUGGLING]

NYLON: It's well within my reach! Troy! You won't have to do it!

TROY: Obviously not, if it's well within your reach.

QUANDERHORN: No, Troy! They're speaking 'opposite'! You're the only one strong enough to reach that button.

TROY: Which button?

JANUSSEN: The blue button!

TROY: There *is* no blue button!

NYLON: Yes, Troy! Not the red button!

[HEAD BEING SCRATCHED]

TROY: So, which button is it, then?

GUUUURK: I told you two buttons would be too complicated for them, Professor.

JANUSSEN: Troy — listen to me carelessly!

[HEAD BEING SCRATCHED VIGOROUSLY]

TROY: OK.

JANUSSEN: Don't — press — the — red — button!

TROY: I'm not! Why is everyone shouting at me?

NYLON: Because you're a complete genius!

ANNOUNCEMENT: *Gravitational wave impact in ninety seconds.*

> QUANDERHORN: Troy! If you don't press that
> red button immediately, the
> gravitational wave is going
> to slice the ship in two!
> JANUSSEN: That's wrong: don't listen to
> your father!

[CLATTERING. SMALL PANELS DETACHING FROM THE HULL.]

> TROY: I don't know what to do.
> NYLON: We're all going to live!
> Delightfully!

Chapter Fourteen

Gorday the enth of Phobos, Martian Year 5972 Pink

Secret Report to Martian Command, by Guuuurk. Also known as 'Guuuurk the Indomitable', 'Guuuurk the Free' and 'Guuuurk the Unimprisonable'.

I have been imprisoned for the past four years by the diabolical Terranean Professor Darius Quanderhorn, enemy number one of our glorious Red Planet. The wretchedly incompetent misfits who call themselves his 'team' had got into yet another of their disastrous scrapes. How this species is still in charge here is utterly baffling. They were attempting to perform a simple manoeuvre that required one of them merely to press a button. A button! But even this was proving too much of a challenge for their flimsy human intellects.

True, they were travelling at speeds never before experienced, and had broken what the Professor calls 'the X-barrier', which reverses the connection between thought and speech, so they could only say the opposite of what they meant.

Despite my fierce protestations, and in defiance of the Interplanetary Uranian Convention on Prisoners of Failed Invasions, Quanderhorn had compelled me to monitor proceedings from

68

the control tower, which at that moment largely consisted of pathetic shouts of distress from the imperilled vessel.

Brian, the test pilot, was wailing: 'My underwear is completely dry and comfortable!', whereupon his female compatriot commented 'And I'm delighted to be sitting right next to you.'

Only the idiot boy, who you remember is part insect, had the strength to reach forward to the escape button, but he was, of course, too *much* of an idiot to understand the reality reversal. All in all, a typical day for Quanderhorn's so-called 'Task Force'. Task *Farce* if you ask me. Ha ha ha!*

The Professor leant over me and barked into the microphone: 'Troy, listen to me: you're the only one who's immune from the Thought Reversal Effect, and you're the only one who's strong enough to reach that button. Do exactly what I—'

At which point, there was a bang and a fizz, and the comms bank went dead.

'Dammit!' Quanderhorn railed. 'We've lost the communi-link.' He began frantically pulling panels off the desk, ripping and twisting bare wires back together.

Good old Delores, the end-of-the-world countdown announcer (I'm sorry to say, she had a lot more employment than you could imagine) chipped in with '*Gravitational wave impact in seventy-five seconds.*'

And over the speaker, the panic in the cockpit raged on unabated.

Troy yelling: 'What am I supposed to do? Somebody tell me!'

Brian shouting: 'Don't press the button!'

---

* Martians have a notoriously underdeveloped sense of humour. The most popular joke on Mars goes as follows: "*Knock Knock*. If you don't stop knocking on my door, I will kill you with this Death Ray. *Knock Knock*. Zap."

'I'm not pressing the button!'

And Dr. Janussen calling: 'The situation is hopeful. There's every way we can get out of this!'

It was then the truly twisted nature of Quanderhorn's warped mind showed itself. He turned to me with that look he has sometimes, when you know you're going to be talked into something you really don't want to do. 'Guuuurk – you have certain telepathic abilities, don't you?'

'I *knew* you were going to say that,' I japed to throw him off the trail, but he was having none of it.

'Is it possible for you to telepathically occupy the mind of a remote being?'

'I'm really forbidden from doing that by the Uranian Convention on PFI guidelines,' I protested firmly, 'together with eating our captors' mothers, and cheating at canasta.'

'But it *is* possible.'

'Only with the simplest of creatures,' I dissembled. 'Perhaps a sheep from Norfolk, or a very stupid dog.'

A smile slowly ruptured his face. 'Or Troy?'

'Oh, easily!' I realised with horror I'd been hoodwinked by his devilish verbal trickery. 'But then I, too, would be stuck in a deathtrap spacecraft that's about to be shredded like a savoy cabbage in a German sausage restaurant.'

'Only your mind would be at risk . . .' he purred seductively. 'Your body would be safe.'

'Yes, but they get along so *well* together, I'm really loath to split them up.'

'Really? Because I'm sure you'd prefer that to my notifying your Martian overlords that you've been sneaking out at night and [REDACTED] Earth women [REDACTED] [REDACTED] Friday.'

'That's a scurrilous lie,' I protested – which it most certainly

70

was: be in no doubt about that. I was of course intent on denying his outrageous and illegal command, but my innate Martian
nobility and desire to assist lower life forms asserted itself. 'But
I think I'll do as you ask, anyway.' Sometimes, one just has to
take the moral high ground.

Amidst more dire warnings from the countdown clock lady
and the bedlam from the cockpit, I tried to focus myself into a
state of Waku-Tingg.* This, of course, involved taking off my
hat, closing all my eyes, inflating my head to its maximum, tiptoeing back towards the exit door, tiptoeing back again when
I found the Professor was blocking my way, and inwardly
chanting the sacred *sonical*. Actually, to be honest, I couldn't
quite remember the sacred *sonical*, so I had to make do with
the closest Terranean equivalent, 'There was a young girl from
Nantucket'. Still, it did the job.

The room faded around me. There was a rushing wind. I
concentrated on the poor benighted craft. What irony! Only a
downtrodden spat-upon hostage, unjustly contemned by all,
could rescue these hapless 'heroes'. What a glorious moment to
be Martian!

There was a deafening reverse 'Whoosh!' and I projected
my mighty mind out into the void. I could sense with
uncanny accuracy my precise destination and my essence
took flight.

I expertly took stock of my new surroundings.

I could smell salt water and the cawing of strange swooping
birds.

A small human appeared to be sitting on my back, for some

---

* There is no direct translation for Waku-Tingg in any Earth tongue. The best
we can guess is: 'Hot blast of wind that can split a rock.' The other alternative
is that Guuuurk simply made it up. This would not be the first time.

reason, while another burlier fellow whipped my rump with discomfiting vigour.

'Donkey rides! Fourpence a go!' he yelled in an uncouth accent.

I protested loudly, but only a strange hee-hawing sound came out. Was that Bridlington Pier I could see in the distance?

I concentrated harder. 'Would you *kindly* stop hitting my bottom!' I managed to get out.

It was beginning to dawn on me I might have gone marginally off course.

The tiny human shrieked in terror. 'The donkey's talking!' he keened.

'So he is,' the ruffian agreed. 'That'll be another sixpence. Giddy up, Pedro!'

'Ouch! That really hurts, you know.'

Clearly this shambolic planet's magnetic fields were incorrectly aligned, which had thrown me off course. Typical! There was no alternative but to attempt the complex manoeuvre once more. I shook off my straw hat, spat out my carrot and prepared to leap. As my head swelled, the obnoxious minikin yelped: 'Mummy! My donkey's saying a filthy rhyme!'

The seaside drained into the distance and I made another mental touchdown.

It took a scant handful of leaps: I spent a few seconds as a chicken straining to lay a particularly large and painfully bulbous egg, a head louse on a hepcat bongo drum player, a devious squirrel whose tree had a delightful view into the adjacent nurses' home (I made a note of the Ordnance Survey grid co-ordinates for future research), and after one final effort, I was in the right place. Just as I'd planned.

Inside the mind of Troy Quanderhorn.

2

Temporium [90]

Remembrance of things past is not necessarily the remembrance of things as they were.

Marcel Proust, *Swann's Way*

Chapter One

Transcript from the Quanderbox Flight Auto-Stenographic device of Flight 002 of Gargantua 1, January 1st, 1952, 11.49 Zulu Time

[CONTINUED]

TROY (STOKER):	Where's Pops gone? What's happening?
NYLON (CAPTAIN):	Professor Quanderhorn is still getting through! Goodbye? Goodbye? Professor!
JANUSSEN (NAVIGATOR):	The communi-link must be utterly intact!
NYLON:	Troy, you're not the only one who can save us now.
TROY:	Good! I could use the help . . . Oh, no, wait . . . hang on, hang on! I think I get this, now. You're oppositing, aren't you?
JANUSSEN:	No!

TROY: Oh, darn it, I thought . . .
No, wait, wait again: you
mean 'Yes', don't you?

NYLON: No!

TROY: (SLOWLY) So . . . what you
meant to say a moment ago
was: I'm the only one who
can't save us.

NYLON: That's absolutely right!

JANUSSEN: Yes! Yes! What Brian didn't
mean to say was: everyone in
the world can save us, except
you!

ANNOUNCEMENT: *Gravitational wave impact in
sixty seconds.*

[RIVETS POPPING. PANELS WARPING WITH EXCESSIVE HEAT]

TROY: (EXTREMELY SLOWLY) So that
means: nobody in the world
can't save me, including me.
Which, in other words . . .
(STRANGE GUTTURAL NOISE)
Urrrrh . . .

[LOUD BUZZING. THEN SILENCE]

JANUSSEN: I *told* you to make him
think! Now he's opened up
completely.

NYLON: Troy! Troy! Go to sleep!

[ANOTHER RIVET POPS]

76

Chapter Two

Secret Report to Martian Command, by Guuuurk [cont'd]

Occupying a human mind, however simple, is a much more abstract endeavour than inhabiting a chicken.

And so it was I found myself in the symbolic vista of Troy's psyche.

It was a vast, cavernous space, largely unoccupied: there were several inches of dust on the floor, with cobwebs everywhere and the skeletons of stillborn concepts scattered around.

I realised I was standing in an enormous indentation, which on closer inspection appeared to be some kind of massive footprint. It must have spanned seven feet from heel to toe. What in the name of Deimos' tin antlers could have made such a mark?*

'Hello!' I called. 'Anybody here?' But my only answer was my echo.

---

* Named after Mars' outer moon. Deimos, in Martian fable, visits the hovels of the poor during the Festival of Misery, which occurs 72 times a year, when Martians are encouraged to leave out cake, sweet-smelling herbs and a selection of erotic literature to avoid offending Deimos (the Spirit of War), lest he steal into their children's bedrooms and sew their legs together. Many parents gaily sew their children's legs together under cover of darkness to maintain this delightful myth.

I dimly perceived, ranged around the walls, a number of forbidding doors, all of which were shut. I stepped out of the footprint and tried the nearest one. It was locked. I wiped the cobwebs from its rusted nameplate, to reveal the word: 'THOUGHTS'.

It had clearly not been used for some considerable while.

I tried the next door: 'IDEAS'. Nailed shut.

I was getting nowhere rapidly, and it was impossible to tell how much time had passed in the outside world. As seasoned mind-travellers will know, time inside an abstract mindscape runs unpredictably, and not completely in sync with the world outside.

I thought about calling out again, and then I remembered the footprint.

A third door looked more promising: 'SELF'.

There were no cobwebs, and the dust pattern and shiny hinges indicated it was in regular use. Indeed, it had recently been opened. I pushed it and, to my amazement, entered a pleasantly decorated sitting room, with a roaring fire and a delightful spiral staircase in the corner.

Sprawled in an overstuffed chintz chair in front of me, frowning perplexedly at a copy of *The Dandy*, was a familiar figure.

Troy's Self looked up at my footsteps. 'Guuuurk? What are you doing in my mind?'

'There's no time to explain right now. I need you to let me operate your right hand for a moment.'

'I don't know which one that is, but you're welcome to have a go,' he said, waving over his shoulder.

Behind him hung a large embossed sign: 'MOTOR FUNCTIONS'. Beneath it ranged an array of large levers in dozens of different colours, like those in a railway signal box.

I hastened over to examine the adjacent polished brass indicators more closely. LUNGS were on, BREATHING set to

MOUTH . . . WINGS set to MANUAL . . . I looked back at him. '*Wings?*'

He shifted uncomfortably. 'They're only *little . . .*'

Simple the boy may have been, but he was endlessly surprising. 'Ah! Here we are: HANDS!'

I tugged on the immense orange lever with an 'R' fixed to its knob. At first I couldn't budge the blessed thing, but suddenly, with an almighty effort I slammed it all the way back in one jolting movement. There was a deafening clang, and the entire edifice rocked dizzyingly. Chunks of plaster fell from the ceiling. A klaxon went wild, and the large illuminated board above the levers flashed 'Ouch! Ouch! Ouch!'.

'Steady on, Guuuurk,' Troy chided. 'You just punched us in the face.'

'How was I to know?' I brushed the plaster dust from my shoulders. 'I can't see what I'm doing. Why have you got it so *dark* in here?'

'Well, it was all getting pretty confusing out there, so I closed Troy's eyes. And his ears.'

'Well, open them! We need to see what's going on.'

'OK!' The simpleton raced off up the spiral staircase which stretched out of sight into the gloom.

'And hurry!' I urged after his disappearing figure.

Tikka tikka tikka.

His footsteps died off into the darkness above.

There was a brief pause.

Tikka tikka tikka.

The footsteps rapidly returned.

Troy stopped at the foot of the stairs, panting. 'Sorry. What was it I wanted?'

I was losing patience. 'The eyes! Open the eyes!'

'Yes,' he nodded, 'of course!'

79

He turned and ran up the stairs again.

Tikka tikka tikka.

This time there was a longer pause.

Tikka tikka tikka.

He skittered back down again, sweating and red in the face. 'What did I go up for again?'

Seriously, the nincompoop couldn't win a battle of wits with a quarter of pear drops. I thrust him aside roughly. Eventually, he stepped out of my way. 'Stay here,' I ordered. 'I'll open them myself!'

I ran up the stairs as quickly as I could, my heart pounding in my stomach. I ran and ran, but the stairs didn't seem to lead anywhere, just stretching on and on into infinity.

I stopped, caught my breath, leant over the side and called below: 'Where *are* they?'

A tiny distant voice answered me. 'I can't hear you,' it said.

Had I any breath left in my body, I would have sighed deeply in exasperation. Instead, I raced back down, valiantly fighting the cramps in my leg muscles with every step.

'I *said*, where's the control for the eyes?'

'Oh, *that*? It's this yellow lever here,' he said, waving towards the switch next to him.

I couldn't believe what I was hearing. 'It's down here?'

'Yes.'

'It was down here all the *time*?'

'Yes.'

'Then why in the name of Norgar's Ravenous Hordes have we been traipsing up and down these bally *stairs*?'*

---

* In Martian myth, Norgar the Loose-Bowelled was a warlord who would only fight armies of women and/or extremely old people. There were, therefore, rarely any spoils to distribute, and his starving troops finally ate him.

'I don't know!'

I bustled the buffoon out of the way again and reached for the EYE lever.

But before I could grab it, there was a strange, echoing noise from the cavernous hall I'd just left, chilling my very blood. Which is not easy, as my blood is normally at a comfortable simmering temperature.

Footsteps! Extraordinarily large footsteps. There was some kind of monster lurking in Troy's mindscape, and it was stamping its way towards us.

Every terrifying step brought it closer. And closer. The room began to shake.

Troy's Self seemed frozen, but I was coursing with noble Martian adrenaline, and bravely leapt to the door which I locked, barred and bolted, then tugged a large sideboard in front of it, and courageously filled the sideboard with rocks, then wedged a ladder up against it.

And still the footsteps came.

Just when it seemed the behemoth was almost upon us, it stopped.

I held my breath. Suddenly, there was a monstrous pounding on the door, and a guttural growl: '*Me! Me! Me!*'

Troy looked somewhat sheepish.

'Troy, please tell me that's not your Ego out there.'

The boy didn't raise his eyes from the floor. 'He doesn't want you in our head.'

More thumps, and the door actually bulged. 'He sounds gigantic!'

'Yes. He is.' Troy shrugged. 'I just think I'm really great, that's all.'

Another thump, and the door began to splinter alarmingly.

I had to work fast. I wrenched back the eye lever and blinds immediately rolled up on the huge picture windows taking up most of the opposite wall. Finally I could see the interior of the stricken craft, and the panic that was going on inside.

But before I could engage the ears, the door finally burst into thousands of fragments, and Troy's gigantic Ego stomped in, bringing the door frame and a good deal of the wall with it, effortlessly shattering the sideboard with a single blow.

It had a huge head. Its features were a grotesque parody of Troy's face, with alarmingly little flinty eyes and two rows of teeth, triangular, sharp and interlocking, as if someone had fashioned a set of dentures from a bear trap. Its arm and leg muscles were hideously inflated, like sausage skins crammed full of basketballs and melons. Also, it drooled rather a lot.

'*Me! Me! Meeeee!*' it roared, beating its mighty chest with fists that could have hammered a concrete pile to the centre of the Earth.

'Quickly, Troy: this is a psychological emergency! The only thing that can subdue him is your Superego!'

'Is he that annoying bloke who's always trying to tell me what to do?'

'That's the chap. Where is he?'

'I keep him in here.' Troy reached under the chair cushion and took out a matchbox.

A *matchbox*.

From inside it, a tiny voice squeaked: 'Let me out! Let me out!'

I sighed. This, I had to admit, did explain rather a lot.

The Ego advanced upon us, hurling shredded furniture in its wake as it bellowed in fury: '*Me! Me! Meeeee!*'

Unperturbed, I was confident, as per the well-known theories of Dr. Kakark Bumpp, our foremost Martian Thinkalyser (whose work was shamelessly plagiarised by that despicable Terranean brain-quack, Sigmund Freud) that however large an ego may grow, it would always be subservient to the moderating influence of even the most underdeveloped Superego. 'Stand back!' I yelled, flipping open the matchbox and liberating the mighty psychological force contained therein.

'Free at last!' the tiny well-kempt Troy squeaked boldly, leaping from the box like a cricket and fearlessly placing himself squarely in the path of the marauder. 'Now listen to me, you—'

And he was gone. Down the monster's mouth, chewed up and swallowed before you could say the 'J' from Jack Robinson.

This was bad. There was now nothing to stop the slobbering behemoth from indulging its vilest bloodlust. I had no doubt in my mind I'd soon be joining the little man on his journey to stomach land.

Desperately, I reached out and threw the switch for the ears . . .

Chapter Three

From the journal of Brian Nylon, 1st January, 1952 –
Iteration 66

Troy was frozen. I tried to reach the button one last time, but I couldn't move a single muscle in my arms, so great was the G-force.

'*Gravitational wave impact in fifteen seconds.*'

I managed, with some considerable effort, to swivel my head slightly towards Dr. Janussen. 'This is the beginning, Gemma. It's all starting now. I want you to know that . . . I hate you so very much.'

She opened her mouth to reply, but then Troy bunched his right fist and suddenly punched himself in the face very very hard and yelled 'Ouch!'

'Troy?' Was he awake? Was there still hope?

Abruptly, his eyes bugged open. And, bizarrely, through his mouth, Guuuurk's voice issued. 'Brian! Gemma! It's me, Guuuurk!' How on earth could such a thing be happening? Nonetheless, it continued. 'I'm here in Troy's brain and I'm in desperate trouble!'

Guuuurk? Inside Troy's mind? And he seemed to be protected from the effects of Reverse Reality. Though I, of course, was not: 'Guuuurk! You mustn't press the button *now*!'

But something very odd indeed was going on inside Troy's head. 'Agh!' came Guuuurk's voice again. 'It's got my feet in its mouth!' There was a pause, and he added: 'It's all going terribly wrong!'

Troy's body lurched forward nonetheless. His hand shot out and shakily moved towards the button.

'You're absolutely nowhere near it!' I shouted encouragingly.

'Almost there,' Guuuurk/Troy strained. 'Ah! No! Get off, you hideous beast! Owwwwww!'

Chapter Four

Secret Report to Martian Command, by Guuuurk [cont'd]

'*Owwwwww!*' The creature had me in its terrible maw. Ignoring the pain completely, I made one last, valiant, self-sacrificing effort to reach the button. And I was close, so close . . . But then, blackness.

And in an eternity that lasted a heartbeat, the rushing winds carried me back to my body, despite all my efforts to bravely and valiantly remain in the danger zone.

For a moment, I was disoriented, still between realms. '*Uuuuurrrrhhhh* . . . It's dribbling on my spats . . .'

Water splashed on my face. I shook my head and opened all six of my eyes to see Quanderhorn in each and every one of them. 'Dammit! Wake up, Guuuurk! Did you press the button?'

Had I reached it? 'I honestly don't know, Professor.'

'Then you've got to go back!'

'I can't!' Desperate as I was to get back to the extraordinarily dangerous situation, mind-hopping is extremely draining, as you all know, and requires a minimum of ninety-six Martian hours of recuperation between jaunts.

'Dammit again! Well, at least we prevented the end of the world. As I correctly calculated, the top of the mountain tumbled directly into the sinkhole, sealing it completely. And all we lost were a few herds of goats and six or seven monasteries. Still, that's no consolation if my brilliant, brave son has needlessly sacrificed his life.'

I was beginning to see how Troy's ego problem might have evolved. 'And Brian and Dr. Janussen, of course,' I added.

'*Nmmmmmmm,*' the Professor mumbled vaguely.

The voice I was dreading blasted out of the speaker: '*Gravitational wave impact in two . . . one . . .*'

We held our breath. A second surely passed. And surely another one. I peered for the blip on the radar screen. It had vanished. Had the ship been destroyed, or had it accelerated out of range? The answer came suddenly:

'*Gravitational wave evaded!*'

The comms desk burst back into life. 'The communi-link's restored!' Quanderhorn roared. 'Guuuurk! Resume the remote controls immediately!'

I dashed to the control panel, grabbed the joystick and hailed the craft.

'Guuuurk to Dustbin Deathtrap! Bringing you home remotely.' I fired the retro-rockets. 'You should be dropping below X-barrier speed any moment now . . .'

Over the radio I heard Dr. Janussen say 'I want you to know, Brian, I don't like *you* terribly much.'

'Sorry?' Brian stuttered. 'What?'

Chapter 5

From the journal of Brian Nylon, 2nd January, 1952 –
Iteration 66

We splashed down in Lake Windermere, where Jenkins was
waiting to take us home. As Troy, Dr. Janussen and I stepped
into his patched rubber dinghy *Gargantua, Goddess of the
Waters*, I looked back at the stricken craft that had borne us. It
was now nothing more than a half-melted lump of amorphous
metal with jagged tears in the structure on all sides, and was
taking in water fast.

With a horrible whispering sound it suddenly fragmented
and collapsed down into itself like a demolished industrial
chimney, leaving a boiling eddy of bubbles and scattered flot-
sam. Amongst it, I spotted my lucky Scout woggle, which I
managed to rescue without the others seeing. I think.*

---

* *From Guuuurk's Report:* 'What the Deimos is that peculiar little braided object
Brian keeps rescuing surreptitiously? Is it something he applies to his genitalia
during the mating ritual in some way, like the red-hot Barbed Hoopno employed
in the Martian honeymoon ceremony? He certainly seems very attached to it
(though not in the way one becomes attached to the red-hot Barbed Hoopno).
We're all laughing behind our hands whenever he gets it out!'

We tumbled, exhausted, into the topless jeep and Jenkins drove us back to the lab.

It was a moonless night, and as we all lay down to try and snatch a few moments' rest, the darkness above us was dispelled all at once by a sudden enchantingly beautiful meteorite shower, bathing us in an ethereal glow.

I glanced over at Dr. Janussen, who was lying on the bench opposite mine. She looked particularly lovely as the soft radiant colours danced over her exquisite face, like fairies on midsummer night.

She opened one eye. 'Brian, your nose is dripping. And there's dried drool on your chin.'

I smiled back at her indulgently. That moment just now on the ship, when she'd claimed she didn't like me terribly much – was that *during* or *after* the X-barrier was reversing our thoughts? Had she really meant she adored me, as I did her?

'You really are disgusting,' she added.

Would I ever know the truth?

Jenkins showed me to my room.

Though I entered it and bade him goodnight with an air of nonchalance, the moment I shut the door, my heart was pounding frightfully. My past lay in this room.

I looked around slowly.

A simple desk, a camp bed, a wardrobe and a washbasin.

I recognised nothing. Remembered nothing. There were no framed photographs next to my bedside, no letters in the drawers of the desk. An inspection of the wardrobe merely turned up a spare set of sensible shoes, two plain brown ties, a couple of tweed jackets and three socks. No inscription on the back of my watch. No wallet or driving licence. No clean underwear.

I collapsed, deflated, onto the smartly made bed. No clues anywhere.

And then it struck me: that piece of paper in my flight suit pocket!

I took it out and smoothed it down. If there were a message in invisible ink, all I had to do was hold it over a heat source.

I scanned the room again. No matches, no radiator, no Primus stove. No heat source of any kind. But then, wasn't I a Boy Scout?

I poked a hole in the mattress and dug out some straw. I opened up the wardrobe and kicked out two slats from the back. Using my shoelaces to fashion a primitive bow drill, I spun a pencil into the remaining slat.

After about seventy-five minutes, the straw began to smoulder, and less than two hours later, it caught fire.

Feverishly I took the paper and held it above the flame.

Nothing happened.

I held it closer.

Letters began to form on the page, from the centre outwards:

ELLAR! EXTREMELY DAN
BOOB

Then it burst into flames, which immediately spread to my sleeve. My right arm was too exhausted from the bowing to actually move, so I had to put the blaze out by rolling on the bed. Which I remembered, just a moment too late, was stuffed with straw. I had to fill my tooth mug with water from the basin with my good arm and rush back and forwards dousing the fire.

After about half an hour, it spread to the wardrobe.

I had to dash into the corridor and hunt down a fire extinguisher. I found several, quite easily, but they were all labelled 'Not Suitable for Fire'. What the devil were they for, then?

When I finally returned, I found absolutely all the furniture had completely burnt out, and nothing remained but several piles of black smoking ashes.

I closed the door quietly, and moved into the adjacent room, which was mercifully unoccupied.

As I switched the light on, I realised I could have simply held the parchment up to the bulb.

I lay on the bed, turning over the message in my head. 'ELLER'? What could that possibly be? Propeller? Fortune-teller? Tunnel dweller? Bookseller? John D. Rockefeller?

'EXTREMELY DAN', I guessed was 'Dangerous', though it could have been 'Extremely dangly' or 'Extremely Danish'.

'BOOB'? A dangerous fortune-teller with extremely dangly boobs? Why the dickens would anyone bother to warn me against such an individual? If I saw them coming, I'd run a mile!

A wave of exhaustion swept over me, and I resolved to sleep and pursue my investigations in the light of day.

I flicked off the light and the room was illuminated by residual bursts of radiance from the dying meteor shower, gently lulling me off . . .

Exhausted, I had an almost dreamless night. There was just one: in a curious violet light, the Professor, wearing a peculiar pair of goggles, was at the foot of my bed, scraping my shins with some sort of strigil. I called out a cotton-mouthed 'Professor?' The dream Quanderhorn held his finger to his lips and vanished backwards into the gloom.

I sank back into peaceful oblivion.

Chapter Six

*From the journal of Brian Nylon, 2nd January, 1952 –
Iteration 66*

I rose late and breakfasted alone in the automated canteen on
synthetic porridge and devilled 'kidneys', from the Professor's
farm. Apparently, for some reason the 'kidneys' were made of
liver. Which was all very well, if you liked devilled liver. Personally, I found it revolting. I took my tea without milk, which
seemed to disappoint the little cow on the table.

At eight, I made my way over to the briefing room. Everyone was waiting. Dr. Janussen, looking fresh and fragrant, was
studying the output from the Telemergency Print-O-Gram.
'The meteorite shower seems to have abated, Professor.'

'Excellent!' Quanderhorn barked. 'That wraps up the sinkhole incident.' He began gathering papers from the desk. 'I'll
be in my office. My door is always open. Jenkins: can you do
something about that damned door? These idiots keep coming
in.' He turned to leave. 'And bring me all the information we
have on that meteorite shower.'

Jenkins grumbled out of the room behind him. 'Another
bloomin' meteorite shower! Still, it's good for the garden.'

And we were left in peace. No end-of-the-world alerts, no

klaxons, no 'no time to explain right now'. Guuuurk noticeably relaxed. By which I mean, he deflated his head noisily. He was resplendent today in a cricket sweater, flannels held up by an Eton tie and a cap with an MCC badge. (I later found out that this stood for Motherwell Cribbage Club.) 'That's that, then,' he grinned. 'The pressure is off.'

Troy perked up also. 'Yeah. I think I might go up and work on my dung ball.'

'On your what?' I asked, not really looking forward to the reply.

'Work out with . . . my . . . *dum*bells.' He sidled out, sheepishly. I exchanged glances with Dr. Janussen.

'Just don't go into his room. Ever. And never let him talk you into a game of croquet.'

Guuuurk hefted a sports bag onto the desk. 'Right! Time for a spot of R&R.' At which precise moment the Professor's voice crackled over the intercom.

'And Guuuurk, I'll want a full report on that sinkhole business on my desk by noon.'

'Absolutely!' Guuuurk's grin didn't waver. He winked at me with three eyes and snapped off the intercom.

The Professor appeared on a wall-mounted TV screen behind him. 'And I don't want you paying a schoolboy to do it for you this time.'

Guuuurk wheeled round. 'That's a scurrilous lie! But understood.'

The TV went dead again.

Guuuurk waited for a few moments to see if the Professor had any more surprises, and then said brightly, 'Right! As I was saying: time for a spot of R&R.'

'What about the report?' I asked.

'Ye-e-e-ess. If you could have it finished by 11.30, so I have a chance to sign it?'

'Why would I do that for you?'

He fixed me with a guilt-inducing stare and tilted his head. 'I don't know, Brian. Why would I selflessly have saved your life at enormous personal risk?'

He started rummaging through his bag. 'OK. Seduction essentials . . .' He pulled out a set of tortoiseshell moustache brushes, a large tub of Brylcreem, a tin of white spray paint, and what appeared to be a passport in the name of Edith Sitwell. A thought suddenly struck him, and he fished out his notebook again. 'Oh, Brian, I was meaning to ask before – these "French letter" thingies – where *exactly* does one get them . . .?'

I realised my face had gone very red. I stammered out some nonsense. 'Well, I, uhm, well . . .' but I was saved by Dr. Janussen.

'Leave Brian *alone*, Guuuurk. You know he's lost his memory, and I need to bring him back up to date.' She thumped a stack of files on the desk.

My heart soared. I'd been desperately wondering how I might persuade the good doctor to spend the morning with me, and here she was, volunteering. At last, some answers!

She flipped through the folders one by one. 'The Failed Martian Invasion; the Second Failed Martian Invasion; the Third Failed Martian Invasion . . .'

Guuuurk looked up from his eyebrow pencil. 'Oh, rub it in, why don't you?'

She ignored him. 'Attack of the Mole People; Hepcats from Under the Sea; Project: Huge Dog . . .' she frowned. 'The Andromeda Thrush; The Man With the X-ray Arse . . .' She turned and narrowed her eyes. 'Guuuurk, have you been tampering with these labels?'

'That's a scurrilous lie! But I get so *bored* . . .'

I was quite keen for Guuuurk to go, so I'd be alone with Dr. Janussen for the first time, but suddenly to my not-very-much-surprise, there was yet another alarm sound – a new one this time, like a particularly piercing telephone ring crossed with the war cry of a pack of baboons – and a light on the wall strobed red and white.

Guuuurk and Dr. Janussen shot upright.

'What's that?' I asked, again not keen to know the answer.

'That,' Dr. Janussen said coldly, 'is the Future Phone.'

Chapter Seven

From the journal of Brian Nylon, 2nd January, 1952 – Iteration 66

We scampered out of the room and round the corner, where there was an armoured door with a strobing red and white beacon above it.

Dr. Janussen unlocked the door with a key on a chain that was round her neck, and we hastened into the room containing this so-called Future Phone.

There it was, spotlighted on a plinth. It looked like a distant relative of a regular telephone, with a bloated riveted base covered in flashing lights. A thick piece of glass in its belly shielded a bright orange flame which was burning up a blob of strange material. There was a faint aroma of scorched linen.

There were two holes on the dial, one labelled 'Yesterday', the other 'Tomorrow'.

I was amazed. 'This is a phone . . . from the future?'

Dr. Janussen's hand hovered over the heavy studded metal receiver. She looked suddenly pale. 'It's only for the direst of emergencies. On the end of that telephone line, one of us is calling from tomorrow.'

'How is that possible? And don't tell me there's no time to explain right now.'

'Well, there isn't. I need to prepare myself. It must be something so terrible, so monumentally awful that—'

But Guuuurk had snatched up the receiver himself. 'Hellllooooo? Yesterday here!'

'Guuuurk – give that to me.' Dr. Janussen held out her hand.

But the voice of another Guuuurk bled out of the speaker. *'Hello handsome!'* it crooned. *'Guuuurk Tomorrow here!'*

'Oh, how lovely to hear from you . . .' Guuuurk eyed us leerily. '. . . Mother!'

Dr. Janussen tilted her head and folded her arms.

I heard the Future Guuuurk hiss: *'Is the coast clear?'*

'No,' Guuuurk offered me a counterfeit smile, 'there are a couple of *birds* on the windowsill, actually.'

'Guuuurk . . .' Dr. Janussen sighed.

'I'll be quick, then,' the Future Guuuurk said, *'Put seven and sixpence each way on* Dandy's Lad, *3.30 at Haydock Park.'*

Guuuurk's smile remained completely fixed. 'I'm sorry to hear your *leg* is still playing up, Mother.'

But Dr. Janussen had had enough of the feeble charade. 'Guuuurk, we can *hear* you on the speaker. And we *know* it's not your mother, because, as you never tire of telling us, you ate her at birth.'

'What?' Guuuurk fizzed with indignation. 'Who *is* this? How *dare* you impersonate my sainted mother, you unspeakable cad?' He slammed down the receiver in mock fury. 'Some people!'

'I can't believe you're using the Future Phone to give yourself racing tips.'

'How else am I supposed to make ends meet?'

'You know every call burns more of our dwindling supply of temporium 90.'

'What's temporium 90?' I asked her.

'It's an incredibly rare natural precipitate of crystallised time. There's only three and a half ounces in the world.'

'Two and a half ounces now,' Guuuurk corrected.

I struggled to understand what had just happened. 'Hang on – Guuuurk, if that was you from the future, why didn't he remember that Dr. Janussen and I could hear what he was saying?'

'Brian, old chap, you're not thinking this through,' Guuuurk purred. 'You see . . .' A look of sudden confusion progressed through his six eyes like momentum through a Newton's cradle. 'Hang on, he's right.'

Dr. Janussen frowned again. 'The best explanation is: you were calling from an alternative future. Something happens over the next twenty-four hours that throws us off track and into a different timeline. You realise the horrible implications?'

'Indeed I do!' the Martian was aghast. 'It means *Dandy's Lad* may well lose at Haydock!'

'And you've wasted a whole ounce of temporium.'

'*Nil desperandum.*' Guuuurk snatched up the phone again and dialled Yesterday. 'I'll just call my past self and warn him, i.e. me, not to take today's call tomorrow.' He grinned winningly. 'Hello, it's Mother here—'

Dr. Janussen snatched the phone away roughly and slammed it down. 'That's another half ounce squandered, you clot.'

I wrestled with the conundrum. 'But surely if Guuuurk had persuaded Yester-him not to take the call today, then Tomorrow-he wouldn't have had to make the call warning Today-him, and we wouldn't have used any of it.'

There was a very long silence.

Eventually, Dr. Janussen said: 'It's not as simple as that.'

'That was *simple*?' Guuuurk wailed. 'I'd hate to hear the complicated version.'

'Every call creates a new time strand, a strand where the people who didn't previously get the call, *do* get the call. The temporium is expended over all the strands *simultaneously*, therefore any strand using the temporium depletes the total store.'

There was an even longer silence.

Eventually, Guuuurk said, 'I was right. I *did* hate hearing the complicated version.'

We all jumped as the phone started ringing again.

We stared at it. 'So,' I ventured, 'do we answer that?'

Reluctantly, Dr. Janussen nodded. 'We daren't ignore it. It could be one of us calling with a critical warning.' She raised the receiver. 'Hello?'

And again we heard some version of Guuuurk on the end of the line. '*Hello! Different Future Guuuurk here. I'm just calling to remind you* not *to answer this call. Otherwise you'll be down to your last half ounce.*'

And in the background on the other end, another Dr. Janussen interrupted: '*Guuuurk? What are you doing? Please tell me you're not calling yourself to warn yourself not to take the very call you're making?*'

'*Good point*,' Different Future Guuuurk agreed. '*Ignore what I just said.*'

The line went dead.

I noticed, with some trepidation, that Dr. Janussen's ear had rotated ever so slightly.

'You idiot!' she snarled at Guuuurk. 'There's only enough temporium left for one more call now!'

The dreaded ratcheting noise was speeding up.

Guuuurk shot me a look that said: *Look out! She's about to blow!*

'Dr. Janussen, you're unwinding,' I ventured carefully. Not carefully enough.

'Get out!' she screeched. 'You useless pair of rubber testicles!'

There really was no call for that sort of sailor talk. 'B-but—' I stammered.

'GET OUT!' she repeated. 'I'll do the report myself!'

'I could just wind it up for you . . . Oh, ow! OK, we'll be off then.'

'And you, you six-eyed loon, stay away from this phone, or I'll deck you!'

'Understood, dear lady.' Guuuurk snatched up his bag and hightailed for the door, and discretion being the better part of valour, I followed him. Very quickly.

We headed down the corridor towards the reception area, not running, exactly, but walking very briskly, and glancing over our shoulders.

'Will she be all right?' I asked, trying to stem the blood from my nose.

'Oh, she'll be fine. She'll burn herself out and fall asleep as usual, and Jenkins will rewind her, safely.'

The aforementioned factotum was behind his desk, apparently counting biros. He eventually looked up. 'Ah! Mr. Nylon. There's a letter for you.' He turned to the wall behind him. There was only one box, with a letter clearly protruding from it, but he made a great show of inspecting every inch of the wall before he 'found' it. 'Ah! Here you go, sir.'

I tried not to snatch it from him. Who on earth would be writing *me* a letter?

Jenkins was looking at me oddly. But then, he tended to look at everyone oddly. He was odd. Mercifully, Guuuurk distracted him.

'Jenkins, old fruit!' the Martian cooed. 'I've been meaning to have a word in your shell-like.' He drew the janitor aside, and they began speaking in low voices I couldn't make out. Clearly, some nefarious piece of commerce was being conducted. That suited me.

Turning away, I examined the envelope.

It was indeed addressed to me: 'Mr. Brian Nylon, Professor Quanderhorn's Secret Laboratory, Somewhere on the road to Carlisle'. I didn't recognise the handwriting, but it was elegant, and executed in fountain pen.

Opening it quickly, I tugged out the missive inside.

It was a torn fragment from an Ordnance Survey map of the local area. The lab, of course, wasn't marked (it never appeared on any map), but the quarry was there, and the old fever hospital within it. There was a hand-drawn 'X' in the middle of the nearby village, with the footpath from one to the other picked out in red, and a time. 10.30 a.m.

I considered requisitioning a vehicle, but, frankly, I didn't want to face any awkward questioning from the nosy janitor. I'd established I was confoundedly bad at lying, and I didn't want any suspicions raised.

I glanced at the clock behind the reception desk. It was already half past nine.

The village was a good three mile walk away. I had to hurry.

Chapter Eight

Booday the argth of Phobos, Martian Year 5972 Pink

Secret Report to Martian Command, by Guuuurk. Also known as 'Guuuurk the Magnificent', 'Guuuurk the Bold' and 'Guuuurk the Bare-faced Liar'.

Having bribed Jenkins to turn a blind eye with a bottle of stout and three saucy postcards, I dabbed on some of the old distemper, fully deflated the noggin and taped closed four of my eyes with stamp hinges.

I admired the effect. Though I say so myself, I cut rather a handsome figure, not a million miles away from the young Dirk Bogarde.

I scurried out to the hut round the back of the septic tank, which I use as my secret garage, and there was the love of my life: my beautiful Morgan Plus 4 drophead sports coupé, *Maureen*, which I had obtained on 'appro' from a rather gullible inbred car salesman in the village. Topping up the tank with the amontillado, I hopped aboard, and sure enough, she started the fifteenth time, meaning my luck was in.

I roared off, my Biggin Hill NAAFI scarf flapping grandly behind me.

I coaxed the beauty around the rough winding country lanes, the sunlight glinting through the naked branches of the trees overhead. I hit a straight, and pushed down on the pedal. *Maureen* replied with an appreciative purr as she smoothly accelerated to top speed. It was a quite glorious January day, crisp and fresh. In a peculiar way, a lesser, more dishonourable Martian than myself might find himself beginning to feel very much at home here. But not me.

I double-declutched, slipped down into growling third, and powered on towards the village.

Chapter Nine

From the journal of Brian Nylon, 2nd January, 1952 –
Iteration 66

I approached the village of Wytchdrowninge over the brow
of a cobbled hill. It was a small but nevertheless horrible
place.

It ought to have been a picture postcard sort of spot, but
there was something *off* about it, something skew-whiffy I
couldn't quite put my finger on. There was a flock of large black
sharp-billed birds I didn't recognise perched along a telegraph
wire. A small tanner's workshop belched yellow sulphurous
smoke which bit into every breath you drew. The front gardens
of the cottages had dried, dead plants in them, and the pub was
called The King's Torso.

As I strolled down the hill quite warily, I passed a blacksmith hammering nails into a disgruntled horse. A hag-like
old woman in a black shawl was entering Slaughter the Family
Butchers, which had unidentifiable organs hanging on hooks
in the window. An ugly baby in a pram was bawling outside a
miserable-looking temperance bar, which had signs on the door
reading: 'Closed Evenings, Weekends and Holidays' and 'No
Dancing'.

I relaxed somewhat to see a policeman on a corner, clipping the ear of a local urchin. He seemed to recognise me, and offered a nod.

I found myself saying, 'Good afternoon, P.C. Mosely.'

I stopped. Now, how on earth had I known that? Could *he* have been the person who'd sent me the map? I was about to cross over to him when I heard a voice whose familiar gravelly timbre gave me pause.

'Chestnuts!' it cried. 'Chestnuts! Buy my lovely hot chestnuts!'

I turned to see the corpulent street merchant at his smoking brazier. He was approached by an amiable fellow in a tweed cap who chirped, 'I'll have six penn'orth, please.'

'Bugger off!' Winston Churchill barked, brusquely dispatching the poor chap on his way.

'Prime Minister!' I hurried over. It was *he* who'd sent me the map.

'Keep it down, Penetrator!' the Great Man rumbled. 'Don't want to draw attention . . .' A housewife passing by eyed us suspiciously, and he suddenly affected a pleasant, vendor-like tone to me. 'Ah! So you'd like some of my chestnuts, sir? Would you prefer them on or off the bone?' He suddenly seemed to lose faith in his rather dismal charade, and leant in again. 'What the devil *are* chestnuts, anyway? Are they still alive?'

'What are you *doing* here, sir?' I felt terribly exposed. I really didn't want word of this encounter getting back to anyone at the lab.

'Communication lines are down all across the country, Penetrator. Something's going on. And mark my words, that despicable scoundrel Quanderhorn is mixed up in it, somehow. What have you discovered?'

'I haven't found anything out at all yet, sir.'

'Well, time is of the essence. Oceanic sinkholes, mountains

decapitated – that insane scoundrel seems to think he can do whatever he pleases. He must be brought under control!'

The urchin had wandered up, rubbing his swollen ear. He fished some filthy coins out of his pocket and squeaked, 'I'll have thruppence worth, please, mister.'

'Bugger off!' the Prime Minister bellowed, cuffing the urchin's other ear to make his point. The lad's face quivered, and he raced off lest we see him cry.

'We have to find out,' Churchill continued unabashed, 'why it's perpetually 1952, and we believe the answer's in the blaggard's cellar. There's something fearful down there. Something so evil and unspeakable it would render the bravest of souls a gibbering, mindless wreck. What we need is a man, a reckless and selfless hero who's prepared to risk his life and even his very sanity for the love of his glorious country. And you are that stupid man.'

He didn't actually say that last bit, but I definitely got the message.

The old woman, clutching a brown paper package drenched with blood from her recent purchase of chitterlings, offered a single coin. 'I'll have a penn'orth, please, sir.'

'Bugger off!' I shouted at the top of my voice. The poor old dear clasped a hand to her heart and opened her mouth in shock, though her teeth stayed firmly clamped. I fully expected her to expire on the spot, but she recovered and scuttled away.

'I say, Penetrator,' Churchill chided, 'that was a bit rude.'

'I'm terribly sorry,' I blushed pathetically, 'but you *are* asking me to break into the most terrifying and dangerous place on Earth. And then what am I supposed to do?'

'Ahh! That's when you employ our Secret Weapon. Here . . .'

He fumbled in the satchel that was slung over his shoulder

and produced, to my astonishment, a live, brightly coloured and rather large bird.

'That would appear to be a parrot,' I said.

'It *looks* like an ordinary parrot,' Churchill smiled smugly, 'but this one has a unique talent. Some of our top boffins have spent many, many weeks and thousands of pounds training him in the art of repetition.'

The Prime Minister seemed so thoroughly delighted with this scientific breakthrough I could hardly bear to break it to him.

'Uhm . . . don't *all* parrots repeat things?'

'*All parrots repeat things*,' the parrot said.

Churchill looked at the bird as if for the first time. 'I need to fire some of our top boffins.'

'So, assuming I survive the cellar, I use this parrot to report back?'

'Yes. Simply teach it your secret message, and when released, it will immediately fly back to Downing Street and repeat to me whatever you taught it.'

'*Secret message*,' the bird squawked rather loudly. It had a rather defiant look in its eye. I was beginning to have my doubts about this parrot's character.

At that moment, I heard a tinny wolf whistle car horn and turned to see Guuuurk parking a rather dilapidated old Ferguson-Brown Model A tractor across the road. 'Prime Minister,' I hissed, 'that chap over there's one of the Quanderhorn team.'

'Quickly, then, Penetrator. And discreetly.' He thrust the parrot at me.

I grabbed it, turned my back and started shoving it into my trouser pocket. The parrot resisted. Vigorously.

'*Awwwwk! We will fight them on the beaches, darkest hour!*'

Churchill hissed, 'Quickly, Penetrator!'

'It's a bit of a tight fit. And it keeps flapping around in there.'

'*Awwwwk! Don't make me beg, Clemmie!*'

'The vicious fiend is trying to peck its way out again.'

The Prime Minister winced. 'Apologies, but they're still working on a smaller parrot.'

'You mean . . . a budgerigar?'

Churchill frowned into the distance. 'I may need to fire *all* of our top boffins.'

'*Waaaarrrk! Narrrzi apparatus!*'

In the end, I had to resort to thrusting the cursed bird down the front of my pants, then tightening my trouser belt considerably so it couldn't escape. It flapped and squawked mightily for several seconds, and then fell into an ominous calm.

'By the way,' Churchill warned, 'it likes monkey nuts.'

He wasn't wrong. It transpired the parrot had merely been positioning itself to launch its attack.

I scanned the street with gritted teeth and tears in my eyes. Had anybody spotted the exchange?

Guuuurk was now backing into the post office's door. I'm pretty sure he'd seen nothing, as for some reason he was holding the ugly baby over his face.

For a brief moment, I felt I was actually getting quite good at this espionage malarkey, when several loud gunshots rang out. One of them hit me in the shoulder.

Through the pain, and with cat-like reactions, I spun round to shield the Prime Minister, only to find him gone, leaving behind, for some reason, the lingering smell of herring.

His abandoned brazier was blazing away unchecked, causing chestnuts to explode and fly hither and thither quite dangerously.

If you've ever tried to douse a dangerous fire with a hungry parrot imprisoned in your underwear, whilst simultaneously dodging exploding conkers and trying not to draw attention to yourself, you may begin to understand my difficulties at this point.

I finally got the disaster under control. Exhausted, bruised, reeking of smouldering tweed, and my poor jinglebells pitted with peck marks, I began to limp back to the complex.

I glanced up the street, and could have sworn I spotted Dr. Janussen walking (with a rather peculiar stumpy gait!) into the hairdresser's, of all places. Curious. She hadn't struck me as a preening sort of woman, and I'd thought she'd said she was staying at the lab. No, it definitely was her. Fortunately, her back was towards me. Still, I pulled my jacket lapels over my face instinctively as I passed the salon window. Which is why I didn't notice the open drain till I fell down it.

Chapter Ten

Secret Report to Martian Command, by Guuuurk [cont'd]

I parked up with a playful toot of the two-tone novelty horn, simulating a human 'wolf whistle', and instantly regretted it. Brian was on the other side of the road with a street vendor. He appeared to be buying a large coloured chicken for lunch. He's a delightful chap, but absolutely *rotten* at lying. I really didn't want him accidently blowing my cover with an ill-judged remark. Thinking quickly, I ducked behind a nearby water company warning sign, which bore the legend 'DANGER! OPEN GRATE', when I spotted Dr. Janussen crossing the road and heading for the hairdresser's, which I realised to my horror was right behind me.

As luck would have it, at that precise moment everybody's head turned towards the rather alarming sound of gunshots. It turned out merely to be chestnuts overheating on a brazier. This was my chance.

I glanced around and spotted a small pig someone had left in a rather ornate wheelbarrow nearby. I hurled the sign aside and snatched up the porker. Using it to hide my face, I backed carefully into the post office, triggering its delightful tinkling bell. I set down the piglet and smacked it to send it squealing on its way, then stepped up to the counter.

As usual, the repugnant old harpy, Mrs. Wiggonby the postmistress, was behind the counter in her moth-eaten wrap-over pinny. Normally, she would be gaily dangling envelopes over the spout of her merrily boiling kettle, but on this occasion she just seemed to be staring fixedly into the middle distance.

'Hail, well met and good morning, Mrs. Wiggonby. And may I say, you're looking particularly ravishing this morning.'

Now this sort of greeting would ordinarily spark a little bit of jolly flirtatious banter. But today, she merely rotated her head in my direction.

'Good morning, sir,' she said, rather slowly and in a dull monotone. 'How can I help you?'

'It's me, Mrs. Wiggonby: Edith Sitwell.'

'Oh, yes, of course, Mr. Sitwell,' she said, but without a glint of recognition.

I peered at her more intently. Her eyes seemed rather glazed, and the pupils were dilated to an extraordinary extent. 'Doris, are you feeling all right?'

'I have never felt more perfect in my life,' she said oddly, in the same monotone.

I shrugged. I would never completely understand Terraneans, and never, ever their unfathomable females. 'Glad to hear it. Now, I was wondering: I see you sell Air Mail letters and registered letters, but do you have any *French* letters?' I raised my top two eyebrows hopefully.

But she merely responded: 'Would you like to see my glowing meteorite, Mr. Sitwell?'

Ah! So we were back to the flirting. Clearly, that was some sort of saucy human innuendo. However, it would be caddish to lead the poor homely creature on. 'I should tell you, Doris—' I smiled kindly '—I do prefer my women to be *very* slightly less repulsive.'

'I really think you ought to see my glowing meteorite. It's just around the back here. It's quite magnificent.'

Clearly, she'd not taken my subtle hint. 'I'm sure it is, old thing, but, er, I am in rather a hurry this morning . . .' I backed out towards the door. 'So nice to have seen you . . .'

Then, through the door pane I spotted the Professor over the road, angrily peeling Troy off a large strip of flypaper in the fishmonger's window. Strange. Hadn't he said he was going to stay in his office? I couldn't risk him learning I was out of the compound. Again. The only other egress was through the rear. This of course meant taking up Mrs. Wiggonby's rather frightening offer. Whatever it was.

'On the other hand, perhaps I *will* just take a quick look at this glowing meteorite of yours.' There was no getting out of it now.

The old trout led me through the multicoloured plastic strips that dangled from the back door frame. I must admit to a certain degree of trepidation. It may come as a tremendous shock to my legion of Martian admirers that Guuuurk the Rampantly Fecund had scant knowledge of Terranean reproduction rituals. Which is to say, none at all. I got into a terrible lather that I had insufficient food supplies about me, and absolutely no murdered flora whatsoever. Moreover, my one and only dancing lesson had been a complete fiasco, when Jenkins and I spent the entire session arguing over which of us should have brought the record player.

'I think I should warn you,' I declared, 'I've never done this before. I do hope you'll take that into account . . .'

We stepped out into a small backyard. I was surprised to see it was crowded with villagers. All of them stared at my arrival. 'Good heavens!' I said. 'This is socially awkward . . .'

And then there was a sound. I've made quite a study of Earth music – the enjoyment of which still eludes me – and this series of harmonic waveforms was indubitably extraterrestrial.

The non-music was issuing from a large rock embedded in the shrubbery, which was pulsing with dazzlingly coloured light.

Mrs. Wiggonby's voice descended to a deeply booming timbre. 'Look deep into the glow, Mr. Sitwell. We want you to be One of Us.'

Slowly, quietly at first, the assembled villagers began to chant in similar low-pitched resonance: 'One of Us . . . One of Us . . .'

I stared into the strangely beguiling luminosity. It seemed to be calling to me. Beckoning . . . beckoning . . .

'One of Us . . .' they chanted, 'One of Us . . .'

Chapter Eleven

The Rational Scientific Journal of Dr. Gemini Janussen,
Wednesday 2nd January 1952 (Again)

Jenkins gently awoke me from my nap. I must confess, I don't recall having dropped off, but we've all been working long hours recently. I was surprised to find I was in my room. Normally it's an extremely efficient, if somewhat spartan affair, but someone, for reasons unknown, had placed jars of sickly scented flowers everywhere. Moreover, there were fragrant candles burning on the mantelpiece, and cushions – *hundreds* of cushions – scattered over every horizontal surface. I *loathe* cushions. What are they *for*? Where did they *come* from?

Even more peculiarly, there was a note by my telephone indicating I'd booked an appointment at the *hairdresser's*, of all things. What a pointless waste of time! Still, it was too late to cancel, and rather than pay for nothing, I decided to take my motor scooter into the village.

When I took it out of the garage, I discovered to my intense horror that during the past week some practical 'joker' had sprayed the entire thing *pink*. Was there never any end to the oh-so 'amusing' japes the adolescent males got up to in this place?

I parked the gaudy vehicle in the woods at the top of the hill, and hid it with bracken. I certainly wasn't going to be seen arriving in the village on such an eyesore.

It was only when I stepped onto the cobbles that I realised I was wearing high heels. I would never choose such an impractical item of ludicrous foot torture. I didn't even know where they'd come from.

I simply snapped the heels off and made my way as best I could down towards the hair salon.

I can't say I was surprised to see Guuuurk arrive in his rather unconvincing 'human' disguise, and his even less convincing 'sports car'. He sounded his juvenile 'wolf whistle' horn and leapt out of his rusting wreck as if he genuinely were a jet set playboy jumping from an Aston Martin convertible.

He spotted me, I think, but clearly didn't want to be seen himself, because he quickly ducked behind a road sign, and skulked there for a while. I was about to go over and order him back to the lab with a flea in his ear, when I heard a series of small explosions. I turned to the source, and there was Brian, one of his sleeves on fire, trying to douse a small conflagration in a chestnut brazier. Really, he is the most useless article imaginable.

When I turned back, Guuuurk had vanished.

I scanned the street to see where he might be lurking, when I was surprised to spot Q. himself outside the fishmonger's. I considered hailing him, but he was staring vacantly into the distance, clearly lost in thought, as was often his wont. Then I heard Troy calling in some sort of panic from inside the shop. Hardly surprising – it rarely took Troy more than a couple of minutes to find himself in intractable trouble, whatever he was trying to do. Hardly bothering to rouse himself from his reverie, the Professor slowly turned and marched inside.

I glanced at the church clock. I had no time for these shenanigans. I had an appointment to keep.

Marcia was just putting the finishing touches to my trim, when her niece, Minnie, burst through the door in rather a blue funk. 'Hey up, Dr. Janussen! They said you was in here. There's some very queer doings over at t'post office.'

'Queer how?'

'People's goin' in there, and they en't comin' out again.'

'Well.' I pulled off my bib and stood up. 'We'd best take a look, hadn't we?'

Chapter Twelve

From the journal of Brian Nylon, 2nd January, 1952 –
Iteration 66

Hampered by my injuries, it took me the best part of an hour
to heave myself out of the disgustingly slimy drain without
further damaging the parrot buried down my underpants. On
top of which, just as I had finally hauled myself almost to the
top of the slippery shaft, I heard Quanderhorn walking past.

He was saying something about 'growing meat and the like'
in his deep voice. Surely those unidentifiable organs dangling
in the butcher's window couldn't have been the discarded
by-products of the professor's liver-substitute experiments? I
resolved to become a vegetarian. And then I remembered his
vegetable experiments and despaired.

Suddenly I caught a glimpse of Troy's distinctive cowboy
boots passing right next to my eye, and had to duck back down
again into the slurry.

Eventually I emerged, unobserved, and staggered to my feet,
muttering a string of words I wouldn't demean this journal by
recording. Whereupon, in the best tradition of one of Mr. Ben
Travers' hilarious Aldwych farces, I turned to find myself face
to face with a vicar.

'*Oh, bugger!*' the parrot said.

I grinned weakly at the kindly old clergyman, who seemed nonetheless unrattled. 'Oh, it's Mr. Nylon,' he beamed. 'Would you like to come with me behind the post office and see the glowing meteorite?'

Well, that seemed a peculiar question. 'Uhhhm, that's very kind of you, Vicar, but I'm afraid I have to be running along. Perhaps another time?'

He put a surprisingly firm hand on my shoulder. 'I really think we should do it now, together, my son.'

I'd read about this kind of thing in the yellow press, so I tugged myself free and stepped briskly away, almost colliding with the old woman who'd tried to buy chestnuts.

'Pardon me, young man. Would you help me?'

I restrained the impulse to give her the Scout salute. (Now, that was one I *did* know: three fingers!) 'Yes, of course.'

'Just take my hand and guide me to the post office to see the glowing meteorite.'

There was something odd going on here, which I couldn't quite get to the bottom of in my mind. I thanked the old biddy profusely and made more excuses. But before I'd gone two steps, the ear-tweaked urchin jumped in my path and shouted, 'Here, Mister – gan wi' us to t'post office and have a goosey at yon shiny rock.'

'Ha ha,' I fake-laughed, 'scallywag!' and ruffled his hair just a tad too violently. I felt a sharp tug at my trouser cuffs. The fat, ugly baby was gumming my turn-ups.

It released me for a second, looked up, and said, 'Goo goo muh-muh meteorite,' then tucked into my cavalry twill again. I glanced behind me. There were a dozen or so more villagers lurching towards me in a curious, stomping half-march, as if possessed. I shuffled free of the infant and started walking briskly.

Heart in my mouth, I gradually quickened my pace, glancing over my shoulder constantly, and unwittingly ran straight into the back of another villager. Mercifully, it was good old P.C. Mosely.

He turned to me with concern. 'Why, Mr. Nylon! Whatever is the matter?'

'I'm sorry, officer, something rather curious seems to be happening to those villagers.'

He looked at them with narrowed eyes and lowered his voice. 'Yes, sir. Deeply suspicious indeed. I've had my eye on them for some time now. It's my opinion they've been possessed by some kind of alien intelligence.'

'Yes. I'm afraid that's what I was thinking, too. The poor devils.'

'Poor devils indeed, sir. Perhaps it would be wise . . .' he snapped a handcuff over my wrist, as his voice began to drop in tone, '. . . if you accompanied me to the post office to see the glowing meteorite.' He clunked the other cuff firmly over his own wrist.

The mob was beginning to chant: 'One of Us . . . One of Us . . .'

There were scores of them now, lurching towards me, their inhuman eyes staring, staring . . .

Chapter Thirteen

From the journal of Brian Nylon, 2nd January, 1952 –
Iteration 66

Instinctively, I knocked the P.C . out with a single blow from my free hand.

I have no idea where that instinct came from, and felt vaguely ashamed of it. It seemed unpredictably violent for me, but predictably stupid. I now had to escape the lumbering mob whilst dragging behind me the dead weight of a rather corpulent village constable.

It was the world's slowest ever chase.

Slowly, and mostly backwards, I hastened at a ponderous crawl up past the fishmonger's and, finally, one desperate heave at a time, the temperance bar next door.

Sweating heavily, I looked back. I'd managed to gain a few precious seconds on the horde – just enough time to clumsily manhandle the unconscious seventeen stone copper I was toting into the conveniently empty pram parked outside.

I began to push it up the hill, barely eluding the grasping lunges of the chanting pack.

I was making much better time, but the pram creaked and moaned with its grotesquely adipose load over the clattering cobbles. I could feel every bump and divot transmitted directly via the rattling handles to my teeth, which were gritted in fear and resolve. Well, to be honest, just fear.

By the time I'd finally put enough distance between me and the mob to rest for a moment, I'd earned quite a ferocious headache, which wasn't helped by the incessant stream of profanities being squawked from my flies. I started to dig through P.C. Mosely's pockets for the handcuff key.

A cluster of furred-up boiled sweets, a whistle, a notebook, a plastic fried egg, three bicycle clips – *why three? What on earth does he do with the extra one?* – a well-licked pencil . . .

'One of Us . . . One of Us . . .'

Come on! A curly sandwich. Very curly. When I held it up to my ear I swear I could hear the sea. A handcuff key, a packet of three Player's Weights – *perhaps he used the third clip around his arm to keep his sleeve up. But then, what about the other arm?* – a box of Puck matches, a warrant card with a rather threadbare cover – *did he keep a spare bicycle clip for a friend? Ooh! Wasn't it something to do with the Freemasons? Didn't they wear a special* – Hang on there. Hadn't I said 'handcuff key'? But where had it gone? I must have put it *some*where.

'One of Us . . . One of Us . . .' Loud now.

What was that rattling in the sandwich? No – just a cockroach . . . Cockroach? *Aghhhh!* Wait, yes, there was the key, glinting between those cobbles!

I scooped it up, jabbed it in the lock and twisted feverishly. The rabble was almost upon me. There was a click that sounded to me like the sweet clarion trumpet of the heavenly host and I was free!

The possessed P.C. was starting to come round. He made a grab for my wrist, but he was still groggy, and I unnecessarily punched him in the face again. Who the devil *was* I?

There was a disturbing humming noise. I spun round to see, with alarm, some of the villagers rolling the meteorite in front of them. As it drew closer, I could hear a kind of unearthly music emanating from it, which seemed to be seeping into my brain.

I turned the pram around and sent it hurtling into my pursuers, scattering them like bar skittles.

I hared off up the hill, over the brow and into the nearby woods. Almost immediately I stumbled and fell over a hard metal object concealed by bracken and fronds. A pink motor scooter!

What an unlucky and cruel twist of fate. Any other colour on the *planet* and I could have ridden it home!

I picked myself up and stumbled on into the unforgiving wood. The path would have been easier, but this way was more direct. And wet. And thorny. And painful.

The sounds of the mob began to fade behind me. Those poor souls!

There was only one way to prevent this nightmare.

And that was to stop it before it happened in the first place.

Chapter Fourteen

*From the journal of Brian Nylon, 2nd January, 1952 –
Iteration 66*

With shattered nerves and shredded clothes, I staggered into the lab reception. Jenkins was scrutinising some kind of report. He pretended not to notice me for a few moments. Then, unexpectedly, he exhaled a sudden cloud of smoke and surreptitiously slipped a pinched out dimp behind his ear with a smooth, practised movement. Only then did he look up.

'Mr. Nylon, sir!' He hiked his moustache. 'You've got yourself in quite a state, there.'

'There's no time to explain, Jenkins.' I raced down the corridor to the room with the Future Phone. I tried the handle. Locked, of course. I banged on the armoured door in frustration.

Jenkins ambled up behind me.

'I need the key to this room immediately!' I yelled.

Jenkins sucked air in through his teeth. 'Sorry, Mr. Nylon, Dr. Janussen left strict instructions in that regard. She said: "On absolutely no account are those two brainless tur—"'

'This is an emergency!' I rattled the handle impotently.

'It's no good you trying to get in, sir, she's got the key with her.'

There came a loud, rude word from my private quarters.

Jenkins coughed and nodded down.

The damned parrot had pecked open my fly buttons! Its multicoloured head was protruding, looking very pleased with itself, I must say. In fact, as I stared at it, its crest slowly raised in delight.

Jenkins ostentatiously averted his eyes. 'Perhaps you'd like to "adjust your dress", sir.'

I stuffed the bird rudely back inside and pinched the gap closed with my fingers. 'Jenkins — I want you to forget what you've just seen.'

'Believe me, sir, I'm trying to.'

My mind swirled through the remaining options. There weren't many. 'Right! We'll have to use the ordinary phone. I need to speak to Downing Street immediately.'

This was one of those moments Jenkins lives for. He shook his head, but couldn't shake the smile from under his tash. 'I'm very much afraid, *sir*, the ordinary phone lines went down with the meteorite storm. And, before you ask, the two-way radio is jammed with what I can only describe as "an unearthly static".'

'Jenkins, listen carefully: that was no commonplace meteorite storm.'

'I'm well aware, sir. This is the information the Professor asked for.' He produced the report from the Telemergency Print-O-Gram machine he'd just been perusing. 'By a hextraordinary coincidence, meteorites landed behind every single post office in the country.'

I grabbed the sheet and scanned it. This was worse than I could have dreamt. Except, possibly, for that dream about Winston Churchill dressed as a Lyons' Corner House waitress — which, come to think of it now, may not have been a dream after all. I stuffed it in my jacket.

This was an invasion, nothing more or less. Unless I could come up with something fast, the entire human race was in peril. But what?

A razor sharp bill suddenly embedded itself in my thigh. Of course – the parrot! 'Wait out here, Jenkins! There may still be one last chance.' I raced into the gentlemen's washroom and locked the door.

I manhandled the parrot out of my trousers and held it firmly so it faced me. It regarded me coldly, the steel of defiance still glinting in its eye.

'OK, parrot: this is your moment. I've got to get this warning to the Government.'

'*Awwwwk!*'

'Here's the message . . .'

The parrot looked at me. '*Here's the message . . .*' it repeated.

'No, that's not the message.'

'*No, that's not the message.*'

Clearly, this was not going to be a straightforward procedure. 'No! Stop! The message will start . . . now.'

The parrot looked at me again. '*The message will start now.*'

'God give me strength.'

'*God give me . . .*'

'Shut up!'

'*Shut up!*'

'No, you shut up!'

'*No, you shut up!*'

I bit my lip. I was arguing with an echo. This wasn't getting me anywhere. Obviously, I needed to go straight to the message without saying anything else. I cleared my throat. The parrot cleared his.

'Don't go to the post office.'

The parrot considered this very carefully, and then said: '*No, you shut up!*'

'No, you shut up!'

'*No, you shut up!*'

I was doing it again! Damn this parrot! Infuriating little . . . I tried again. 'Don't go to the post office.'

'*No, that's not the message.*'

'Yes it is! It *is* the bloody message!'

'*God give me strength.*'

I composed myself and tried one last time.

'Don't go to the post office.'

There a very long silence. The parrot mulled it over. It put its head on one side and said: '*Go to the post office.*'

'No no no no no no no! That's the very opposite! Listen. Now listen very carefully. We'll do it one word at a time: Don't . . .'

'*Don't . . .*'

'Go . . .'

'*Go. . .*'

'To . . .'

'*To . . .*'

'The . . .'

'*The . . .*'

'Post . . .'

'*Post . . .*'

'Office.'

A glint of comprehension dawned in the parrot's eye. He puffed out his chest feathers, and in a confident tone declaimed, '*Go to the post office.*'

I'm afraid at that point my patience ran out, and I made it rather brutally clear to the parrot what his options were.

There was a discreet knock on the door, and Jenkins called,

'Is everything all right, sir? Only, I heard a lot of hideously tortured squawking going on in there.'

'Out in a minute, Jenkins!' I held up the hopefully chastened bird. 'Right, this is your last chance, Buster. Don't go to the post office.'

'*Don't go to the post office.*'

'No no no . . . hang on, though. What?'

'*Don't go to the post office.*'

'Yes, yes. That's it! You beauty! I could kiss you!'

The bird was extremely pleased with itself. It started bobbing its head up and down and repeating very excitedly: '*Go to the post office! Go to the post office! Go to the post office! Go to the post office . . .*'

Clearly, this was hopeless. I had no option but to stuff the wretched creature back in my trousers. Serve him right, too.

The obstreperous janitor was waiting outside, pretending he hadn't been listening at the door.

'Jenkins! Any second now, an angry possessed mob of villagers is going to swarm up that road . . .'

Jenkins rolled his eyes. 'Oh, not again.'

'I'll try and hold them off for as long as I can. In the meantime . . .'

I scribbled out a note as best I could on a sheet of Izal:

> Urgent and important:
> Broadcast on all channels across the world:
> 'DON'T GO TO THE POST OFFICE!'

I handed it to him. 'You've got to get this to the Prime Minister somehow.'

Jenkins took the note and openly read it, which I considered

127

rather disrespectful. 'Very good, sir. I'll slip out the back gate . . .'

He hastened out of a nearby side door, as my mind raced ahead. Would the Professor's security devices be sufficient to keep out a violent mob? And if not . . .? My thoughts were abruptly interrupted by a familiar voice, but with a rather dark and unusual tone.

'Hello, Brian.'

I turned. It was the Martian.

Chapter Fifteen

From the journal of Brian Nylon, 2nd January, 1952 –
Iteration 66

I smiled, but the grin rather froze on my face. 'Guuuurk – didn't I see you going into the post office?' I asked as casually as I could. 'Did they happen to show you the glowing meteorite at all?'

'Yes, they did. It's rather . . .' The Martian paused. Various eyes opened and closed so rapidly his face looked like a pinball machine. 'Oh I see,' he finally concluded. 'You're "One of Us"?'

Damn! He'd been turned!

I had no choice but to pretend they'd got me as well. 'Yes . . . I am . . . One of Us.'

'And so am I.'

We looked at each other uneasily. There was a long, embarrassing silence.

'Shall we do the chant?' Guuuurk suggested.

'I suppose so,' I reluctantly conceded. Neither of us seemed eager to chant first, so I rather feebly attempted to take the lead. 'One of Us . . . One of Us . . .'

Guuuurk joined in in a rather cursory fashion, before breaking off apologetically. 'I'm not very good at the chanting, actually.'

'No, neither am I.'

'We'll take it as read, shall we?'

That was a relief. 'I am looking for the Earthling Dr. Janussen,' I lied as best I could, 'to, uhm, stop her using the Future Phone to warn Yesterday-us not to go to the post office tomorrow. Today. Do you know where she is?'

'I'm right behind you, Brian.'

I wheeled around, shocked. 'Dr. Janussen!'

Guuuurk seemed similarly taken aback. 'Gemma! Did you hear what we were just saying? At all?'

Her eyes took us both in for a moment, then her voice seemed to take on a deeper timbre. 'Every word. But have no fear – I am also One of Us.'

This was a terrible, terrible blow. The beautiful, brilliant Dr. Janussen subsumed by an alien intelligence – perhaps forever! I should have realised there was something amiss when I'd seen her curious lumbering walk in the village. I had to struggle to wrestle the emotions from my face.

I was about to speak, when Professor Quanderhorn himself stepped forward out of the shadows and boomed, 'I am also One of Us.'

I couldn't help myself. Before I could stop them, the words 'Oh, Rats!' had fled my mouth.

The others turned towards me as one. 'Perhaps I got the Earthling expression wrong,' I squirmed. 'I mistakenly thought rats were good things. I meant to imply I was just so utterly delighted the Professor is another One of Us.'

Quanderhorn nodded. 'Troy is also One of Us, aren't you, Troy?'

Troy stepped out of the shadows himself. 'Actually, I don't feel any different. But if you say so, Pops.'

So. My worst fears had been made manifest.

Everyone had been taken over except me.

Chapter Sixteen

Booday the argth of Phobos, Martian Year 5972 Pink

From the Secret Report to Martian Command, by Guuuurk. Also known as 'Guuuurk the Intelligent', 'Guuuurk the Mighty' and 'Guuuurk the Sartorially Superior'.

Everyone had been taken over except me.

Obviously the dreary meteorite hypnotism couldn't possibly work on my superior Martian brain, but I'd cunningly managed to dupe the rather simple-minded zombies behind the post office into believing I had been converted. As soon as the *tedious* chanting really got going, I made my excuses and left. I succeeded in starting Maureen in a lightning-fast twenty-three minutes, teased her up to almost 12 mph, foot flat down, and zipped out of town like wax off a floozy's hairpin.*

Encountering Brian alone in reception, I realised just in the nick of time that he, too, had been 'absorbed'. Unsurprisingly, it quickly emerged that the entire useless so-called 'Invasion

---

* Clearly, this is one of Guuuurk's many Martian expressions which fail to translate into any Earth language. Thank goodness.

Prevention Team' had fallen to the same device. How these sorry nincompoops ever managed to beat off the might of Mars on three consecutive occasions is a mystery wrapped in an enigma, folded up in a conundrum and stuffed inside a paper hat. With 'I don't know' written on the front in brown crayon.

It was child's play persuading the alien Brian that I was also 'absorbed'. But maintaining the subterfuge now all four of them were possessed was going to prove very trying and extremely dangerous.

'Oh!' I exclaimed. 'We're *all* One of Us, then. How lovely!'

There was a rather worrying pause. I broke the silence by suggesting we tried the chant again, but alien Brian mercifully demurred. 'I'm afraid I have to go off now . . .' he declared, 'and do . . . evil alien . . . thingumabobs. Gemma Alien, could I possibly have the key to the Future Pho—'

'Stay where you are, dammit!' the alien Quanderhorn barked. 'I sense that one of us is *not* One of Us.'

I heroically resisted wetting myself. 'Are you saying one of us is . . . One of Them?'

'There's only one way to root out the imposter,' Quanderhorn insisted. 'Extreme physical violence.'

'Good idea,' I said quickly. 'I'm sensing it's Brian.'

The alien Brian looked shocked. 'No, it isn't,' he stammered.

'That's just what Not One of Us would say,' I cleverly countered, 'if he was One of Them.'

'Very well, let's see.' Quanderhorn turned grimly to Troy. 'Punch Brian in the face.'

The lad seemed confused. 'Won't that hurt him?'

'Exactly the point. If he's truly One of Us,' alien Quanderhorn said, 'he will feel no pain.'

'Actually,' alien Brian squirmed, 'I turned my ankle earlier, and oooh . . . no pain at all. Just nothing. So it's obviously not—'

Troy punched him in the face.

'Ow! H. . .*owwww* did you not hurt me, Alien Troy, when you punched me so *viciously hard*?' A rather large and painful-looking bruise seemed to be swelling across his jaw.

I could see Quanderhorn was about to shift his attention towards me. Thinking fast, I yelled: 'Let's try kicking Brian in the shins.'

'Uhm . . .' Brian started to protest, so I had no choice but to quickly deliver the first vicious boot myself. The others joined in enthusiastically.

I could have sworn Brian's eyes glazed over, but obviously, I was imagining it.

'Ahddnngg! Unnnghhh! Ha ha ha,' he screeched with an un-convincing half-laugh. 'See? If that had hurt at all, I wouldn't be able to dance a hornpipe now, would I?'

He staggered forward, took a single step and immediately fell over. He started flailing about on the floor humming a sea shanty. 'See? I think Guuuurk's the traitor! It's definitely Guuuurk, not me.'

Quanderhorn picked up a sturdy wooden chair and handed it to alien Gemma. 'We have to be sure. Break this over his head.'

'All right! All right! I admit it!' Brian confessed. 'I'm a human, and proud of it. I was playing for time. And it worked! Ha ha. Jenkins is warning London as we speak. So do your worst, you filthy alien swine.'

Bravely, and without any thought for my personal safety, I interposed myself between the evil aliens and Brian, and made my heroic stand. 'You're not alone, Brian, for I, too, am One of Them. If any of you despicable alien fiends want him, you're going to have to come through me.' I struck my sensei Shaku-wocky fighting stance and defied them to make a move.*

---

* Guuuurk often boasts of his proficiency in various Martian martial arts. Oddly, they are never called the same thing twice.

Chapter Seventeen

*The Rational Scientific Journal of Dr. Gemini Janussen,
Wednesday January 2nd 1952 (Again)*

Guuuurk fell to his knees and grovelled disgustingly before the possessed Q., tears running down all his cheeks. 'All right! All right! I was immune to the meteorite! Please, I beg you, don't inflict the extreme violence on me. I'll do anything to help you conquer this planet . . . or *my* planet. Mars is ripe for the picking. We're all useless fighters anyway. Our Death Rays don't even work! Just don't hurt me.'

I resisted the temptation to break the chair over *his* head.

Personally, I'd never even made it to the post office. Just crossing the street, I'd been approached by five different villagers, obviously in some hypnotic fugue state, who'd tried to insist I look at their wretched meteorite. Clearly, it was no ordinary space debris: it was some kind of extraterrestrial life form bent on exerting its deadly thrall on humanity. I could see only one chance to save life on Earth – to get back to the lab and call Yesterday-us with a dire warning.

I found it rather shocking to overhear that both Brian and Guuuurk had apparently been taken over. Swallowing the key to the Future Phone was pure rationality – who knows what havoc these demons might wreak with such a device!

But, now with Guuuurk and Brian both unmasked, the situation was altered: we humans outnumbered the aliens.

I stepped forward. 'You may as well know, I didn't look at the meteorite, either.'

Brian started hauling himself unsteadily to his feet. 'Dr. Janussen!' he grinned stupidly, 'Gemma! You're – you! How very marvellous!'

Q. sighed. 'And so am I. Troy also.'

Brian wrinkled his brow. 'So . . . none of us was ever "One of Us"? But I saw you and Troy in the village, Professor.'

'We'd gone to examine the nearest meteorite, but it soon became apparent it was dangerous to approach it. When I saw you'd all been subsumed, my plan was to get you to knock yourselves out one by one. I'm afraid this required a certain amount of creative deception.'

'And I didn't mean a word of what I said just now about being a miserable snivelling traitor.' Guuuurk patted down his trousers to clean the knees. 'Ha ha. I bet you completely fell for it!'

Troy smiled. 'I've no idea what's going on. But I quite liked kicking Brian.'

'Sorry, Brian, no offence,' Guuuurk apologised. 'But actually it *was* surprisingly enjoyable.'

Brian plonked himself into a chair and winced. 'At least we don't have to do that appalling chant again.'

At which precise moment, we heard it, from outside the walls:

'One of Us . . . One of Us . . .'

Barely audible at first, but getting inexorably louder. Of course, the inevitable klaxon sounded and the announcement we'd been dreading came over the tannoy.

'*Angry mob storming the outer compound! Engaging primary security protocols.*'

'Not to worry,' the Professor snapped. 'We'll simply call Yesterday-us on the Future Phone, and tell them the dire—'

'I've swallowed the key,' I confessed. 'Don't all look at me like that. I thought you were all alien invaders. It was the only expedient course of action.'

'Not to worry.' The Professor was unfazed. 'Nylon has the situation covered. Good old reliable Jenkins will have delivered the message to London. He should be back here, according to my calculations . . .' He pulled out a slide rule and fiddled about with it '. . . assuming he took his usual bicycle and didn't get a flat . . . He'll be here . . .'

Jenkins burst back in through the side door, panting and sweaty. 'I done it, sirs!'

'. . . any moment . . .'

'I delivered the message!'

'. . . now!' Quanderhorn looked up. 'Jenkins,' he scolded, 'you're early'.

'I greased the chain yesterday, sir.'

'Well, why didn't you tell me, dammit? How am I supposed to calculate anything properly when you're randomly adjusting parameters all over the place, willy-nilly?'

'I didn't know it was a parameter, sir. It just looked like a normal chain.'

It beggars belief. There was a baying crowd of alien invaders outside, and these useless males were bickering about bicycle components. I steered the conversation back to sanity. 'Hadn't we better turn on the wireless?'

'*Angry mob penetrating outer defences!*'

'And hadn't we better do it quickly?'

'Excellent thought, Dr. Janussen. Jenkins – take the

largest forklift truck to warehouse number nineteen and load up Gargantua – the portable Quanderadio. And a very long lead.'

'Or,' I suggested, 'we could just use the set in the briefing room.'

'Almost as good, Dr. Janussen. Almost as good.'

I arrived first, immediately tuned into the Home Service and twisted up the volume. The reassuring honeyed tones of the BBC announcer filled the room:

'Here is an urgent and important announcement on all frequencies: Go to the Post Office! Go there at once and look at the glowing meteorite! I repeat . . .'

Horrified, I twiddled the tuner to another station. Radio Paris:

'Au Bureau de Poste! Y aller à la fois et regarder la meteorite glowing! Vite! Vite! . . .'

I zipped through the medium wave:

'Go zur Post! Gehen sie dort sofort und blick auf die glowing meteorite! Schnell! Schnell!'

'Ichido sugu ni yūbinkyoku ni ikimasu!'

'перейти к почтамту сразу сразу!'

A dark cloud was forming on Quanderhorn's brow. 'Jenkins? Did you send that message by telegram?'

'I did, sir.'

'And where did you go to send that telegram?'

'Why, the post office, of course.' A strange, cold grin bled over the janitor's features as his voice descended below the depths of human pitch. 'And soon, you will all be One of Us.'

Chapter Eighteen

The Rational Scientific Journal of Dr. Gemini Janussen,
Wednesday 2nd January 1952 (Again) [cont'd]

It's extraordinary to record at this moment that throughout all of this protracted situation none of the men, not a single one of them, had mentioned my rather striking new haircut. Not that I wanted them to, of course, but the sheer poverty of their observational facilities never ceased to amaze me.

For the record, and not that it matters in any way, I'd elected to have a Doris Day bob, because it was the most efficient style on offer. The sheer expediency of it, by coincidence, also subtly flattered my oval face, which I'd have thought would have been apparent to all. Clearly, I was wrong. Again, not that it matters. Frankly, this was not the time to be concerned with such piffling trivia. I can't think why it had crossed my mind. My hand went up instinctively to my right ear. I've no idea why – what an odd thing to do!

The alien who had hijacked Jenkins had produced from his pocket what appeared to be a banana, and was holding us at bay with it, as if it were a gun.

'Stay where you are. You will all be absorbed shortly.'

'I say, Jenkins.' Brian sidled forward with a rather

unconvincing nonchalance. 'Ha! You chaps have a lot to learn about our Earth weapons.' He leapt and made a grab for the banana, which emitted a bright electric arc, repelling the foolhardy idiot across the room into the back wall with a rather sickening thud.

'You've a lot to learn about *our* weapons,' the Jenkins monster crowed. 'Ho ho ho.' He looked up, as if receiving a telepathic signal. Clearly he was operating as a component in some sort of hive intellect. 'We are approaching the main gates. Soon you will be subsumed.'

Q. barked: 'Delores, seal the main gates!'

'*Sealing main gates now.*'

'That should hold them for a few hours.'

'*Crowd broken through main gates.*'

I heard a loud crash in the distance, and the chant suddenly grew in volume and, distressingly, fervour.

'Dammit!' Q. thumped the desk. 'What idiot thought it was a good idea to install chocolate gates?'

That person, of course, was him. He'd claimed he could make them stronger than vanadium steel. We'd all had our doubts after the caramel submarine disaster.

'Ho ho ho,' the Jenkins alien laughed mirthlessly. 'A little thing like chocolate gates can't stop us!'

I estimated the marauding horde would achieve total incursion within seven minutes and thirteen seconds, with a probability of .97 recurring they would ingest us into their collective.

Guuuurk's voice almost reached dog whistle pitch. 'Chocolate gates! *Chocolate gates!* What were we expecting? An attack by Hansel and Gretel? What's the next line of defence? A wall of meringues? A marzipan drawbridge over a pink blancmange moat?'

The alien waved his banana tauntingly. 'It'll take more than confectionery fortifications to stop us.'

Q. rounded on him with a cunning expression. 'What *will* it take then, Jenkins?'

The human part of Jenkins was clearly battling his alien interloper, because he hesitated just an instant – the sound of His Master's Voice had somehow got through to him – but the alien regained control. 'You can't trick us with your intellectual shenanigans, Professor! We'll never let on about the music.' The alien's face twitched in irritation. Bravo, Jenkins! He'd managed to slip us a clue!

Brian had hauled himself back into the fray. 'What does he mean, musi—' He stopped and stared at me rather unnervingly. 'I say, Dr. Janussen, have you changed your hair?'

Typical shallow male! How could he be thinking about such trivialities at a moment like this?

'You've had it cut, haven't you?'

I sighed. Might as well get the nonsense out of the way. 'Well, yes, if you must know.'

'It's rather fetching.'

'I don't care.' I waited. No doubt this conversation was going to drag on for some considerable while, ranging over various irrelevant aspects of my appearance. I waited a little longer. And a little bit more. Nothing!

'And now,' the Jenkins creature waved his bizarre weapon at us, 'if you'd all like to queue up politely, it'll be quicker to absorb you into the hybrid swarm.'

Q. closed his eyes wearily. 'Troy – push that idiot into the broom cupboard and bolt it shut.'

'OK, Pops!'

Jenkins pulled a lopsided grin. 'You can try, sir, but you'll find I have the strength of ten—'

The banana weapon was snapped in half and the alien was in the broom cupboard quicker than wax off a floozy's hairpin.*

'Oh. Well done, Master Troy.' Jenkins' muffled voice issued from the cupboard. 'You're a lot more muscular than I thought.'

This delighted Troy of course, who is Vanity incarnate. 'I am though, aren't I?' He flexed his arm. 'Would you like to feel my biceps?'

'Very much, sir.'

Before we could stop him, Troy had released the bolt and it took Guuuurk, Brian and myself combined a great deal of effort to push the door shut again. Clearly Jenkins was drawing strength somehow from the collective.

'Hey!' Troy protested. 'What are you doing? He wanted to feel my biceps.'

'He wanted to *escape*, Troy,' I pointed out.

'Wow! These aliens must have like super-duper intelligence of some kind or other. I never saw that coming.'

'Sorry, sir,' came the muffled voice, 'I can't hear you properly.'

'Nice try!' Troy called. 'Fool me once, shame on you – Fool me twice . . .' He paused, frowning. 'What was it again?'

'*Shmmmm ogggg yggg,*' came faintly from the cupboard.

Troy pulled it open. 'Sorry – what was that?'

This time it took all four of us to close it. The alien's strength was increasing all the time, presumably as the horde got closer.

Brian was braced against the cupboard door, panting. 'I was just saying, what did he mean about music back then? Only, I did faintly hear something strange coming from the meteorite.'

Guuuurk, who was the only one of us to have actually

* The other members of the crew clearly picked up a number of Guuuurkian expressions along the way.

encountered the thing at close hand, said, 'Music . . . ye-e-es. There were some kind of peculiar, unearthly tones vibrating from it.'

'Just a minute.' Q. ruffled through the papers on the desk. 'Where's that meteorite report, dammit?'

And from the cupboard: 'Mr. Nylon hasn't got it in his jacket pocket, that's for sure!'

'Thank you, Jenkins.' Q. held out his hand. Brian unfolded the report and passed it over.

Q. scanned it quickly. 'Of course! Look at these waveforms.' He slapped the report with the back of his hand. 'The meteorites must exert control with a sequence of harmonic emissions. All we have to do is generate blocking soundwaves in the directly opposing frequencies!'

Guuuurk half-closed all his eyes. 'I hope nobody's going to suggest we form a barbershop quartet. Because I'd have thought we'd have learned our lesson from the deadly sing-off with the Cockroach Kaiser's Battle Choir. I still have mandible scars on my throat.'

Troy was exasperated. 'I *said* I was sorry! We hadn't eaten in three days!'

'*Crowd has broken through the marzipan drawbridge—*' The Professor avoided Guuuurk's gaze '*—and overcome the attack penguin.*'

'Attack penguin!' Brian exclaimed. 'So *that's* what was in the sentry box!'

'*Occupation of this building estimated in five minutes.*'

Q. snapped into action. 'We'd better get moving. What we need is some kind of device that can reproduce a succession of tones on a variable harmonic scale. We'll have to construct some sort of jerry-built Hammond organ from what's available in this room. Everybody: what do we have?'

We all scattered around the briefing room, calling out what we found:

'A broken chair . . .'

'Half a banana . . .'

'Three slices of National Loaf . . .'

'A paraffin heater . . .'

'The other half of the banana . . .'

'A fire axe . . .'

'A ream of foolscap paper and a Hammond organ . . .'

PROFESSOR PROBLEMS

'Splendid!' The Professor clapped his hands. 'We need to move fast! Start chopping up the Hammond organ with the axe, and we can combine the keyboard with the slices of bread and rolled-up strips of paper to fashion a sort of primitive hurdy-gurdy . . .'

Again, we were all thinking it, but this time I was the one who spoke. 'Or we *could* just plug in the Hammond organ and play that.'

The Professor regarded me blankly for a moment. 'Well, if you insist on being hidebound by conventional thinking . . .'

Guuuurk had plugged the organ in and flicked the switch. A low hum began to swell as it warmed up. 'But what will we play on it?'

The Professor flipped open the organ stool and grabbed a sheaf of manuscript paper.

'Here!' He scribbled quickly and handed the sheet to Guuuurk.

'"Order . . . larger . . . penguin?"' he read, baffled.

'Professor?' I urged. 'The tune?'

'Of course.' Consulting the meteorite report, he deftly scrawled down a series of elaborate musical notations on the manuscript paper and held it out with a flourish.

There was the sound of breaking glass from round about the reception area.

From the cupboard, the Jenkins thing crowed. 'We're breaking into the main building!'

Which provoked the irritated response from the tannoy: '*Are you trying to do me out of a job, Mr. Jenkins? They're* officially *breaking into the main building.*'

I grabbed the sheet music, propped it up on the stand and started to play. Surprisingly, what came out was a jerky little gavotte. Strangely catchy, too.

There was a distressed rattle from the cupboard, and the door seemed to bulge. Could the music, by any miracle, be working?

'I think I know that tune . . .' Brian's face scrunched up, as if he were in pain. 'I can't remember where I've heard it. Somewhere. I can't recall . . . Play it again.'

I did, this time pulling out the *Trompette Militaire* stop. The Jenkins creature wailed in anguish and hurled itself around the cupboard. Dust began to erupt around the architrave. '*Arrggh!* Not the opposing tonal frequencies!'

'It's working!' Q, yelled. 'Keep on playing!'

'Stop it! Pleeeeease! I can't stand it!'

I literally pulled out all the stops and played. And played.

There were banshee shrieks and deep glottal groans as the alien thrashed around in intolerable agony. Then it abruptly fell totally silent.

I stopped.

We all watched the cupboard door leerily. Was the creature trying to dupe us again? If we approached, would it suddenly burst out and overpower us? Brian took a tentative step forward, then stepped right back again as whatever was inside let out a sudden groan.

Finally, there was a respectful tap on the inside of the door, and Jenkins meekly called, 'Can I come out now, sir?'

We exchanged glances. Was this yet more subterfuge?

Brian, always too soft-hearted for his own good – and often everyone else's – gently unbolted the door and gingerly pulled it open.

There Jenkins swayed, blinking in the light weakly. He stumbled to the nearest chair and collapsed into it.

'Jenkins?' Guuuurk asked tentatively from the back of the room, under a table.

Jenkins took out a hip flask, and took a generous slug from it. For once, he didn't even bother to do it surreptitiously. 'Ooh, I just had the most terrible dream.'

Q. leant over him. 'And what *was* this dream exactly, Jenkins?'

'I dreamt I'd been possessed by bodiless aliens from another galaxy.'

'Bodiless aliens?'

'Yes, sir. They roam the voids of space, riding meteor clusters, endlessly seeking host creatures to occupy.'

Guuuurk pretended he'd found what he'd been looking for on the floor and stood. 'That's just like the Martian nursery rhyme "The Beta Centaurans" . . .'*

'Tantalising.' Q. straightened. 'Such creatures are spoken

---

* THE RIME OF THE BETA CENTAURIANS
Translated from the Martian by the Venerable Kruunkk

> Beware of the Beta Centaurans,
> All children had best run and hide,
> They're looking for bodies to jump in,
> And have lots of fun when inside!
>
> They ride through the stars quite unnoticed,
> Inside clouds of meteorites,
> So avoid glowing rocks if they're singing,
> And sew up your earholes at nights.

of not just in Martian fable – I've seen them mentioned in a number of ancient alien inscriptions. It's obviously not a mere legend, but some kind of race memory. They have different names, but always the same story: a species so advanced, they evolve beyond corporeal form, and exist only as pure thought. No pain, no death. No wants, no needs. Sounds like Heaven, doesn't it? Unfortunately, after several rather dull millennia, they realise that spending eternity as brainwaves can't match up to the simple pleasure of eating a crisp, juicy apple, or five minutes alone with a hoochie coochie dancer from the travelling carnival.'

Brian asked, rather naïvely, 'But what do they do with these bodies they occupy?'

The Professor raised his eyebrows. 'They indulge them, Nylon. They indulge in relentless hedonism. An endless orgy of feasting and, yes, rutting. They rut and eat and rut and eat and rut until the bodies are burnt-out husks.'

'So they're like Frenchmen, then?' Brian asked. I don't know if he was serious.

'And then they hitch a ride on the next passing meteor cloud, and the whole messy business begins again.'

All of Guuuurk's pupils dilated unnervingly at the same moment. 'So that's what they're after? They want to subject our poor defenceless bodies to relentless wanton sexual abandonment?'

Q. nodded. 'I'm afraid so. It doesn't bear thinking about.'

'No. No it doesn't . . .' Guuuurk seemed to drift off.

A faraway expression enveloped Brian's face. 'Hmmmmmmmm . . .'

At the mere mention of sex, the male's power of reason immediately downs tools and goes on a wildcat strike. And woe betide any sane thoughts that try to cross the picket line.

Jenkins shook his head. 'I tell you, Mr. Nylon, when they were inside my head, the things they was planning to do to each other . . .' He took another belt from his flask. 'Unrepeatable!' He shot a not-too-subtle look in Guuuurk's direction. The Martian looked up with sudden interest. 'Though I may be persuaded to set them down in vivid detail in a little book, for the right consideration.'

There was a hammering on the automatic storm doors, less than three hundred yards away – the last line of defence! The chant was growing ever more frenetic.

Time to haul the transfixed cavemen back to reality. 'Can we please focus! They're getting very close. We have to connect the organ to the tannoy system . . .'

There was more hammering and the sound of splintering wood. Inexplicably louder now, as if suddenly in the room itself. I spun round to see Troy chopping away at the organ with the fire axe. 'Troy! What are you doing? Stop!'

'I'm chopping up the organ.'

'*Don't!*' I pulled the emergency Flit Gun from my handbag, and drove him back. But it was too late – the organ was matchwood.

'Ow!' Troy wiped the tears from his eyes. 'What was that for?'

'Why did you *do* that?'

'Imagine what the aliens could do if they got hold of it!'

'What could they do?'

'Well, they could . . . they might . . . Sorry – what was the question?'

'*Apologies for the interruption*,' the tannoy announced, '*but they're through the storm doors and heading for the briefing room.*'

Chapter Nineteen

From the journal of Brian Nylon, 2nd January, 1952 –
Iteration 66

We formed a human/Martian chain and piled as much of the furniture as we could against the door, but we all knew in our hearts it wasn't going to hold them for very long. Or, indeed, at all.

There was no other way out, except for a tiny fanlight high on the outer wall, which nobody could fit through. Although Guuuurk did try. Very vigorously.

The Professor was pacing. He suddenly whirled round and pointed at me. 'Nylon! You say you *recognised* the tune on the organ.'

'Yes. Well, I thought I did, but—'

'Dammit, man, you *have* to remember!'

'I *can't* remember! I can hardly remember *anything*!'

'Brian.' Dr. Janussen gently cupped my chin with her hands and stared straight into my eyes. 'You need to *think*. Where did you hear it?'

'I don't know!' I wrenched her hands away in frustration. 'I can't remember! I lost my memory! What's wrong with you all?'

'You didn't forget *everything*. It's all in there, somewhere.'

Guuuurk stepped in. 'Was it something on the radio?'

'Yes. No. I don't know.'

'Dammit, Nylon! *Think!*'

My head was spinning. 'Why won't you all leave me alone? I'm not a monkey on a string!'

'A what?' Dr. Janussen grabbed me again. 'What did you say?'

'I said I'm not a . . . That's it! That's the song! "Monkey on a String" by Ethel Smith, First Lady of the Hammond organ. 'I *did* hear it on the radio. When I was with . . . Virginia.'

Everybody shuffled uncomfortably at the mention of Virginia. The Professor's expression took on a very dark tone. But try as I might, I couldn't remember much more than flashes from that afternoon on the riverbank . . . the barges chugging by . . . the two of us side by side eating watercress sandwiches . . . a portable radio the size of a small house . . . Ginny saying: 'The tanks will blow us all apart . . .' And then just foggy nothing. Tanks? Was she talking about the army?

'The music, Nylon!' Quanderhorn snapped me from my reverie. 'You're certain it's identical to this "Monkey on a String"?'

I grabbed the sheet music and ran it over in my head. Identical. I nodded. 'Note for note.'

'Splendid!' Quanderhorn barked. 'All we need to do is get *Housewives' Choice* to play that record over national radio. That will easily release enough people from the aliens' thrall to quash the invasion.'

'Trouble is, Professor,' Jenkins' cheeks were glowing red from his hip flask indulgence, 'the phone lines is down, and the shortwave's shot, an' all. There's no way to get a message through.'

I heard the ominous sound of a large boulder rumbling along

the corridor towards us. The meteorite! It could easily be employed to batter the door in, before it imprisoned us all with its 'fluence.

There was no point keeping my secret any longer. 'I think I have something here that may help.'

Before anyone could react, I reached into my flies, fumbled about and pulled out the parrot.

There were gasps. Everyone stared.

'What the devil is this, Nylon?' The Professor eyed me cautiously. 'Some kind of pornographic magic show? Because it's scarcely the time or place.'

The parrot looked at me with distaste, blinked, then squawked: '*I like Gemma's bottom!*'

The foul-beaked little rascal! I have no idea where he'd heard that. Honestly. It's not a thing I'd say. My cheeks felt like they'd been slapped with hot flannels. 'I-I . . . would *never* say that,' I stammered.

'Why?' Dr. Janussen folded her arms. 'What's wrong with my bottom?'

'Nothing!' I squirmed. 'I like it! No! I don't like it! I mean it's perfectly . . . it's where it should be and it does the job. Whatever that job might be—'

'Oh, shut up, Brian.'

I happily did.

Quanderhorn grabbed the parrot and studied it. 'Excellent preparedness from our resident Boy Scout. Right – here's the plan: first, we use the back of the fire axe to flatten the parrot and slide it under the door—'

'Professor . . .'

'No, you're right. I've got a better idea.' He studied the parrot intensely. 'Its beak is a perfect miniature loudspeaker – if we squeeze it tightly and whistle the tune up its little anus . . .'

Much as I'd like to have seen the bird suffer thus, I felt I ought to step in. 'That may be slightly over-elaborate, sir: the parrot is trained to fly to London and repeat whatever it's been taught.'

'Why didn't you say so in the first place, you clown, instead of distracting us all with your ill-judged prestidigitation?'

'*Mob now directly outside the room.*'

A mighty thumping began against the door. The furniture tower shuddered, but held firm.

Quanderhorn held the parrot six inches from his face. The surly psittacine was clearly sizing him up, like a boxer at a weigh-in. 'Right, parrot, here's the message—'

'I must warn you, Professor, the bird is somewhat—'

'Oh, we haven't got time for that! Right! Message begins: This is Professor Darius Quanderhorn speaking . . .'

The parrot blinked. '*Professor Quanderhorn speaking.*'

'Don't abbreviate!' the Professor scolded. 'Message continues. To avert subjugation of entire human race it's imperative you instruct the incumbent presenter of *Housewives' Choice* to play the following phonographic record, repeatedly and without pause: "Monkey on a String", by Ethel Smith, brackets First Lady of the Hammond Organ close brackets. Yours et cetera, et cetera . . .'

There was a long silence.

'Professor, that may be *slightly* too complicated for—'

'*Awk! To avert subjugation of entire human race it's imperative you instruct the incumbent presenter of* Housewives' Choice *to play the following phonographic record, repeatedly and without pause:*'

'Excellent!' Quanderhorn beamed.

'. . .*The Runaway Train by Vernon Delhart.*'

'Get the axe.'

'*Awk! "Monkey on a String", by Ethel Smith.*'

Quanderhorn nodded. 'That's better.' He climbed on a table and released the bird through the fanlight. It perched on the outer frame for a moment, relishing its freedom. Slowly, it turned its head fully 180° to face us and squawked: '. . .*I like Gemma's bottom!*' Then it spread its wings to their full span defiantly and soared away. I watched it go until it was barely a speck on the horizon.

'Hang on,' I said, 'isn't that north?'

But my words were lost under a thunderous crash as the stacked furniture collapsed spectacularly, sending shards and splinters flying all over the room.

And the door gave way.

3

50% Acrilan, 20% Cotton and 70% Anaconda

That time either has no being at all, or *is* only scarcely and faintly, one might suspect from this: part of it has happened and is not, while the other part is going to be but is not yet, and it is out of these that the infinite, or any given, time is composed. But it would seem impossible for a thing composed of non-beings to have any share in being.

Aristotle, *Physics*

3

50% Acrilan, 20% Cotton and 70% Anaconda

Chapter One

*Hansard, 2nd January, 1952**

EMERGENCY DEBATE ON CURRENT CRISIS
HC Deb 2 January 1952 vol 552 cols 2786–8

Mr. Somerville Hastings (Barking)
Would the Prime Minister care to explain what, precisely, is being done to deal with this astonishing spate of unbridled fornication and gluttony currently enveloping the country?

Cries of 'Hear! Hear!'.

The Parliamentary Secretary to the Board of Trade (Mr. Henry Strauss)
I share my hon. Friend's concern. Fifteen pie shops in my constituency have been denuded in the past two hours alone!

Cries of 'Scandal!' and 'Shame!'.

---

* This document, a single page torn from Hansard, was pasted in a scrapbook discovered in the Quanderhorn cache. From the rather daringly 'Gallic' nature of certain of the snapshots in the book, we may assume it was compiled by Mr Jenkins.

Mr. Speaker
Order! Order! If the hon, Ladies and Gentlemen in the back rows do not put their clothes back on and stop what they're doing immediately, I shall be forced to eat this enormous plate of cream cakes. Ummm. Delicious.

Sir Lynn Ungoed-Thomas (Leicester North East)
Will the Prime Minister tell us when, if at all, he intends to come and see the glowing meteorite behind Westminster Post Office?

Cries of 'Hear! Hear!' and 'Meteorite!'.

The Attorney General (Sir Lionel Heald)
I concur with my hon. and learned Friend. Yes or no? We must have an answer! It's imperative that – I yield to the hon. Lady. Ooh! Honourable Lady – please keep doing that!

The Prime Minister
Let me assure the Attorney General: we are not standing idly by. This very afternoon, I sent a messenger to mobilise the Armed Forces, only to discover they are rogering each other senseless all over Aldershot. But to be fair, they usually are.

Mrs. Bessie Braddock (Liverpool Exchange)
But what about the *meteorite*?

The Prime Minister
You may go and see the meteorite if you like, Mrs. Braddock, but you'll still be a fat ugly old cow in the morning!

Much raucous laughter and slapping of knees throughout the Chamber.

Cries of 'Very witty, Prime Minister!'.

Lieut-Colonel Marcus Lipton (Brixton)

Has the Prime Minister yet called upon the services of the excellent Professor Quanderhorn, one wonders?

Cries of 'Hear! Hear!' and 'Good old Quanderhorn!'.

The Prime Minister

I should be delighted to oblige my esteemed colleague, if he could perhaps explain how, in the absence of working telephony, I might accommodate such a request.

Lieut-Colonel Lipton

In that case, might the Prime Minister at least cheer us all up by calling Mrs. Braddock a fat ugly old cow again?

Riotous merriment for several minutes.
Loud metallic clang.

Mrs. Braddock is ejected from the Chamber for striking the Honourable Member for Brixton on the head with the Mace.

The Debate ends as Prime Minister leaves the Chamber to take charge of the developing crisis personally. He is heard to mutter: 'That reprehensible blackguard Quanderhorn is behind this, mark my words.'

Pandemonium ensues.

Chapter Two

From Troy's Big Bumper Drawing Book

[PICTURE OF A STICK MAN WITH BIG SCRIBBLED BLOBS ON THE TOP OF HIS ARMS, LABELLED 'ME!']

HA hA hA. We're hiDing in the AttiCk. There right unDerneAth. They CAnt see us. I MADe A hole in the seAling. We CliMMeD uP. I FilleD the hole Agen With My WAX. Its grAte uP here. There's stuFF. There MAKing noises Down there. I Dont no whAt there Doing, but it sounDs like sports. LouD sports. There going grunt grunt grunt. Its Fun. I like this. Ive tAken My shirt oFF AgAin. OW. Just bit My tong. TAstes niCe. We PlAyeD snAP. I Won. Hoo rAy Four Mee! This is grAte!!!!!!!!!!!!!!!!!!

Chapter Three

Franday the rth of Phobos, Martian Year 5972 Pink

From the Secret Report to Martian Command, by Guuuurk.
Also known as 'Guuuurk the Fastidious', First Archimandrave
(Removed) to Krrrrgg, the Quite Cruel, Driller of Holes in Un-
mentionable Places

Seventeen hours!

Seventeen hours hiding in a ceiling cavity with a bunch
of hapless humans, a nest of woodlice and thirteen bats. And
frankly, the bats and the lice were better company.

I had managed to save the feckless crew by making a hole
in the ceiling (don't ask me how!), selflessly shooing everyone
up there before myself, and persuading Quanderhorn Junior to
plug the gap with some of that vile gunk he constantly secretes
from a gland in some peculiar place in his body.

It's hard to decide what the highlight of the long tedious
night was: the game of seven card stud using three slices of
National Loaf as cards and woodlice as poker chips (I lost every
louse I had to the stupid boy), or the indoor cricket, using real
bats. The pitiful squeaking alone is enough to put you off your
stroke.

Oh! I had also rather cleverly remembered to rip the huge radio set from the wall (plaster and all!) and haul it up with me (what a feat of Martian muscle!). But we dared not switch it on until the stroke of 9 a.m., when the *Housewives' Choice* programme began, lest the revelling mob below us were alerted to our presence.

And, heavens to Betsy, was that mob revelling.

I tried peering through a crack in the ceiling, but it didn't offer a sufficiently wide field of vision. Whatever they were up to, they were doing it with unbridled gusto, I'll give them that. I heard several peculiar phrases being called out repeatedly, which I couldn't adequately translate. I made fastidious notes of them for later, intending to check them against Jenkins' forthcoming 'little book'. To improve my vocabulary, I mean.

Troy, ravenous as always, had made himself a tongue sandwich. With his own tongue. Everyone immediately shushed his inevitable 'Ow!'. It was getting close to nine, and we couldn't take any chances now.

Brian glanced at his watch for the umpteenth time. 'The parrot *must* have got there by now.'

I raised my second and fifth eyebrows.* '*If* he managed to find his way to London without being swooped on by birds of prey, *or* blasted out of the sky by one of your inbred aristocracy, and *if* he remembers the message correctly, and doesn't just bowl up and regale everyone with an account of how much he likes Gemma's bottom.'

Brian blanched and blushed at one and the same time. He practically resembled a barber's pole. 'For once and for all – I never *said* that! The bird just made it up on its own.'

---

* The various combinations of Martian raised eyebrows (there are 720 different permutations) are detailed in appendix 4: Martian Ocular Signalling System.

'Of course it did,' Gemma smiled. Was I imagining it, or was she looking at Brian with surprising gentleness? 'Brian . . .' she began.

'Yes?' The lad sprang to attention like a puppy to a Bonio.

'Just in case this . . . doesn't work out . . .'

'Yes?' the young infatuate panted.

'I feel I ought to clear things up a little . . .' She reached into her pocket. 'There's something I've been meaning to—'

But Jenkins spoiled all our fun by butting in with: ''Scuse me, sirs and miss: it's nine o'clock coming up.'

Quanderhorn, who'd apparently been dozing against the back wall, snapped immediately to attention and crawled quickly over to the radio. His hand hovered over the knob. 'Ready?'

We lowered a wooden pallet over the loosely plugged ceiling gap and stood on it. If the horde heard us, we might keep them out for a few seconds, but no more. Though from the noises below, I suspect they wouldn't have been disturbed by a kookaburra playing the cymbals perched atop a battleship's foghorn at Krakatoa.

The Professor twisted the knob, and we all winced at the sound of the Greenwich Time Signal pips. Below, there was no obvious reaction. We held our breath.

'*This is the BBC Light Programme. And now, a very special edition of* Housewives' Choice, *hosted by a Most Important Person . . .*'

The familiar signature tune started up. There was a slight hiatus in some of the pandemonium underneath. We heard one or two footsteps shuffling towards the ceiling gap, and braced ourselves.

The strains of 'In Party Mood' faded away to the gruff, familiar voice every Martian child has learned to despise. The cursed Churchill himself.

'*Good morning, housewives everywhere.*'

There was a groan and the rustle of script pages, and an off-microphone mumble of '*Do I have to say that?*' After a garbled reply from the producer, Churchill continued. '*Oh, very well.*'

He began reading somewhat reluctantly. '*I have a special request from a Professor Darius Quanderhorn*' (he could barely bring himself to utter the name without actually spitting) '*to play a certain record . . .*'

There came a scratching on the ceiling beneath us. It started to grow more urgent, and there were unearthly murmurings instead of the erstwhile frenzy.

'*Please turn up your volume knob to maximum and hear . . .*'

He exhaled painfully and, off-microphone again, whined, '*I know he's just doing this to humiliate me.*' He exhaled once more, and forced himself onward.

'*Ethel Smith – brackets – First Lady of the Hammond organ – close brackets – play that lovely melody . . .*'

Covering the microphone with his hand, he moaned, '*Oh, for heaven's sake!*' and finally announced: '*Monkey on a String.*'

Yes! Against all odds, the parrot had made it!

There was a violent thump on the ceiling, and we were rocked on the pallet, just as the perky melody blared forth from the nation's radio sets.

It took effect almost immediately.

The thumping noises ceased, and were replaced by a cacophony of pained moaning and whining, and desperate cries of 'No! No! Make It Stop!' and 'Not The Music! Please!'

Quanderhorn's eyes burned with delight. 'It's working!' He twisted up the volume.

On the radio, behind the music, we could hear a chair being pushed away from a desk, and Churchill declaiming: '*No – I have absolutely no intention of saying anything concerning Gemma's bottom! Whoever she is, and however callipygianous it may be!'* and the door slamming as he left the studio.

The opposing modal frequencies had done their job. The hung-over grumblings of the mob shaking free of their enchantment wafted up between the joists. It was going to be quite a disturbing shock for whomever came to and found themselves attached to Mrs. Wiggonby. And, indeed, there came the sudden desperate screech I associated with just such an event.

We were so caught up in the celebration we all quite forgot Gemma had been about to tell Brian something terribly important. We were not to discover the full horrifying consequences of the omission until it was far, far too late.

News

No. 25,133 FRIDAY, JANUARY 4, 1952

QUANDERHORN

Huge Debt of Gratitude

The people of Great Britain once again owe a huge debt of gratitude to the great genius, Professor Darius Quanderhorn, as he single-handedly averted yet another alien invasion yesterday. Alerting the authorities in the nick of time, his daring solution to the horrifying parasitical incursion drove out the menace without spilling a drop of human blood!

Skilful deduction

As all over the country a massive wave of appallingly un-British behaviour threatened to eliminate our superior moral standards entirely and set a poor example to less civilized members of the Empire overseas, he skilfully deduced the aliens' weakness: a popular tune on a gramophone record! Its tones exactly inverted the communication signals upon which the invaders relied, disrupting their hive intellect, returning the victims to their natural state of paralysing embarrassment which is so essential to our way of life.

Story continued on Pages 2 – 17. See also Leading Article, p 7:
"A KNIGHTHOOD FOR QUANDERHORN?"

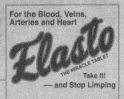
SAVES THE DAY!

Heroic Inventor

Fleets of Army Lorries, especially adapted for the purpose, patrolled the entire nation, through village and town alike, blasting Monkey on a String, by Ethel Smith, First Lady of the Hammond Organ, through gigantic loud speakers, day and night, until every single victim had been released. And the heroic inventor of those magnificent loud speakers? Why, none other than Professor Quanderhorn himself!

Saviour of the Nation

The aliens' meteorites, blocked from interacting with their occupants, ceased glowing and crumbled into harmless piles of coalite, which will keep the Post Offices warm all winter! Of course, the Saviour of the Nation is far too modest to make any public acknowledgement of his virtuosity, but rest assured his place in all our hearts is secure for all time.

Better than Winston Churchill

Prime Minster Churchill was unavailable for comment. An anonymous number 10 spokesman, however, between puffs on his cigar and sips of brandy, said: "This adulation is pernicious twaddle. The truth is no one can cope with these crises better than Winston Churchill. The PM would like to thank Quanderhorn for his minor role in assisting the government, and in gratitude, offers him a very big V sign."

See also From our Political Correspondent, p 8:
"CHURCHILL IS A BIG FAT LOSER!"

Chapter 5

The Professor thanked us all, but mostly himself. We crawled back to our rooms, all except for Quanderhorn, who rarely seemed to need sleep, and Jenkins, of course, who had a good deal of extremely unpleasant cleaning up to deal with.*

I tried to rest – I hadn't had a wink in twenty-four hours – but my mind just wouldn't stop buzzing. After four days I was still no clearer who I was or what the devil was really going on here.

I wandered back downstairs and snagged a notebook from the stationery cupboard. I thought somehow if I kept a journal I might be able to make sense of things just a little. Also, should my memory ever be wiped again – apparently a distressingly likely eventuality – the entries would yield valuable clues to my amnesiac future self. Sitting back down at my desk, I

---

* In the Professor's own notebooks, there are many sketches of an 'Alpha-Matic Sleep-Speeder' headset, which supposedly compacts eight hours of sleep into two and a half minutes. Some accounts claim the Professor had stocked up on considerable reserves of sleep while attending a Beat Generation interpretation of Wagner's Ring Cycle, featuring bongo-playing Valkyries in black leotards.

unscrewed the top of my fountain pen and began to write.

'*The journal of Brian Nylon . . .*' I stopped, staring at the script.

The note I'd found in my flight suit previously *was my own handwriting*. Clearly, it had been a warning to myself, and I'd be a fool not to take it seriously.

Of course, that note was ashes now. Feverishly I rifled though the shards of my splintered memory – what had it said?

Something about dangly boobs, I remembered that for some reason. Something else about a fellow named 'Dave'? Or was it 'Don'? And a reference to a fortune-teller. No, wait: it had actually said 'Ellar!' It seemed obvious now: the word was 'Cellar'.

'Don'? Done? Donkey? Don Quixote? Don Quixote's down in the cellar? You never know in this place. There's always some kind of bizarre danger lurking behind every . . .

'Danger!' The name wasn't 'Don', it was 'Dan'! I was warning myself about something dangerous in the cellar. The same thing that Mr. Churchill had portended. And just who might that other someone be?

There was a rap on the door. Instinctively, I went to stuff the journal between some clothes in my drawers, then I realised I didn't have any clothes in my drawers, or anywhere else for that matter.

'Just a minute!' I called. 'Just . . . winding my watch up.' What a dismal excuse! 'With no trousers on,' I added. Which made it worse.

I ran backwards and forwards stupidly for a few moments, then jammed the tome under my mattress, struck an assumed casual pose on the bed and called 'Come in!'

The Martian poked his enormous head around my door. 'Brian? I thought I heard you moving about in here.' He stepped in, notebook in hand.

'Couldn't sleep,' I confessed. 'You neither?'

'Oh, Martians only sleep one year in seven. That's why a full Martian breakfast has eighty-two eggs. And then you get constipation for the following six years. Listen, old boot: can you tell me what "tennis whites" are?'

'Of course. It's sort of white plimsolls, flannels and a white shirt and pullover.'

'So, cricket whites, then?'

'Yes. No!'

'What's the difference?'

'Well, if you turn up for cricket in tennis whites, everyone would laugh at you.'

'I seeeee . . .' He clearly didn't. 'Only I'm giving lessons this afternoon to a group of sixth-form girls from St. Winifred's.' He turned to go, then poked in again. 'Also, I need to know what "tennis" is.'

'Actually, Guuuurk.' I was aware I had to be very circumspect about my plans. He seemed like a pleasant enough fellow, but I still couldn't bring myself to completely trust a Martian. 'I was wondering if you could remind me which way it is down to the cellar . . .'

Guuuurk shut the door quickly. 'You don't want to go down to the cellar, old fruit,' he hissed. 'Remember what happened to poor old Virginia. Morning – face of an angel. Afternoon – huge pile of oozing broccoli.'

So Virginia had ventured down to the dreaded cellar. How had she got down there? 'It's that special lift, isn't it?'

Guuuurk looked suddenly serious. 'There are some things that, around here, you just don't ask,' he said under his breath. 'Now then,' he continued brightly, 'I managed to hire a "racquet" from Jenkins, but I need to know a little more detail . . .' He picked up his notebook and naughty pen again, sat down on my chair and crossed his legs like a shorthand typist. 'Go.'

It was a very long night. When you try to explain tennis to someone who doesn't understand it, very soon it begins to make no sense whatsoever. Particularly the scoring. And everything else. When we'd finished, I felt I knew considerably less about it than when I'd started.

Guuuurk eventually left, practising his forehand smash with what I couldn't bring myself to tell him was actually a frying pan, and I finally felt very tired indeed. But just as I lowered myself onto the mattress, closed my eyes and began to drift into blissful oblivion, that annoying woman blurted out over the tannoy:

'It's 7.30 precisely. All personnel proceed to the briefing room immediately.'

Chapter Six

From the journal of Brian Nylon, 4th January, 1952 – [cont'd]

I couldn't take much more of this. I dragged myself upright and staggered over to the washstand for a quick basin bath with rusty water and carbolic. As I'd burnt the remainder of my clothes, I attempted to rinse what I had under the tap and put them on again.

Pulling sopping Y-fronts up my cold legs, I envisaged any number of horrors that might be awaiting me. But there were no existential threats, no comets hurtling towards the Earth, no imminent invasions. In fact, the scene, when I arrived, was calm.

I sat on the radiator and steamed lightly.

Guuuurk was lounging in his whites – heaven knows where he'd managed to muster them from – shirt collar up and pullover looped over his shoulders, trying to jam his frying pan into a racquet press.

Troy hadn't arrived yet, but Jenkins lurked in the corner, eyeing us all insubordinately over his steaming tin mug of compo tea.

Dr. Janussen, as ever, looked radiant and fresh, like she'd just stepped from a fragrant garden where she'd bathed in crystal waters with nymphs and been wafted dry by the sweet breath of a scented zephyr. I noticed the Future Phone key was around her neck again. I didn't want to think about how she'd retrieved it.

The Professor breezed in cheerfully. He rubbed out the word 'CRISIS' on the blackboard, and chalked up the word: 'BREASTS'.

Guuuurk immediately dropped his frying pan, whipped out his notebook, and leant forward with fierce concentration.

'Right, let's get the necessaries out of the way.' Quanderhorn glanced around the room. 'Did I remember to congratulate myself after yesterday's triumph?'

'Yes, Professor.' I nodded just a tad too enthusiastically. 'But congratulations, anyway.' The others looked at me with disdain, but my mission to the cellar meant I had to maintain a 'teacher's pet' *façade* to avoid suspicion. Although, come to think of it, I was exactly the sort of person who would have been the teacher's pet.

'Excellent crawling, Nylon! Time, then, for the business of the day ... I present my latest revolutionary cross between science and underwear.' The Professor picked up a little bell from his desk, tinkled it and stared at the door.

Nothing happened.

Quanderhorn sighed, and said again in a slightly louder voice: 'I present my latest revolutionary cross between science and underwear.' He tinkled the bell more loudly and stared at the door.

We all stared at the door.

Nothing happened.

Eventually, from outside, Troy called: 'Was that the bell?'

'Yes! Yes!' the Professor yelled back, testily. 'When you hear the bell, wheel the thing in, remember?'

'OK. So, when the bell goes, then.'

'Right.' The Professor tinkled the bell again.

We all stared at the door.

Nothing happened.

'Didn't you hear that, Troy?'

'No – sorry. Someone keeps ringing the doorbell, just when I'm ready.'

'We don't *have* a doorbell.'

'Yes. That's what's so annoying about it.'

'Let's forget the bell, shall we? Just wheel it in.'

'All right.'

Troy trundled in a large cage, draped with a dust sheet. Whatever was inside was clearly very big, very angry, and very not human. It roared and snapped and hurled itself repeatedly against the cage with considerable enthusiasm.

The Professor gathered himself again. 'I present . . .' He whipped away the dust sheet with a flourish. '. . . et cetera et cetera!'

Secured inside the cage was a most curious animal – certainly not a Child of Nature. It was quite squid-like, though an angry pink with a lacy sort of skin, like a pig's caul. It had no eyes I could make out, but two large gooey, gummy mouths on each of its twin bulbous heads.

'Sweet Lord Baden-Powell!' I cried. 'What *is* that?'

The Professor beamed proudly: 'The Living Bra: 50% Acrilan, 20% cotton and 70% anaconda.'

The hellish chimera reared both its demonic heads and began spitting in fury.

I shook my head firmly. 'I'm sorry, Professor – I really can't allow Dr. Janussen to put that on.'

The Professor frowned. 'Of course not. That would be far too dangerous. No. This is a job for our very brave Product Tester.'

Everyone seemed to be looking at me again for a very long time.

I sighed. I was beginning to learn what *that* meant.

'Take your shirt off, Nylon!'

I immediately flushed red. 'I don't want to take my shirt off,' I stammered, trying not to catch Dr. Janussen's eye. 'I don't like taking my shirt off.'

'Really?' Troy seemed genuinely surprised. 'I like taking my shirt off.'

'Do you even *have* a shirt, Troy?'

'Yeah! Course I do. This pink one with the two nipples . . . Oh, wait . . .' He stared at his chest as he slowly processed the implications.

The cage rocked as the beast roared and flung itself against the bars violently.

Guuuurk took four or five steps back. 'That thing looks more vicious than an eyeball-sucking Martian tiger-maggot.* Are you absolutely sure it's safe for *anyone* to put on, Professor?'

'No idea. Come on, Nylon, off with it.' He nodded at Jenkins, who staggered over dragging a large trunk.

I disrobed as discreetly as I could, inconspicuously shielding my nipples with my thumbs in front of a lady. My shirt made a

---

*THE EYEBALL-SUCKING TIGER-MAGGOT
from *More Nonsense Tales for Martian Minnows*
by *Tynggg the Unrhymable*

A marvellous thing is the bold Tiger Maggot:
It's mostly all tail but it seldom will wag it
in joy, when its Master gets home

Instead it will pounce from some shadowy corner,
Reducing its Mistress at once to Chief Mourner,
That optical orb-gastronome.

wet splat as it slid heavily off the back of the chair.

Quanderhorn rooted in the trunk and pulled out what looked like a pair of opera gloves made of chain mail, studded with metal spikes. 'Dammit, Jenkins,' he cussed, 'I told you to bring the *really* armoured gloves!' He also produced a pair of giant tongs, about two and a half feet long. 'And I wanted the *extremely* long tongs.'

'Sorry, sir: they're at the blacksmith's being repaired after when you put that thing *in* the cage, yesterday.'

'Oh, well. Let's hope it's worn itself out trying to bite through the solid titanium bars in a frenzy of bloodlust. Right!' He braced himself, tongs extended fully in his armoured hands. 'Arms in the air, Nylon! Stand back, everyone else!' he added, unnecessarily.

I raised my arms and closed my eyes.

'Open the cage!'

There was a tremendous, unhuman roar, and a series of banshee screeches, over the Professor's struggling grunts as he tried to wrangle the beast into position.

I took a deep breath and prepared to die.

Chapter Seven

*The Daybook of 'Jenkins' Jenkins, RQMS Royal Fusiliers
(dishonourably discharged), Friday the 4th of January, 1952*

Jeyes Fluid bulk delivery tomorrow. Order more rubber gloves.

You should see the look on Mr. Nylon's face as they puts that
thing on him. It's hard to tell what's whiter: his pigeon chest
or his face. As soon as it slaps against him, the creature stops
growling and slithers round his ribcage, gentle as a baby octopus hugging its dear old mum.

'And there we are,' the Prof says. 'Comfy?'

Mr. Nylon finally opens his eyes and looks down. 'No,' he
says.

Mr. Guuuurk, the Martian chap, chimes in: 'Actually I think
it's rather becoming. I'm getting quite aroused.'

I'm hoping he isn't, 'cause the Jeyes Fluid ain't coming till
tomorrow.

The Prof leans in and peers at the creature. 'The question is:
if you actually had breasts, would it be giving you support?'

Young Master Troy pipes up with what we was all thinking:
'He does sort of have breasts.'

'I do not!'

Dr. Janussen says: 'They're bigger than mine, Brian.' Which sends him all of a dither again.

'No they're not! Not that I've looked . . . Or wanted to look . . . or seen how big . . . or not . . . Not that there's anything wrong with them whatever size they are . . . Oh Lord . . . somebody help me, please.' The Prof obliges:

'How does it feel?'

'Well, it feels very . . . uuuuuuuuh . . .' he says, or noises to that effect. His eyes go round and round like the fruit in the one-armed bandit at the King's Torso, and he starts sweating more than a pig doing jankers. 'Uhhhhhhhhhhhhhh . . .' he goes. Hard to tell whether it's terrifying him or titillating him. 'It's strangely . . . nuuuuuuuuuhhhhhhhhhh . . .'

'I think we can call that a success,' says the Prof. 'Women everywhere will not only have firm support, but also something to fetch the newspaper in the mornings.' That's the Prof for you: always thinking of other people's convenience. Everyone starts putting their things away, then Mr. Nylon chirrups:

'Can I take it off now?'

Well, that thing growls like it knows every word he's saying.

The Prof frowns: 'Ah. Well. That might not be advisable right at the moment.'

'Thing is, Mr. Nylon,' I says, 'we haven't fed it today. Or actually ever.'

Well, he pulls such a face, like a Jerry I once garrotted with my bootlace. 'Unghhhuhhhh,' he groans. 'It's contracting! Get it off!'

The beast don't like that kind of talk, that's for sure. It growls so loud you can feel the floor rumbling underfoot.

'*Don't startle the bra!*' the Prof yells. 'It could be dangerous.' He's not wrong. Now you may think Mr. Nylon is a gutless wonder with no spine to speak of, but you'd be wrong. I know something about him what would change your mind, but I cannot share it in these pages.

'Get it off me! Get it off me!' he screams in his high-pitched voice.

'If you insist.' The Prof turns to yours truly. 'Bring me the rifle.'

Somehow, Mr. Nylon's face finds an even paler shade of white. '*What?*' he squeaks.

'I'm afraid the only way is to shoot it off,' says the Prof. 'Don't worry: everyone in the Army told me I'm a crack shot.'

Well, I couldn't let that stand. 'Beg pardon, Professor: they told you you was a *crap* shot.'

He waves his hand at me. 'Don't bother me with pettifogging details! The rifle!'

Ours not to reason why. I reaches into the trunk and hands him the trusty Lee-Enfield No. 5 Mk 1 'Jungle Carbine', loaded and safety catch off, as per standing orders.

He raises the weapon. 'Everybody stand back.' To be honest, everyone was still standing back from last time, but Mr. Guuuurk managed somehow to stand back a little bit more.

The Prof takes careful aim at the bra from two feet away, squeezes the trigger, and scores a direct hit on the Telemergency Print-O-Gram, a good ten feet to the left, blowing it to smithereens.

'Actually,' Mr. Nylon says, surprisingly calm, like, 'it's starting to feel quite comfy now.' You can tell he's lying, because he's squirming something rotten, and a gasp of pain hisses out of him as the creature tightens its grip.

The Prof yells: 'Stand still, dammit!' and shoots again, this time missing ten feet to the right, and blasting Alaska out of the globe on his desk.

'Please stop shooting, Professor,' poor Mr. Nylon pleads,

sounding quite breathless now. 'It's making him very tense.' He can hardly get those last words out.

There's a crack – everyone hears it, and he croaks quite matter-of-fact: 'I think that was one of my ribs.'

And blow me sideways, there's another crack, and he nods and rasps just: 'Yup!'

The Prof starts rooting through the trunk. 'I'm afraid we may have to use the flesh-eating virus pistol to get it to release its grip.' I didn't have the heart to tell him I'd lobbed it into the Obliteration Chamber after that last horrific fiasco.

But poor old Nylon doesn't know that, does he? 'No, no. I wouldn't dream of putting you to all that trouble, Professor,' he babbles. 'I'll just keep wearing it for a bit.'

The bra loosens off a bit when it hears that, and starts a sort of purring noise.

Mr. Nylon quickly slips his shirt back on. Not much point. It's so wet, you can see the bra right through it.

'OK! That's it! Demonstration over.' The Prof starts dumping all the equipment back in the trunk, no thought to putting it in any kind of order, of course. 'Nylon!' he yells. 'A word.' And nods towards his office.

Well, of course, there's plenty of mess to be cleared up, as per, so I grabs my trusty broom and starts sweeping up behind them as they walk towards the Prof's office and go in. By amazing coincidence, I just happens to catch the beginning of the conversation before the Prof looks up, spots me accidentally watching him, pulls down the venetians on his office door and slams it shut.

So I can't make out another bloomin' word after: 'It pains me to say, Nylon, that we have a traitor in our midst . . .'

Chapter Eight

From the journal of Brian Nylon, 4th January, 1952 –[cont'd]

I wandered into the Professor's office. I'd glanced in before, but had never (at least in my memory!) actually been inside. I tried to scan the room on the q.t. It was crammed with half-completed prototypes, stacks of dog-eared notepads and skeletons of creatures not to be found in any encyclopaedia. Quanderhorn followed close behind me.

'It pains me to say, Nylon, that we have a traitor in our midst.'

He shut the venetian blinds and closed the door as I tried to stop my ears turning red by sheer willpower. I doubt I was successful. My eyes fell on a pair of goggles on the desk that seemed oddly familiar. Quanderhorn quickly swept them into a drawer.

He was too agitated to notice. 'A snake in the grass!' he went on. 'A double-crossing Judas, passing as one of us and reporting to that pompous egotist Churchill. Or as I call him . . .' He affected the most disdainfully childish expression and voice: "*Cheeuuuurchill*".' I would have been rather taken aback by the vehemence of his loathing, had I not been scared so utterly witless.

'A traitor?' I tried to ignore the increasingly urgent signals now transmitting from my bladder like the order to arrest Crippen, and focused instead on the pain in my ribs. 'Surely not, Professor?'

His face struggled to adopt a kindly expression, which was thoroughly unfamiliar to it. 'I know to someone as basically decent as yourself, Nylon, such a thing is too disgusting to contemplate. Which is why, before your memory . . . went away, I engaged you to root out this lying, despicable, backstabbing turncoat.'

Which circle of Hell had I wandered into here? Which ward of Bedlam was this? I had been recruited by Quanderhorn to hunt down Churchill's agent, *who was also me*? I forced my features into a facsimile of a smile. 'And I said I'd do it?'

'Yes. You vowed to find out who this foul, two-faced, weaselling ingrate was, so they could be eliminated.'

'And by "eliminated",' I offered hopefully, 'I meant given a jolly good ticking-off and sent home without—'

'No.'

'No, of course not. I meant dock their holiday pay and—'

'You meant – they would have to be . . .' He fixed me with a stare that left no ambiguity. '*Taken care of*.'

'I meant *that*?' The fake smile was dying on my face.

'Yes, like you did with Virginia, when you transmuted her into the giant broccoli monster.'

'What?' I felt the ground had opened beneath me and I was falling into an abyss from which there would never be any return. 'That was *me*?'

'Oh, of course – you've forgotten: when you discovered she'd been down to the cellar, what choice did you have but to blast her with the Vegetablising Ray?'

The more I found out about my past, the less I wanted to recover any more of my memory. The man I'd been – I didn't want to *be* him again. Duplicitous, violent, ruthless. None of it felt right. None of it at all.

'B-but then,' I stammered, 'surely we've already *dealt* with Churchill's agent?'

The Professor shook his head sadly. 'I fear another, more dangerous imposter is still at large. We suspect their codename is: Agent Perpetrator.'

I almost corrected him, but only allowed the first syllable to escape before I caught myself. 'Pen—'

'What?'

'I was just looking for a pen. Ah! Here it is. Here in my pen pocket. Where it always is. I'll just make a note of that on my hand: *Perpetrator.*'

If the Professor found this odd, he didn't let on. 'Nylon – I'm relying on you to smoke out this vile, amoral, self-serving vermin, and give them the brutal treatment you usually mete out.' He looked me up and down, as if appraising me for the first time. 'Who could have realised that pathetic, wet, incompetent exterior concealed the stony heart of a sadistic, merciless bastard? Certainly not I.'

A small buzzer sounded in the corner of the office, and Quanderhorn strode over to monitor some experiment he was conducting with a rat, a drainpipe and some vicious-looking electrodes. He didn't dismiss me, he just seemed to forget I was still there. And who could blame him, contemptible creature that I was? I slunk towards the door, but as I opened it, I saw the Professor glance at me out of the corner of his eye in a curious way.

Were there more, even darker secrets buried in my past?

There was a flash of light, a puff of smoke and a plaintive rodent squeal.

I shuddered and left.

Chapter Nine

From the journal of Brian Nylon, 5th January, 1952 –
Iteration 66

I stumbled up to my room, quite thankful not to bump into any of the others, except Jenkins, whose gaze I avoided.

I sank onto the miserable bed and tried to muster my painful thoughts. What was the truth? Could I believe the Professor? Why would he lie to me?

The only way I could ever get to the bottom of this whole thing was to go down to that terrifying cellar and find its secret.

It was a long and difficult day. There were a lot of preparations that had to be made. I needed some boot polish for facial camouflage, a dark balaclava, some shoes that made no noise, lock-picking equipment, a jemmy and some kind of climbing rope.

On the pretext of securing some fresh clothes, I managed to persuade Jenkins to let me have the key to the stores (it cost me my watch!). The shelves were surprisingly empty, with only the occasional item on view.*

---

* There are several instances in Jenkins' daybook where he refers to the warehouse as 'The Shop'.

For genuine, daily use, I did manage to rustle up a couple of pairs of itchy wool trousers, some string underwear (which I loathe, but needs must), and some grey shirts made of an odd synthetic material which sparked if you rubbed the sleeves together. There was no boot polish, but I managed to find some gravy browning. No balaclava either, but I did discover a rather large sock I might cut a hole in for my face. Not ideal, but beggars can't and all that. As for the noiseless shoes, though, no sign.

I was hoping perhaps for gym pumps, but Guuuurk had presumably taken the last pair for his tennis apparel. After an hour of increasingly desperate rummaging, I came across a pack of balloons amongst the Christmas decorations. If I stretched one of the long thin ones over each of my brogues, it should, in theory, muffle them sufficiently. Make do and mend, as Mumsie used to say.

Surprisingly, the storeroom did yield a crowbar and a rather professional-looking lock-picking kit. What on earth they were doing there, Lord alone knows. I stuffed the whole lot in a military duffel bag and hoisted it over my shoulder.

Fully stocked, I now had to chew over the problem of getting it all past the eagle-eyed Jenkins. Mercifully, as I headed back to the main building, I saw him scuttling off towards the village on his bicycle, presumably to get my watch to the pawnbroker's before it closed.

Safely back in my room, I laid the equipment out on my desk. I could hardly make my cellar incursion in broad daylight, so I closed my eyes for just a few minutes, and didn't wake up until night had fallen. Obviously, I had no idea of the actual time, but an angry moon was flooding the room with white light.

I made my preparations.

It was quite difficult to get the right consistency of water to gravy browning, and mixing it up made me feel incredibly hungry. I smeared it over my face and checked the mirror.

So far, so good.

The balaclava would conceal most of the drips and streaky bits. I pulled on the argyle sock. It was a snug fit, and the colour-ed rectangles made me look a little bit like a violent Harlequin, but on the whole, professional, though it did have a tendency to ping off my head if I turned too quickly.

I had the devil of a time stretching the red and green party bal-loons over my shoes. Several of them went out of the window, and one almost took my eye out. They didn't quite do the job as well as I'd hoped, because I now squeaked quite gratingly with every step, setting my own teeth on edge. Still, better than the sound of my clodhoppers, so long as the dangling coloured overhangs at each toe didn't trip me up.

I tucked the rest of the equipment in the bag, and crept to my door.

I opened it just a chink.

There was no light under Dr. Janussen's door. I slipped out. I crouched and listened at her keyhole. I could just about make out the gentle rhythm of an extremely delicate, feminine snore rattling the door.

Satisfied, I straightened and turned, and almost jumped out of my balloons to find Guuuurk standing right next to me.

'Hello, old sport!' he chirped. His various eyes roamed over my outfit. I was suddenly acutely aware I was smeared in gravy browning, wearing a sock on my head, balloons over my shoes, and carrying a bag that made a clanking noise every time I moved. 'On your way to a little "assignation"?'

'Certainly not!'

'No, neither am I.' He winked. 'The very idea of tennis les-sons at midnight is a scurrilous lie.'

'You're probably wondering why I'm dressed like this . . .'

'Like what?' He seemed genuinely baffled.

'Nothing. In my typical earth night-walking outfit.'

'Really? How interesting. Not sure about the balloons, though. And you do smell . . .' he wrinkled his Martian nose, '. . . rather meaty.'

'That's to repel the mosquitoes.'

Guuuurk chewed this over and finally said: 'I thought the whole *point* of mosquitoes was that they *liked* meat.'

'These are vegetarian mosquitoes.'

'Vegetarian mosquitoes!' He shook his head sadly. 'This planet is *such* a shambles. Evolution clearly took a detour around you lot.' Then he slipped off down the stairs ahead of me, mouthing 'Cheery bye' as he disappeared.

I ran a quick check at Troy's door. He was obviously within . . . was that the sound of him rubbing his legs together?

Jenkins was undoubtedly boozing away my watch money in the King's Torso, so there was only the Professor to worry about.

Only the Professor!

I crept down to the reception area.

Deserted.

I tiptoed squeakily towards the bank of lifts. I found my shoulders loosened themselves when I spotted one of the lifts was on the forty-third floor of the High-Rise Farm. Hopefully, Quanderhorn would be up there, squeezing cows into the wee small hours.

Nonetheless, my hand was shaking as I reached out to summon the Professor's private lift.

Chapter Ten

From the journal of Brian Nylon, 5th January, 1952 [cont'd]

I half-expected all kinds of alarms to go off as I pressed 'Call', but the doors slid open smoothly, and I stepped inside the car. They clanged shut behind me again very quickly. I tried not to feel trapped. Who knows what Jenkins had meant by 'security devices'?

I forced myself to keep calm and studied the array of buttons. They were marked with the usual impenetrable symbols, which presumably only the Professor would understand. A fish; a portcullis; a moon; a ghost . . . And what was that one? Siamese twins? None of them evoked 'Cellar' to me, or anything like it, so I simply pressed the bottom button, but nothing happened. Clearly, they were not yet activated.

I started as the metallic voice of that damned woman issued from the speaker. '*Please state your identity and destination.*'

I gulped back the growing feeling of dread that rose like so much bile in my throat, and pulled off what I honestly think was a pretty brilliant facsimile of the Professor's growling, angry voice. 'It's me, Quanderhorn. Dammit!'

There was a short pause, and a strange whirring noise while

the mechanisms, whatever they were, assessed my verisimili-
tude. I aged about seven years.

Finally, old metal-voice kicked in: *'Welcome, Professor.
Where can I take you today?'*

Triumphant, I quickly replied: 'The cellar, of course.
Dammit.' I really think I got the impatience level just right.

'Certainly,' she said. I was on my way!

But then she went on: *'Simply answer the security questions,
to verify that you are not a shape-shifting troglodyte from beneath
the Earth's crust. Who is the current Prime Minister of Great
Britain?'*

Ah! I knew this one. *'Cheeuuuurch*ill!'

More whirring, but less tension this time. I'd got that bang
on.

'Correct. Level two security question . . .'

How many questions were there going to be? I tried to think
as Quanderhorn might . . . 'Don't bother me with pettifogging
details, dammit!'

'Is the correct answer. Level three . . .'

'I really need to get on. Dammit. Emergency override.
Dammit.' Was I over-doing the 'Dammits'?

This time there was a much longer, louder whirring. Hopefully I hadn't pushed my luck too far . . .

Suddenly a small hatch slid open about waist height in the
wall panel.

'Quandermetric Emergency Identification Reader activated.'

I had pushed it too far.

*'Please place the designated body part into the aperture
provided.'*

I looked at the aperture provided, and its height above the
ground. 'Which body part would that be?' I asked, really
hoping I was wrong.

The metal-voiced harridan taunted: '*You may need to unzip.*' Good grief. Why on earth would anyone *install* such a device?

'Remind me again—' what had Guuuurk called her? '—Delores! Why did I fit this particular precaution?'

She sighed. '*The troglodyte shape-shifters only mimic what they can see of a person, so will not have this particular appendage. Please place the designated body part into the aperture provided.*'

I looked at the aperture again. She couldn't be serious. Could she?

'*Alarms will be activated unless the designated body part is inserted into the—*'

'Yes! Yes! I'm doing it! I'm doing it right now!'

And I did. There was an electronic swishing sound and a bright blue light slid across inside the aperture, rather disturbingly.

More whirring. Then:

'*Have you put it all in?*'

'Yes! Yes! Please hurry up!'

Another swish and the bright blue light again. And more whirring.

'*Are you sure?*'

'Come onnnnn!' Was she teasing me, the witch?

'*Thank you, Professor. Please leave it in there for the duration of the trip.*'

The lift clunked into action and shot down rapidly.

I was on my way to the infamous cellar. So focused had I been on getting there, I'd completely forgotten to be utterly terrified.

But now I remembered.

Chapter Eleven

I spent most of the day trying to restore my room to its simple efficiency. I can't understand how it had got so disordered: I only come here to sleep and wash and change clothing. Is Jenkins subletting my room to someone else in the hours I don't use it?

I boxed up all the perfume bottles – why would anybody need more than one? – took down the Tony Curtis poster, threw all the cushions and soft toys out of the window, collected up all the shoes (dozens of pairs!) and discovered, of all things, a Plus~a~Gram record player under the bed! Not only that, there was a collection of disgustingly maudlin Johnnie Ray records beside it. Honestly, each time I put on a new song, thinking it might be better than the last, it turned out to be even *more* syrupy and sentimental.

For some reason, I suddenly needed a tissue. Hay fever, I expect, as it was January. I went to my bag, only to discover it had been switched with one made out of some kind of lizard leather. Most impractical. Really, I'm going to have to have this business out with Jenkins, once and for all.

191

I rooted through the unfamiliar bag. Needless to say, it had been cluttered up with all kinds of lipsticks, compacts, scented unguents and some sort of strange greasy black pencils, which I can only assume were meant for scribbling on your face in some frivolous way. I came across the letter I'd almost given Brian last night in the attic, when it looked as if our number might be up. Virginia had asked me to give it to him the last time I'd seen her, and I'd been waiting until the fog cleared from his memory loss, but that didn't seem to be happening. If anything, he seemed to be getting foggier. As the thought of Virginia crossed my mind, I noticed a faint tickle on my cheek. Curse this wretched pollenosis!

But wait: the letter had been opened! When can that have happened? It's certainly not something I would ever do.

Still, now the seal had been broken, as it were, and presumably the contents scrutinised by someone unknown, pure rationality suggested I should read it.

So I did.

And what I read changed everything.

Chapter Twelve

From the journal of Brian Nylon, 5th January, 1952 –
Iteration 66

The lift finally lurched to a stop. And so, for a second, did my heart. My nerves jangled like a set of cowbells dropped on the floor in a funeral parlour.

'*The Cellar,*' the metallic voice announced, and the doors slid open creakily.

I snatched my 'designated body part' from the aperture, zipped up and stepped out.

'Thank you,' I tried to say, but only a hiss of wind escaped my throat.

'*Maximum safe exposure time: three minutes.*'

'What?'

The doors shut behind me.

'Wait! Wait! What d'you mean, "Maximum safe exposure time"?'

But all I heard was the sudden rapid whine of the lift's electric motor as it wisely fled back to safety, taking with it my only escape.

I was alone.

But I did not feel alone.

Slowly, I turned. The cellar was not as I'd imagined. It was more like a huge tunnel, hewn through the limestone, presumably created during the quarry mining phase. The white walls seemed wet, but when I touched them, my hand came away coated in some sort of vile, sticky slime.

There were strips of dim fluorescent lighting running along one wall. Some of the tubes were old, almost black at either end, some were dead, and others flickered off and on at random.

The tunnel stretched away ahead, fading into an impenetrable gloom.

And was it my fevered imagination, or did that sound like a not-quite-human cry in the distance?

Now, I'm not a believer in ghosts and spirits and such foolishness – though I admit my beliefs were being challenged in this place on an almost hourly basis – but every hair on my neck was telling me there was something down here.

Something not of this world.

I bit my lip hard. The pain helped me pull myself together. Three minutes? I didn't have long. Nor, in all honesty, did I want long. I took a tentative step towards the source of the sound, and then another. And somehow, without having to muster up the courage to do so, I was walking.

Each footfall echoed around the curved walls. The fluorescents buzzed and sputtered into the distance. Occasionally, I'd imagine I'd heard something skittering behind me, but when I wheeled round, there would be nothing there: just the fading impression of my footprints on the damp floor.

There were a number of doors lining the tunnel wall, with foreboding messages like 'Do Not Open This Cupboard Under Any Circumstances!', and 'Under No Circumstances Open This Cupboard!'. There was an ominous angry buzzing sound behind one of them. I had every intention of obeying the instructions.

Suddenly, I realised I'd had to start hunching my shoulders, as the ceiling got lower, and eventually, I was shuffling along in a crouch.

As I grew closer, what I'd thought had been the sound of a human voice became a throbbing harmonic hum, a babble of incoherent buzzing that was at one and the same time in the background, yet also drilling deep into my subconscious. Somehow both plaintive and sad, like a million dying wasps all trapped in a giant bottle.

I became aware that the air was getting thicker, in some way. Soupier. As if I were being enveloped by a mink-lined fog.

Then, in a sudden flicker of light, I saw something inexplicable.

The space at the end of the tunnel pulsed and warped, as if reality itself had no hold in this place. That, or my mind didn't have the capacity to interpret what it was seeing, as if I were a caveman wandering into Battersea Power Station. I stood transfixed as the warping resolved into a shifting series of impossible shapes, and I perceived I could step forward through a small opening.

Instantly, the sound became deafening. All around me, stretching up into a vast vaulted chamber, were huge, shining metal tanks. Although they seemed solid, their actual shape was beyond my comprehension.

Then all the sounds resolved at once into a single voice. And the voice was saying:

'Help us.'

The voice was mine.

Chapter Thirteen

*From the journal of Brian Nylon, 5th January, 1952 –
Iteration 66*

'Help us!' Where was this strange omni-voice coming from?
I peered at the closest 'tank'. Its surface shimmered as if in a
heat haze, and became filmy and opaque, then melted away to
translucence, and I was staring straight at me.

But not quite me. I looked slightly older. Harrowed. My hair
was parted in the centre now, not quite disguising the thinning
locks. This other me banged his fist against the tank. Somehow,
it made the whole chamber shudder.

'Help us!' he howled.

'You . . . you're me?'

He was roughly pushed aside by another figure. Another me.
This one considerably older: stooped and with even less hair.
'We're all you!' he yelled, his open maw exposing a distressing
poverty in the tooth department. But worse by far was the
hollow stare of his yellowed eyes where hope had died some
time ago.

And then another me thrust his face forward. Middle-aged
and gone to seed. Would I really let myself accumulate such a
paunch without caring? 'You've got to get us out of here!'

I stepped back. The tank seemed to wobble and bulge, as if it could barely maintain its integrity. And now there were dozens of 'me's: Some young – though none younger than my present age – some old, some positively *decrepit*. All of them elbowing each other aside for attention. All of them pleading with me.

Looking at them, these ragtag editions of myself who were never incarnated –these phantoms who had never had the chance to *be* – I felt the deepest pity in the hollow of my soul. Didn't Quanderhorn realise the unspeakable consequences of his infernal time loop? And presumably not just to me: to everybody. The innocents who never got to exist. The millions and millions of lives unlived.

'You've come before,' an eighty-year-old me with a hearing aid croaked. 'And you *never* help us!'

'What do you mean I've come before?' I cried back at them. 'When? When did I come before?'

And then others took up the cry: 'You never help us! You never help us!'

'How? How *can* I help you?'

And as one, a giant chorus of Brian Nylons howled back. 'Releeeeeeeeease us!'

I had to do something. I stepped towards the tank again and took a closer look. I couldn't perceive any kind of hatch or gateway, nor any controls that might operate such a thing. There were patches of peculiar-looking deposits at its base, like glowing orange frost, as if there was some curious seepage. I had a vague idea I'd seen it somewhere before, but who knows where?

Slowly, tentatively, I reached out to touch the bulging, pulsating walls of the silo. Perhaps I could . . .

A deafening siren screeched into life.

'Cellar breach attempt!'

As one, the Brians reared up and keened the most plaintive, miserable wail, then swirled into a vortex as if they'd been stirred up by a giant spoon, spinning away from me, shrieking as they were snatched into the maelstrom: 'Help! Help us! Let us live!'

'Wait! Wait! What do I have to do?' But the tank was solid again, and the only sound was that infernal siren. Red warning lights were strobing accusingly.

'*Unauthorised personnel detected . . .*'

'No, no, Delores! It's me! The Professor. Dammit!' I staggered back towards the entrance to the chamber. Suddenly, a magnesium flare flashed straight into my eyes, momentarily blinding me, and for a terrifying few moments, I couldn't locate the exit at all. I thrust myself forward, but persistently found myself back where I'd started, without any apparent travel. Then, finally, a wild desperate charge and I burst through whatever orifice had borne me here, and back into the tunnel.

'*Deploying anti-intruder defences . . .*'

'No, don't do that!' I pleaded, scrambling wildly along the narrow passage as fast as a crouch would allow. I had just managed to haul myself upright when the metallic voice continued:

'*Releasing slow-motion gas . . .*'

Slow-motion gas?

With a flash of insight, I realised just too late that the invisible ink note had been warning me the cellar was 'BOOBY TRAPPED'. I cursed my dunderheadedness as I pumped my legs in the direction of the lift. I thought I could make it before . . . Suddenly, there was an ominous hissing from all sides.

And I slowed motion.

Suddenly, it took all the muscles in my body straining to their maximum to move forward just a tiny fraction of a step at a time.

It was frustrating, physically draining, and, given the terror that was thumping thickly through my heart, oddly boring. Every half inch of progress was like running a marathon while pushing a cricket roller.

The lift was only three yards away, though my advance was now so languorous it would surely take me weeks to get there, and I feared I'd be completely exhausted within a couple of minutes.

The lift doors slid open. I don't know why. But it gave me hope. The light inside spilled out a warm glow of safety. I strained every sinew for a desperate sprint. I might just make it . . .

'*Dropping ball bearings.*'

I wasn't going to make it.

Chapter Fourteen

The Rational Scientific Journal of Dr. Gemini Janussen,
Saturday 5th January 1952 (Again)

The lift doors opened onto a tumult of sirens and flashing lights, and amidst it all, to my surprise, there was Brian.

For a second I thought he was frozen to the spot, then I noticed his leg moving forward slightly, and realised he must have triggered the slow-motion gas. Far from standing still, he was actually running for his life.

'*Dropping ball bearings.*'

Brian's eyes widened slowly. Very slowly. His body inched towards the lift almost imperceptibly. 'Ooooohhhhhhh ... Shhhhhhhhiiiiiiiiiiiiiiiiiiiiiiiiiiiiiiiiping ... Foooorecaaaaaast,' he drawled, as the hatches opened overhead and discharged their painful load.

Being non-organic, the ball bearings were not subject to the effects of the gas. They rained down upon him like hail from a blunderbuss, clunking off his skull with sickening regularity as he ineffectually attempted to dodge them like Tom Brown running the gauntlet past Flashman and his cronies. '*Ooooooooowwwwww! Ooooooooowwwwww! Ooooooooowwwwww!*'

Covering my mouth with my handkerchief, I reached out my arm. 'Brian! Grab my hand! Quick!'

'I'mmmmmmmmmmmm tryyyyyyyyyiiiiing . . .'

'*Engaging corridor flame-throwers* . . .'

Already I could feel the gas beginning to slow me down. If I didn't grab him right now, all would be lost.

I stretched as far as I could, fingertips straining, and managed to grip his flailing hand. I pulled him to me with all my might, simultaneously kicking the 'Door Close' button with my heel, praying it wasn't too late.

I heard more hatches flying open in the cellar walls, and caught the distinctive garlic-like odour of phosphorus.

There would be no second chances.

With a terrible roar and a blinding flash, the phosphorus spontaneously ignited in the moist air and a giant fireball bloomed towards us.

I hugged Brian tightly and closed my eyes, preparing for the worst. There was a jolt, and I opened them again.

The lift doors had finally closed.

I prayed they'd hold back the intense heat long enough for us to get out of there. They began to glow as the pungent stench of scorched air seeped under them.

Then suddenly we were on our way upwards. We could begin to breathe without fear of scorching our lungs as the air began to cool. We took in great gulps of it, gratefully.

Slowly, I became aware Brian and I were looking into each other's eyes, our chests heaving, still locked in a close embrace which, on reflection, might no longer have been appropriate.

'Oh! Sorry!' I tried to disengage, but my arms seemed to have developed a will of their own – a side effect of the slow-motion gas, no doubt. Strangely, Brian didn't attempt to disengage either.

'Yes!' he burbled. There was a very, very embarrassing pause whilst we looked at each other, then several ball bearings fell out of Brian's bra and clattered to the floor, mercifully breaking the spell.

We hastily separated.

'That was close.' I brushed down my skirt quite unnecessarily.

'Yes,' Brian agreed wittily. 'That was close.' He tried to make it look as if a man casually plucking metal spheroids out of his cleavage was the most natural thing in the world. He failed.

He looked up and caught me staring. His eyebrows contracted. 'Wait a minute: how did you manage to work this lift? Surely you need . . .'

I didn't want to go into that, most definitely, but my hand involuntarily checked the clasp of my crocodile bag was firmly shut. I changed the subject skilfully. 'Never mind that. What were you doing down there?'

He looked, for a second, as if he genuinely wanted to answer. But then the impulse passed. 'What were *you* doing down there?'

Somebody had to make the first move. I heaved a sigh. 'Brian. There's something you really need to know . . .'

There was a *ping*! '*Ground floor.*'

The doors slid apart on a very animated Troy. 'Brian! Gemma! There's an intruder in the basement!'

Guuuurk pushed his way past the lad into the lift. 'Exactly. Delores – take us to the roof.'

'No,' Troy stepped in behind him, 'the intruders are *down*.' He bustled Guuuurk away from the button array. It was like watching schoolboys squabbling over the last Wagon Wheel at the tuck shop window.

'And that,' Guuuurk ducked under Troy's arm, 'is why we're going *up*!'

Brian and I knew, naturally, that there was no intruder. At least, not any longer. 'The optimal course of action is for us all to leave the lift right now.' But as I stepped forward, the doors slid shut in my face. I reached down and pressed the 'Open' button, but for some reason it was unresponsive.

'In which case,' Guuuurk tilted his head in that annoying interrogatory way he has, 'what are you doing in the lift in the first place?'

I glanced round at Brian. His face was circulating though that strange array of expressions he adopts when he is struggling to make up one of his dismal untruths. Fun as it was to watch him, I decided to step in to the rescue. 'We were heading down to try and find the intruders, weren't we, Brian?

Brian opened his mouth, but a few baby sounds were all that escaped: 'Buh . . . Maaah . . . Hnuuuh?'

Hopeless. I had to rescue him, as usual. 'Then we realised only the Professor can operate this thing.'

'It always works for me,' Troy grinned. 'Lift! Activate that button over-thing, where it all lights up and does stuff!'

I suppose the Quanderhorn voice pattern must have been similar enough to fool the device, because the bank of peculiar hieroglyphics illuminated obediently.

'*Manual override enabled.*'

I tried to open the doors again, but that button was still dead. Curious.

Guuuurk studied the console without comprehension. 'Right! Which one is the roof?'

Troy bustled him aside. 'No – we need to go *down* and catch those intruders. They may be dangerous.'

'The thing is,' Guuuurk looked down at his tennis outfit, 'I really can't be seen by dangerous intruders in my plimsolls. It gives such a bad impression . . .'

'We're going to the very bottom,' Troy insisted, 'and that's that.' And he pressed a button.

Brian looked perplexed. 'Troy – that was the very top button.'

'No, bottom. That's the one at the top, isn't it?'

The lift jolted and started winching us upwards. The rate of acceleration was quite alarming. I had to grip the handrail. Brian's hand was already there, and mine fell on his. I didn't want to embarrass myself further by making an issue of it, so I left it there.

Guuuurk steadied himself in a corner, both hands braced against the lift walls. 'What on earth have you done now, you mutton-headed dolt?'

'Nothing . . .'

'Next stop: Lunar Station.'

Brian literally squeaked. '*Lunar?* This lift goes to the *Moon*?'

Trapdoors sprang open in the walls, and benches with harnesses attached unfolded out of them.

Guuuurk raced over to the console and started punching buttons wildly. 'No! Delores! Stop! No Moon! No Moon! Reverse! Reverse mechanisms! Stop!'

'Manual override deactivated. Please secure yourselves.'

Guuuurk gave Troy his Death Glare, then carefully slid down onto the nearest bench and started buckling himself in. 'Well,' he smiled pleasantly, 'that's another delightful *contretemps* you've ingeniously masterminded.'

4

Oxygen

`. . . late on in the game I stupidly slapped a Bayern player across the face, after he had been kicking me all the game and was sent off.

Albert Quixall, *interview for Retro United*

Chapter One

From Troy's Big Bumper Drawing Book

[PICTURE OF ANOTHER STICK MAN WITH BIG SCRIBBLED BLOBS ON THE TOP OF HIS ARMS, STANDING ON A BIG CIRCLE LABELLED 'MOON!']

HAhAhA. I prest A buttun. weer on the Moon! HoorAy! Its grAte here. Theres no Air. Theres A Moon yot. JnD A supur spAys stAtion. weer All going to Dye, sAys My FrenD Gurk. Hes stupiD. He sMels. Theres An Erth in the sky. Its Just like ours only FAr AwAy.

Chapter Two

Dr. Janussen removed her hand from mine and sat down. She clearly hadn't noticed they were touching, though, personally, I still felt a warm, tingling glow on the back of my hand where hers had rested. I didn't say anything. Frankly, my mind was a bit of a mess. The experiences in the cellar had quite knocked me for six. And what was it Dr. Janussen kept trying to tell me? There really was never time to explain anything, here.

And now we were heading for the Moon.

I fastened my own harness and gripped the bench. Could it be true? The Moon? The actual *Moon*? Anything was possible, with Quanderhorn. But how long was it going to take us? The Moon was, what? A quarter of a million miles away, give or take? If we were travelling at the speed of sound, which was . . . can't remember – surely, if I was a pilot I ought to know that – but say, five hundred miles an hour, that would take . . . Start again. If a train leaves Ipswich at 11.35, travelling at . . .

And suddenly, we stopped!

Everybody looked around nervously.

208

'*Destination: Moon.*'

The doors slowly parted on the most extraordinary vista. Through the panoramic window of the small outpost outside, the sky was perfect black, yet pierced by a million glittering stars. The ground was chalky grey, undulating and studded with craters.

Unless I'd taken leave of my senses, we really were on the Moon! 'How did we do that? It should have taken hours! Days! Weeks!'

Dr. Janussen shrugged. 'Meta-acceleration, I assume. Q.'s been working on it for a while, now. Is everybody uninjured?'

Troy had already unbuckled and had bounded outside like an excited toddler on his first trip to the beach. 'Hey! Come out here and look!'

Guuuurk didn't leave the bench. 'I am not stepping out of this lift into what I can only describe as an ineptly converted bus shelter with corrugated iron nailed over the gaps.'

That seemed a bit harsh to me. 'Nonsense!' I countered. 'There's official signage in a futuristic typeface. See? It specifically says "Advanced Lunar Station Q".'

'*Advanced!*' Troy repeated emphatically.

Something about the Byzantine arcanity of Troy's tortuous logic always seemed to get Guuuurk's goat. He completely forgot himself, leapt up and frogmarched me outside. 'Ad*vanced*? Look: it's a *bus shelter*! See: there's a timetable for the 43 to Highgate Woods!'

He did have a point. There was supposedly a bus due in ten minutes.

'And here!' He gestured animatedly. 'A poster for the Tufty Club! Only on your preposterous planet would a squirrel be the spokesman for road safety. Squirrels are *hopeless* at crossing roads. I've never even *seen* one that wasn't flat. Crossing the road is the very *least* of their talents.'*

Dr. Janussen tapped me on the shoulder. 'We really ought to go straight back. Troy, tell the buttons to switch back on again.'

But the lad was rapt, staring at the sky. 'What's that big blue thing up there?' he asked in wonder.

Dr. Janussen said, quite matter-of-factly: 'That's the Earth, Troy. Now, come on – we're wasting time. Let's get back in the lift.'

It crossed my mind to mention to her that the lift doors had just shut again, but at that moment, like the others, I found myself mesmerised in the thrall of the Earthglow. It bathed the lunarscape in its majestic blue radiance, and glinted tantalisingly off the myriad crashed spacecraft that pocked its surface as far as the eye could see.

'Oh, wowzer! Look at all those beauties.' Troy's face was a perfect picture of innocent delight.

Guuuurk, however, wasn't quite so captivated. 'It's like a bally ships' graveyard out there,' he whined.

Dr. Janussen tried to steer us all back to sanity. 'Clearly a

---

* It's about time we went into this. Here are the 'rules', it would appear, of the Time Loop:

People who die in one version of 1952 are not resurrected in subsequent iterations.

So, although in the first iteration, George VI was the King, succeeded by Elizabeth II, she would remain monarch for all further iterations (unless she were to die) and remain the same age.

In the timeline you and we enjoy, Tufty was not created until 1953, but we can assume from this journal entry that in this alternative time Elsie Mills, his creator, devised him in one of the previous 1952s. Things (and people) that are created in *one* of the 1952s persist into future iterations – babies, for instance are not constantly born and then stuffed back into their mothers.

very dangerous environment. Which is why we should leave here immediately.'

An electronic buzz-crackle snapped us out of our reveries, and the Professor's distorted voice echoed from a speaker above a small, circular screen in a box above the advert for Sharp's Brazil Nut Toffees.

'Advanced Lunar Station Q . . . Come in, Advanced Lunar Station Q . . .'

The circular screen fizzled, and a phalanx of zigzag lines resolved themselves into a jerkily moving image of the Professor's face.

'Advanced Lunar Station Q, respond . . .'

We bounded over. Gravity here was distinctly different. I could easily have covered six yards in a single leap without any kind of exertion, although I did bang my head on the tin roof rather badly.

Dr. Janussen found the transmit button and pressed it. 'Advanced Lunar Station Q responding. Over.'

The Professor's disembodied head scrutinised us with disdain. Clearly, this was a two-way visual link. 'What are you doing up there, you idiots?'

Guuuurk was affronted. 'I'll thank you not to take that kind of tone, Professor. How were we to know the lift *went* all the way to the Moon?'

'You're not even supposed to *be* in that lift.'

Dr. Janussen asked: 'Are you saying it's unsafe, Professor?'

'Well, its experimental, owing to the difficulty in maintaining the tensile strength of the cables.'

There was the tortured creak of metal rending, bolts shearing, and then a mighty twanging, snapping noise, followed by the rather unmistakable sound of a lift plummeting uncontrollably two hundred and fifty thousand miles back down to Earth.

'Dammit!' Quanderhorn keened. 'What idiot decided to make them out of liquorice whips?'

Not even Dr. Janussen felt inclined to provide the slightly obvious answer to this question.

Chapter Three

The Daybook of 'Jenkins' Jenkins, RQMS Royal Fusiliers (terminated on moral grounds), Saturday the 5th of January, 1952

Running short of Izal.
Collect football pools money.
Steam off stamps and burn football pools.

An intruder in the cellar = lots of mess. And guess who has to clean it up? Muggins, of course. So the ball bearings are all swept up, and the pools of incandescent phosphorus nicely mopped away – takes a long time with this slow-motion gas hanging around, I can tell you – and I'm just in the porcelains relieving myself – it's lasted sixty-five minutes so far – when yet another perishing alarm starts its caterwauling. Turns out the, ahem, 'crew' have been and gone and taken the lift up to the flipping moon.

I ask you.

The Prof's calling me, so I interrupt my business without proper shakings and start rushing towards him fast as I can, but this gas means I'm moving slower than that Son of a Samurai in Burma whose hamstrings I severed with the jagged lid of a bully beef tin.

I finally drags meself into the briefing room, and there they are, on the screen, looking all little boy lost and forlorn. I can hear them all speaking over the moon radio as I gets closer.

'How are we going to get back down there without the elevator?' Mr. Guuuurk's asking.

Elevator? I ask you. How that Martian can call himself an Englishman, I just don't know. Martians? Don't like 'em.

'We're working on a better cable,' the Prof says, 'by feeding silkworms with Brillo Pads. I'm hoping for a breakthrough shortly.'

'What kind of breakthrough?' asks young Nylon.

'The kind where silkworms don't die after eating Brillo Pads. On the plus side, we *have* produced some delightfully bullet-proof camiknickers.' That's the Prof for you. Always turning disaster into triumph.

Dr. Janussen steps up. 'How long do you think it might be before you can effect a repair, Professor?'

The Prof don't even have to think about it. 'It shouldn't take more than three weeks.'

'And how much oxygen do we have up here?'

The Prof gets out that fancy Dan ruler of his and starts sliding bits backwards and forwards. 'Enough for four hours.'

I did the sum in my head. They were several hours short.

Mr. Guuuurk went straight into one.

'So,' he wails, 'this is how it ends for Guuuurk the Mighty, Second Reserve Novice Nose-Ring Polisher to the Emperor's Deputy Concubine Twice Removed. Suffocated to death, fruitlessly waiting for a 43 bus on the moon. My only comfort: a series of poster-borne platitudes from a tree-dwelling rodent with negligible traffic knowledge.'

He goes rabbiting on like this for a good five minutes more, working hisself up into quite a lather. If he don't watch hisself, that Dr. Janussen might have to give him a fourpenny one to calm him down.

'No need for hysterics,' the Prof coos. 'Naturally, I have a plan.' He always has a plan, him.

Young Master Troy pipes up from the moon: 'Great, Pops! What is it?'

'To replace you all as quickly as possible,' the great man says without blinking. 'Must run along and get straight on with that now. Well done, everybody, but mostly me.'

He snaps off the moon radio, and turns to me, rubbing his hands. 'Right, Jenkins – when you eventually get over here – we have work to do.'

'Should I place an advert in the *Exchange and Mart* for new lab assistants, as per usual, sir?'

'That won't be necessary. I have the replacements in hand.' I wonder what he could have meant. 'Get a move on, man!' he says, getting irritated.

'Running all the way, sir.' I'm still six feet away, and not likely to reach him much before lunchtime.

The Prof tuts and rolls his eyes. 'Jenkins. Have you ingested slow-motion gas by any chance?'

'It's very possible, sir.'

'Here.' He tosses me a funny-looking garibaldi with glowing raisins. 'Eat this fast-motion biscuit.' Ah well. In for a penny . . . I raises it to my mouth . . .

'Can't you eat it any quicker than that?'

'Not really, sir. Where are we getting these replacements you mentioned?'

He smiles to himself all secret-like, and his eyes goes over to those peculiar goggles with the violet light I sometimes see him creeping around in at night.

'You'll see, Jenkins, you'll see . . .'

He worries me no end when he goes like that. It usually means what I'll see is trouble.

Chapter Four

Franday the rth of Phobos, Martian Year 5972 Pink

Secret report to Martian Command, by Guuuurk 'the Magnificent', Deputy Sand Lord of the Third Pit, Vice Guardian of the Sacred Bag of Dust, et cetera et cetera.

Dr. Janussen finished smacking my face to snap herself out of her hysterical ranting fit.

'Thank you, Guuuurk,' she said gratefully. 'I needed that'.

'You're quite welcome, dear lady.'

I find crises like this bring out my native chivalry. I pretended to sob loudly a little longer, and pounded the floor with my fists to make her feel better.

'What did he mean by "replace us"?' the naïve young Nylon asked.

'No.' The man-boy-ant shook his head. 'Pops would never do that.'

'Oh, you think he would never leave his only son, his chief science consultant, his test pilot, and his closest friend and *confidant* to asphyxiate to death on an airless satellite in the name of Science, do you?'

'Which one of those is me?' Troy asked.

'You're the *son*! You're the bally *son*! Who the devil did you think you were? King Haakon the Seventh of Norway?'

'I thought I might be his closest confidence.'

'No! *I'm* his closest confidence. And it's not "confi*dence*" it's "confi*dant*".'

Brian looked confused. 'I thought Dr. Janussen was his closest *confidant*.'

'No! *Me!* I am!'

Dr. Janussen started smacking me again for some reason. She really was quite unstable. 'Pull yourself together, you Martian milksop!' she ranted. 'If we're going to get out of this, we need to concentrate. All right. What resources do we have?'

We all began scavenging for supplies. The station was, well, bus-shelter sized, but it was dark, and stuffed with boxes and lockers and piles of bric-a-brac.

Brian found some rations in a locker: live chickens in a toothpaste tube, a packet of dehydrated pigs, and a gallon of powdered water, the proper use of which had clearly not been thought through. He scrutinised the labels. 'Look at this: "Contains 200 pigs. Do Not Drop in Bath."'

'Let's drop it in the bath!' Troy inevitably suggested.

Mercifully, the simpleton was distracted when Dr. Janussen's torch alit on what at first appeared to be a pile of filthy washing, but turned out on closer inspection to be four complete spacesuits discarded willy-nilly over a stack of boxes. Did I dare to start hoping?

'Right!' I said, commandingly asserting myself over the hapless crew. Or it may have been Dr. Janussen. 'Our only chance is to put on these spacesuits and find one of those ships out there we can repair. Quickly.'

I grabbed a suit. It seemed heavier than it ought to have been, and it rattled oddly. I tipped it upside down and a collection of human bones tumbled out. Round about an entire person's worth, I would have guessed.

'Someone's stuffed mine full of bones,' Troy announced.

'They're all full of bones,' Brian pointed out.

'Just tip them out and get into them quickly,' I or Dr. Janussen commanded. It may not have been me, actually, because I answered.

'Do we *have* to?'

'Do you want to live?'

I was going to explain in considerable detail exactly how much I wanted to live, but I didn't *particularly* want to be smacked in the face again. So, to my eternal shame, I reluctantly obeyed the Terranean shrew.

I suppressed a shudder and choked back a tiny spasm of vomit as a femur plopped out of the leg when I pushed my own through. It was gruesome, but there's no denying: this really was our only hope of survival. And surviving is my second favourite thing. My most favourite is surviving with a crisp, white fiver in my pocket. But I digress.

Suited up, oxygen tanks checked and working, we stepped towards the airlock. I say 'airlock', but it was actually an up-and-over garage door, wedged in place by garden gnomes.

Advanced Lunar Station Q!

We kicked the gnomes out of the way, the doors snapped up, the remaining air escaped with a terrifying whoosh, and the chicken Troy had squeezed out exploded with a squawk.

All we had now was the oxygen in our tanks, and our helmet radios were our only contact with each other.

Delores piped up: '*Leaving Advanced Lunar Station Q . . . And remember: Tufty says "When crossing the Moon, watch out for Moon monsters."*'

'Oh, highly amusing,' I smiled through gritted teeth. 'Thank you.'

Chapter Five

Feed boiler.

I eat the whole of that fast-motion biscuit, which turns out to be
a mistake. I start racing round like Mussolini when he spots the
enemy. I do get a lot done, but my heart's thumping through
my ribcage fit to burst.

I nip down to the village chemist's in two and a half minutes.
I would have gone faster, but the friction in my trousers was
a worry. Old Mr. Gerber says he could rush the film through
in four weeks. We haggle, and he decides two hours would be
plenty. I put the revolver away. Course, I haven't been able
to get the bullets since 1949, but one sight of my well-oiled
old Webley tends to encourage co-operation in even the most
stubborn negotiator.

Quite keen to see that snap when printed up. I wonder who it
might have caught? I has my suspicions, but I'm foresworn not
to share them on these pages. It could raise some embarrassing
questions round this place.

As I'm making such good time, I decide to pop into the Torso for a quick elbow-tilter, where I find Bill Blagstone celebrating. He's just told his foreman exactly what he thinks of him, and where he can stuff his job, on account of what he thinks is a football pools win. I don't have the heart to burst his bubble. But I do accept several pints.

Oddly enough, the drink doesn't hit me like usual, and I get back to the lab in double record time. I have to stop every once in a while to scrape off all the insects splatted on my face, but then I'm off again, sprightly as ever.

When I get there, I find the Prof's locked himself in the isolation lab. I press my ear to the door, but I can't make anything out, before Himself bursts out of the door and hands me a list.

'We need all of this right now, Jenkins.'

I studies it. A ton of nappies? Fourteen gallons of formula milk? Army size drum of talcum powder? 'It'll take a while, sir,' I tells him. 'Here they are.'

'Too late!' The Prof dashes off another note. 'Now we need this.'

I studies it. Eighteen Dick and Dora books, a gross of wax crayons, and half a dozen potties. 'I'll have to go further afield for that lot, sir,' I says. 'Here they are.'

But he's already handing me another note. I'm beginning to form an impression of what might be happening here. Four hundred and seventy blue exercise books, nineteen Fuzzy Felt kits, three train sets, a football and assorted dollies.

Mark my word, he's growing people in there.

And he's growing 'em fearsome quick.

Chapter Six

Franday the rth of Phobos, Martian Year 5972 Pink [cont'd]

Secret report to Martian Command, by Guuuurk, et cetera et cetera.

Walking on another planet's surface seemed to excite the hopeless Terraneans beyond all reason, though of course to me, it was just another miserable hike over rocks and craters. Not that I'm comparing it to Mars, where the rocks are rockier, and craters infinitely more craterous.

'I can't believe it!' Brian kept banging on. 'We're all actually on the *Moon*!' Well, hooray and put out the flags. It was bleak, airless and dusty. Which, coincidentally, is a top Martian singing group.*

---

* Bleek, Hairless & Dusty have so far released 22 albums, including such number one smashes as: 'The Emperor Ate My Family, Made Me Feel So Sad', 'Rockin' Round the Rocks With Rocks', 'Dust Gets in All Six of Your Eyes, Unfortunately', the classic 'Boy – It's Hot Here (Except When It's Freezing)', and their runaway hit 'Kill the Accursed Earthlings With Death Rays (Then We'll Be Dancin' All Night)'. They were recently inducted into the Martian Hall of Imprisonment For Offences Against The Emperor.
Srce: Fragment from Martian Teen magazine Just 32, edition 4955

I must also register my objection, here, to the arrogant way the Terraneans call it *the* moon, as if it were the only one in the entire bally universe. It's not even a particularly splendid moon, as these things go. Either of ours could knock it for sixpence. They also have the temerity to call their planet *the* world. What hubris! Everyone knows Mars is *the* world, and that's a fact.

'Hey!' Troy was bounding around like a Mexican jumping bean who's had too much coffee. 'There's a moon yacht tethered round the back here!'

This so-called 'moon yacht' turned out to be a battered old Morris Minor, with the back seats ripped out and replaced with huge accumulator batteries and a brace of queer-looking electric engines. I thought mournfully of my beautiful Maureen. Would I ever drive her again?

'There's only room for two,' Brian pointed out.

'Well, that's fine,' Dr. Janussen said. 'It's more efficient to split into two groups, and double our chances of survival.'

Immediately, my wily brain whirred into action. 'Right!' I said, skilfully seizing control of the situation. 'Let's pick teams!'

Dr. Janussen pursed her lips to say 'OK', but before she got past the 'O', I jumped in with 'I pick Troy!'

The dreadful Terranean scold didn't even bother to hide her disappointment. 'Damn! That means I'm stuck with Brian.'

'*Stuck* with?' Poor young Nylon's face was quite a picture. Even through the glare glinting off his smeary helmet you could see he was utterly crestfallen.

'I'm on Guuuurk's team!' Troy grinned. 'Great!' I would have taken delight in the notion that he was happy to be paired with me, but frankly, if a giant bolide came crashing out of the sky and incinerated us all in a fiery cloud of white hot death he'd have said 'Great!'.

He pulled open the passenger door and craned inside. 'Who gets the moon yacht?'

For an idiot, he had a point. That vehicle could mean the difference between life and death. I know Delores had been joking, but there really were Things out there – Dangerous Things you really didn't want to meet out in the open.

Resourceful as aye, I lit on the notion of suggesting a game of Martian Closey-eyesy, a schoolyard prank that wouldn't dupe a Martian toddler with a punctured head.

'Martian Closey-eyesy?' Brian asked, intrigued. 'How does that go?'

'Well . . .' I relished the moment, 'you see that distant ridge over there, in completely the opposite direction?'

'What? That big pointy one?'

'Nooooooo . . . a little to the left of that . . .'

'Where the dust cloud is?'

'A bit further along the horizon. Do you see it now?'

'I think so. Is it the jagged one?

'Yes, yes: the jagged one. See it?'

'Yes! But where's the Closey-eyesy bit?'

'Oh, you don't need to close your eyes *now*,' I chirruped, releasing the Morris Minor's brake and waving genially as Troy and I drove off. 'You've already lost the game!'

Hahaha. So long, suckers!

In the rear-view mirror, I could see the sad look of resignation and disdain Dr. Janussen was shooting at an even more crestfallen Brian, the poor sap.

Troy, meanwhile, was staring me down angrily, for some unknown reason. 'Guuuurk – why did you pull me inside like that?' He was genuinely cross. 'I really wanted to see that ridge you were talking about.'

The more discerning reader might be questioning the wisdom of my team selection right now. Well, my logic ran thus: should we encounter danger, the insect-brained mutant would make the bigger meal, so I could happily scarper off while they're eating him.

I must say, the moon jalopy handled rather well. Almost – though I'd never admit it in front of her – as well as old Maureen. No atmosphere and low gravity certainly helped us pootle along quite nicely. I began to wish I'd brought my driving gloves and my favourite pipe. And perhaps even a blonde or two!

I steered us due north-east towards a promising-looking cluster of wrecks. They were further away than they first appeared, which I'm afraid meant there was no way of avoiding that most dreaded of all things: a conversation with Troy.

'Do you miss Mars, Guuuurk?' he crackled over his radio.

Not wanting to alert these Terraneans to my undying devotion to Mother Mars, I dissembled somewhat. 'I don't miss squatting down a dust hole. Or the diet of Martian dust. Or the perpetual dust storm. It's the dust I don't miss, principally.'

He stared out of the windscreen, surprisingly maudlin. 'If I thought I'd never see our dear old abandoned fever hospital near Carlisle again, I don't know what I'd do.'

I studied him for a great deal of time, to see if I could detect the slightest spark of irony, but there was none.

'I mean,' he went on, 'you must want to get back home very badly.'

'Obviously, as a loyal and honourable Martian, it's my duty to attempt escape at every opportunity,' I admitted.

He peered at me more closely. 'You wouldn't double-cross me and steal one of these ships back to Mars, would you?

'I imagine your incredible strength and fierce devotion to Earth would easily thwart me.'

'Would it?'

'Please say it would.'

The lad suddenly jerked over to his left. 'Wow! D'you see that?'

'What?'

'I just tried to go left, but I went straight on.'

I narrowed my top two eyes. 'Yes, Troy. That's because *I'm* the one that's driving.'

'Oh yeah. I got confused because the Moon's usually in the sky. Not on the floor.'

'Ye-e-e-esss . . .?'

'Well, don't you see? It means everything's the other way round.'

Oh dear. Troy *thinking*. This is exactly what I'd been hoping to avoid. 'I don't follow,' I said, rather foolishly pursuing the issue.

'Well . . .' He screwed up his eyes and concentrated as hard as he could. 'If we're upside down that must mean that your left is my right. And – therefore – you must be me because you're on the left, so I'm *you*.'

'I'm getting a frightful headache.'

'Oh no! Should I take an aspirin?'

The more discerning reader will by now have given up trying to figure out why I selected my team as I did. I know I had.

'Perhaps we should stop talking,' I said, 'to preserve our dwindling oxygen.'

'You're right! Look how the dials on our suits have gone down already!'

Great Deimos! If he wasn't right about this! I'd absolutely failed to notice it really was draining very much faster than I expected. I floored the accelerator. It was all over if we didn't reach those wrecks soon.

Very soon.

Chapter Seven

Troy and Guuuurk had headed north-east along the ridge, so we
struck out north-west, directly across the plain, which would,
according to Dr. Janussen, 'Optimise our potential search grid'.

We made good time, covering perhaps five or six yards with
each bound. We'd started off in silence. I was still chafing from
her blatant disappointment at having me as her team member,
and she was still stewing over the Closey-eyesy business.

Finally, I snapped. Enough was enough.

'I'm terribly sorry. Excuse me for bringing this up, but were
you serious back there? About preferring Troy to me?'

'It's more efficient if we don't speak,' she countered coldly.
'But to answer your question: it's pure rationality. Troy is
ridiculously brave, superhumanly strong and utterly malleable.'

I couldn't let that pass. 'I'm pretty darned brave.'

She let out a short sharp breath. 'No, Brian – you really are
not. Think of all the times you literally scream.'

Well, that was hardly cricket. Everyone has their quirks.
'Well, I'm quite strong.'

'Again: no.'

'On the other hand, I do agree: I'm not very malleable. I'm extremely strong-willed.'

'Shut up, Brian.'

'OK.'

I bounded on in grumpy silence for a few minutes, which was foolish, really: there was so much I needed to talk to her about. A lot had happened in the last few hours, but my thoughts were flitting around from question to question, like an indecisive bee at the Chelsea Flower Show.

I desperately wanted to ask her just what it was she'd been going to tell me in the lift, and in the attic, but there were some things I had to get off my chest first.

'I don't blame you for loathing me, actually.' I took a deep breath. 'I'm not sure if you know this, but *I'm* the callous swine who turned poor Virginia into a subhuman cruciferous vegetable.'

There! I'd said it aloud, and I was glad I'd done it. I braced myself for her righteous and thoroughly deserved disdain.

Instead, surprisingly, she said: 'You did no such thing.'

'You don't have to protect me. I'm not a child. The Professor told me everything.'

'I have no idea why he'd say that, but Virginia did it to herself.'

I stopped in my tracks, panting. 'What? *What?*'

'Keep bounding. She left you a note. I read it. I know I shouldn't have, but I did. She said *she* was going to sacrifice *herself* to "literally beat the clock".'

'My word! Is that why she was climbing up Big Ben? It's somehow connected with this Time Loop business?'

'She thought so, I assume. She said it was the only way. That she'd seen what she called "the horrors" of the cellar, and it had to be stopped.'

I shuddered involuntarily. My own experience in the cellar had been petrifying. Of course! That's what she'd meant in my riverside reverie: the tanks she'd spoken of weren't military tanks, they were the bizarre tanks in which those horrifying spectres were trapped!

To think of poor Virginia down there, all alone, presumably experiencing terrifying phantoms of her failed future selves . . . And a thought occurred to me. 'So . . . that's why *you* were going down there when you rescued me: to see for yourself what she'd found there.'

Dr. Janussen nodded. 'And what were *you* doing down there?'

Well, I'd started making a clean breast of things, I might as well go all the way. I sighed. 'There's something else I need to come clean about, Gemma: I'm a spy.'

'Yes, I know.'

She *knew*? But *what* did she know? That I was a spy for Churchill? Or that I was a spy for Quanderhorn? I had to be careful . . .

'You *know*?'

'You and I are both spies for the International Scientific Ethics Authority.'

My courage failed me again. 'Yes, that's exactly the spying I was talking about.'

'I thought you'd forgotten about it, with the memory loss and everything, but obviously, you hadn't.'

'Ha! How could I forget the . . .' *What the deuce was it called?* '. . . the International Ethical Agency Society . . . thing? And their lovely headquarters in . . .' *Oh Lord, why did I have to keep on talking?* ' . . . New York.'

'Geneva.'

' . . . in Geneva!' *Shut up now, Brian, while you're still getting away with it.*

But Dr. Janussen wouldn't let it go. 'And the world-renowned scientist we report to is . . .?'

Confidence is everything when pulling off a deception. I went straight in with: 'Thomas Edison.'

'Who died in 1933.'

'. . . when he handed the reins over to . . .'

Thankfully, she gave me a clue. 'Albert . . .?'

'Albert Speer!'

'The Nazi architect?'

'Albert Schweitzer . . . Albert Camus . . . Albert Quixall . . .'

Oh, God, Brian. What are you burbling about?

She put me out of my misery. 'Einstein.'

'Of course, Albert *Einstein*! Why would a Sheffield Wednesday footballer be the head of the International . . . whatever it was?'

'It doesn't matter if you've forgotten, you clot. You really are the world's worst liar.'

It's sadly true. 'I know. I'm *terrible* at it. Why the devil am I a *spy*? I'm really not cut out for it.'

She gave me a look . . . I'd never seen it before, not on *her* . . . I'm not entirely sure what it meant – was it – dare I even think this? – affection? Whatever it was, it passed away again very quickly. But it made me feel rather . . . intoxicated.

We bounded on a while. I noticed my stomach was starting to growl. I couldn't remember the last time I'd eaten. I had a couple of tubes of chicken in my pocket, but the thought of squeezing them out and then, presumably, slaughtering and cooking them, didn't appeal.

It was then I spotted it, not fifteen yards ahead of us. In case it was some kind of lunar mirage, I asked Gemma: 'Do you see that?' rather tentatively.

'Yes,' she said. 'Of course I see it.'

'It's a hot potato stand.'

'Yes.'

'On the *Moon*!'

'I know what it is.'

'But I'm ravenous.'

'Remember what Delores said, Brian. Just ignore it.' She bounded past the hot potato stand, giving it a rather wide berth.

Bewildered, and very, very hungry, I reluctantly bounded after her.

Chapter Eight

Secret report to Martian Command, by Guuuurk, et cetera et cetera.

We'd almost made it to the wrecks in blessed silence, when the lad snapped out of whatever reverie he'd been in and started bouncing animatedly on his seat.

'Wait! Stop the yacht! Stop the yacht!'

I wrenched up the handbrake and we careened round in a cloud of grey moon dust.

'What? What is it?'

'Over there!' He gesticulated wildly behind us. 'We just passed a little cobbler's shop! It had those sweet little windows with the swirly bits in the middle, and little mechanical elves hammering on a brogue in the display.'

'Ye-ess . . .'

'I was just thinking I need some new shoelaces . . .'

'Were you *really*?'

'I mean, what are the chances? A shoelace shop on the Moon, just when I need one? It's about as unlikely as me seeing a . . . Oh, look! A barber's! I was just thinking I needed a trim round the back. Do you think they have that rubber thing that puffs talcum powder down your neck? I love that.'

I heaved a deep sigh. 'Troy, I need to explain to you about a creature called "the Lunar Mantrap" . . .'

'Hang on a minute. I just need to nip over to that cute little sweet shop and get a quarter of gobstoppers.' He was actually unhooking his seat harness. I laid a gentle hand on his shoulder as I accelerated away and tried again.

'The Lunar *Mantrap* is a deadly plant life form which lures the unwary traveller into its jaws by picking up our thoughts and mimicking objects of our immediate desires. Do you understand?'

'Oh yes! You mean . . . no, I don't understand.'

'They're carnivorous shape-shifters. They read your mind and morph themselves to look exactly like the thing you want to see.' He was still struggling. 'They're Nasty Things That Want to Eat You, so They Copy Things You Like.'

This seemed to sink in. 'The filthy swine!' he cursed. 'Pretending to be toffee shops!'

'So you see − we have to be on our guard at all ti—' I hit all the brakes at once. Would you believe it − right in front of us was the most splendid saucy gentleman's club! It was a riot of flashing signs: 'Open All Nite!', 'Gals Galore', 'Free For First Timers', and 'Beautiful Loose-Moralled Ladies Cavorting in Their Barely Adequate Nether Garments'.

'Wow!' Troy gawped. 'That's a *lot* of neon.'

I unhitched myself and threw the car door open. 'Let's *go*! I've got a whole wad of luncheon vouchers burning a hole in my tennis flannels. Tally-ho!'

'I'm right behind you!'

We scampered towards the lush red carpet that beckoned us towards the warm glow of the doorway. There was a poster beside it, advertising 'Unlimited Complimentary Cocktails for Martians and Part-Insectoid Humans Every Saturday'. What a stroke of unbridled luck! It *was* Saturday!

I was just about to set my foot down on the carpet and step inside when the idiotic troll grasped my elbow with his muscular hand like a G clamp, holding me back. 'Wait!' he yelled. 'What if it's one of the Bad Eaty things?'

'Let go of me, you addle-brained ape, I'm going inside!' I knew what he was up to, the bounder: he wanted first pick of the showgirls. Well, nothing was going to stop a violet-blooded Martian like me from getting to the floozies first. I stamped hard down on his foot, and he released me.

It's a bit of a blur from that moment. I remember my feet sticking to the 'carpet' as it began to roll up behind me, and banks upon banks of bayonet-sharp teeth emerging from the darkness beyond the doorway, dripping with what looked like acid. I was propelled helplessly towards them. I tried to move, but my feet were mired in its glue-like saliva. I was done for. The only honourable thing was to embrace my fate with all the calm dignity in my noble Martian breast.

'Help! Help!' I shouted, just to make the Terranean lad feel better, really. 'I'm too handsome to die!'

But the scoundrel had gone! There was no sign of him whatsoever. He'd simply left me there to be chewed and digested. And I thought he was my friend!

If only I could liberate one arm, I could perhaps tap the broadcast button on my breast and warn the others of the danger, as a last heroic act of heroism. I kicked savagely at the beast's cheeks, and managed to momentarily distract it enough to rip my hand free and hit the switch.

'Brian and Gemma! This is the last message I shall ever send! It's curtains for me. Don't try and reach me – you'll never make it. But you young things still have a chance at life – for heaven's sake watch out for the Lunar Mantraps.'

There was a terrible roar as the savage creature reared to deliver its death blow. I punched it violently in the eye. He wouldn't forget *this* meal in a hurry.

'I go now. This is the end for Guuuurk the Beneficent: I die as I would have wished: sacrificing myself for the greater glory of Mother Mars. I peacefully await the end, and my undeniably befitting transition to Bzingador.*

'Thus ends the life of a legend. Weep not for me. Weep only for Mars, who has lost her favourite son . . .'

'Guuuurk out.'

---

* Bzingador (*silent 'b'*) is a kind of Martian Valhalla, where the souls of the bravest Warriors are welcomed for an eternal slap-up meal at the legendary Long Table, at the head of which sits the Lord Phobos himself, brandishing his Mace of Fog, his Orb of Drizzle and his Mantle of Intermittent Showers. Each warrior has a twelve-breasted serving wench at each knee who pops sausages into his mouth, and isn't allowed to argue, remark upon his personal hygiene or make him shop for furniture.

It is most unlikely Guuuurk would even get to ring the doorbell, as a pit would open beneath the entrance, and cowards and traitors are whisked straight down to Croydon, the Martian Hades. Most Martian historians maintain it inspired the name of the London borough, and suggest that anyone who doubts this should pay a visit to Croyden power station on a Saturday night.

Chapter Nine

Clearly, Brian's hunger was not abating. Everywhere we looked there was a fully formed fish and chip shop, or a transport café, or the Aerated Bread Company. In frustration, he scooped up a pebble and hurled it at a small Italian trattoria, which immediately morphed back into its base form: a rather revolting giant Venus flytrap sort of plant, its gaping maw lined with savage teeth.

This delighted the schoolboy cricketer in Brian. He grabbed a handful of pebbles and started targeting the lunar plants with gusto. He could hurl a stone quite a distance in the low gravity here, without breaking his step.

Eventually, we left the outcrops of vegetation behind, and found ourselves in a large, dusty basin, with a cluster of promising-looking craft on the far ridge.

I was feeling the exertions, now, and my breath was coming in gulps, which was inefficient. I held up my hand and shouted: 'Stop!'

Brian paused, panting. 'Are you sure? We've got less than thirty minutes of oxygen left.'

'Well, how much is that? That could be any amount at all right down to zero.'

'Ye-es, but if you had ten minutes left, for example, you wouldn't say "less than thirty", would you?'

'But that *would* be factually correct.' Honestly, the vague way this man's mind worked! How on earth anyone such as myself could find him remotely attractive was quite beyond comprehension.

'OK – so we have twenty-eight minutes left. Approximately. And I still don't understand why we're stopping.' He gave that funny little half-smile of his.

'The more we strain, the more oxygen we burn. Our most efficient course is to rest for exactly three minutes.'

We both caught our breath.

I was beginning to feel a little light-headed. I checked my oxygen feed for blockages, but everything was fine. Suddenly, a tiny wisp of light flared from a nearby ditch. And another. 'Over there!' Brian started. 'What are those things?'

'They're luminects.'

'Whatinects?'

'A sort of moon glow-worm.'

He relaxed and started breathing more normally. 'They're beautiful.'

Objectively, I had to admit: they *were* an appealing sight. 'If you tune in your helmet, they say you can hear them chirruping.'

I twisted my own tuner, and sure enough, there they were. A beautiful chorus of basso song drifting in and out on the solar wind. 'Isn't that lovely?'

Brian was pulling a face. 'Not *really*.' He actually scratched his helmet. 'They sound like . . . a room full of terribly flatulent old men.'

Pitiful. What was wrong with this boy? 'Widen the frequency and you can hear the moon crickets, too.'

And a harmony of soothing baritone blended in to form a peerless symphony of lunar Nature, making me almost giddy with the wonder of it all.

'Is it me,' Brian asked tentatively, 'or do they sound like they're belching?'

Oh, this was typical. 'There's absolutely no romance in your soul, is there?'

'*Romance?* That one over there sounds like it's throwing up!' There was an awkward pause, while the philistine shuffled uneasily. 'Where are we exactly?'

'The Sea of Tranquillity. Isn't it romantic?'

He kicked at a pebble. 'No. Not really. There's a bit too much farting and belching and vomiting for my taste.'

'Do you want to put your arms around me?' I said, suddenly. I don't know why. I seemed to be feeling increasingly frivolous.

Brian was staring at me strangely. For some reason, my hand automatically went up to the right side of my helmet. 'Your ear . . .' he said, unhelpfully.

'What about my ear?'

'It's . . .' He seemed strangely reluctant to tell me.

'What *about* my ear?' I repeated, quite cross with him.

'It's . . . it's winding down.'

'Winding down?' My hand shot up again. Why did it keep doing that?

'And we can't reach it through your helmet.'

'What do you mean, "winding down"?'

But the truth was: I already knew the answer. I'd been denying it, pretending it wasn't happening, but all those strange goings-on: the pink motor scooter, the cushions and the make-up . . . Could that have been . . .? It *must* have been . . . *me!*

Johnnie Ray records?

Crocodile handbags?

Actually, thinking about it now, I did quite like Johnnie Ray, particularly 'The Little White Cloud That Cried'. And that crocodile bag was pretty snappy (ha ha!).

Oh my Lord! Winding down? It was blindingly obvious now. The right-hand side of my brain – the rational, logical side – was powered by clockwork!

Clockwork!

And there was a part of me that always knew that.

'You're going to be all right, Gemma.' Brian smiled gently and stepped towards me. It was quite a sweet smile, when you thought about it. 'You're going to be just fine. You'll simply start to feel increasingly emotional and intuitive, that's all. It's still the same old clever custard Dr. Janussen at the helm in there.'

He was right. I could fight this. It was just a question of focusing on pure rationality and expediency. We were in mortal danger, and if we didn't . . .'Kiss me!' I demanded. Right out of the blue. Honestly. How forward!

Brian shifted nervously on his feet and kicked another pebble.

'Go on, kiss me,' I positively demanded.

'I feel . . .' He squirmed. 'I feel I'd be taking advantage of you. In this . . . condition.'

'I *want* you to take advantage of me, you wonderful idiot!' I tilted my head back and puckered up. Resist that if you can, boy!

But he didn't move. 'Gemma, it's pure rationality. We're both wearing space helmets. If we took them off now, our eyes and tongues would boil, literally *boil*, long before our lips touched. That is if our lungs hadn't already imploded.'

'I don't care about boiling lungs. Kiss me.' My hands actually reached for the clasps of my helmet. I don't know if I'd have gone ahead and wrenched it off, but I was interrupted by a transmission from Guuuurk:

'*Brian and Gemma!*' BZZT! '*This is the last message I shall ever send, unless you drag your arses over here sharpish and—*' ZZZTSSS! '*some kind of fallacious floozy flophouse. That stinker Troy—*' FZZZZT SSSSS! '*cowardly bas—*' FZZZZT! '*Ahhhh! It's digesting me! I don't want to die! I'll give you anything if you get over here quick and—*' BZZZT! '*I'll even betray Mars! For heaven's sake reply. Do you read me? Do you rea—*'

I snapped the radio off.

Brian was fiddling with his receiver. 'I didn't get that. What did he want?'

'Nothing. Now: tell me what you think of my eyes . . .'

In my headphones there was a sudden outburst that sounded undeniably reminiscent of flatulence and belching, just like Brian had been describing.

'Sorry.' He kicked another pebble. 'Those were all me.'

Chapter Ten

The Daybook of 'Jenkins' Jenkins, RQMS Royal Fusiliers (AWOL since 1945), Saturday the 5th of January, 1952

Groom boiler.

The Prof's scampering in and out of that isolation lab like that Eyetie POW we chased round the Colosseum with bayonets fixed.

I finally manage to attract his attention: 'Any news from the crew on the Moon, sir?'

He looks surprised I've even asked. 'Oh, it's pretty hopeless for that bunch. As far as I can tell, there's only one discarded ship up there that can conceivably be rendered spaceworthy. And frankly, I doubt they have the wherewithal to work out how to use it.'

'I put all the gubbins you ordered over there, sir.'

'Oh, bring it in. Bring it in. We're going to start needing it shortly.'

Sometimes with the Prof, it's best to come straight out and ask. 'Am I right in thinking you're . . . growing people again, sir?'

'Yes. But I think I've got it right this time.' I clutches an armful of baby gear and follows him into the Iso lab. 'I've been scraping the dead skin from the subjects while they slept for the last nine months.'

'In your night vision goggles, sir, would that be right?'

He fixes me with one of his looks. Sometimes, it ain't best to come straight out and ask.

'Yes. Well spotted, Jenkins.' And there's a little bit of a threat in the 'Jenkins'. 'Anyway, I've gathered sufficient bio-material to grow duplicates rapidly. Very rapidly.' He hits a button, and a panel in the wall slides aside and there's a window behind it. 'If I hung around waiting for years for people to grow up properly, there'd be no end to it.'

The window looks on to this quaint little nursery room. There's four cots: a baby boy in the first, a baby girl in the next one, then a baby Martian, of all things, and something odd in a cocoon in the last one. The Martian one has a special muzzle on, to stop him eating the wet nurse.

As I watches, I can actually see them growing! In less than five minutes, they've outgrown their cribs and are crawling around on a mat.

'How are they going to learn things, sir?'

'That's the beauty of it: by the time they're fully developed, they'll have inherited the entire knowledge of their donors. No need to teach them anything! Imagine that: no more schools, no more teachers, no more rules!'

Just then, the little Master Quanderhorn duplicate bursts out of whatever pupa thing he's been growing in, and starts stacking up the cots like alphabet bricks.

'I'm the best!' he's saying. His very first words!

'Put those beds down!' says the purple baby, lighting a tiny miniature cigarette. 'This place is an absolute shambles.'

The Prof's watching approvingly. 'They should be fully

grown adults by 3.37 this afternoon.'

Young Dr. Janussen crawls over to young master Nylon, who's heavily involved in his Brio train set. 'Give us a kiss, Brian,' she says, and plants one on his cheek.

He leaps up like he's been stung by a rattler and starts rubbing his face with considerable vigour. '*Yewgh!*' he yells. 'Smelly girl! Go away!' Ha! He'll be regretting that in about forty minutes if my arithmetic is right.

'So they're going to be completely identical, sir, to the original crew, are they?'

'Perfect replicas,' he nods. 'Almost.'

Oh dear.

'Almost, sir?'

'Obviously,' he says, with that terrifying glint in his eye, 'I've made one or two improvements.'

Chapter Eleven

Franday the rth of Phobos, Martian Year 5972 Pink [cont'd]

Secret report to Martian Command, by Guuuurk, et cetera et cetera.

I didn't seem to be standing at the sacred Gates of Bzingador, where pain and suffering are washed away forever by the tinkling Fountains of Serenity. Instead, I was in considerable pain, and suffering rather badly. There was a gruesome smell, which led me to believe I may have soiled myself, my feet were screaming in agony as if being *digested*, and I could hear the most *ghastly* clanging noise.

When I opened a few of my eyes again to check why I wasn't dead, I saw Troy outside the roaring behemoth's gaping maw, banging it roundly over the head with what looked like a huge section of jagged steel ripped off from some structure.

'Stand back!' he cried, unnecessarily. I wasn't moving anywhere. I was rolled up in the creature's tongue like Cleopatra wrapped in an Axminster.

'Where the devil have you *been*?' I croaked weakly.

'Getting this!' He brandished the giant *ersatz* axe. 'I pulled it off a crashed ship – take *that*, Moon Monster!' He brought it down again to a horrifying screech from the Mantrap and a massive spurt of bilious sap from a huge gash in its hide.

The tongue unfurled and spat me out like used chewing tobacco. I tumbled, winded and slime-covered, onto the lunar surface.

Troy swung again and again. The creature was lunging at him ferociously. He yelled over his shoulder: 'Get back in the yacht, quick!'

I didn't need telling twice. To be honest, I didn't need telling *once*. I was already slamming down the accelerator when he just managed to jump in beside me.

'Guuuurk – I nearly didn't make it!'

'Do you really think I would leave you behind?'

He thought for a second. 'Probably, yes.'

'What? After you risked your life to save me from almost certain death?'

He pondered again. 'Probably, yes.'

That, to me, is the essence of friendship. When you know each other *so* well.

'What an ignominious end that would have been: savaged to death by a hotsy-totsy parlour.

We motored on. The pain in my feet gradually subsided to a dull throb. I drove resolutely past an All-Nite Stripperama, the Lunar Playboy Club, and the combined Racy Cummerbund Shop and Swedish Massage Emporium.

I glanced round at the lad. He was worryingly gullible. 'We really need to keep our wits about us with these Mantrap demons,' I admonished. 'We have to remember: they always appear as something you urgently desire.'

'Right.' Troy nodded. He was gloriously quiet for a moment. It didn't last. 'Like, say, when we found this yacht.'

'Yes . . . No! . . . *What?* No. That's nonsense.'

'Think about it. We really wanted a moon yacht, and *bam*! There it was.'

'No.' I chuckled. 'They can't mimic moving objec—'

'The yacht's one! The yacht's one! Jump out! The yacht's a monster!'

Before I could protest, he'd wrapped his arms round me and leapt backwards through the passenger door, bringing us both down in the moon dust with a sickening crump. The vehicle plunged onwards, dizzily out of control. It veered wildly to the left, swerved to the right, smashed into a large boulder which sent it spinning into the air. It finally embedded itself in a rocky ridge, throwing up a slow-motion plume of severed metal parts and scattered debris.

Slowly and painfully we got to our feet.

'I think you panicked a bit there, Guuuurk,' the simpleton castigated. 'Turns out it *was* just a moon yacht after all.'

'And now,' I pointed out, though it hardly seemed necessary, 'it's just a useless farrago of smoking metal detritus.'

'You give up too easily, Guuuurk.' He slapped me on my back with more gusto than I'd have liked. 'I'll just haul it over there to that handy moon yacht repair garage.'

I glanced over to it. The sign by the petrol pumps read 'Completely Smashed Moon Vehicles Repaired in Ten Minutes! No Wreck Too Wrecked!'. I sighed.

'Troy, Troy, Troy, Troy, Troy.' I shook my head genially. 'However many times do I have to explain this: the creatures disguise themselves as something you want to see . . .'

'Ye-e-e-e-esss . . .' I swear I could hear his mighty brain whirring.

'Something that's not normally found on the Moon . . .' I think I was beginning to get through.

'Ok-a-a-a-ayyy . . .'

'. . . But is familiar to the person they're trying to trap!'

His eyes widened alarmingly. I could see what he was think-ing. Again, I chuckled. 'No,' I smiled kindly, 'they can't do peop—'

And that's as far as I got . . .

Chapter Twelve

From Troy's Big Bumper Drawing Book

Its Gerk! The monstr is Gerk! Gerk is the monstr! Heres A Droring oF Gerk:

[STICK FIGURE WITH HUGE HEAD AND LOTS OF EYES]

AnD heres A pikture oF whAt he reelly look likes when hees A Monstr:

[CRUDELY DRAWN PLANT WITH A MOUTH]

i hAve to kil hiM, whiCh is A pitty beCus hees My best FrenD.

BAM bAM bAM i go on his helMut. its beginning to CrAk oFen. BAM bAM bAM.
He's trying to sAy soMethink but i wont lissen.
BAM bAM bAM.
BAM bAM bAM.

Chapter Thirteen

From the journal of Brian Nylon, 5th January, 1952 — [cont'd]

As if it wasn't hard enough trying to make it to the cluster of wrecks before our oxygen ran out, I had to expend enormous amounts of energy, time and valuable air trying to get Gemma to focus on the mission. Everything was a distraction for her. Wasn't this a lovely pebble? (No, it was just another dull little rock); if we settled down here, where's the nearest school? (The Earth).

I couldn't get her to tell me what Guuuurk had actually been saying in that transmission. In the small snatch I'd been able to make out, he'd sounded rather panicked. Worrying.

My helmet radio picked up a dull, mighty thump in the distance, and I wheeled around to see a massive plume of smoke hurling debris above the horizon from roughly their direction. 'Merciful Heaven! I hope nothing's happened to the others!'

But Gemma seemed quite unperturbed. 'Oooh. That would mean we were the only two people left on the Moon. Just you and I under the twinkling stars of the Milky Way.'

My indulgent smile was wearing out, but I pasted it on one more time, and ploughed on.

We'd encountered a couple of ships that appeared potentially spaceworthy, but it had quickly become obvious they were beyond salvation. The Moon was a savage mistress. She took a heavy toll on things that stayed here too long, and she would surely take *us* if we lingered in her arms.

Just when I thought all was lost, we rounded a dune to find an absolutely magnificent immense vessel, apparently intact, at the end of a long trench, embedded at an angle of thirty degrees in the encroaching scree. If it was still operational, it shouldn't take much to blast it free.

It appeared undamaged: defiant and sleek, a bold, glossy metallic red. It tapered towards the top, then swelled again into a sort of bulging head, with an arrangement of portholes and grilles that made it look for all the world like a scowling demon timelessly caught in a perpetual rage. It was intimidating, but no doubt, that was the point. For us, it was beautiful. It was hope.

But was it real?

Just to be sure, I flung a pebble at it. It pinged off the sturdy hull without making the slightest mark.

Definitely real.

'Oh, must we look at *another* ship?' Gemma followed me reluctantly, deliberately dragging her feet. 'It's so *boring*.'

'Just one last one.'

She rolled her eyes. 'Why can't we have some *fun*?'

I'd given up checking the remaining oxygen. It wasn't helping, and checking for oxygen levels wasted . . . valuable oxygen. But we could only be mere minutes away from depletion.

Trying to keep my mounting excitement from causing me to breathe any faster, I circled the craft's mighty girth. Two of its fins were indeed embedded in the ground, though I had no doubt the powerful-looking launch engines would blast it free without too much kerfuffle.

But for the life of me, I couldn't find an entrance.

The highly polished lower hull was diamond-hard and entirely featureless. There didn't even appear to be a seam.

'Gemma, I need some help here. We've only got a couple of minutes of oxygen remaining—'

'Oxygen, oxygen: that's all you think about.' And she began dry coughing.

I glanced down at the dial on her breathing apparatus. Her supply was out.

She looked at me, confused and afraid. 'Why can't I breathe, Brian?'

'We've got to get into this ship. We've got to get inside it right now.'

'My legs feel . . . heavy.' She physically wilted.

I bounded over and caught her. 'Here . . .' I uncoupled my remaining tank and swapped it with hers. Rather unchivalrously, I fear, I took a final gulp of air before I did.

She started breathing again, the panic drained from her eyes, and the colour of her lips returned to beautiful. They gradually raised into a cheerful arc, then wavered once more. 'But what will you breathe?'

'Don't worry. There's still a few minutes' worth left in my suit.'

She smiled an infinitely sad smile. 'You really are a terrible, terrible liar, Brian.' Then she gave me that look which had induced in me such giddiness earlier on.

'I know' I said.

I banged the unrelenting metal surface desperately one last time, to no avail whatsoever. There was no discernible door of any kind.

'Gemma? I need a little rest. I'm just going to close my eyes for a while. Promise me, you'll get inside there, whatever happens.'

'How? Brian? Brian . . .?'

Hers had been the first voice I could remember hearing, and it appeared it would be the last. I felt myself disconnecting from this world. It wasn't all that unpleasant, really. I sank to a crouch, then collapsed ingloriously to my bottom. I managed to raise my head just a touch, to see the iridescent blue glow of the earthlight, haloing the stunning face of the woman I adored.

Not a bad way to go.

Chapter Fourteen

The Daybook of 'Jenkins' Jenkins, RQMS Royal Fusiliers (missing, presumed dead), Saturday the 5th of January, 1952

De-worm boiler.

Kids? Don't like 'em. Oh, the chaos! Things starts getting dodgy round about half past eleven, or as I likes to call it: 'puberty'. We has to separate the young duplicates into individual rooms, for their own safety. The mess! The smell! The discarded clothing! I'm shovelling packets of crisps in there like there's no tomorrow and carting out filthy laundry by the pallet load. There's pimples and bumfluff moustaches and the monthlies and dumb insolence – that's what I can't stand, the bloomin' dumb insolence. And skiffle, whatever that is. Can't keep a washboard in the kitchen for five minutes. Good thing they sleeps most of the time.

As if that's not enough, the Prof's also given me a huge list of materials to pack into Gargantua, the Super Quandertechnicon. I'll be honest, he does tend to call more or less everything 'Gargantua', the old Professor. I've no idea why. It's not as if he's a stupid man. I suppose he feels it's a waste of his brain space, thinking up new names for all the whatsits and whosits he's inventing all the time.

Anyways, I'm busy driving Gargantua, the Quanderforklift, hither and thither. Warehouse to truck, to lab, to warehouse. Perculiar list of stuff I have to shift, too: Cutting equipment, pitch torches, mobile generators, lights, protective overalls, and five hundred titanium shovels. I don't know what it is he's preparing for, but it's definitely something big.

The Prof don't bother explaining to yours truly, of course: he's busy tormenting that poor rat of his again. I tell you: that rodent has it easy compared to me.

When the Great Man finally breezes in, I asks him: 'Just a thought about the duplicates, sir: what happens if the others come back again?'

'The others?'

'The real Dr. Janussen and that. Would we have to . . . take care of these young perishers?' I've got this old Gurkha kukri what would do the job nice.'

'Oh, there's no chance of that, Jenkins: Those poor devils are never coming back. Their oxygen will have run out . . .' he glances at his watch, '. . . six minutes ago. Now: how about rustling me up some of your devilled liver kidneys?'

Chapter Fifteen

From the journal of Brian Nylon, 5th January, 1952 –
Iteration 66

I really hadn't expected to wake up. I opened my eyes in the
most peculiar environment: everything was red! For a moment,
I thought I might be in Hell. Or Woolworths. It took me a minute
or two to realise I was actually still alive and on the flight deck
of the alien craft.

Everything here was that same furious scarlet, except for
clusters of strange symbols everywhere in incandescent crimson, which I presumed was alien writing of some description.
Below the scowling portholes was a rank of what I assumed
were control consoles, but they were shiny, smooth and featureless, with no apparent mechanisms.

Gemma was standing in the cockpit area, studying the blank
panels. Her helmet was off. My hands shot up to my head. Mine
was off, too. 'Gemma!' I called, but my throat was ridiculously
dry, and hardly any sound issued.

She heard me anyway, and turned. 'You're all right, I assume?'

'Yes, I . . . I think so. What happened?'

'I'm not entirely sure. I suspect I wasn't . . . completely
myself for a while.'

I noticed her ear had been wound back into position, but her look defied me to mention it.

'I remember I was . . . furious,' she went on. 'Quite out of control, really.' It was clearly a strain for her to talk about it. 'Furious you were dying, and I couldn't find a hatch. Then, suddenly, a portion of the hull just sort of . . . gave way.'

'Gave way how?'

Her scientific curiosity reasserted itself. 'As if the metal temporarily became fluid and a hatchway just sort of melted into existence. I pulled you inside, but the rest of the ship was dead. I couldn't believe it! To have got this far . . . it was intensely frustrating. I'm afraid I cursed the whole stupid ship!' She looked down, ashamed at that. 'And suddenly the life support just activated itself. Lights, atmosphere, everything.'

I climbed to my feet and lurched unsteadily over to her. 'So is it spaceworthy?'

'I've no idea. I can't work out how to access these controls, if that's what they are.'

'Are you sure this is the main control deck?' It did indeed appear to be the pilot position. I glanced through the oddly shaped viewports. There was a cloud of dust on the horizon I'd never noticed before. A storm? On the Moon? Was that possible?

'There's a couple of small chambers behind us.' She nodded with the back of her head. 'Nothing useful in any of them.'

'Maybe the controls are hidden behind more of that liquid metal stuff?'

'Of course. It's axiomatic.'

We both ran our hands over the sleek surfaces. Nothing. I noticed when our hands accidentally brushed, she gently moved hers away without comment.

We stood back. 'What exactly did you do to get the hatch to work?' I asked.

She shook her head and tried replaying it in her mind. 'Absolutely nothing. It just seemed to know I wanted it to open.'

'OK, let's try that.' I cleared my throat and announced, in my best BBC voice: 'I wish to use the controls.'

We stared at the 'console'. Nothing happened.

'Oh! Of course!' I slapped my forehead. 'I didn't say "please". What must it think of me? *Please* I would like to use the controls to get back to Earth, if you please. Thank you.'

And again, nothing.

Gemma started: 'Perhaps if you—'

'No, no.' I waved her away. 'I think I'm getting there.' I started again. 'Please, very kind machine-ship, grant me the favour of revealing unto me the hidden bounty of your marvellous controls . . . No no no, that's far too obsequious. No wonder it isn't taking any notice of me.'

I raised my voice. 'I command you, in the name of Her Majesty Queen Elizabeth the Second, by the Grace of God, of Great Britain and the British Dominions beyond the Seas, open the hidden hatch now!'

I fixed the panel with my very best schoolmaster's stare. 'I mean it. I'm not joking. I'm *waiting*.'

I crossed my arms for further effect. 'I'm still waiting. Nobody's going *anywhere* until you open the hidden hatch.'

'Brian,' Gemma interrupted gently, 'I don't think that's really going to—'

'No – wait: you said you cursed it.'

'What?'

'You cursed the ship. What did you call it?'

'I can't remember . . .'

'OK, you damn ship!' I tried. 'You think you're so blasted

clever, don't you?' I gritted my teeth and forced myself to swear at it. 'You . . . you . . . you filthy machine bastard!'

'Brian – why don't you let me . . .?' she offered.

'I'm *trying* to save our lives, woman!' I exploded in desperate frustration. 'Can you *please* control these *incessant* interruptions?'

There was an electrical whine, and the deck lit up. The surfaces melted away, revealing bank upon bank of mysterious blinking lights – all red, of course – and strangely shaped glowing crimson screens.

'See? I told you.' I relaxed and breathed out. There was still a chance we could survive. I shuffled uneasily. 'Gemma, I'm awfully sorry if I got a little heated there. I was . . .'

And the deck died again.

'Curious,' Gemma said, and started studying the surface again.

'Don't worry,' I smiled, smugly. 'Turn on again, you filthy machine bastard!' But nothing happened. 'You dirty, snivelling toerag!' I tried, glancing over at Gemma apologetically. In truth, I only knew two or three swear words, and I was getting to the end of my supply. 'You . . . you . . . vicious little *snot*!'

But the panels remained defiantly dead.

I heard a dull buzzing sound coming from the back of the flight area. I turned my head. 'What's that noise?'

Gemma stooped so her eyes were parallel with the surfaces, studying them for slender cracks. 'Your helmet radio. It could be Q.: he might be able to help.'

I hurried back, pulled my helmet on and turned up the volume on the earphone.

And I heard the single word: '. . . *traitor!*'

Chapter Sixteen

From the journal of Brian Nylon, 5th January, 1952 – [cont'd]

My stomach suddenly contracted like a jellyfish being poked with a stick. 'Pardon?'

'*I said: come in, Penetrator.*' Even a quarter of a million miles away on a short wave transmission, the growling voice of the Prime Minister was unmistakable. '*Agent Penetrator, come in . . .*'

Gemma glanced over her shoulder. 'Who is it, Brian?'

'Ohhh, I . . . can't quite make out. I'll have to go over here . . .' I found a handle recessed into the bulkhead. '. . . into the Communications Room . . .'

I tugged open the door.

Immediately I was hit by an avalanche of crockery.

A giant tower of dinner plates toppled over like a felled redwood and crashed into the deck and shattered to smithereens. I had barely recovered from the shock when a second tower, obviously held in place by the first, cascaded over me as well. Wave upon wave of suicidal crockery seemed intent on hurling itself to the floor, till the final plate fell with a horrible smash.

'. . . into this alien crockery cupboard,' I extemporised nicely. 'Where the . . . reception is better.'

'What on earth are you doing?'

'Shhhhh! I think closing the door might help.'

I crunched my way into the tiny cupboard and wrenched the door shut behind me, dragging all the shattered fragments noisily back in with me.

'Sorry about that, Prime Minster,' I whispered. 'We're in a bit of a pickle at the moment . . .'

'*Speak up, man! The radio link might fail at any moment. You're on the Moon, you know.*'

'Yes, I'm sorry about that—'

'*Stop whispering, Penetrator. You're barely audible.*'

'I'm afraid I can't really speak up.'

'*Just attend to me, then. I have new and urgent information. On no account must you go down to Quanderhorn's infernal cellar until you have disabled the hidden security camera.*'

Hidden security camera? Then it hit me: that flash when I was fleeing the cellar! It must caught me full on. I doubt even my gravy browning camouflage and sock balaclava would be sufficient disguise. I was rumbled!

'But, Mr. Churchill:' I hissed, 'I've already—'

'*Just thought I'd better warn you, Penetrator. Now, enjoy your spot of French leave. It's coming out of your holiday days, you know.*'

'Mr. Churchill . . .'

But there was only the dead buzz of static. And for some intangible reason, the lingering sound of herring. I jumped as Gemma dragged open the door.

'Brian, we're still in serious trouble out here. Who knows how long this life support's going to hold out.'

'All done, now.' I crunched back over the plates and shut the door behind me.

'Who was it?'

'I . . . I couldn't quite make it out, perhaps it was Guuuurk repeating his message.'

Gemma looked pained. She was clearly wrestling with a recollection that she found especially difficult. 'Brian, I'm so sorry. I should have told you this before. I tried calling them when . . . when we got here, but there was no response. We have to face facts. They're way past their oxygen limit. I'm afraid the pure rationality is: we're never going to see Guuuurk or Troy again.'

I actually smiled. I don't know why. It hardly seemed appropriate. The very thought seemed somehow impossible. 'What?'

'They're gone, Brian. We're on our own.'

I barely had time to accommodate this devastating news, when a hatch melted into the bulkhead and Guuuurk stepped through, removing his helmet.

'There you are, you absolute rotters! I've been ringing the blasted doorbell for five minutes!'

Chapter Seventeen

From the journal of Brian Nylon, 5th January, 1952 – [cont'd]

'There's a *doorbell*?' I echoed, incredulously.

'Of *course* there's a doorbell. Where d'you think this is? *Pluto?*'* He turned and dragged Troy up the ramp, boots first. 'We're not all *savages*, you know, just because we're alien. And the Galactic Convention, carefully laid down over millions of years and observed across cultures throughout the known universe since time immemorial, is that when someone outside *rings* the wretched thing, someone on the inside bally well *answers* it!' He let Troy's feet fall to the deck, and the hatch sealed itself behind him.

Gemma tilted her head. 'It's probably in a frequency beyond our hearing range'

'That's what the Plutonians always say. But that's just an excuse for being skiving layabouts.'

---

* Plutonians have a reputation for being the most slatternly and uncivilisable beings in the Solar System. A year on Pluto lasts approximately 247.9 Earth years, meaning the average Plutonian lifespan is measured in weeks, so a Plutonian farmer won't live to see the harvest he's planted because it won't occur for several dozen generations. As a consequence, they can't be arsed to plant anything, or do work of any kind. Or anything.

I looked down at the prone Troy. His face was quite blue. I knelt and unscrewed his helmet quickly. 'Is he . . .' I began, and his eyes blinked open.

'Can I stop holding my breath now?' he wheezed.

Guuuurk looked puzzled. 'When did you start doing that?'

Troy climbed to his feet and swayed, still holding his breath. 'When the air ran out half an hour ago.' He gagged. 'I'm feeling very—' His eyes rolled back in his head and he fell poleaxed to the deck again.

Guuuurk shook his head wearily. 'Don't worry. It's just lack of oxygen to the brain. It'll make very little difference, honestly.'

'We saw the explosion from the basin,' I said.

Guuuurk held up his helmet. It was latticed with a filigree of spiderweb cracks. 'There was a slight misunderstanding,' his eyes cursed Troy, 'resulting in the rather unnecessary demise of my radio. We did try waving to you. But Dr. Janussen here was busy drawing romantic doodles in the moon dust, and you were intent on dragging her away.'

'Romantic doodles!' Gemma scoffed. 'I was doubtless trying to explain an advanced scientific concept.'

'Yes,' the Martian smiled. 'Using a giant heart with an arrow through it.'

Troy rasped. 'Can . . . I . . . breathe . . . yet?'

'Yes, you knuckleheaded twit! Breathe!'

Troy just lay there, his eyes flitting from side to side. Finally, he asked: 'How do you do that again?'

Guuuurk hung his head. 'In out, in out.'

'Oh, yeah. Then shake it all about!'

'That's not breathing, that's the *hokey cokey*!' He turned to us. 'You *see* what I've had to endure? It's a miracle we survived. Happily, you don't need nearly as much oxygen as humans if you're a Martian, or a half-insect, half-moron.'

'Hey!' Troy raised his head. 'Was that an insult?'

Guuuurk narrowed five of his eyes. 'Only a moron would think it wasn't.'

Troy got to his feet again. 'Well, that's where you're wrong, because I'm one, and I think it was!' He marched over and thrust his face into Guuuurk's. 'I've had it up to here with your rudeness, you huge-headed purple-faced ...' He reached for the worst taunt he could muster. It turned out to be: 'bad, bad man.'

And suddenly, there was the electrical whining again.

'The deck's up,' Gemma called.

'Wow!' Troy cooed in childlike wonder. 'This ship is pretty darn hep!'

And just as rapidly, the electrical whining ceased.

'. . . and the deck is down.'

'Well,' Guuuurk said, 'just power it back up again.'

'We don't know how.' I shrugged.

'You don't know? Well, how did you get into the ship, then?'

'We don't know.'

'You don't know?'

Gemma stepped in. 'Would you kindly stop saying we don't know and tell us what we do need to know?'

'I thought it was obvious.' Guuuurk crossed to the consoles. 'Didn't you notice the scowling portholes?

Troy giggled. 'Yeah – they look really really cross!'

Guuuurk rolled many of his eyes. 'This is a Mercurian Star Clipper.'

We all looked at each other, slightly baffled. 'Meaning?' I asked.

Guuuurk sighed in exasperation at the poverty of our intergalactic species knowledge. 'Mercury's either ridiculously cold or insanely hot, so the Mercurians are per*petually* cheesed off. I mean: absolutely *fuming*. If you bump into one in a dark alley, you'd better have your estate in order and a fully paid-up funeral plan. *Ergo*, they power their craft with their biggest natural resource: raw anger.'

'It's powered with *anger*?' I struggled to understand how that might work in practice, but Gemma got it immediately.

'Of course!' She beamed that delightful radiant smile which always accompanied a new scientific insight. 'That's entirely consistent with our experience. I was angry when we got into the ship, remember? And you were angry with me when the console lit up.'

'Oh, I wouldn't say I . . . well, I suppose I was.'

Guuuurk stepped away from Troy. 'That's why I was mildly irritated when I first came in. I'd had to work up to that pitch to open the hatch. Of course spaceships don't have *doorbells*, you idiots, but I had to get angry about *something*. Honestly. Sometimes I think you credulous shower will believe anything.'

I was shocked to my core by this admission. 'You've never lied to us about anything else, have you, Guuuurk?'

'Brian!' he gasped. 'You cut me to the quick! I swear to you as an Englishman: I have never lied about anything else whatsoever.'

'Well, that's all right, then. I apologise for implying any such thing.'

'Apology accepted.' A thought occurred to him. 'Actually, this may be a bad time to ask, but d'you remember that five pounds you owe me?'

'No.'

'Oh, no: of course you wouldn't remember. What was I thinking? In actual fact, I've a notion it might have been *ten* pounds. But I won't hold you to that. Let's call it seven guineas and draw a line under the whole messy business. Now I will take cheques, and personal items of an accredited value—'

Gemma took control, as usual. 'Can you all please concentrate? There's a permanent lunar storm, and it's closing in on us.' She nodded through the scowling portholes.

The cloud of dust seemed to have grown in size quite alarmingly, and was indeed heading our way.

She turned back. 'If we don't get up and running before it hits, the ship could be buried too deep to blast free. Then we'll be stuck here for ever.'

Chapter Eighteen

From the journal of Brian Nylon, 5th January, 1952 – [cont'd]

I broke the horrible silence. 'So what do we do, then? Get angry, somehow?'

Gemma nodded. 'Troy, get angry with Guuuurk again.'

'Why? What's he done?'

'This!' Guuuurk trilled, and slapped him.

Smack!

'Ow! That really hurt!'

The controls started powering up.

Gemma called: 'It's working. Slap him again.'

Guuuurk complied.

Smack!

'Ow! Do that again, and I'll get really . . .'

Smack!

'. . . angry. Owwww!' Troy rubbed his face. 'Stop doing that!'

Smack! Smack!

And now the consoles were thrumming with electrical life. 'We have power!' I buckled myself into the pilot's seat. Through the viewport, I could see the swelling dust storm was distressingly closer.

Gemma pointed to a meter on the console. Its needle was hovering in the red zone below the redder red zone, which wasn't quite as reddy red as the utterly red zone at the top. 'We're going to need more anger.'

'I'm smacking him as hard as I can,' Guuuurk protested.

Smack!

'Owwwwwwwww! I think he is,' Troy agreed, rubbing his ruddy cheeks.

Gemma looked over at them. 'Maybe you should try shooting him with one of your useless Martian Death Rays.'

All Guuuurk's eyes turned steely. 'I'll have you know . . .' He paused to slap Troy with some venom.

Smack!

'*Owwwwww!*'

'. . . our Death Rays are the best in the Solar System!'

The humming got louder and the needle wavered up towards the slightly more red area.

'In fact, the intergalactic magazine *Popular Xenophobe* gave Martian Death Rays an unprecedented five-skull rating, when compared with other species' Death Rays in a totally randomised, double-blind—'

Troy slapped Guuuurk quite hard.

Smack!

'*Ow!* What was *that* for?' He slapped Troy back.

Smack!

'*Ow!* I'm trying to make *you* angry!'

'Well, I can't say you're not succeeding.'

Smack!

'*Ow!*'

Smack!

'*Ow!*'

Gemma called: 'Keep slapping each other! The storm is

almost on us! Don't stop, whatever happens.'

There followed a tit-for-tat slapping spree, reminiscent of the traditional Bavarian dance, only without the annoying accordion.

The power was building, but we still needed more.

I glanced over at Gemma, who'd reached the same conclusion: one of *us* needed to get angry.

She shook her head. 'I'm afraid I'm fully wound. I can't *get* angry.' There was a dolorousness in her eyes at this. It was clearly a painful admission.

There was nothing else for it. 'All right!' I yelled. 'Somebody make *me* angry. Quick!'

Troy, eager to please as always, leapt in first with: 'Brian, you're stupid!' *Smack!* '*Ow!*'

'I know,' I agreed. 'I am pretty dense, I'm afraid.'

Guuuurk tried. *Smack!* '*Ow!* You're hopeless with women!' *Smack!* '*Ow!*'

'True,' I sighed. 'Come *on*! We're losing power.' The vanguard of the storm was already here. I could hear the myriad tiny pebbles it swept before it pattering against the hull.

'Brian, you're smelly!' *Smack!* '*Ow!*' was Troy's rather dismal contribution.

Smack! '*Ow!* You're a dithering milksop!' was Guuuurk's.

'You'll have to make me much angrier than that, if we're going to create enough energy for a lift-off!'

Gemma had been thinking quietly to herself. She turned to me and said: 'Brian, England is a dreadful place.'

I was shocked. What on earth did she mean? 'There really is no call for that kind of—'

'Her Majesty the Queen,' she added, 'is not a very nice woman.'

There was a sudden surge and the needle leapt into the upper red, really really red zone.

'Now, that is *completely* unfair,' I protested, barely containing myself. 'Everyone says she's quite the most delightful lady—'

'Scones,' Guuuurk chipped in coldly, 'are not as good as apple strudel.' *Smack!* 'Ow!'

'What absolute *tosh*! Everyone knows German cakes are *useless*. Have you ever eaten *dampfnudel*? It really is like chewing sweaty socks.'

And as if that weren't enough nonsense, he added: 'Queuing is stupid!'

Well, I've never heard such out-and-out balderdash. 'Don't be ridiculous – it's the very *cornerstone* of civilisation!'

There was a huge roar, and the main engines blasted into life. The whole ship shook as it struggled to pull clear of the lunar rubble.

The slapping had apparently become unnecessary, now.

Guuuurk was starting to enjoy himself. Rather too much, if you ask me. 'Steak and kidney pudding tastes like donkey urine!'

'Well, that actually is true.'

The power began to wane.

'Vera Lynn,' Gemma tried, 'is an *appalling* singer.'

I opened my mouth, but words wouldn't come out.

The engines throbbed back to full power.

Guuuurk added: 'And George Formby isn't funny.' Well, that was just plain Wrong. The man's an absolute caution!

Then they all started pitching in.

Guuuurk: 'A nice cup of tea does nobody any good.'

Troy: 'Cricket is *stupid*!'

Gemma: '*The Archers* is incredibly boring.'

Guuuurk: 'Shakespeare was French.'

Troy: 'Cricket is *stupid*!'

Guuuurk: 'Florence Nightingale was a heartless bitch!'

Gemma: 'The British never play fair!'

Now, that really was beyond the pale. I was fairly sure we'd racked up enough energy by this point – the needle was actually bending against the upper marker – but Guuuurk was unstoppable:

'Beer tastes better when it's chilled! Public schools are just for thick people! The BBC is *not* the envy of the world! A bow tie doesn't make dinner taste any better! And "Britons never shall be slaves"? What a joke! You've been persistently invaded by any nation who could rustle up three boats and a set of carving knives. The Italians, the Danes, the Swedes and Norwegians, the French, the Dutch, the Germans . . . Yes! There's a headline for you: your Royal Family are all Krauts! They're not really called "Windsor", but "Saxe-Coburg-Gotha"! The clue's in the *name*!'

I could actually hear the vein in my temple throbbing now. 'That's quite enough of that!' I shouted, rather rudely. 'This is *beyond* irritating.'

'Well done, Brian,' Gemma wheeled in her seat to face me. 'You can calm down, now. See: we're clear of the Moon and heading for the Earth's atmosphere.'

'Cricket is *stupid*!'

'That's enough, Troy.'

'But it really is!'

I looked through the viewport. The Earth was indeed looming towards us, or, more accurately, her gravitational pull was dragging us in.

'We've done it!' I cheered. 'We're safe! We're free-falling back to Earth.' Somebody started screaming.

272

Chapter Nineteen

Transcription of Mercurian Flight Recorder, Flight
DIS-TA-GRAKK, Date: Gakrr i Nar di trlll (estimated
*Earth equivalent: 29th September, 1949)**

TEE-POL (PILOT): Look at that shitty blue
planet down there! Those
bloody Earth bastards think
they've got the bloody lot,
don't they?

POL-TEE (CO-PILOT): Those two-armed stuck-up
monkey cousins make me *puke*!
They're all *[MIMICKING]*
Ooooh! Look at us with all
our water, and our frozen
poles and our equatorial
warmth, and everywhere in
between *[LA-DE-DAH VOICE]*

---

* Translated by Gargantua, the Linguaphonic Quanderlator, at an unknown
later date. This document is outside the chronology of the main sequence of
events, but it offers an interesting insight into the origins of the Star Clipper
and we make no apologies for its inclusion. But we do apologise about the language, and have tried to shelter you from the more toe-curling instances.

'*temperate*'. Wouldn't last two minutes on [PROFANITY EXPUNGED] Mercury!

TEE-POL: No, they'd be like: 'Ooooh, my feet have literally caught fire in the scorching rays unfiltered by the atmosphere.'

POL-TEE: Bloody 'atmosphere'! Jammy bastards! *[LA-DE-DAH VOICE]* 'We've got an '*atmosphere*'! I can't wait for the heat death of the Universe, when the sodding Sun turns to a big red giant and literally incinerates the smug bastards while they're having their 'cups of tea' and their 'pizza pies' and their 'beef quesadillas'!

TEE-POL: Oh, yes, *[LA-DE-DAH VOICE]* 'cups of tea'! They don't have to put up with liquids that boil so fiercely they could melt your shoes, or frozen so solid, when you try to drink them, they stick to your skin and you literally have to rip your own lips off just to get sustenance!

POL-TEE: Shut up!

TEE-POL: You shut up, you [PROFANITY EXPUNGED] [PROFANITY EXPUNGED]!

274

POL-TEE: Shut *Upppp!* There's a transmission coming in!

QUANDERHORN: *Professor Darius Quanderhorn here, speaking on behalf of the Human Race, via a remote link somewhere on the road to Carlisle. Alien vessel: we wish you no harm. Just follow the signals and this space beacon will guide you safely down to our planet, which we call 'Earth', where we can discuss peaceful co-operation between our two great peoples.*

TEE-POL: What did he say?

POL-TEE: Didn't understand a [PROFANITY EXPUNGED] word, the stuck-up Terranean ponce. Let him have it!

[MASSIVE SALVO OF WEAPON FIRE. HUGE EXPLOSION. TINY FRAGMENTS OF BEACON DEBRIS SPATTERING ON THE VIEWPORTS.]

TEE-POL: Ha ha ha! Got it right up the [PROFANITY EXPUNGED]. That bastard beacon is now space dust!

POL-TEE: Look out, here comes their moon!

TEE-POL: Oh, yes, *[LA-DE-DAH VOICE]* 'We've got a *moooooooon!*

Mercury hasn't got a moon,
but we've got a great big
[PROFANITY EXPUNGED] of a
moon.'

POL-TEE: We're coming in too fast, you
dick! Swerve! Swerve!

TEE-POL: I *am* swerving, you daft
[PROFANITY EXPUNGED]. What
d'you call this, if it's not
a swerve?

POL-TEE: It's a crap swerve.

TEE-POL: Oh, you think you can pilot
this better, do you? Here,
here, put on the pilot
sucker. Here it is!

POL-TEE: Put it back on, you stupid
[PROFANITY EXPUNGED]. You're
going to kill us all.

[SHIP GOES INTO SPIRAL DEATH DIVE]

POL-TEE: [PROFANITY EXPUNGED].

TEE-POL: [PROFANITY EXPUNGED].

POL-TEE: Activate the [PROFANITY
EXPUNGED] shields!

TEE-POL: Oh yes! The [PROFANITY
EXPUNGED] shields should
easily repel an entire
[PROFANITY EXPUNGED]
moon, you dozy [PROFANITY
EXPUNGED]-wit!

POL-TEE: Better get into the escape
pods, then.

TEE-POL: Where the [PROFANITY EXPUNGED] are the [PROFANITY EXPUNGED] escape pods?

POL-TEE: You were supposed to load the [PROFANITY EXPUNGED] escape pods!

TEE-POL: What am I? Head of [PROFANITY EXPUNGED] escape pods?

POL-TEE: Yes, you [PROFANITY EXPUNGED] are! It's embroidered on your [PROFANITY EXPUNGED] pocket!

TEE-POL: [PROFANITY EXPUNGED].

POL-TEE: [PROFANITY EXPUNGED].

[DEATH SPIRAL WHINE INCREASES]

POL-TEE: [PROFANITY EXPUNGED].

TEE-POL: [PROFANITY EXPUNGED].

POL-TEE: Right. It's parachute time.

TEE-POL: Where the [PROFANITY EXPUNGED] are the [PROFANITY EXPUNGED] parachutes?

POL-TEE: You were supposed to pack the [PROFANITY EXPUNGED] parachutes!

TEE-POL: What am I? Head of [PROFANITY EXPUNGED] parachutes as well now?

POL-TEE: Yes, you [PROFANITY EXPUNGED] are! It's embroidered on your other [PROFANITY EXPUNGED] pocket!

TEE-POL: [PROFANITY EXPUNGED].

```
POL-TEE:  [PROFANITY EXPUNGED]. I'm
          getting out of here!
TEE-POL:  No! Don't open that hatch!
          We'll both be sucked out into
          [PROFANITY EXPUNGED] space!
POL-TEE:  You stay if you want, you
          kamikaze [SHORT PROFANITY
          EXPUNGED], I'm bailing.
```

[HATCH OPENS — RUSH OF WIND]

```
TEE-POL & POL-TEE: Ohhh - [MULTIPLE PROFANITIES
                   EXPUNGED]!
```

[RECORDING ENDS]

Chapter Twenty

The Daybook of 'Jenkins' Jenkins, RQMS Royal Fusiliers (deserted), Saturday the 5th of January, 1952

Call vet re: boiler foot rot.

Students! Don't like 'em. The duplicates is all that age now, which means, of course, they knows *everything*. They're all busy drinking Woodpecker cider, smoking stinking French cigarettes and reading John Paul Satire while playing the bongos. 'Cept for the Martian, who's obsessed with reading *The Will to Power* by Neacher whilst listening to Vargner. I hates the music, but I do like them pigtailed blondes in horned helmets and pointy metal breasts on the record sleeves. Can't get enough of high culture, meself.

In other words, at this stage the duplicate crew is pests. On the whole, I tries to avoid them. I just shovels in the fags and the cider and the Valderma antiseptic balm, and leaves 'em to sort *themselves* out.

The Prof's none too interested, neither. At least, not for the moment. He's busy looking for that bloomin' rat of his. Somehow, the little blighter's managed to escape from his maze. It must have been a fairly elaborate escape and all: he left behind a dummy rat made of matchsticks and bird droppings.

While he's busy running round calling, 'Here, Ratty! Here's a nice piece of cheese for you,' I cough to draw his attention. 'If everything's OK, sir, I'll just pop to the front desk to see if that intruder photograph's arrived.' Truth is, I'm well behind in my begging letters, and I needs to go through the obituaries again.

He doesn't look up from his searching, or even put down the cattle prod and the gunny sack. 'Yes, Jenkins, that would be—'

And blow me, if yet another bloomin' tocsin doesn't start up.

'*Alert! Alien spaceship approaching Earth rapidly.*'

Well, the Prof drops the prod and the bag now, and runs straight into the Space Defence Operations Centre, with me on his tail. He's busy switching on screens and turning on radars, oscilloscopes, cosmic arrays and, for some reason, *Workers' Playtime* on the Home Service.

'What idiot turned that godawful music on?' he yells.

'Sorry, sir, I'll get rid of it at once.'

'You know I *hate* Anne Shelton.'

I didn't, but I clocks it for future reference.

'*Alien spaceship now entering Earth's exosphere.*'

'Punch it up on Gargantua, the Giant Space Tellyscoppy-screen, Delores.'

'*Initialising.*'

The seven-inch screen starts up. We watch the little light in the middle for a bit.

'*Valves warming up.*'

'Oh, come *onnnnn.*' The Prof taps the desk impatiently.

'*Valves still warming up.*'

Then, all of a sudden, the picture blossoms out from the centre. There's this huge ship powering towards us with a really angry-looking face. I'm sure I've seen its kind before . . . but I can't place where.

'Dammit, Jenkins: looks like a Mercurian Star Clipper!'

Oh yes. I remembers now. Mercurians! Don't like 'em. 'Shall I activate the peace beacon, sir?'

'If you recall, Jenkins, the last lot of hooligans in one of those vessels blasted the previous peace beacon to space dust.'

'So they did, Professor. What shall we do then, sir? They're getting closer.'

'Can we afford to give them the benefit of the doubt a second time?'

'It's hardly my place to say, sir, but I don't trust them slippery snarky swines. Not one inch.'

'I hate to say it, Jenkins, but I'm afraid you're right. For the security of the whole planet there's only one course of action we can take. Actuate Gargantua, the Dangerous Giant Space Laser.'

I glances over at him. There's this strange look in his eyes I ain't never seen before. What he's suggesting is not only a potential Act of Interplanetary War, it's also premeditated cold-blooded murder. On the other hand, they *is* only aliens.

The actual firing barrel of the Dangerous Giant Space Laser is up there in orbit of course, but we controls it from a remote gunnery panel right here. So, I takes a deep breath, marches over to the laser vault door, selects the key on my fob and puts it in the upper lock. The Prof puts his own key in the lower one, and we nods, and turns them in unison.

I heave open the door, and there she is: the Dangerous Giant Space Laser Control Turret, in all her terrible glory. It's enough to give any red-blooded Englishman a stirring. And I don't mean in his breast.

'Alien vessel breaching thermosphere.'

I shins up into the seat and straps meself in. A circle of blue lights burst into life around the pedestal base, and the target overlay illuminates all orange and pretty and plots out the course of the target vessel. 'Got 'em in my sights, sir,' I says.

The Professor looks uncommon grave. Normally something like this wouldn't give him pause for a moment. Eventually, he says: 'We really have no choice, Jenkins. No choice, I'm afraid.'

'*Alien vessel penetrating mesosphere.*'

On the screen, the huge orbiting solar-powered laser barrel turns majestically in space towards its prey, and begins to initiate its warm-up sequence.

'*Alien vessel entering stratosphere.*'

This shakes the Prof out of his funk. 'We can't let them breach the troposphere, Jenkins. You'll have to blast them.'

Now, I'm not saying I enjoy pressing the button on this thing, 'cos that might make me sound like a sicko, and this is a weighty business. Still, ready to do my solemn duty, I pops a humbug in my mouth, starts humming 'Rule Britannia', and flexes my index finger in small circles over the trigger. 'Locked on target, sir.'

'What are you waiting for, man? Fire.' He turns and leaves the room quietly muttering 'Dammit,' under his breath.

I lets 'em have it.

The explosion! It's like Guy Fawkes Night round at the Aga Khan's in the middle of the Blitz in Hiroshima. When the blast clears, there's nothing left at all.

Absolutely nothing.

Not even the splattered remains of unidentifiable organs.

Chapter Twenty-One

*News strip recovered from Quanderhorn's Telemergency
Print-O-Gram, 4.53 p.m., 5th January, 1952*

```
REUTERS NEWS AGENCY FLASH....................................................
4:53: MYSTERIOUS INCIDENT PICCADILLY CIRCUS.........MORE FOLLOWS.........

BIZARRE ERUPTION CLOSES LONDON PICCADILLY CIRCUS UNDERGROUND STN.........
AREA ROPED OFF. MET POLICE REQUEST BACK UP FROM ARMY...................



4:54: REPORTERS BANNED FROM AREA. DOWNING ST. "NO NEED TO PANIC".

THOUSANDS PANIC.........MORE FOLLOWS.......................................

@0ISOLATED REPORTS CLAIM STATION PLATFORM DESTROYED. WITNESSES REMOVED IN
BLACK MARIAS. THOUSANDS MORE PANIC.......................................


TOMORROW'S WEATHER: INTERMITTENT DRIZZLE..................................



4:55: JOKE OF THE DAY....................................................

LITTLE GREEN MAN: "I SAY, MR CHURCHILL, TAKE ME TO YOUR LEADER".........
MORE FOLLOWS.............................................................
MR CHURCHILL: "I'M SORRY, BUT PROFESSOR QUANDERHORN IS OUT AT THE MOMENT!"..


JOKE ENDS...............................................................
```

Chapter Twenty-Two

Three minutes earlier, from the journal of Brian Nylon, 5th January, 1952 – Iteration 66

'We've done it!' I cheered. 'We're safe! We're free-falling back to Earth.' Somebody started screaming, '*We're free-falling back to Earth!*'

'Please pull yourself together, Brian,' Gemma chided. 'We're going to need all our energy to get sufficiently furious to power the landing rockets.'

Suddenly, the lights all glowed a brighter red and a peculiar sound erupted from speakers somewhere.

'It's a red alert!' I called.

'Well, of course,' Guuuurk drawled. 'Have you *seen* this ship? What other kind of alert could it be?'

'I think it's about as red as a red alert can get. Even here.'

The sound erupted again.

'Pardon me,' Troy apologised.

'That's not you, Troy,' Gemma said.

'Are you sure? It sounds like me when I've burrowed into too many cabbage leaves.'

The sound again.

'Pardon me.'

Gemma was scouring the readouts. 'I think the ship may have detected some sort of threat.'

I could make neither head nor tail of the displays. 'What's it saying on this screen, Guuuurk?'

'Oh, yes. Because all aliens must know each other, I can magically read Mercurian now.'

'I'm sorry, but it's just gibberish to us.'

'It's gibberish to me, too.' He started feeling under the desk. 'I was hoping it wouldn't come to this – we'll have to use the emotional interface.'

Gemma and I stared at him blankly. Troy also stared blankly, but I don't think he was joining in with us.

'Very big on emotions, the Mercurians, remember?' Guuuurk answered our gapes. 'So they use one of these . . .'

He found what he was looking for under the console and tugged out a flexible tube, like a cross between a slimy octopus tentacle and a vacuum cleaner hose with a plunger on the end. It was, of course, red.

I eyed it with deep suspicion. It seemed to be secreting a sort of gloopy gunk from the end and making a slight slurping noise. 'What are we supposed to do with that?'

'*You?*' Guuuurk threw back his head and laughed. 'Your puny Terranean minds wouldn't be able to cope with the forces of overwhelming mental strain. Leave it to a Martian.'

With another derisory laugh, he attached the sucker in the middle of his forehead between his top two eyes. Instantly, his expression fell and his head deflated with a terrible trumping noise.

'*AAAAAAArgh!* Fear! Fear! Fear!'

Troy yelled: 'Unplug him, quick!'

'Fear! Fear! Fear!'

'No,' Gemma insisted. 'We need to know what's happening.'

Guuuurk managed to twist his head round sufficiently to shoot her a look of intense hatred. 'Fear! Fear! Fear! Terror! Gut-wrenching horror! Argh! Argh! Please! Please unplug . . . Fear!'

'Oh, for heaven's sake.' Gemma reached for the plunger.

'Fear! Fear! Overpowering dread!'

She tugged the sucker off Guuuurk's forehead with a hideous ripping sound. He collapsed to the deck, but his head started to reinflate reassuringly.

'I didn't completely get the entire nuances and subtleties of the message,' he said, pretending to ignore the rivulets of sweat cascading from his swelling forehead, 'but I'm going to go right out on a limb here, and say: something quite frightening is happening.'

Gemma looked at me. 'We'll have to plug Brian in.'

'Oh!' I wasn't entirely sure I was up to that. 'Me? Really?'

'Well, I'm not likely to have much luck with an emotional interface, am I? And we can hardly leave it to Troy. No offence, Troy.'

'Why,' Troy asked belligerently, 'would I know a *fence*? I'm a *person*.'

'Yup,' I nodded, 'you've convinced me.'

And without any ceremony, she jammed the sucker onto my brow.

Chapter Twenty-Three

*From the journal of Brian Nylon, 5th January, 1952 –
Iteration 66*

All at once, the scene before me melted away into a fog. I perceived the ship as an entity, flying through the atmosphere.

Then I *was* the ship itself.

I was zipping happily downwards towards the beautiful blue Earth, the rushing atmosphere just beginning to caress my hull, warming me up pleasantly. It looked nice and welcoming down there, and I was looking forward to firing my splendid retro-rockets for a smooth and luscious landing. Then a strange feeling overtook me . . .

'Hmmm,' I said, quite unconsciously. 'That's slightly annoying.'

Somewhere off in the distance, I heard Guuuurk exclaim 'What?' as if affronted.

The strange sensation seemed to be emanating from somewhere a little below, and off my starboard bow. The feeling was . . .

'What is it, Brian?' I heard Gemma ask through the haze.

. . . a threat! There was a threat of some kind. My vision tunnelled into the darkness and I saw it! A floating platform. A huge tubular pipe, ringed with oscillating neon-esque ellipses. A cannon!

'It's . . . it's some kind of huge space gun.'

I heard the disbelief in Gemma's voice: 'Not the Professor's Dangerous Giant Space Laser!'

'Fear!' Guuuurk shouted. 'Fear! Fear! Stomach-churning panic!'

Gemma pointed out tartly that Guuuurk wasn't even connected any more.

'I don't need to be,' he shot back, then squeaked quietly under his breath. 'Fear! Fear!'

'It's rotating towards us,' I warned. I was starting to sense growing anxiety.

'Don't worry,' Troy piped up. 'Pops would never fire at us!'

'It's beginning to power up!' Extremely worried now.

Gemma said soberly: 'He doesn't know it *is* us.'

'No, Pops, no!' Troy yelled very loudly indeed.

'He can't hear you, Troy.'

'Guuuurk!' the lad shouted, quite disturbed. 'Quick! Do your thinky-leapy mind thing and tell him.'

The Martian shook his head. 'I can't leap into a fully developed mind.'

'You leapt into mine.'

'Precisely.'

'We can see the barrel through the viewport, now,' Gemma called. 'Yes – the tip's starting to glow.'

I tugged off the sucker. The sense of mounting terror immediately drained away.

Then, as the viewport swam back into focus, it came flooding back again.

The laser was indeed getting brighter by the moment. I reached for the joystick, but I must still have been connected to the ship in some way, because I was instantly aware that firing the retro-rockets wouldn't be sufficient to escape. 'We have to get out. Are there escape pods? Parachutes?'

Guuuurk shook his inflating head. 'Nothing like that. I happened to check that the very first moment I came aboard, by sheer coincidence'

'So,' I tried to keep the desperation out of my voice, 'is there nothing we can do?'

Guuuurk frowned for a moment, then smote his forehead. 'Of course! What was I thinking? The shield!'

'We have a shield?'

'Of course! Every Mercurian ship is fitted with a ceramic-powered weapon shield.'

On top of the burgeoning terror, I began to feel slightly nervous. And sick. 'A what?'

Guuuurk clambered to his feet and started fighting his way to the back of the flight deck. 'An impenetrable energy shield that can repel anything – even a Martian Death Ray.'

Unhelpfully, Gemma murmured: 'I have a sequinned *bag* that can do that.'

Guuuurk pretended he hadn't heard. 'It's powered by ceramic oscillation. A series of discs fit into that slot there.' He waved his hand at the console. 'They're the exact dimensions and structure to create the perfect resonance.'

'Ceramic discs?' I asked. For some reason, I was beginning to sweat a great deal.

'Yes.' Guuuurk began opening and closing various doors and hatches.

'You mean like . . . dinner plates?'

The Martian snorted. 'I suppose so, to the untrained eye. Yes. Fortunately, every vessel has a large store cupboard full of them.'

He opened *the* door. The couple of plates I'd managed to leave still intact slipped off the shelf and smashed into the rest of the detritus, with a horrible final crash.

'What the blazes?' Guuuurk squeaked. 'It's like a Greek wedding in here!'

'I may have chipped one or two of them earlier,' I admitted.

'Chipped? *Chipped*? They've been pulverised to *powder*!' On his knees, he started rooting through the debris, trying to find a plate that was more or less whole.

Troy was at the viewport. 'Laser thingy's going all blue! I think it's about to blast us!'

No time for guilt! 'Could we glue some bits together?'

'Oh yes!' Guuuurk scooped up handfuls of ceramic fragments and let them dribble through his thumbs. 'We have ample time to painstakingly reconstruct an entire dinner service from what is essentially dust, and perhaps paint it daintily with a lovely willow pattern and sign it "Josiah Wedgwood" in our *remaining two seconds of life*!'

There was definitely a lingering connection with the ship's emotional interface, because I felt a sudden surge of energy in my stomach, and the needle on the console's power indicator leapt simultaneously.

Gemma had spotted this herself. 'Calm down, Guuuurk – you're overloading the anger engines.'

'Calm down? *CALM DOWN!?*' His face began to take on a rather dangerous tint of orange, and his head started swelling alarmingly. 'I've been *very* patient with all of you up till now, even though you're an utterly useless *shower*!' I'd never seen his head quite so swollen. 'I've been catapulted to the *Moon*, forced to project myself into the head of an *imbecile* and locked in an *attic* for twenty-four hours while a possessed village performed a ceaseless cacophony of uncontrollable *rumpy pumpy* in the room below.'

I opened my mouth to try and reason with him, but he was in full flow now.

'I've been *tortured* by Mole People, *imprisoned* by shape-shifting troglodytes and painfully *stamped* on by a giant sandal in the *Attack of the Forty-Foot Bishop* . . .'

The power needle had leapt off the scale, and the whine of the engines had grown to a deafening roar. 'Guuuurk . . . you'll blow us sky-high!'

He simply ranted on and on. 'But this *really* puts the skin on the Ambrosia Creamed Rice, this does! Our one, solitary, slim chance of survival, and Brian, a man who was drummed out of the *Quakers* for being excessively placid, suddenly takes it into his head to go on a senseless rampage of crockery destruction – like a deranged Italian housewife who's just discovered her husband in bed with the *Pope*.'

I could barely make out what he was saying above the shrieking engines now.

'*Why*, Brian? *Why?*'

I felt a hand in mine, and looked down to it. Gemma mouthed: 'I'm afraid we've really had it this time.'

Guuuurk raised his voice above the cacophony. He was raving and shrieking now. 'And as if *that* weren't enough, at the end, the only companions of Guuuurk the Magnificent, Patronome-In-Waiting of the fifteenth biggest gas puddle on Phobos, are a clockwork-brained *female*, an insectoid *simpleton* and a *pottery-hating psychopath* who—'

We were all enveloped by a blinding flash, and I actually felt my component atoms scatter in a million directions.

5

Chiffon

What a chimera . . . is man! What a novelty, what a
monster, what a chaos, what a subject of contradiction,
what a prodigy! A judge of all things, feeble worm of the
earth, depository of the truth, a sewer of uncertainty and
error, the glory and the shame of the universe!

Blaise Pascal, *Pensées*

Chapter One

The Daybook of 'Jenkins' Jenkins, RQMS Royal Fusiliers (on the run), Saturday the 5th of January, 1952

Keep an eye out for Intruder photo arriving.

I'm at the front desk, poring through the obits, as per – I spots Albert Rawtenstall, the Black Pudding King, is now sadly demised, owing to an unexpected encounter with his own meat-reclamation scraper, thereby making poor old Mrs Rawtenstall a lonely widow woman. Rich, bereft *and* vulnerable: the holy trinity. I makes a note in my begging book. I'll be getting out the Basildon Bond later on.

Just then, the postman arrives and passes over the envelope from the chemist's.

Of course, there's never five minutes' peace in this madhouse. Just as the kettle's starting to steam nicely, that particularly annoying telephone ring starts up. The one that sounds like three fire engines manned by escaped lunatics from Bedlam banging on saucepans. The special stripy light on the wall behind me starts flashing again.

It's the Future Phone.

I stuffs the envelope in my pocket and charges to answer it.

Thankfully, the Prof's ordered the door kept unlocked since the last how's-your-father, so I gets to it pretty quick.

When I picks it up, I'm surprised by the voice on the other end.

'*Quanderhorn here. I need to speak to Quanderhorn.*' Just like the prof to spend the very last bit of Temperaryum on a Future call to himself.

The actual Prof comes into the room behind me and I holds out the receiver to him. 'It's *you*, sir, for you.'

'Tell him I'm out.'

'*And I know he isn't out. I'm in the* future, *dammit!*'

I turns back to my Prof. 'He's most insistent, sir.'

'Oh, very well. I'd better not be wasting my own time.' He snatches the handset off me roughly. 'Hello?'

I cranes over to hear, without looking as if I'm craning at all. Years of practice pulls it off. '*Listen, Quanderhorn, there isn't much time,*' the other one says. '*The advanced technology in that Mercurian vessel has stirred a powerful alien artefact, a giant ziggurat, slumbering these many millennia under Piccadilly Circus.*'*

'Oh, really?'

'*Anyone who penetrates the heart of its structure will discover astonishing secrets beyond human understanding.*'

'I see. And why are you bothering to tell me this?'

'*To be honest, I don't have the faintest idea. I need to get to the point.*'

'Well, get to the point, then.'

'*Well, if you'd just stop interrupting me, I would get to the point—*'

---

* The atrocious spelling in this reported speech has been corrected for the purposes of clarity.

'You're interrupting *me*!'

'*No* – you're *interrupting* me. *Just listen: I must give you this dire warning . . . whatever you do, don't*—'

And then, there's this operator's voice: '*To continue this call, please deposit more temporium.*'

'Dammit!' The Prof chops his hand down on the cradle repeatedly. 'We don't have any more temporium! Hello? *Hello?*'

Furious, he slams the receiver down. 'What idiot would not put the dire warning first, if he knew damn well we were going to run out of temporium?'

'Begging your pardon, sir, isn't he you?'

He turns slowly. 'One phone call to the Military Police, Jenkins, mentioning your Post Office savings book—'

Well, that's quite uncalled for, in my humble. I'm only trying to defend him. From him.

[SQUEEZED IN BETWEEN LINES AT A LATER DATE IN GREEN BIRO:]
And I must point out for legal purposes, according to my union rep, that the implication of these allegations are entirely without substance, and a jury of my peers would almost certainly ex-honourate me.

[ORIGINAL JOURNAL CONTINUES:]

'What I meant to say, sir, was: what a idiot!'

He gives me that chilling look. 'He's me! Are you being deliberately insulting now, Jenkins?'

Well, I'm all a-fluster. 'No. I mean yes. I mean . . . that's a rum do, that Piccadilly Circus business, isn't it, sir?'

'Oh, I already knew about all that.' He tosses over a strip of ticker tape. 'This came in earlier over the Telemergency Print-O-Gram.'

I studies the tape. 'Blimey, sir. The other you was right! Mysterious Hincident in Piccadilly Circus.'

'Ye-e-es. I wonder why he didn't remember I already knew it?'

All this Future Phone business does my head in, if you want to know the bald truth.

'We'd better get down to London. Fast.'

'Ha ha. Have you seen this joke at the bottom, sir? Very funny. "Take me to your leader!" Ha ha ha. 'Cause, you see, Mr Churchill is *supposed* to be the leader, sir, but really, it's you, is what they're saying. Ha ha. Oh, that's tickled my funny bone, that has.'

He just looks at me, quite grim. 'Is that Quandertechnicon loaded, Jenkins?'

'Yes, sir. I'll get the starting handle right away.'

Then, I kids you not, there's yet *another* alarum going off. This time, though, it's only a little ping of a sound, and it's coming from the Professor's watch.

He glances at his wrist. 'Perfect timing! The duplicates are ready.'

Chapter Two

*Secret Report to Martian Command, by Guuuurk
(Unknown)*

'. . . *pottery-hating psychopath, who – hang on! What's going on?
Where are my feet? Come to that, where is any of me?*'
Those were my initial thoughts, recorded purely for scientific
purposes, you understand. I'd hate to inaccurately imply that a
courageous Martian warrior such as oneself would in any way
be in a complete and utter blind panic. Although I *was* literally
blind. And I was, theoretically, panicking. I seemed to be floating about somewhat aimlessly in lots of tiny unconnected parts.
I defy any Martian to wake up to *that* bag of toffees without
panicking just a *soupçon*.

Here I was, haplessly wafting about space as a sort of molec-
ular cloud – an evaporated, diluted, dispersed version of my
magnificent solid self.

Quite honestly, I wouldn't have been in this *appalling* position were it not for the hopelessly inept bunglings of those
brainless Terranean knuckle-draggers I'm compelled to work
with.

To think that I, Guuuurk the Uncomplaining, Interim
Sub-Manager of refurbishments to the Sacred Temple of

Grrrronk, (Car Park Surfacing Underdepartment), fifteenth half-cousin of His Flatulence the Archbishop of Mars – twenty times removed – could end his days... Ohhh, I just can't be *arsed*.

I admit, I'd begun to drift away, quite defeated by the futility of it all, into some kind of oblivion . . .

* * * *

From the journal of Brian Nylon, No Time.

This is jolly hard to explain. I know it may sound like some of that French philosophical gobbledygook, but I just can't think how else to put it – I was, and yet I wasn't.

Perhaps this is what the poor devils in the cellar felt like: being and simultaneously *not* being – those nomad souls ever wandering an unrealised hinterland in the gap between Form and Consciousness. Innocents condemned to a lifeless twilight? What kind of *demons* could compel a man to do that? Oddly, none of that seemed to particularly matter to me now.

I had no body, but everywhere was my body. And I was a part of everywhere. I was a planet forming from dust and rocks, I was a spiralling galaxy, I was the heart of a supernova. For a brief, fleeting moment I was the entire Universe itself, expanding everywhere into the Void. And just for this glorious instant, I knew everything.

Everything. And suddenly it was all beautiful and all made utter sense.

I began to drift into a lazy, wonderful daydream. It was like slipping into a warm bath of silky oneness.

There was no point resisting it.

It was inevitable.

* * * *

From Troy's Big Bumper Drawing book.

[PICTURE OF A STICK MAN WITH LIMBS AND HEAD DE-
TACHED AND 'ME!' WITH VARIOUS ARROWS POINTING
TO THE BITS]

iM An AtuM! its grAte. Theres other AtuMs too, AnD theyr
Me. iM More AtuMs thAn Gerk is. His AtuMs sMel. HA hA.
woooA! Here i go. iM A sun. its hot. iD tAke oF My vest,
but AtuMs Dont hAve vests. i like sMAshing My PArtiCAls
together. They MAK big brite bAngs!!

BooM! BooM! BooooooM!!!
iM stAying heer FoR EVR.

* * * *

The Rational Scientific Journal of Dr. Gemini Janussen.
Unknown time.

This was most interesting. Pure rationality would suggest our
existence had come to an end, but that didn't seem to be the
case. I still had awareness. In fact, I hadn't felt so totally complete for some time.

Could it be that being released from my physical self had
freed me from the battles that daily bedevilled me? My thoughts
were somehow . . . pure. Pure me, unhampered by mechanical
interfaces. Unworried by physical imperfections.

What was happening? Unless this *was* death, the only fea-
sible explanation was that Guuuurk's overloading the anger
receptors had caused the engines to go into a super-nuclear
eruption, disintegrating us all to our very atoms and propelling

301

them through some kind of quantum tunnel.

But something was wrong. I could feel my component molecules racing away from the source of me, like ripples fleeing a stone tossed into a lake.

It was not an unpleasant sensation, but I had an impression that the process was diluting my very Self.

I could sense the others around me, all expanding away, losing themselves to the thrall of the Universal Mind.

I wondered if I might not be able, by an effort of the will, to arrest the dispersal. It's not a simple matter to exert one's will without the benefit of a physical brain of any description, but it was imperative I succeeded.

I concentrated, really concentrated.

I reached out my mind to the furthest flung parts of all of us and started hauling them back to our cores.

Chapter Three

The Daybook of 'Jenkins' Jenkins, RQMS Royal Fusiliers (stripes torn off), Saturday the 5th of January, 1952

7:30 Thursday: Cod Supper with Mrs Rawtenstall.* N.B. Shampoo moustache beforehand. And afterwards.

The fully loaded Quandertechnicon is a stubborn beast to handle. Very hard to swerve when a deer crosses the road, but I manages to hit most of them and stuffs them in the back. Same with the pheasants. Why the dozy beggars don't fly more, I really don't know. They walks more than is good for them, that's for sure.

The Prof's way off ahead of us in his streamlined sixteen-skeins rubber band car, and the duplicates is following in the jeep. I'm bringing up the rear, which is how I likes it.

Wedging my pork pie in the air vent, I steers with my knees while I pulls out that envelope from the chemist's. No time for fancy Dan steaming now. I rips it open with my teeth and slides

---

* Jenkins often reports he is partaking of a 'Cod Supper' when dining with a lady friend. Whether or not this involves the consumption of actual food is a moot point. Certainly, there is no record of there ever having been a fish and chip emporium in the village of Wytchdrowninge.

out the photograph of the cellar intruder.

What I see shocks me to my very marrow. And I can tell you, it's a pretty big marrow.

Chapter Four

From the journal of Brian Nylon, 5th January, 1952 – [cont'd]

Can you imagine a startling explosion that smashes you to your component atoms happening backwards? A sort of de-splosion? Well, that's how it felt. With a final, sickening slamming sensation, we found ourselves literally reconstituted on the deck amid the smoking ruins of the Mercurian ship.

A tremendous sense of loss washed over me – the residual effect of my connection with the vessel, as I realised it had crashed very heavily somewhere, and was, in fact, dying.

There was smoke. Small fires had broken out all over the flight deck. The viewports were fogged on the inside with a thick layer of soot, and on the outside with some kind of mud.

'That,' Guuuurk dusted himself down, '*really* hurt.'

'Yes,' Troy agreed, climbing to his feet. 'Can we do it again?'

Through the smoky mist, I looked around anxiously to see if Gemma was OK. Mercifully, there she was, efficiently beating out the fires on the console. Even though she had a cute little sooty mark on her nose, she looked as perfect as ever.

'Did anyone else feel that . . .' I hesitated to ask. It seemed so existential-y and French '. . . that molecule thing?'

'Yes, Brian.' Gemma doused the final flames. 'We all exploded into a billion particles. We *felt* it.'

'OK. I was just worried I might have—'

'No, no. It really happened.'

'Yes,' Guuuurk snapped tartly. 'And the odd "thank you" wouldn't go amiss.'

'*Thank you?*' I could barely contain myself. 'For completely disintegrating us?'

'In the nick of time! So the laser couldn't blast us to pieces!'

'So you killed us . . .' Troy reasoned rather painfully, '. . . to stop us being killed.'

'Nobody got *killed*. You all just got very slightly *atomised*.'

Troy struggled with this a while, and then concurred: 'OK. Thanks, daddio!'

I was still somewhat baffled. 'So, what actually happened?'

Gemma unconsciously checked her ear. 'Guuuurk's right: his little temper tantrum overloaded the engines. They blasted us into . . . whatever that reality was.'

I turned to her. 'And did you . . . you brought us all back, didn't you? You saved us.'

'Ha!' she snorted grimly. 'Saved us for what? We could have crashed anywhere in the universe, known or unknown. Plus, we're trapped on a dead ship.'

Not quite dead, but almost. I could feel the last vestiges of its life ebbing away as the colour drained from the bulkheads – once a ruby red, now an anaemic pale pink. A terrible thought struck me – presumably the reason for Gemma's grave expression. 'But if the ship dies – there's no way of opening a door! We'll never get out!'

But it was too late. The final tint of colour had bled away, leaving the hull a deathly white.

Chapter Five

From the journal of Brian Nylon, 5th January, 1952 – [cont'd]

The lights dimmed to almost nothing. I became conscious of the acrid air supply dwindling terminally. We had fifteen minutes, at best. All the oxygen tanks were dead, of course.

Gemma was examining the area where the door hatch had appeared. 'There doesn't seem to be any manual override . . .'

'There's always this one!' Troy yelled, and grabbed the bulk-head with both hands.

'Not yet!' Gemma yelled. 'We don't know if the atmosphere out there is . . .'

With a terrible ripping sound, Troy yanked out a section of the hull leaving a huge, jagged hole.

'. . . breathable.'

'Ooops!' Troy grinned. 'Beg pardon!' And with another horrible metallic screech, he rammed the metal back into place, rather unevenly, like a jam jar lid pushed over a manhole.

Guuuurk actually smacked his forehead like I'd seen Edgar Kennedy do in the pictures. 'Oh, well done! Another gold for England in the Stupidity Olympics!'

Gemma shook her head. 'It doesn't matter really. If there's no oxygen in the atmosphere out there, we're finished anyway.'

She prodded Troy's handiwork with her finger, and it fell outwards with a ghastly clang. She stood on the rim. I realised too late what she was about to do. I yelled, 'No, Gemma!' But she ignored me, steeled herself and took a very deep breath.

Time seemed to be frozen. To come back from the dead like that, and then just lose her again . . . that would be beyond cruel.

She exhaled slowly, turned to us and nodded.

'You should have let me do that,' I protested.

'Why?' she shrugged. 'So I'd have lived thirty seconds longer than you?' There was something uncharacteristically melancholic about her, since the lunar business.

'Cheer up!' I smiled encouragingly. 'It may never happen.'

'What?' Guuuurk cried. 'What may never happen? Because I'm running out of terrible things that possibly *can* happen. What's left? What have you got lined up for us next, Brian? Do tell, because I must make a note in my diary. The twelfth: we all get boiled alive in a giant lobster creature's tureen. Afternoon of the fifteenth, we get kidnapped by face-eating daffodils from the ninth dimension . . .'

There were a lot more of these, but I haven't bothered to record them. We let him rant on, though. I think we were all slightly hoping the tirade might bring the ship back to life, but sadly, it didn't.

I glanced back over at the tear in the hull, and spotted with some alarm that Gemma had stepped out through the hole.

I followed, of course.

Outside, it was pitch dark and fearfully cold. The air stank of smouldering foliage. We were in some kind of dense overgrown forest, as if sculpted in gnarled old wood by an insane hand. At least there was life here. Plant life.

Gemma was staring up at the heavens through the tangled

canopy of bare branches. Beyond them, the stars glittered coldly. I couldn't recognise any of the constellations, but then I never did get that badge. From time to time there was a short burst of a call from some kind of creature. A bird? A badger? Some kind of flying badger?

Troy stepped up behind me. 'Where are we?'

Gemma shook her head. 'I really don't know.'

Guuuurk, having realised no one was listening to him any more, had followed us outside. 'Fortunately for you,' he declaimed, 'all Martians are born with an encyclopaedic race memory of every constellation in the Universe. Nooooowww-ww . . .'

He squinted three of his eyes, formed a parallelogram with four of his thumbs, and peered at the skies through it. 'I would say without any question of doubt we're on a small jungle-like planet . . .'

We all watched, impressed, as he appeared to make a number of complicated mental calculations. '. . . somewhere in the Crab Nebula.'

This was devastating news. '*The Crab Nebula?*'

'Definitely. Quadrant 54, unless I'm *very* much mistaken.'

Gemma was equally crestfallen. 'That's six and a half thousand light years from home.'

'Woah!' Troy groaned. 'Are you saying we're going to miss today's broadcast of *Muffin the Mule*?'

'I keep *telling* you,' Guuuurk snapped, 'it's *not* a real donkey.'

'Isn't it?'

'*Every* time!'

'But he's so *clever*.'

'He's a *marionette*!'

'The truth is, gentlemen.' Gemma turned. 'We may as well put all memories of Earth behind us.'

This rather knocked the stuffing out of me. 'What do you mean?'

'Pure rationality, I'm afraid. It's an impossible distance. I mean we will never get back.'

There was a shocked pause. Eventually Troy said: 'I *wondered* how it fitted on top of a piano. *I* tried that with a donkey and there was a terrible mess afterwards.'

'So,' Guuuurk mused, '*that's* what happened to my baby grand.' He paused, then added: '*And* what that zebra was doing in my room.'

'Well.' Gemma brought us all back to Earth. Or not, in the circumstances. 'Accentuating the positive: we are on a class M planet, so we can breathe. There is plant and, it would seem, animal life. So we're not going to starve to death. We can use the husk of the ship for shelter, at least until dawn. Assuming there is a dawn here.'

'Yes,' Guuuurk agreed cheerfully, 'there are planets in this quadrant where nightfall lasts for millennia.'

'It's already getting colder,' Gemma continued. 'We need to build a fire. There should be plenty of kindling and firewood about. Suggest we split into teams I want Troy,' she added, without a decent sporting pause.

'Fine!' Guuuurk kicked a tree stump. 'Though, first, why don't we play a quick game of Martian Closey-eyesy . . .?'

But Gemma and Troy were already deep into the forest.

'Well, Brian,' Guuuurk smiled with thinly veiled disappointment. 'Looks like it's just us.'

Chapter Six

From Troy's Big Bumper Drawing Book

[PICTURE OF A BADGER WITH WINGS, AND AN ARROW POINTING AT IT, LABELLED: 'NOT ME!']

weer on A Aliun planit. its grate! its six millium billium trillium Miles in lites From carlisle. weer going to hav A Fier. my FrenD JeMA tole Me orF For pikking up tree trunks beFor they Fallen Down. i bet we get Mor wooD thAn Gerk. He sMels. my FrenD BrAin sAys to wACh out For Flying bAgers. i still think muFin is reel or how CuD he DAns?

311

Chapter Seven

I can't say we made rapid progress. Guuuurk walked in a low crouch, hands poised in a sort of *ersatz* judo ready position, wheeling round regularly at the slightest sound, and chopping at the air, quite often making himself jump by stepping on dried bracken.

I thought I might calm him with some chat. 'Guuuurk – back there . . .'

'Oh, yes. Of course, I actually wanted to have you on my team, so I rather cleverly tricked Gemma into picking Troy.'

'She picked him before you could say anything.'

Guuuurk nodded. '*That's* how clever it was.'

'Actually, I was talking about when you were making me angry on the ship—'

'Ah, yes. I did want to apologise for some of those things I may have said.'

'One or two of them *were* rather—'

'Indeed. And it pained me greatly to be forced to say them. I want you to know that, in actual fact, I consider myself an Englishman first, and a Martian second.'

'Well, that's what I thought.'

We stumbled on in silence for a few minutes, grabbing up twigs and so on. Finally, I couldn't hold it any longer. 'But what you said about George Formby—'

'Oh, good grief! Perish the thought, dear boy! The man is an absolute *caution*.'

We both chuckled.

'That song he sings about peering through windows pleasuring himself while watching women undress and honeymoon couples in the act of mating. It's a *riot*!' I couldn't help thinking Guuuurk hadn't quite got the idea of what the song was about. Or, upon careful reflection, perhaps *I* hadn't.

Guuuurk suddenly became terribly interested in his feet. 'And speaking of mating, old fruit. What exactly were you and the delightful Dr. Janussen up to out there on the Moon? Ever since, she's been more morose than a camel with three humps and I notice *you've* suddenly started calling her "Gemma".'

Had I? My face was surely glowing like a paraffin heater. 'It's nothing really. She just – became more aware of her – you know – clockwork brain thing . . .'

'You've been listening to Jenkins, haven't you? It's not her *brain* that's clockwork, old sport, it's *electrical*, but it's *powered* by clockwork. Otherwise she'd have to strap a heavy duty industrial battery on her head. I fancy even Signora Schiaparelli herself couldn't conjure up a hat ghastly enough to disguise it.'

'Anyway. She knows now. I think she's always known in some buried part of her.'

'Well, that's probably for the best. Once she gets over the shock of it. And the calling her "Gemma" business?'

My face was now as incandescent as a three bar electric fire. 'Oh, well – you know . . .'

'I do. I do know indeed, my dear chap. And take it from one who has been . . . in a similar position, if you know what

I mean, on many, many occasions. And if I've learned one thing, it's this.' He paused dramatically 'Never take them to the pictures when they're showing Woody Woodpecker. He's a complete passion killer. I think it's his *laugh*.' He shuddered uncontrollably. 'Quite unnerving. And never put your arm around them until *Pathé News*. If you're in luck, something unspeakably hideous will have happened, and they'll need manly succour—'

This stream of no doubt priceless romantic advice was cut short by our rounding a particularly large tree and rediscovering Gemma and Troy in front of the crashed ship. They were warming their hands over an enormous bonfire, the like of which I hadn't witnessed since VE Day.

'I say!' I called, 'isn't that rather overdoing things? We don't want to attract any predators or anything.' And as if on cue, I *definitely* heard the snuffling squawk of a flying badger.

We tossed our meagre bundles of twiglets into the blaze, where they were consumed in seconds, and started preparing to spend the night.

While Gemma and I laid out makeshift beds with fire blankets rescued from the ship, Troy squeezed out a couple of chickens from the tube, which, of course, escaped immediately, so he and Guuuurk had to set off chasing them down.

Which pretty much left me alone with Gemma. 'I suppose,' I said, 'this is going to be our life from now on.'

'It very much looks that way.'

'We'll be growing old together.'

I offered a rather winning smile, but just got back a rather chilly 'Yes.'

I took a deep breath, mentally. 'Look: I've been hurled along on quite a tumultuous emotional roller coaster over the past twelve hours. And now we've ended up here, together, frankly, it doesn't seem quite as unbearable a thing any more to come out and – yes – speak my mind clearly. Say what I have to say without any tedious rambling, or beating about—'

She folded her arms. 'For heaven's sake, Brian, get to the point.'

'You and me . . .' My voice cracked, just right exactly when you wouldn't want your voice to crack. 'Do you suppose there's a chance we could ever—'

'No.'

'Understood!' I shot back quickly, as if that cold final rebuff had been the most expected and natural thing in the world, and hadn't in any way ripped my very soul into tiny shreds like the man who does paper-tearing tricks in the music hall.

She straightened and brushed a bang from her forehead. 'No, you *don't* understand: it's never going to happen for us; the rational side of my brain is literally *inhuman*. I'm calculating, cold and heartless, and who could love that? And there's no denying it to myself any longer, but when I wind down, I'm hysterical, reckless and juvenile. And who could love *that*?'

'Me,' I said, proudly. 'That's who. Both the impossible sides of you. There's no rhyme or reason to it, is there? When you feel a certain way about a certain person . . .'

'Kiss me,' I think she said. Yes, she definitely did.

'What?'

'You didn't last time. I won't ask again.'

She didn't have to. We kissed. And it was undeniably the most glorious kiss of kisses . . . and yet . . . it ignited a torch in some dark corner of my memory. I had been kissed like this, exactly this, before! Yet, I couldn't recall a face or a time for it. But what did it matter? This was now, and it was real. And it was my Gemma.

Somehow, we parted. 'Was that . . .?' I hesitated to ask,

because the wrong answer would dash my soul against some very cruel rocks. '. . . is your ear winding down?'

'No, Brian. It makes no sense to me whatsoever. . .'

'But it does! You're finally allowing the two sides of you to communicate – you're incorporating your emotions with your reason – and it's wonderful!'

'You could be right!' she beamed. 'And I think that I'm very much in—'

A chicken hit me in the face, squawking, as it fled the lumbering figures of Troy and Guuuurk.

'Oh, well done, Brian! You practically had it in your hand. We'll never catch it now.' Guuuurk turned to Troy. 'Squeeze out another one.'

'Tube's empty.'

'Seriously? You mean we've lost all *thirty* of them?'

''Fraid so.'

'This entire planet's going to be populated by angry chickens!'

Troy creased his brow. 'Why d'you think they'll be angry?'

'You can't expect them to be *pleased* – they've spent who knows how long squashed into a toothpaste tube!'

I looked over at Gemma, but even though she returned my smile, once again the moment had passed for us.

Still, I must admit to feeling schoolboy happy as we all sat cross-legged, staring into the bonfire, trying to fry three eggs on the end of a stick. I even considered suggesting we sing 'Ging Gang Goolie', but the thought of having to explain it all to Guuuurk, and especially to Troy, put me off completely.

Guuuurk stood and clapped for attention. 'We have to face facts, chaps and chappess,' he announced. 'We're going to be stuck here in this *shocking* place for the rest of our naturals. We can't go on as we were, however much we might have liked to. There must be changes. First, we must elect a leader.'

'Hang on.' Troy cocked his head. 'I think I can hear a bus coming.'

A bus! We all laughed. Even Gemma giggled slightly.

'I seriously doubt,' Guuuurk chuckled, 'that buses come *quite* this far, young Master Quanderhorn. A leader,' he repeated. We all turned to Gemma. Guuuurk pretended not to notice, and pressed on. 'Now, I know what you're thinking, but it need not necessarily be the most *obvious* candidate amongst us. What we require is a sort of rakish *wisdom*, from someone who is undeniably a member of the ruling class, and who, ideally, has first-hand experience of surviving on another world.'

There was a worrying glow of something approaching in the distance through the thicket of trees right behind Guuuurk, and a faint, disturbing growling sound, which was growing louder.

Oblivious, the Martian continued: 'Naturally, this *fêted* person, whoever she – or perhaps more likely "he" – may be, would have the pick of the food, the women, any spare cash lying around, animal furs, a splendid shelter built by the other, lesser members of the tribe, and first dibs on the nattiest clothing. Now, modesty forbids my suggesting any individual in particular, but I'd say six eyes were an absolute prerequisite— What *is* that bally noise?'

There was no ignoring the rumble now. It sounded like the engine of an AEC RT Regent III bus, with bodywork by Eastern Coachworks at Oulton Broad.

Which was precisely what, at that very moment, drew up beyond the mound behind him.

'I think,' I replied, 'it's the number 43 to Highgate Woods.'

Guuuurk turned slowly and stared in disbelief. 'I didn't know there *was* a Highgate Woods in the Crab Nebula!'

But by then, we were all running over the mound towards the road.

'Come on, you dozy lot!' the conductor complained, hanging off his platform. 'We can't hang around here all evening. We got 'omes to go to.'

Earth! We were on Earth!

Then I remembered my Scout Camp Laws. 'Hold that bus!' I yelled. 'I've just got to put this fire out.'

Chapter Eight

Lumpy the blith of Deimos, Martian Year 5972 Pink

Secret Report to Martian Command, by Guuuurk 'the Infallible', fifteenth Minnow of Gaaaark 'the Unfathomable', and his ninety-third concubine, Bong.

After a rather unpleasant *contretemps* with the over-officious bus conductor, involving some Peruvian coinage and a twenty-seven bolivar note from Venezuela, we found ourselves rudely ejected from the bus at the very next stop, in Highgate Village.

I was acutely aware my face colouring was drawing unwanted attention, even in the dark, so I persuaded Brian to pop into Timothy White's and get me a bottle of calamine lotion, which I slapped on in the absence of distemper. If anything, it looked even better than the paint. It gave me the glowing, tanned aura of a young Randolph Scott. With the masculine tang of zinc oxide.

The general plan was to get to a telephone of some kind, but the booth on the high street had been annexed by a gang of juvenile delinquents, who were beating at the coin box with crowbars. I was slightly cheesed off there were no postcards with tempting telephone numbers on display therein, which that moustachioed mountebank Jenkins had promised were all over the place in London.

Still, plenty of other intoxicating naughtinesses to investigate now we were On the Loose and In the Smoke!

Hardly able to contain my excitement, I skilfully persuaded the others that an unvandalised telephone would most likely be found in the saloon bar of the Wrestler's Arms. Licking my lips at the prospect of some actual hard liquor – not the rancorous filth Jenkins distils in the professor's laboratory, or that dreadful rot gut they decant at the Wytchdrowninge ironmonger's – I was first through the inviting etched-glass doorway. 'Ales', it promised. Ales! 'And Stout'. Stout! Imagine! I'd no idea what stout was, but it sounded the very ambrosia of the gods.

Imagine my disappointment to find the way to the bar blocked by a huge scrum of inebriated humans, clustered around a wireless set.

As we drew closer, we heard one of those dinner-jacketed BBC types droning on about something bizarre happening at Piccadilly Circus. Some kind of pyramid object – 'a ziggurat of great antiquity' – long buried under Eros, had forced its way up from the Earth's crust into the Tube station.

Honestly, these Terraneans get distracted by the slightest thing. I was just about to fight my way to the counter and demand the best stout that money could buy (on the slate), when blow me, if the next voice on the radio wasn't old Quanderhorn himself.

'*Stand back!*' he was calling on his megaphone. '*Stand back from the ancient alien artefact!*'

Damned if my slight hesitation didn't allow Dr. Janussen to grab my forearm. 'Guuuurk – where d'you think you're going?

We're wasting time. We're clearly needed—'

And then, oddity of oddities, Dr. Janussen's voice was also issuing from the wireless.

The BBC chap introduced her as 'one of the Professor's associates, the lovely Dr. Gemini Janussen.' I could feel the real Dr. Janussen's grip tighten on my arm in shock.

'*Good evening, everyone,*' this other Dr. Janussen replied. '*And thank you for the charming compliment.*'

I realised, on reflection, that her voice was almost the same as the real Gemma's, but not quite. Slightly . . . gentler. And – dare I say it? – more feminine.

Brian looked as if he'd applied some of my calamine lotion to his own face. 'How can you be there and here at the same time?' he asked Gemma.

'*Actually,*' the radio Dr. Janussen trilled, '*being merely a woman, I just make the tea and stuff around here.*'

I screamed in pain as the real Dr. Janussen's fingernails dug deep into my arm. I swear I thought they were going to meet in the middle!

'*What?*' She thundered in a terrible voice. 'Is she *mad*?'

I patted her hand with my working arm, and craftily slid the other one out of danger's way. Thank heavens I did, too, because the next words out of the radio might well have caused her to snap it in two.

'*We should all put our faith,*' the radio Gemma went on, '*as I do, in my fiancé, our brave test pilot – Brian Nylon.*'

Brian, as usual, had fixated on the wrong part of the sentence. He half-smiled: 'Fiancé?'

'She *is* mad,' I muttered to myself. And now there was another *Brian* on the radio.

'*Hello, everyone,*' declaimed this second pretender breezily, in a much more confident version of young Nylon's whiny tones. '*Nothing to worry about, now. I've got it all in hand. Two sugars for me, darling.*'

'*You're sweet enough already, darling,*' the radio Gemma cooed, and the two of them laughed gaily for very much longer than one would have expected.

'Does anyone have a vomit bag handy?' spat the real Dr J.

Ha ha ha. The look on Brian's and Gemma's faces! Quite clearly, they'd been replaced, and their pitiful egos couldn't cope with it. It really was quite jocund when you think about it. Honestly – these vain creatures have absolutely no sense of humour when it comes to themselves.

And then, horror of horrors, the presenter made a rather more startling announcement. '*And unless I'm mistaken,*' he said, '*they're followed by none other than* Edith Sitwell!'

'*What?*' I found myself exclaiming. And then some appalling parody of my own mellifluous voice started ranting: '*Death to all Earthlings! Soon you will all be overrun by the superior warriors of the planet Mars and fry in the white heat of our inescapable Death Rays!*'

The reporter chuckled indulgently. '*Marvellous new poem, Dame Edith.*'

How dare that stinker pretend to be me, pretending to be Edith Sitwell? Was he utterly devoid of morals and ethics? 'He's nothing but a scurrilous liar,' I protested.

'What is going *on*?' Brian demanded.

Gemma had managed to gather herself. 'Somehow, the Professor's duplicated us all. Only, not quite.'

'Not quite? "Death to all Earthlings"? Is that something I regularly say to you over breakfast?' I mean, obviously I secretly agreed with the fellow's sentiments, Death to all Earthlings et cetera et cetera, but it seems frightfully *infra dig* to come right out and say it to their *faces*.

322

But the radio fellow wasn't finished with the treats. *'And here comes young Troy Quanderhorn, the Professor's son with the matinée idol looks.'*

'Ooh,' our Troy crooned, 'he's my favourite.'

'Troy – a word for our listeners.'

This duplicate Troy, quite frankly, sounded indistinguishable from our own lummox. *'I don't know any words,'* he said. *'Oh – except "herringbone". Is that a word?'*

Our Troy threw back his head and laughed. 'Ha! That Troy fellow's an idiot! Everyone knows "herringbone" isn't a word.' He shook his head pityingly.

'So,' the penguin-suited popinjay concluded, *'with the Professor and his crack team about to descend to the Tube line and break into the mysterious ziggurat – hopefully to discover momentous secrets hitherto unrevealed to humanity for millennia – we return you to Max Jaffa and the BBC Palm Court Orchestra, resuming tonight's* Hungarian Hoo-Hah.'

'No, no!' I yelled impotently at the wireless set. 'Go back! We need to know what's going on with those unspeakable imposters!'

But the ghastly racket of horses' tails being scraped across cats' intestines started up, and the crowd immediately began to disperse. I was bundled out of the way as absolutely every last one of them headed for the bar. Was I never going to get my glass of stout?

Brian's brow was as furrowed as Mrs Wiggonby's goitre. 'If they're supposed to be duplicates, why are the other "us"s so different?'

'Clearly,' Gemma answered somewhat stiffly, 'Quanderhorn couldn't resist making "improvements" to us. The arrogant fool.'

I found this actually quite shocking. I'd never heard anyone on the team directly criticise the Professor, much less the stalwart Dr. Janussen herself. She was normally so dispassionate about everything.

'There's nothing for it,' she announced. 'We have to get to Piccadilly Circus.'

Piccadilly Circus! The heart of Soho! *Now* we were talking.

'Follow me, everyone,' I ordered, heading back through the scrum for the doors.

In my head, I stared singing:

'In the day time Grandad's searching for truth,
But at night time he's searching for his youth
In Piccadilly, Piccadilly, dear old London's broad highway . . .'

Chapter Nine

Outprint from Gargantua, the pocket Quanderdictoscribe.
Dateline: Saturday the 5th of January, 1952, 19.37 hours

JENKINS: . . . and this just clips
under here, sir . . . I just
switched it on.

NEW BRIAN: Got it! Testing, testing
. . .

JENKINS: Yep! It's printing out the
other end lovely. Not too
heavy, is it, new Mr. Nylon,
sir?

NEW BRIAN: No. Nghh.

JENKINS: It *is* less than forty pounds.
Miracle of miniaturisation,
it is. Off you go then, sir.

NEW BRIAN: (CLEARS THROAT) I am standing
deep in the heart of
Piccadilly Circus Underground
Station, where a gigantic
pyramid-like structure has
forced its way from the

bowels of the Earth to the
top of the platform . . .

JENKINS: Just near the chocolate
machine.

NEW BRIAN: Yes, thank you, Jenkins, you
can go now.

JENKINS: (MUMBLING) You tries and
gives them colourful detail,
it gets thrown back in your
face.

NEW BRIAN: It's impossible to tell how
deep the edifice goes. There
appear to be the markings
of a doorway inset into the
hard, rough grey granite-like
material of its surface.
There are two huge closed
eyes carved in relief above
the 'doorway', somewhat
reminiscent of Egyptian and
Aztec hieroglyphs. On the
crumbling remains of
the platform before it,
gangs of Irish navvies
stand by, pickaxes at the
ready, awaiting the Prof's
instructions as to how we're
going to smash our way in,
and give old Johnny Alien a
shellacking he won't forget.

NEW GUUUURK: Ha! Enjoy that pitiful
illusion of human

superiority while you can.
When our mighty fleet lands,
you'll be bending the
knee before your Martian
overlords!

NEW GEMMA: What shall *I* do, Brian
darling?

NEW BRIAN: You're already doing it, my
poppet: just stand there and
be gorgeous.

NEW TROY: I don't know if it will
help, but I'm going to rip
open my shirt and expose my
magnificent oiled chest.

NEW BRIAN: You're not wearing a shirt,
old chap.

NEW TROY: Nyaaaaah. Anyone got a needle
and thread?

QUANDERHORN: Stand back, everyone! This
is a job for Gargantua, the
giant Quandersaw. Bring her
forward, Mr. O'Reilly!

O'REILLY: (DISTANT) Assuredly.
Bejabers.

[SEQUENCE OF MECHANICAL SOUNDS]

NEW BRIAN: (LOUD) I'm looking at a
colossal chainsaw rumbling
forward, with three
atomic-powered turbine drives
spinning fifty titanium
technic axles and a, what?

327

A thirty-foot diameter blade
. . .?

QUANDERHORN: Thirty-five. Spinning at
fifteen million revolutions
per minute, made of specially
reinforced chiffon.

NEW BRIAN: Sorry, sir? Did you say
'chiffon'?

QUANDERHORN: Yes. What of it?

NEW BRIAN: The giant whirring blade
is lowered into position
. . . makes contact with the
granite doorway . . .

[VARIOUS SOUNDS]

NEW BRIAN: . . . and just sort of flaps
impotently for a couple of
seconds, then rips to shreds.
And the Professor cuts the
engine.

[BRIEF SILENCE]

QUANDERHORN: What idiot thought you could
reinforce chiffon?

NEW BRIAN: The Professor is now looking
at me rather angrily.

QUANDERHORN: Do you *have* to keep up
a running commentary on
absolutely everything that
happens?

NEW BRIAN: Well, yes, sir. Those are my
orders from you.

[SEQUENCE OF UNRECOGNISED SOUNDS]

NEW BRIAN: Professor! The wall!

QUANDERHORN: Describe it, man, describe it.

NEW BRIAN: I hardly know what I'm seeing. The ancient stones on the face of the edifice are sort of . . . sliding around . . . rearranging themselves. The eyes! The great stone eyes are opening! It's looking at us! It's actually looking at us!

QUANDERHORN: Tantalising!

NEW GEMMA: Hold me, Brian, I'm frightened.

NEW BRIAN: There's nothing to be— Oh, my God! The mouth's opening! It wasn't a door, it was a mouth all the time! It's speaking!

[UNRECOGNISED SOUNDS. SCREAMING AND PANIC]

Chapter Ten

Lumpy the blith of Deimos, Martian Year 5972 Pink

Secret Report to Martian Command, by the real <u>actual</u> Guuuurk 'The Adventurer', Assistant Assistant to the Assistant Assistant's Assistant Stick Sharpener, temple of Draaaag (leap years only).

The Tube trains were all cancelled, of course, and as we neared Piccadilly on foot, the roads and pavements became absolutely crammed with fleeing cars and panicking Terraneans. So our progress through Soho along Brewer Street was disastrously slow. Not as slow as I'd have liked, though. Everybody kept tugging me onwards whenever I stopped to ask directions from the ladies standing in doorways, who seemed only too eager to offer helpful advice and even, for some peculiar reason, Gallic language tuition.

Eventually, I was dragged to the corner of Great Pulteney Street, where our way was completely blocked by a police cordon. Brian tried to explain to one of the officers that we were the *real* Quanderhorn crew – unlike those swizzlers from the radio – but his troubles only earned him a thump on the head from a truncheon.

A great Martian general, at this point, would come up with a strategy so ingenious that it would reduce his followers to slack-jawed, dewy-eyed awe.* And so it was when I hit upon the rather ingenious notion of our doubling back and taking a short cut through the Windmill Theatre.

The others could scarcely contain their utter adulation, and barely tried to restrain me at all as I dashed in through the stage door with Brian literally hanging off my shirt tail.

In my giddiness, I rather clumsily happened to stumble into, of all places, the showgirls' dressing room! Being a gentleman, of course, I immediately averted my eyes from the array of half-stockinged legs, suspender belts, peek-a-boo *brassières*, feathered G-strings, sheer silk *negligées*, lacy *peignoirs*, and, in one or two cases, entirely naked bodies! Of women!

And dash it all, if I hadn't completely forgotten about the Gentleman's Novelty Instant Camera which I'd hidden in my buttonhole when coaching the St Winifred's upper sixth tennis team, for evaluating tricky line calls. For some reason, it chose *now* to start going off.

It might not have induced such loud screaming and rushing about had it not been for the blizzard of snaps popping out of my breast pocket, and the blinding flashgun which I'd rather thoughtlessly concealed in my flies.

---

* This is doubtless a reference to the great Martian general 'Groooog the Impervious': when surrounded on all sides and under siege by the armies of his mortal enemy (and ex-wife) Borbindaxxx the Terrifying, he instructed his followers to eat their own feet rather than starve. It wasn't an entirely successful tactic, as it transpired that Borbindaxxx had grown bored and left the area with her forces weeks before. And when Groooog opened the city gates to check, a pack of Martian sloth-wolves slunk into the compound. Normally these lazy predators are quite easy to outrun, simply by strolling away at a leisurely pace, but on this occasion the entire army was casually nibbled to death in their immobile state over a period of several months.

The bouncers were terribly understanding about the whole business, and as a warning broke only three of my thumbs.

Escorted to street level via a window that really ought to have been open, I rejoined my colleagues, only to be furiously congratulated by Dr. Janussen with a cricket bat. (I assume she'd somehow obtained it from the theatre's props room.)

I managed to dampen down her excitement by observing there was now only one way past the police cordon.

Down.

Young Troy easily lifted a rusted manhole cover. In order to distract the growing attention of the milling crowds, I had him hurl it in the air like a discus, and yelled: 'Look! A flying saucer! It's probably those *awful* Martian stinkers!' (which is obviously the most terrifying prospect on the *planet* for the feeble and cowardly Terraneans), and while everyone calmly got out their mirrors, one by one we slipped down into London's dank sewers . . .

Chapter Eleven

The Daybook of 'Jenkins' Jenkins, RQMS Royal Fusiliers (on the run), Saturday the 5th of January, 1952

Boil dishcloths.

Well, I thought I'd seen everything, what with being the Prof's *Ada-de-camp* all these years, but a talking pyramid was a new one on me.

I can see right deep into its mouth, which is a sort of corridor with steps disappearing down the epiglottis.

They all stands there, gawping at it, as it comes out with a perculiar lingo in a voice like a foghorn jammed up an elephant's jacksie (which takes me back to that day in Tobruk, when we'd had a little bit too much of the laughing juice).

Me, I do something useful: I tries writing down what it's saying. It comes out as: 'Tugggggah shhhhhhhhpkkkk! Vuuuuuk com com dooooooffffahhh!' or thereabouts. Could be Italians. Italians! Don't like 'em.

The Prof snatches the paper off me and starts typing it into one of his Gargantua things. This one's got a big speaker on the side. Blow me, but after a minute, it starts chittering out proper words. Now I writes down exactly what it says:

'Greetings, intelligent life forms. An advanced alien species called, but you were apes. We'll pop back in a billion years. All the very best, the Planet Seeders.

'P.S. A relic which will unlock the Secret of the Eternals is buried deep in the heart of this ziggurat, for those intelligent enough to survive the labyrinth.'

'Blimey, Professor,' I says, 'that's more or less what Tomorrow-You exactly said.'

The Prof says: 'Ye-e-ess,' all long and drawn-out and dripping with suspicion.

He walks over to the mouth, which has now fallen still and silent, and become an entrance to Gawd knows where. He peers inside, tapping it with his knuckles.

'It seems to be a kind of invitation,' he says. 'Perhaps we should take it up?'

'Yes, but remember, Professor, begging your pardon, You also told yourself: "Whatever you do – don't."'

This doesn't sit well with the Prof. He don't like being told what to do, even by himself.

'Dammit, Jenkins, if I started not doing anything a future me told me not to do, there'd be no end to it!' He turns and calls to the duplicates: 'Everybody suit up: we're all going into that ziggurat!'

He goes to leave, then turns back and adds: 'But mostly not me.'

Chapter Twelve

From Troy's Big Bumper Drawing Book

[PICTURE OF A STICK MAN UP TO HIS NECK IN BROWN
SCRIBBLE, AND AN ARROW POINTING TO HIM, LABELLED:
'ME!']

weer Cronling thru the sooers. Its grAte! I Cnt even sMel
gerk!

Chapter Thirteen

Lumpy the blith of Deimos, Martian Year 5972 Pink

Secret Report to Martian Command [cont'd]

I was quite dry and comfortable as we crawled along the sewer tunnels. What I'd forgotten, of course, is that humans, for the most part, don't have handy suckers on their palms and knees. Ha ha ha. They were making quite a brouhaha as they scrabbled along in the aromatic unmentionableness below.

'Thank you, Guuuurk,' Brian whined, 'for providing the perfect end to the perfect day.'

'How was I to know you couldn't crawl along the ceiling, like any respectable species?'

'I *could* do that,' Troy grinned, 'but I don't want to. I like it down here, where it's all warm and sludgy.'

'We've just got to put up with it,' Dr. Janussen called. 'It's the only way through. Now, stop bleating and let's move on. We must be almost adjacent to the Tube platform by now.'

And, sure enough, Brian found a door inset into the brickwork up ahead. 'Here!' He waded quickly towards it. 'This must be it!'

He tugged open the door, and I swear to you, an absolute

cascade of crockery teetered over like the Leaning Tower of Pisa in an earth tremor and positively *hurled* itself into the tunnel in a miasma of shattering fragments.

'What the devil?' he groaned, as sugar bowls and teapots narrowly missed his head and committed ceramic hara-kiri before our eyes.

'What *is* it with you and crockery, Brian?' I shook my head in disbelief. 'Are you some sort of deranged porcelain-hater? Are you unable to pass an intact dinner service without experiencing irresistible murderous tendencies?'

Brian simply stood there agog. Dr. Janussen pointed out a sign on the door which indicated it was the basement storage vault for Swan and Edgar's department store. She shut it firmly and waded over to an adjacent door, this time an iron one with a London Transport roundel cast into it, and a large, rusty hatch wheel below.

As Brian strained to turn the wheel, we all prayed it wasn't the Underground train drivers' canteen pantry.

Fortunately it wasn't.

'Wow!' Troy was wide-eyed in wonder. 'There's a whole spare Tube station in *this* cupboard!'

Chapter Fourteen

The Daybook of 'Jenkins' Jenkins, RQMS Royal Fusiliers (never formally charged), Saturday the 5th of January, 1952

Darn dishcloths.

While the replacement crew is off putting on their safety suits, the Prof finally asks me the question I've been dreading.

'Do you have the photo of the cellar intruder, Jenkins?'

There's no getting away from it now, is there? I fishes in my pocket. 'The envelope fell open whilst I was driving, sir.'

'I imagined that might happen.' He kept his hand held out.

'Prepare yourself for a terrible shock, Professor,' I warns him, when, blow me, I'm the one shocked!

The access door behind me clangs open, and I hear someone say: 'Wow, there's a whole spare Tube station in this cupboard!' which can only be young Master Quanderhorn hisself! The original one, I means, not the carbon.

He squeezes himself through the orifice, and sure enough, the others tumble out after him. I don't know what to say.

'Master Quanderhorn, sir! And the rest of you! Bless my soul, we thought you'd all perished on the Moon.'

338

The Prof's gone deadly quiet. For a moment, I'm thinking he's had an attack of some kind.

'No, Jenkins,' Dr. Janussen says in a voice that's dripping acid. 'We were in that vessel someone tried to obliterate with the Giant Space Laser.'

'You wasn't!' I don't know where to put meself. I mean, I've killed a lot of people with friendly fire over the years – who hasn't? But this was the biggest SNAFU of 'em all. 'What about a nice cup of char,' I suggests, 'and a lovely fig roll for the weary travellers?' But there's no deflecting the stream of venom.

'Yes, *Quanderhorn*,' the Martian spits, surly as I ever seen him, 'I think you have a few questions to answer.'

The Prof unfreezes, sharpish, and starts fiddling with some machine or other. 'You're alive,' he says, all matter-of-fact and dum-de-dum. 'That's most inconvenient.'

Well, the Martian turns a colour I've never seen him go before and fairly bites through his cigarette holder in fury. 'Incon*venient*? Incon*venient* is when you're forced to hide in your paramour's wardrobe because her husband has unexpectedly returned from Malaya. Incon*venient* is when the play you wanted to go and see is banned by the Lord Chamberlain simply for featuring a nude woman in a wheelbarrow. Getting blown to your component atoms by a deadly Giant Space Laser is a little bit more than Incon-bloody-*venient*!'

'For me, it's inconvenient. I've gone to all the bother of replacing you. Or rather, *upgrading* you.'

And this is what gets Mr Nylon's goat. 'In what way *upgrading*? What makes you think we *need* upgrading?' he queries, all defiant like.

Don't faze the Prof, though. 'For instance, you, Nylon, I made more assertive. You comply far too easily with what other people want.'

'Well,' Mr Nylon says equitably, 'that seems fair enough.'

'It does *not*!' Dr. Janussen cuts in – she's changed her tune on him, that's for sure. 'It's Brian's humility that makes him what he is: what makes him special.'

'Well, thank you, Gemma,' he says, all beaming like a schoolboy who's conker's just become a twelver. 'That's a jolly nice thing—'

'Oh, shut up, Brian,' she snaps.

'Right-ho!'

Gemma now, is it? I wonders what went on up there on the Moon? Nocturnal manoeuvres with full kit, I shouldn't be surprised.

'Dr. Janussen,' the Prof ploughs on regardless, 'I made you more agreeable. None of this "having opinions" nonsense.' Quite right, an' all. Confuses the men.

Dr. Janussen is dumbstruck by this. For a change, I have to say.

'And Guuuurk, I dispensed with your appalling dishonesty.'

'That's a scurrilous lie!' The Martian fishes out a cheap medallion. 'As you can clearly see, I was recently awarded, by Her Majesty Queen Elizabeth, this Empire Pedal for Consticuous Honesty. Pay no attention to the spelling. They're terribly short-staffed at the Royal Mint, apparently.'

'What about me, Pops?' the young lad chirrups. 'You can't improve *me*.'

'Ah, Troy. I magnified your intelligence a thousandfold.'

'Woah! That's more than seven!'

'Unfortunately, that only amounts to a couple of extra IQ points.'

'Woah! That's more than seven!'

Mr. Nylon is looking all bewildered and hangdog about the whole business. But I notice he's put his hand all gentle and that on the small of Dr. Janussen's back. And she don't even bat it away! Least said . . .

'But where does this leave us?' he asks.

The Prof rubs the dust off his hands and turns back. 'Much as it pains me to say this: I'm afraid, my erstwhile colleagues, it leaves you . . . replaced.'

Chapter Fifteen

From the journal of Brian Nylon, 5th January, 1952 – [cont'd]

Replaced!

And, right on cue, they emerged from under the canvas of the makeshift tent, clad in white, one-piece protective coveralls with the hoods pushed back. It was an extraordinary shock to see their faces. The new Gemma was wearing peachy lipstick and rouge, and, unless I was mistaken, a rather heady French perfume. She'd eschewed the white wellingtons the others had donned, and instead was teetering on rather impractical if undeniably flattering heels.

The new Troy, on the other hand, looked indistinguishable from our own: brawny and permanently bewildered. The replacement Guuuurk had a cold, reptilian look of fanatical hatred burning in all of his eyes. His features were more pinched – *meaner*, somehow. And was that really a Hitler moustache, or just a shadow under his nose?

But the other Brian – that was flabbergasting. He looked *exactly* like me. Only, strangely, more handsome. How did he pull that off, exactly? Was it the hair? His manner? His whole *bearing*, perhaps?

'Well, blow me down!' he laughed rather rudely. 'If it isn't the bag of misshapen seconds!'

'No,' Troy shot back, '*you* are.'

His bulky lookalike snapped: 'No, *you* are.'

Whereupon they entered a battle of wits:

'No, *you* are!'

'No, *you* are!'

'No, *you* are!'

'No, *you* are!'

'No, *you* are!'

'No, *you* are!'

'No, *you* are!'

'No, *you* are!'

'No, *you* are!'

'No, *you* are!'

'No, *you* are!'

'No, you *really* are!' the duplicate announced triumphantly.

'Damn!' poor Troy vented. 'I didn't see *that* one coming!'

Gemma was regarding her fluffy double with undisguised contempt. 'You may as well know that you're not needed, now that we're back. So you can just spray on another gallon of whatever perfume that is – I presume French Tart Number 9 – cake your face with even more powder if that's remotely possible, and hobble off on those ridiculously improbable stilettos.'

'Ooh, I don't like the other me at all!' her replica squeaked. 'She's so aggressive and shrew-like.'

'Take no notice of her, my darling.' My double literally patted his Gemma on the head. I waited for her inevitable retaliatory punch in his kidneys, but it never came.

The pseudo-Guuuurk had squared up to his counterpart. His voice was flatter and more – I don't know – *robotic* than our Guuuurk's. 'I propose,' he droned, 'we Martian brothers massacre all the humans and eat them, in preparation for the glorious invasion.'

'Good plan,' Guuuurk nodded indulgently. 'Only, I have a *terrible* feeling they might put up a *teeny-weeny* bit of resistance.'

'Ha!' his counterpart snorted. 'And if we are slaughtered in the heroic attempt, so much the better!'

'Ye-e-e-s.' Our Guuuurk carefully screwed another lavender Sobranie cocktail cigarette into his holder. '*Although* . . . I *do* have a doctor's certificate here that regrettably excuses me from suicide missions until my impetigo clears up.'

Outraged, the new Guuuurk slapped him in the face. 'Worm! You are a despicable turncoat and a miserable coward.'

'Have you been reading my business card?' Guuuurk enquired, I think quite seriously.

'Stand aside.' My double rather boorishly bundled our Martian friend out of his way. 'Let the streamlined *primo* team-o take care of this.' He even *sounded* better than me. Was he deepening his voice somehow?

Still, boorishness like that shouldn't be tolerated. 'Listen, old chap, it's not a competition, you know. Why don't we all just shake hands and—'

The Professor, who'd been watching the whole thing with amused fascination, abruptly piped up: 'What if we were to *make* it a competition?'

My double threw back his head and laughed like Errol Flynn in *The Adventures of Robin Hood* when Basil Rathbone pulls out his rapier. 'Excellent notion, Prof! Both teams face the petrifying dangers of the ziggurat, to see which can reach the relic concealed in its heart without being horrifically butchered by the unknown terrors that undoubtedly lie within!'

'Ye-e-e-es,' Guuuurk said again, '*although* . . . I do have *another* doctor's certificate . . .'

'You're *lower* than a worm!' pseudo-Guuuurk snarled.

Troy stepped in to defend our lad. 'No, *you* are!'

'No, *you* are!' duplicate Troy shot back.

'No, *you* are!'

'No, *you* are!'

'No, *you* are!'

'No, you really *really* are!' the duplicate announced triumphantly.

'Damn!' poor Troy vented. 'How does he keep *doing* that?'

'Professor, you *can't* allow this,' my Gemma protested calmly. 'It's *beyond* childish.'

'Well,' 'Errol' grinned – even his teeth were whiter! It was really irritating. 'If you Old bods are too lily-livered to do it, we New Improved bods'll go in alone.'

'No!' Troy snapped, eying his duplicate with loathing. 'I want to beat me, and beat me hard. I want to show everybody what a useless idiot I really am.'

The Professor sighed. 'Very well, both teams will go in, and the winners will get to keep their positions.'

'And the losers?' the new me asked, before Gemma could object again.

'Good point,' the Professor conceded. 'We can't have two sets of you wandering around willy-nilly. It could cause all manner of misunderstandings.'

'Fine.' My double raised an arrogant eyebrow. Surely he hadn't actually been *tweezing* that? 'In the unlikely event we *lose*,' he chuckled, 'my whole team will voluntarily enter the Obliteration Chamber.'

Obliteration Chamber? I'd never heard of any Obliteration Chamber.

What else did this other 'me' know that I didn't?

It occurred to me for the first time that this other incarnation of myself might have access to my entire memory. The answers to *everything*.

345

'Oh, Brian,' the lacy, frothy version of Gemma swooned, 'you're so *heroic*!'

I saw my Gemma looking at me meaningfully. Well, I'd show *them* who was heroic. 'And if *we* lose,' I announced defiantly, 'so will we!'

'Nooooooo!' Gemma screamed, punching me rather effectively in the kidneys. 'You *idiot*!'

'Excellent!' The Professor nodded, and having suddenly registered the rather extended tea break in which the navvies were still indulging, he wandered off to gently berate them.

'To the death, then,' he remarked casually, over his shoulder. 'Get your safety suits from Jenkins, and let battle commence!'

Chapter Sixteen

*The Daybook of 'Jenkins' Jenkins, RQMS Royal Fusiliers
(innocent until proven), Saturday the 5th of Janury, 1952
[cont'd]*

Well, what a how's-your-father! Mr. Guuuurk doesn't look none too pleased by this battle-to-the-death development, as they all walks behind me towards the changing tent.

All hissy quiet-like, he goes: 'Brian, are you *insane*? If we don't get hideously killed in the Ziggurat of Certain Death, we have to step into the *Obliteration Chamber*. I can't be obliterated! Not at my time of life – I'm a despicable turncoat and a miserable coward!'

Which is true. I picked up his business cards from the printer's.

'Sorry. I just don't know what came over me.' Mr. Nylon is genuine upset. 'That so-called "duplicate" of me jolly well gives me the pip!'

Dr. Janussen is made of sterner stuff. 'Oh, what's the point of worrying, anyway? We're up against an insectoid meathead, a Martian Nazi, Captain Loves-Himself and his flibbertigibbet girly-girly girlfriend. Quite honestly, if we can't beat that lot, we deserve to be obliterated.'

347

The relief on Mr. Nylon's face! I swear he's more worried about her reaction than he is about facing oblivionisation!

Then Master Troy chirps: 'Where do we *buy* these Cigarettes of Certain Death? They sound great! Mine are just filter-tips.'

Dr. J. begins to patiently explain as they all steps through the tent flap. I looks around furtive, like, and sure enough, the Prof's off down the far end of the platform, busy herding the navvies. I clears my throat pointedly before Mr. Nylon follows the others. 'Ahem. Could I possibly have a quick private?'

'What is it, Jenkins?'

'It's about a certain photograph, sir. Here.'

I hands him the dreaded envelope. He looks puzzled, but then he slides out the photo, and he gets my drift, quick enough.

'My goodness!' he exclaims, a bit too loud for comfort.

'You were the intruder in the cellar, sir. It was you.'

'Yes, well . . . Um, I can explain that—' He starts his usual blathering.

'No, don't, sir. You're a truly terrible liar, begging your pardon.'

'Well, that . . . That's true enough.'

'We both know you're a spy.' Well, I have seen men suddenly go deathly pale – usually because of those giant leeches that lurk down the khazi in the Burmese jungle – but Mr. Nylon beats 'em all. He looks like an albino dipped in icing sugar at the North Pole, singing 'White Christmas'.

'Do we?' he stammers.

I puts him out of his misery. 'We're both spies.' Now he goes a completely different colour.

'Are we?'

'On behalf of the British Operatives for the General Biological Research Union of Sanitation Handlers,' I announce proudly.

I can see him trying to work out what they call the 'acronym'. 'We don't refer to it by its initials, of course. For obvious reasons.'

I think I hears him mutter: 'Is there any organisation I'm not a spy for?' but we're talking so low, like as not I've misheard.

'In the light of which developments, comrade brother,' I winks at him, 'as shop steward, I have to employ my endeavours to find some way of *not* showing that photograph to the management, *viz.* to wit and i.e., Professor Quanderhorn.'

'Could you draw a moustache and beard on it?' he asks.

'It's already got a moustache and beard,' I points out.

'No,' he says, 'that's gravy browning.'

I don't ask. Dr. Janussen starts calling him from the tent. I pats my boy on the shoulder. 'You'd best be off, comrade. Don't worry, old Brother Jenkins'll think of something. Be like Dad – keep mum.'

'Brian!' she calls again. And he scampers off obediently, like Lassie to a mineshaft.

Think of something? All very well saying that, old Brother Jenkins. But what?

Then there's this tap on my shoulder, and the Martian pops back out of the tent, in his white boiler suit. He's adding a cravat and a spotted silk hankie in the top pocket.

'Jenkins, old bean,' he hisses, 'can I have a private?'

'I have to tell you, Mr. Guuuurk, I'm in a bit of a rush at the moment.'

'I think you'll find time for this.' He reaches into his inside pocket – I notice he's got tape round three of his thumbs. 'I have a fresh consignment of particularly ... *artistic* photographic studies of the most tasteful nature taken backstage at the Windmill Theatre.'

The Windmill! I feel a tiny drop of drool forming under my

moustache, which I wipes away all surreptitious-like. You don't want these Martians aware you're keen in negotiations.

'Knowing you as a well-travelled gentleman of the world and a long-standing connoisseur of pulchritudinal portraiture—' he spiels.

'I do like big ones, sir, and that's for sure,' I blurts, before I can stop myself.

'I was wondering if you might be interested in obtaining them, as per our usual financial arrangement. Which, I recall, is a crisp, white fiver.'

I narrows my eyes and stares him down.

'Fourpence,' I says. 'Take it or leave it.'

He looks like he's about to have a heart attack while sucking a bowl of lemons. '*Fourpence?* You cut me to the quick!' he wails. 'Here am I trying to make a meagre crust from the pathetic scrapings of a miserable existence and you insult, nay, *mock* me with your derisory offer! Three pounds!'

'Fourpence', I fires back.

'You're stealing the bread out of my children's mouths! I know I don't have any children at the moment, but I plan to have some, and feed them bread! Two pounds!'

'Fourpence.'

'Let's split the difference.'

'Agreed. Fourpence.'

'Oh, very well,' he groans, handing the snaps over. 'Mind you, I shall want a written receipt for tax purposes. Shall we say for five hundred pounds?'

'I'll write one for three shillings and elevenpence ha'penny,' I says. 'And that's my final offer.'

'Done!' He certainly has been. He's solved my problem. But him, poor blighter, his problem's just beginning. I've seen what that Obliteration Chamber can do.

Chapter Seventeen

Private Diary of Winston Leonard Spencer Churchill:
Saturday the 5th of January, 1952.

Tea break over, I packed away the Fortnum's hamper and silver champagne tankard. Retying the knotted string around my trouser knees, slipping back the false red nose made from an old tomato, and reinserting the signed photograph of Joseph Locke into my wellington, I resumed my erstwhile persona as 'Mr. O'Reilly', the simple Irish navvy.

Of course, no one had recognised me in this impenetrable disguise, and I had therefore been able to witness in person the sinister alien apparatus issue forth its terrible declamation.

The Secret of the Eternals! Should such a prize fall into the hands of the accursed Quanderhorn, he would become unstoppable, and this great nation of ours could never be liberated from the pernicious snare of his infernal Time contraption.

The years of tremulous waiting must end. The hour of action had been finally thrust upon me!

But before I could put my ultimate plan into action, there was one question that demanded an answer.

And at last I spotted Agent Penetrator himself, hovering around the mouth of the ziggurat, reconnoitring. As fortune would have it, he was blessedly alone, at least for a moment or two. I hurried over to him, keeping to the shadows cast by the malignant alien edifice.

'Pssst. Begorrah and bejabers,' I brogued expertly, 'do you have a light for a simple bog Irishman's shillelagh?' I still have no idea what that is.

'Mr. Churchill!' he exclaimed, rather indiscreetly.

I hushed him. 'Indeed it is, Penetrator. You're a hard man to track down.'

'I didn't know you'd been looking for me, sir.' There was something different about the fellow. He seemed more assured, more dauntless. He even looked slightly *taller*. Clearly that holiday on the Moon had worked wonders on his constitution.

'I have to tell you, sir,' he went on, 'this is all being recorded and transcribed.'

'I'm aware of that, Penetrator. Don't concern yourself – my people will tear off and destroy the printed version when we've finished.'

'Your people?'

'Yes, Penetrator. None of these men is actually a genuine navvy.'

One nearby pipes up: 'Oi am, sir.'

'You're sacked.'

'Fair enough. I'm orf to da pub.' He tossed his shovel aside and trundled off happily.

'*Now* none of these men is an actual genuine navvy, so we can speak freely.'

'Roger that, sir.'

'So, to the important business: I need to know precisely what you found in Quanderhorn's cellar.'

He looked completely mystified. 'I didn't find anything in the cellar.'

I *knew* it! That scabrous fox Quanderhorn had been talking the whole thing up to thwart any manoeuvre against him. But I needed to be certain.

'Nothing dangerous down there at all?' I persisted.

'Not to my knowledge.'

I looked deep into his eyes, as I'd looked deep into Stalin's. I can ascertain whether or not a man's telling the truth. Stalin wasn't. Penetrator indubitably was.

'That's excellent news!' I slapped the fellow on the back. 'There'll be a medal in this for you, young rapscallion! Though regrettably it won't be the Empire Medal for Conspicuous Honesty. We've had a lot of trouble with cheap forgeries, recently.'

He looked momentarily perplexed. 'I'm afraid I really don't know what all this cellar stuff is about, sir—'

'Of course you don't.' I winked. 'And neither do I. Carry on, Penetrator. But don't be *too* successful.'

Leaving him behind, I hastened to the transcribing device to supervise the immediate destruction of any record of our conversation. I was finally free! Free of the confounded restraints that had prevented my moving against Quanderhorn.

Free as the goddess Nemesis herself to deliver that final, delicious and richly merited thunderbolt.

Chapter Eighteen

The Daybook of 'Jenkins' Jenkins, RQMS Royal Fusiliers (pleas taken into consideration), Saturday the 5th of January, 1952

'Good God in Heaven!' The prof's veins all knot in his forehead.

'I told you to prepare yourself for a shock, sir.'

'But this!' He slaps the photo with the back of his hand. 'What devilish agency would infiltrate my top secret cellar in G-strings and rotating nipple tassels? The Russians? The Martians? The Elastic-eating Mothmen from Trappist-1?'

'Oh, I remember them Mothmen, sir. Nasty bits of work. The amount of bloomers that fell down after *that* attack!' Mothmen? Don't like 'em.

Corner of my eye, I see some navvies tearing up bits of paper. Why can't they just use bog roll, like civilised people?

The Prof's eyes is flittering from side to side, his mind churning nineteen to the dozen. He don't usually get agitated like this. 'Whoever it was, the blundering buffoons were threatening the very essence of existence.'

Blimey. 'If you'll forgive me, sir, d'you mind me asking how?'

He goes all quiet for a moment, then shoots me this look

which really frightens me. 'Yes, Jenkins, as a matter of fact, I mind very much.'

Knowing what's good for me, I hastily changes the subject. 'The duplicates are ready to go in, sir. The originals are still arguing who gets to hold the flaming torch.'

'I'll deal with all that, Jenkins.' His veins don't look much less purple. 'We can't risk any more incursions into that cellar. You have to get back to the lab urgently and shore things up. Double the slow-motion gas, triple the ball bearings, quadruple the flame-throwers and raise the invisible shield.'

'If you remember, sir,' I reminds him, 'you put the invisible shield down somewhere, and now we can't find it.'

'Dammit! Secure that cellar *at all costs*!'

Well, I don't know exactly what he's got going on down in that cellar, but I ain't never seen him scared like this. Never.

Chapter Nineteen

Dr Virginia Whyte's diary, December 31st, [the very first]
1952

I can't honestly say I knew precisely what it was in London we
were on our way to, but it was thrilling, nonetheless. I'd never
seen Darius look quite so exhilarated, as he powered the Jaguar
XK120 roadster down the A1, snow-covered fields flashing past
on either side. Despite the temperature we had the roof down,
and I was rather thankful for the woolly scarf and mittens Aunt
Alice had knitted for me for Christmas. The wind ruddied our
faces and occasional flecks of snow stung my cheeks before
melting.

As night fell we stopped off at a transport café to put the
roof up. We sat, gratefully cupping our hands round hot mugs
of cocoa, amid the gruff lorry drivers and intense-looking
young men in leather jackets and tight blue workman's
trousers. What a hoot! It was, quite frankly, a tremendous
adventure!

I managed to hold back until we finally purred into central
London, then I could supress it no longer. 'So, are you finally
going to tell me, you beast?' I asked.

'Tell you what?' He grinned.

'Whatever it is, you silly goose! I can see you're bursting to come out with it.'

'Virginia.' He positively gleamed. 'Remember when we first started out, with barely enough money to keep body and soul together?'

'I'm not likely to forget that. We had to live a whole week on that *awful* soup I cooked up.'

He laughed heartily. 'Yes, I can still taste it! I've got a confession: I fed most of it to that funny little dog you had.'

'My chihuahua? Gargantua? You didn't! You could have killed him!' I punched Darius playfully on the shoulder.

'And remember,' he grinned on, 'how we'd sit up into the wee small hours, telling each other fine stories of how one day we would do some work – important work – that people would remember us for for ever?'

I laughed. 'Yes! Pipe dreams of the young and foolish!'

'It may have seemed like a pipe dream at the time—'

'Darius – what are you telling me? You've finally got the Vegetablising Ray operational?'

'No, not that . . .'

I almost missed a heartbeat. 'Not the *Möbius Project*? Have you found a way to make it work? But that's enormous! And you kept it to yourself?'

'I didn't want to raise false hopes. But if I'm right, Virginia, this is it! Our masterpiece! Our *magnum opus*!'

'Come on, Q-horn – don't keep me hanging. How will we pull it off?'

As usual, once unleashed, there was no stopping the Professor in him. 'Well, what we needed, of course, was to identify the precise location where the conflux of temporal energies are most powerfully focused.'

'Yes, clearly, but—'

He held up his driving-gloved finger. 'By fracturing the very continuum itself only at that precise spot, the ruptured time stream would be forced out under tremendous pressure along the path of least resistance to find egress at another precise location elsewhere.'

'But we already knew all that. We simply don't have the geomaths to calculate either of those points.'

Grinning unbearably, he reached into his door bin and handed me a battered exercise book.

I skimmed the formulae-strewn pages greedily. 'This . . . If this is correct—'

'It is.'

'Then the emergence point would be precisely beneath the old fever hospital we converted into our laboratory!'

He nodded, rather smugly. 'Directly into that cavern we made into our cellar . . .'

'Our *cellar* . . .? I wondered why you chose that curious site.'

'Where the excess years can be safely stored in a five-dimensional array of polytopic hyperspheres!'

'So *that's* what all that equipment was!' I raced through the rest of the calculations as best I could. 'And that would make the origin point . . .'

He smiled to himself as we rounded New Palace Yard, slithered to a stop, and gazed up the yellow illuminated face of the clock popularly (and incorrectly) known as 'Big Ben'.

It was half an hour to midnight, and the revelries were in full swing. We pushed through the milling throngs below, into the Palace of Westminster. We ran giddily through the maze of stone corridors and slipped in at the base of the clock tower. Darius took my hand and led me quickly up the stairs.

'So,' I panted, 'starved of fresh tomorrows, Time would loop over and over – a temporal Möbius strip – and it would be perpetually 1952!'

'We'll be virtually immortal – of course people will still die, but not of old age any more. We'll stay just as we are for ever! It's the single most important contribution anyone's ever made to humanity.'

I stopped to catch my breath. 'But what about people who are miserable, people who are in pain? Aren't we condemning them to perpetual suffering?'

'But I'll have *time*, Virginia. Time to find a cure for all diseases. To end all suffering. Time to pursue *all* my projects—'

'You mean all *our* projects.'

'Yes,' he said too slowly. He didn't mean it. '*Our* projects. Of course.' There was a distant look in his eyes. 'But mostly mine,' he added rather strangely. He began climbing again.

'But, Darius – people may not *want* to stay the same for ever, have you thought of that?'

He was several steps ahead of me by now, 'People! What do we care for *people*? People don't *think* – they have no *idea* what's best for them! We're giving them stability. Constancy. No more fear of things changing – it'll be a perpetual golden age no one need ever look back to!'

We rounded the last twist of the stairway and he pushed open the door to the clock chamber. I stepped in after him, lungs and legs aching.

The ticking of the colossal mechanism was deafening, but what startled me was the bewildering and complex series of relays, switches and devices which had been jury-rigged to the famous workings. They beeped, buzzed and burred, lying in wait like some monstrous insect that had made its atrocious nest in our national monument.

'Y-you've already set the whole thing up?'

'I told them it was a minor weather experiment.' He laughed rather unkindly. 'They're so easy to dupe, it's almost cruel.'

A horrible realisation flooded over me. 'Now I see why you waited 'til New Year's Eve to tell me.' He didn't even register my disappointment. I'd naïvely assumed he was being romantic. 'You're going to activate it *tonight*!'

'It's already activated, Virginia! I wanted you to be here to witness it firing up with me.'

He looked over the terrible creation with something like pride. Or was it obsession?

I *had* to deter him from this path. It was madness. 'We can't just go ahead with this – there are so many things we need to work through—'

'Plenty of time to work them through after midnight has struck. All the time in the world, in fact!'

'But the polytopic hyperspheres are finite. They won't hold more than ten years safely. Twenty at the most.'

'Agreed, but we'll have found another way to safely dissipate it long before then.'

I checked the reverse clock face; it was almost midnight. 'Darius, we have to disengage this right now—'

But as I spoke the giant minute hand tocked up to the twelve and the chimes began, shaking the chamber and forcing my hands over my ears.

'You *have* to listen to me,' I shouted. 'The storage array will eventually become unstable. Please wait!' But the machinery was already gathering speed, and each new chime was getting closer to the last.

'Impossible!' he yelled back. 'Now it's in motion, the Time-Splicer can't be stopped. It'll automatically fire up at the end of every year to keep the Möbius time stream turning back on itself. It's synchronised to the final stroke of midnight.'

'Darius! No! Once those tanks reach capacity, the slightest tremor in the cellar could cause a temporal fissure that would split the planet . . . maybe even reality itself!'

The final chime rang out. The sound seemed to hang in the air, and then reversed itself, like a genie being sucked back into its bottle.

I thought I felt a slight wind, but it didn't seem . . . physical, somehow. It didn't hit me, so much, but passed through me, like a wave.

We stood in blank silence for a second or two.

Then, suddenly, after a slightly bemused hiatus, the crowd below began to cheer and sing 'Auld Lang Syne'.

He grinned. And as I stared into his eyes, I realised with deep sadness and not a little dread, that the Darius I knew had gone.

'Happy Old Year,' he said.

Chapter Twenty

Private Diary of Winston Leonard Spencer Churchill:
Sunday the 6th of January, 1952

I positively skipped over to the dark archway where my men had concealed the field telephone. My hand was uncharacteristically steady as I raised the receiver and jauntily cranked the handle.

'Hello? Is that the Air Chief Marshal?'

'It is, Prime Minister. Awaiting your orders.'

I gleefully savoured every syllable: 'I'm activating Plan 43. Scramble the newly formed Advanced Laboratory-Blasting Squadron.'

'I'll need the code phrase, sir.'

I gave it to him. And feeling capriciously frivolous, I added: 'Oh, and toss in the massed bands of the Royal Scots Dragoons, to give the attack a more carnival atmosphere.'

'Acknowledged!' and he yelled, off the phone, *'Scramble the Lab Busters!'*

I slowly clicked down the receiver. 'Twas done. And done well.

Tonight, once and for all, that maniac Quanderhorn's laboratory complex shall be wiped from the face of the earth!

6

Trinitrotoluene

There will come a time when our descendants will be
amazed that we did not know things that are so plain
to them. Many discoveries are reserved for ages still to
come, when memory of us will have been effaced.

Seneca, *Natural Questions*

Trinitrotoluene

Chapter One

From the journal of Brian Nylon, 6th January, 1952 – [cont'd]

It took a mite longer than anticipated, suiting up. We all had to undergo a rather thorough and degrading hosing down, except for Guuuurk, who'd avoided the worst of the drains. But he still managed to keep us all waiting as he squirted on lashings of his disgusting gentleman's aftershave – *Ladykiller*,– which he'd got in a job lot from the ironmonger's, though beneath the handmade label, the square can looked suspiciously like 3-in-One oil.

It would have been unkind of me to say so, but I had no doubt the fumes would certainly kill any lady foolish enough to venture too close to it!

Troy had somehow found a pair of corduroy shorts, which he thought made him look much 'hepper' than his duplicate, and no amount of cajoling could persuade him otherwise. He refused to wear his safety suit at all. Or any kind of shirt.

I even saw Gemma surreptitiously brushing her hair! She would never previously have done that in public. When she caught me looking at her, she unexpectedly smiled.

I smiled back as I spent a sensible scant twenty minutes practising my knots in the climbing rope, just in case the situation called for a quick taut-line hitch with a double fisherman up the other end.

Still, when we were finally ready to go, we were well and *truly* ready, and chomping at the bit to face the challenge. We stepped out of the tent.

Up the platform, I spotted the duplicate crew heading into the ziggurat. 'Come on, chaps – we're falling behind already.'

Troy grabbed the flaming torch.

'Wait a minute,' Guuuurk protested. 'We can't let the Man With No Brain carry the flaming torch! He'll incinerate us all!'

He reached to grab it, but Troy lifted it away. 'But *I* want to hold it. Look! I can hold it highest.'

'It doesn't have to be *high*.' Guuuurk rounded on Troy. 'Wherever it is, it's not going to get any *brighter*. Just like *you*.' He used this little moment of triumph to snatch the torch for himself.

'For heaven's sake!' Gemma grabbed it off him. 'It doesn't *matter* who holds the flaming torch.'

'Actually, it does,' I corrected, taking it gently out of her hand. 'If Troy *does* hold it too high, it could ignite the ceiling.'

I was suddenly drenched by the entire contents of a fire bucket.

'I thought I'd better put it out before we use it,' Troy explained, taking back the black, smouldering stick it had now become. 'Just to be on the safe side.'

I brushed off the excess water, to no great avail. 'Now I'll have to go back and change again!' I grumbled, but Gemma had ignored the event and was marching resolutely towards the gaping mouth of the edifice. We really had no choice but to follow in her lovely wake.

I felt the strange thrill of trepidation as we gingerly entered the jaws of the ziggurat. Immediately we were inside, the sound took on a deadened, claustrophobic feel, draining away our bravado. For a moment we stood at the top of the steps and stared down into the gloom. Of the duplicate crew, there was no sign.

'I believe,' Guuuurk broke the silence, 'that this might be a good moment to invoke the "No Claustrophobic Alien Ziggurat" clause in my contract—'

'*Or*,' Gemma raised her eyebrows, 'we could invoke the "Compulsory Martian Vivisection" clause . . .'

'Oh!' Guuuurk slapped his thigh. 'Let's not get bogged down in picayune legalese. We're all in this together, chaps.' He still didn't move.

Troy peered down the staircase, holding out the dead smoking twig in front of him. 'Can't see a darn thing down there. This torch is almost useless.'

'May I remind us all,' I said, 'if we don't beat the duplicates to the relic, we are literally dust. And they've got a head start.'

'That's not an advantage.' Gemma started boldly down the stairs. 'They'll encounter the traps first. They'll either neutralise them, or get snared. Either way, we'll easily catch up.'

'*Traps*? Nobody said anything to me about *traps*!' Guuuurk followed her closely, clearly feeling that proximity to Gemma might be his safest course. 'How are we all meant to *see* these bally *traps* without that flaming torch?'

'No problem.' Troy raced ahead, overtaking us all. 'I'll just pull down my corduroy shorts a smidge—'

'*What*? No!' Guuuurk yelped.

But the darkness below was suddenly chased away by a glowing incandescence emanating from Troy's posterior!

'Good heavens!' Gemma started. 'Are those sort of glow-worm buttocks you have there, Troy?'

'I had no idea Troy had a light-emitting bottom!' I exclaimed, partly in admiration, and partly in horror.

'There's lots about my bottom people don't know.' Troy smiled. 'This way!'

We carefully descended the slippery stone treads one by one.

'Actually,' Guuuurk whinged, 'there's precious little I don't know about Troy's bottom, after that year we spent sharing bunk beds. And, frankly, I'd rather forget most of it . . .'

I knew why he was burbling on like that. There was one thing on all our minds we didn't want to verbalise.

Traps.

What were these traps? And when would we find the first one?

Chapter Two

Outprint from Gargantua, the pocket Quanderdictoscribe.
Dateline: Sunday the 6th of January, 1952 00.59 hours

NEW BRIAN: The other group is
squabbling, as usual — they
can't seem to move two paces
without falling into some
contretemps or other! We've
stolen a march on them, and
entered the ziggurat first.
The air is slightly warm, but
surprisingly fresh. Hard to
believe it's been sealed for
many thousands of years.
We've been descending these
stone steps for four or five
minutes, now. Levelling off
into a short corridor. I can
see a tiny portal at the
end . . . I presume we're
supposed to enter it . . .
Oh! It's much bigger in

here! We now find ourselves in
a circular vault. Watch out!

NEW TROY: Woah!

NEW BRIAN: Gemma — take my hand. There's
a pit of some kind right in
the centre, leaving only a
narrow ledge running around
the perimeter! We'll have to
inch our way around, keeping
our backs to the wall . . .

[SOUND OF HUGE STONE GRATING]

NEW BRIAN: A heavy door just slid shut
behind us, along some sort of
greased channel carved into
the floor! No turning back
now!

[SOUND OF BOOTS SCRAPING AGAINST STONE]

NEW GEMMA: Brian! I'm scared.

NEW GUUUURK: Why is your subordinate sex
so decorative and frail?
Our females are ugly and
terrifying! As you will see
on the Day of the Glorious
Invasion, when you're
all dragged, chained and
screaming, into their tents!

NEW BRIAN: Pay no attention to him,
lambikins! Keep holding my
hand. I can see an exit on
the far side now.

NEW GUUUURK: Wait! If your Earth eyes weren't so feeble, you'd see some of the ledge stones ahead of us are hinged — they'll send us straight down into the pit!

NEW BRIAN: You may be an unpleasantly outspoken fellow, but bless your Martian low-light vision, you're right!

NEW GEMMA: Brian! I can hear something scurrying around down there in the pit!

[UNKNOWN SOUNDS, REMOTE]

NEW BRIAN: What is it?

NEW GEMMA: I can't tell! Whatever it is, I think it's heard us!

NEW TROY: I could lure it away by throwing it a piece of liver.

NEW BRIAN: Troy — remember what I told you before? Your liver has to stay . . .

NEW BRIAN/NEW TROY: (TOGETHER) . . . on the inside!

NEW TROY: Yes.

NEW BRIAN: OK, everybody, *nil desperandum*. Just put your feet exactly where Guuuurk's have been, like good King Wenceslas' page! All the way round — that's right . . .

371

[FURTHER UNKNOWN SOUNDS, SLIGHTLY LOUDER]

   NEW GEMMA: I can still hear those things
        scuttling down there . . .

   NEW BRIAN: Come on, everybody — *nil*
        desperandum!

  NEW GUUUURK: I think I can almost
        reach the handle . . .
        thank Phobos! If I had to
        listen to any more of that
        caterwauling, I'd throw
        myself into that (PROFANITY
        EXPUNGED) pit!

[SOUND OF STONE DOOR SLIDING OPEN, WITH DISTANT
     WATERFALL BEYOND]

   NEW BRIAN: This way, everyone — before
        this door closes too!

  NEW GUUUURK: I'm through!

   NEW TROY: And me!

   NEW BRIAN: Gem-gem?

   NEW GEMMA: Ow! I can't make it! I think
        I've turned my ankle! You'll
        have to leave me.

   NEW BRIAN: Nonsense! I'll just pick you
        up. Here!

   NEW GEMMA: Woo! Thank you, kind sir.
        (WHISPERED) I haven't turned
        my ankle at all! I just
        wanted you to hug me!

[SOUND OF STONE DOOR CLOSING]

```
NEW BRIAN:  You little minx! Come on — we
            can't let those old fogeys
            catch up!
            We are entering a vast—
```

            [SHEET ENDS]

Chapter Three

The Daybook of 'Jenkins' Jenkins, RQMS Royal Fusiliers (Empite Medal of Consticuous Gallantry and bar), Sunday the 6th of January, 1952

I arrive back at the lab in treble quick time, thanks to the Prof's rubber band car and an entire packet of fast-motion garibaldis. 'Course, there's a number of cats embedded in the radiator, but that's just the price of progress, I suppose.

I have meself a little chuckle thinking of them frozen in the headlights, going: 'Me? – *Ow!*' Ha ha. You've got to laugh, or you'd cry.

That's what I tells meself when I finds meself a few moments later lying at the bottom of the secret cellar service stairway with a broken leg.

Bad, too. It's bent over backwards.

I agonisingly fishes out the walkie from my back pocket and calls the Prof. 'Professor? Jenkins here, over.'

He shoots back with: '*You took your time, dammit! Are you down in the cellar yet?*'

'Yes, sir. But small problem in that department. The good news is: I've found the invisible shield. It was lying across the stairs. The bad news is: I lost it again when I tripped over it, fell down the steps and wound up at the bottom with a compound fracture of the lower tibia. It's rather painful, actually, sir. It's bent over at a bad angle. And I think I can see a piece of bone protruding through my trousers.'

'*Dammit, Jenkins – I'm relying on you.*'

'I'm very sorry, sir. Dragging myself along the floor as best I can, sir. Anything you could do that might alleviate the situation would be most appreciated.'

'*Alleviate the situation? I can't be in two places at once! Wait!*' He thinks for a moment. I wonders what's going through his head? Meanwhile I bites on my key fob and pushes the bone back as best I can. I'm almost blacking out as I hears him say: '*Yes – I can be in two places!*'

'How's that, sir?' I grunts through gritted teeth.

'*Years ago, I created a duplicate of myself for just such an emergency.*'

I tries to say 'Splendid news, sir,' but all I can manage is: 'Gnnnurrhuuurgunhuurnur!' as I shoves it right back in.

'*Did you hear what I said, Jenkins?*'

I ties a stair rod into a makeshift splint using my regimental tie. 'Yes, sir, splendid news. Where is this other you?'

'*He's in suspended animation, in a cupboard just down the corridor. It's marked* "Under No Circumstances Open This Cupboard!"'

'I see it, sir. Dragging myself over to it now, sir.'

'*Hurry up, man! We haven't got much time!*'

'Still dragging myself, sir . . .'

I hears him sigh, more than once.

'Still dragging . . .'

Dragging goes on for some time. As does the sighing.

'*Are you there yet?*'

'Yes, sir. It's right in front of me. This is the one, isn't it, sir?

"Do Not Open This Cupboard Under Any Circumstances!"'

I reaches up, unlocks it and manages to tug down the handle. The door springs open, and I'm face to face with a huge yellow-and-black striped buzzing winged monster insect, hovering menacing-like, staring at me with red-eyed fury and a sting on its arse like a Cossack's sabre.

Well, I seen some pretty big mosquitoes when we was liberating the Philippines, but this beauty knocks 'em all into a cocked hat.

'What's all that noise, Jenkins?'

'It's a giant psychopathic wasp, sir!'

'Don't let it out! Shut the door! Shut the door!'

'I'm trying, sir!' Believe me, I was, and all. 'Only the wasp don't want me to.'

I was putting my shoulder into it, but the bloomin' wasp was the size of Rocky Marciano. I pulled the stair rod out of my splint and started beating the blighter with it. He goes to sting me, and I manage to slam the door shut. The sting comes straight through the wood and misses my head by a whisker. I hammers the barb crooked, so the varmint can't pull free, and locks the door again.

'What's going on now?'

'Just putting my splint back on, sir.'

'Why on earth did you open the giant psychopathic wasp cupboard?'

'Because it said "Do Not Open This Cupboard Under Any Circumstances!" sir.'

'What idiot would open a cupboard that said that?'

'Begging your pardon, sir, but you told me to.'

'No, no! I said: open the cupboard marked: "Under No Circumstances Open This Cupboard!"'

'Ah! That would be the other cupboard, sir. Just dragging

myself over . . . Still dragging, sir . . . Still dragging . . .'

'*For goodness sake, can't you drag yourself any faster?*'

'Nearly there, sir. Nearly there.' I decide it's best to make some conversation. 'This other "you" I'm looking for, sir: have you in any way . . . "altered" him at all?'

'*Only slightly.*'

Oh dear.

'*I've given him ethics.*'

'But don't you always says that thing about ethics, sir. How's it go? "The pursuit of Scienticifal Truth, and that, is the only Ethical Poppy—"'

'*The pursuit of Scientific Truth is the only Ethical Boundary one ever needs; the rest is just poppycock.*'

'That's it! So what did you want to give him *ethics* for, if I may be so bold?

'*To weaken him. He has to be weaker than* me, *in case he should try to usurp me in some way. But he should be more than capable of helping you for the present.*'

'Very foresighted, sir. Ah! Here I am. "Under No Circumstances Open This Cupboard!" Do you really think I *should* open this cupboard, sir?'

'*Yes! Yes! We're wasting time!*'

'Fingers crossed then . . .' I says, hauls meself as upright as I can, and opens it.

And there he is! The Professor himself! Or rather his ringer. Covered all over in a big cellophane sheet, like dry cleaning.

I tears off the wrapper and looks at him for signs of life. Nothing. He's like a waxwork. Then, just as I'm peering close at his face, his eyes pop open! Just like he's just been having forty winks.

'Jenkins!' he says.

'Thank heavens, sir,' I says into the walkie. 'The duplicate Professor is all right.'

'*Duplicate?*' snaps the Prof in front of me. 'I'm the *real* Quanderhorn, you idiot! It's *that* charlatan who's the imposter!'

Chapter Four

After descending the stone stairway for a good few minutes, we found ourselves in a short corridor with a tiny portal at the end. Troy's buttocks disappeared into it, and we had to scramble after him to avoid being left in the dark.

It led to a large, round chamber. We narrowly avoided falling into a dark pit in the centre, and found ourselves balancing precariously on a four-inch ledge.

'That must be the aforementioned trap!' Guuuurk announced. 'I must say, I was expecting something a *little* more creatively fiendish.'

The door suddenly shut behind us.

'Yes,' Guuuurk nodded. 'More like that.'

I peered into the gloom. 'No sign of the other crew.'

'D'you think we beat them to it?' Troy asked, hopefully.

Gemma shook her head. 'Not yet: we'd have passed them.'

'What if they turned off down some other passageway?' I asked.

'It's a labyrinth, not a maze.'

'Meaning?'

'A maze has alternative paths, a labyrinth just one.'

379

'Looking on the bright side,' Guuuurk mused, 'perhaps they fell here, at the first hurdle, and their poor, broken bodies are rotting down there in the pit.'

This thought, rather callously, cheered us up enormously.

Gemma went on: 'Everybody keep facing the drop. We're going to have to inch our way around the rim. I imagine the egress is somewhere on the far wall.'

We began a slow and perilous shuffle along the ledge.

'Wait!' Guuuurk yelled. We halted, tottering. 'I can just about see something on the ledge ahead, with my Martian low-light vision!'

'You never told us you had low-light vision,' Troy protested.

'And you never told us you had an incandescent bottom!'

'Well, I wouldn't have needed an incandescent bottom if you'd told us about your low-light vision-ness.'

'And I wouldn't have needed my low-light vision if your glowing behind actually had a few more *lumens* to it.'

Gemma rolled her eyes. I stepped in – this was no time for squabbling. 'What is it you've spotted, Guuuurk?'

'Don't get your hopes up, but it looks for all the world . . . like a crisp, white fiver!' He recklessly turned and crabbed around to it, but as he stooped, the stone he was standing on suddenly tilted . . .

I cried 'Guuuurk! No!' but too late; he teetered backwards and fell straight into the void before I could reach him. I almost stumbled in after him, but just managed to steady myself in time, ricking my ankle rather painfully in the process.

'Oh no!' Troy wailed. 'Poor Guuuurk!'

Gemma craned over to peer into the abyss. I held her back. 'Don't look, Gemma. There's no point. We've lost him.'

'Yes.' She cast her eyes down. 'I know.' Did I actually see a tear on her cheek? 'He's . . . gone.'

Troy stared at the pit in disbelief. Gemma and I hung our heads.

'What are you *doing* up there!' Guuuurk chirped from the darkness. 'It's only a couple of feet *deep*! I'm fine.'

'What's down there?' Troy asked.

'Hard to see much, really. The floor's strewn with something soft and downy . . .'

But there came another noise, from the far end of the pit. A sort of scuttling.

Gemma and I exchanged looks. 'Guuuurk – get out of there,' she yelled urgently.

'Just a tick. I'm sure that crisp, white fiver is around some-where . . .'

And another burst of scuttling.

Guuuurk heard it this time. 'What's that? There's something down here!'

'Guuuurk – get out of there, *now*!'

I got out my rope and looked for something to tie a taut-line hitch to.

'Brian – it's two feet deep,' Gemma pointed out.

I mumbled an apology, and started winding the rope back up.

More scuttling now. Much more. Growing closer and closer . . .

'Something's coming!' Guuuurk's voice wailed in the dark. 'I can see its pitiless eyes glinting in the gloom!'

'Over here!' I shouted desperately leaning over as far as my throbbing ankle would allow. 'Take my hand!'

'Great Phobos!' There was a petrified pause. 'It's a *duck*!'

'A what?'

'It's a duck! It's a duck!' he screamed in complete terror, and started racing aimlessly round the pit below. We could track his progress from the loud quacking noise and flapping that followed him.

Gemma was horrified. '*A giant duck?*'

'Who said anything about a *giant* duck?' Guuuurk yelled. 'It's a normal-sized duck! It's after me! Get away! Get away!'

The quacking and scurrying and yells of terror reached manic proportions.

'I could lure it away by throwing a piece of liver,' Troy offered.

'Troy, remember what I told you before,' Gemma said gently. 'Your liver has to stay . . .'

And together they chorused: '. . . on the *inside*!'

The screaming and quacking continued in the background:

'It's a duck attack! It's a duck attack! Get away from me! No! No! It's going to spring!' and so on *ad taedium*.

'Why on earth,' I asked Gemma, 'would ancient aliens set a trap with a *duck*?'

She shrugged. 'It was a billion years ago. They had no way of knowing what would emerge as the dominant species. This is probably designed to ensnare creatures who evolved from worms.'

'For mercy's sake, will you two stop wittering on like a pair of idle hairdressers and get me away from this vicious monster!'

'Calm down, Guuuurk, it's just a *duck*.'

He stopped suddenly, panting. 'Oh yes. Just a duck. Of course. I don't know what came o—'

And then there was another quack.

'*There's two of them!*' He raced off again. 'Ducks! Ducks!'

'Shall I pull him out?' Troy asked.

'Two ducks! Double duck attack!'

'No, just ignore him,' Gemma said. 'Troy, can you reach that handle over there?'

'Yes,' he replied confidently. 'Yes. Absolutely. Absolutely.' There was an uncomfortable pause, breached only by Guuuurk's incessant pleas and the odd flurry of feathers. 'The – *what* was it?'

'The sticky-out thing that opens the door.'

'A *pair* of ducks! A small pack of vicious ducks!'

'You mean *this*?'

'That's it. Pull that down.'

The stone exit door slid open.

The light it shed was enough for Guuuurk to find the ledge and finally let us haul him back onto it. 'You saved those ducks in the nick of time,' he panted. 'One minute longer, and it would have been orange sauce overcoats for the evil little blighters!'

Troy had already slipped out through the portal towards the sound of cascading water, leaving us in near blackness. Gemma bundled Guuuurk out after him, then turned back to me. 'Brian – what are you waiting for?'

There was no escaping it any longer. I hung my head. 'Dash it all, Gemma! I didn't want to say in front of the others, but I seem to have twisted my ankle.'

'Don't worry, you'll manage—'

'No – it's bad. Very bad. I can't walk at all. Don't argue – you're just going to have to leave me behind.'

Chapter Five

Mission log. Flight number 001, Advanced Laboratory-Blasting Squadron ('The Lab Busters'), Wing Commander William 'Wee Willy Winkie' Watkins, Office Commanding. Dateline: Sunday the 6th of January, 1952 01.18 hours

This whole circus is dashed odd. Being ordered to bomb a target in one's own backyard rather goes against the grain. I'm assured it's in the national interest, but it still rankles. Still, ours is not to reason why.

Took off at 00.52, on the direct orders of the Old Bulldog himself, and on course to deliver payload at . . . 03.13 hours.

Wing consists of six B-29 Superfortresses, fully loaded with the old bunker-busting bangers, so they handle a tad on the reluctant side, even for a Yankee kite!

Off the record, the bloody pipers in the back are driving me bonkers! 'Ride of the Valkyries' played on those god-awful things is the ghastliest racket you could ever imagine.

Best not to upset the Jocks, though. They've been nipping at the old Highland giggle water since ten. Plus, they're all wearing kilts and none of them have their legs crossed. It's the stuff of nightmares, I can tell you.

At least the infernal din is taking my mind off things.

Chances are this whole business is nothing more than a dry run, and we'll get the recall codes any time now.

My eyes keep flitting to the incoming message light.

The bagpipes play on.

The light remains dead.

Chapter Six

The Daybook of 'Jenkins' Jenkins, RQMS Royal Fusiliers (confused), Sunday the 6th of January, 1952

This other Professor, he ain't such a bad type. He sorts out my leg in double quick time, injecting it with his quick-hardening plastic bone substitute. Then he sprays on his Experimental Insta-Skin. 'Course, me leg will be covered in fish scales from now on, but that's the price of progress, I s'pose.

While I'm walking about a bit, testing my weight on it, he's switched off the alarms and that, and taken a quick gander in the secret cellar bit. Never been in meself. Not without the black goggles and sound-deadening helmet. Never had no inclination to, neither. What with the noises what come out of there.

He emerges all ashen. 'What in the name of all that's holy has my maniac duplicate been up to? There are some places even science shouldn't venture.' he shudders. 'I see now I didn't create a mere duplicate: I created a dangerous monster!'

'Begging your pardon, but the Professor told me *you're* the duplicate Professor, Professor.'

'Of course he's saying *he's* the real Professor. He *lies*! I rather foolishly removed his ethics to make him more efficient!'

'So *he's* the duplicate?'

'Yes. He trapped me in suspended animation many, many years ago.'

Well, this gets my brain in a proper spin. It makes sense, doesn't it? Evil duplicate overpowers Original and locks him away like in *The Man in the Iron Mask*, starring Louis Hayward. On the other hand, this could be the evil duplicate trying to undermine the *real* Professor, like in *The Man in the Iron Mask*, starring Louis Hayward.

Whichever one he is, he's ranting away: 'I can't believe he's stored all this surplus time in these unstable conditions! It's insanity! The slightest tremor could trigger a cataclysmic extinction event!'

Well, that might be so. On the other hand, he might be the wrong Professor. I has to be sure, somehow. 'If you'll just excuse me for one minute . . .' I turns away and takes out the walkie. 'Professor!' I says, 'The Professor here says he's the real Professor.'

'*Of course he* thinks *he's the real Professor! It's the only way he could function.*'

The other one chimes in: 'Obviously, I programmed *that* one to think he'd programmed me to think I'd programmed him.'

I'm getting quite the headache now. And it's not from the fishy smell of my leg.

'*Look,*' the one on the walkie barks, '*there's no time to explain right now. Just shore up those defences, the pair of you. That cellar cannot be compromised. Understood?*'

'On that we do agree,' says the other one. 'I just pray we're not too late.'

Chapter Seven

Perhaps it was both disingenuous and foolish, but I was gripped by an overwhelming desire to witness Quanderhorn suffer his richly warranted come-uppance at first hand, and, as it were, in the flesh. The Germans have a word for it: *Bezirksschornstein-fegermeister*. Or is that the word for 'head chimney sweep'?*
No matter.

The brigand had terminated a clearly fractious walkie-talkie exchange, and was rabidly studying the printout from his transcribing machine, when suddenly he looked up and sniffed the air, like a predatory coyote. 'Is that you over there, Mr. O'Reilly?'

And even though I was a good fifteen feet away from him, and in deep shadow, he turned slowly and looked directly at me!

'Or should I say, Mr. *Cheeuuuurch*ill!' He slurred that distinguished nine- hundred-year-old appellation in such a way as to make it sound like a Rumanian gypsy's curse!

---

* Yes, it is.

I returned the favour. 'Indeed, it is I, Qu*wwaaaaaa*nderhorn!'

'Did you really think that pathetic leprechaun disguise would fox me for one moment?'

'What gave me away?'

'The smell of herring. You're the only person I've ever treated with the Experimental Insta-Skin.'

'And I curse that Mephistophelian day I heedlessly allowed you to cause my testicles to forever shine like a stickleback. Better I had died from the shrapnel wound.'

'If you're trying to stop me, you're too late, you dipsomaniac has-been.' He held up the printout with something approaching triumph in his manner. 'In just a few short minutes, my team will be at the heart of the ziggurat, and the powerful relic therein will be in my hands!'

'Much good it will do you, you maniacal Bedlamite!' I speared the end of a fresh *Romeo y Julietta* with a match, ignited it and inhaled, to deliver the delicious *coup de grace*. 'At this very moment, a crack squadron of bagpiping bombers is *en route* to reduce your disreputable monster factory to ashes!'

Well, that stopped the fellow in his tracks!

But I had scant opportunity to relish my victory. I expected him to be angry, to rant and curse; perhaps even throw himself on the ground and pound the floor with his fists, like the gigantic, thwarted toddler I took him to be.

Instead he seemed to age ten years before my eyes, and something in the sinking of his shoulders chilled me to my very soul.

'Prime Minister,' he croaked with sudden deference, a look of genuine fear flooding his features. 'There's something you really have to know . . .'

Chapter Eight

Outprint from Gargantua, the pocket Quanderdictoscribe.
Dateline: Sunday the 6th of January, 1952 01.24 hours

```
           NEW BRIAN:   Well, we got through the
                        Mirror Maze of Lightning
                        Death in no time at all! I
                        thought the Waterfall of Glue
                        was simple, but this was
                        really easy.
           NEW GUUUURK: The Collapsing Stairway of
                        Strangling Vines was so
                        elementary, it wouldn't even
                        have duped a Venusian carpet
                        salesman.* It's an insult
```

---

* There are three species of Venusians: Empapaths, Cheatopaths and Aggropaths, and only Empapaths are allowed to become salesmen, in order to ensure that customers are not ripped off or beaten up. Unfortunately, an unscrupulous Cheatopath can prey on the generosity of the Empapath salesman, and persuade the unfortunate devil not only to hand over the product for nothing, but a large portion of his salary to boot. The Aggropaths simply thrash them soundly to the same effect. It's no coincidence that carpet sales on Venus are the lowest in the Solar System.

to my superior Martian
intelligence.

NEW TROY: The Corridor of Huge,
Dangerously Swinging Weights
was great! Can we go back
there?

NEW BRIAN: (CHUCKLE) All in good time,
Troy. And they'll have to
come up with worse things
than armies of poisonous
scarabs flooding out of the
walls if they're going to
stop us getting to the
centre.

NEW GEMMA: Silly old aliens not as
clever as my Bri-Bri.

NEW TROY: Hey! Is this another of those
sticky-out thingies?

NEW BRIAN: A handle! Yes. Well done,
Troy — you're learning. Let's
go!

[SOUND OF DOOR SLIDING OPEN, THEN CLOSED]

NEW TROY: I hope there are big spikes
in this one! Spikes are
great!

[SOUND OF ROARING FLAMES]

NEW BRIAN: I think we're on the final—

[SHEET ENDS]

Chapter Nine

From the journal of Brian Nylon, 6th January, 1952 – [cont'd]

'Those huge dangerously swinging weights nearly took my testicles off!' Guuuurk wailed. 'All eleven of them!'

'Troy,' Gemma grunted breathlessly, 'you can turn off your bottom now. It's light enough in here.'

'I can't . . . really . . . talk at the . . . moment,' Troy rasped. 'I've got strangling vines round my . . . neck.' He began recklessly hacking at them with his Bowie knife.

Gemma turned her face to me. 'And I absolutely refuse to carry you any further, Brian.'

'I'm afraid you'll have to,' I apologised. 'My trousers are still stuck together from the Waterfall of Glue.'

She set me down quite brusquely anyway. 'You'll just have to hop.'

Things had not been going quite so well between the two of us. She seemed to become less fond of me the further she carried me. I don't know why. Well, I do know why – I really was the most hopeless article imaginable.

However, on the positive side, I discovered that, since being savagely bitten by the army of poisonous scarabs that poured out of the wall, my ankle had gone completely dead, and it had no problem holding my weight again.

I turned to assess this latest challenge we'd wandered into, and nearly jumped out of my skin.

I was face to face with my duplicate!

The ziggurat had clearly taken a toll on the wretched creature – instead of the handsome dashing hero I'd seen before, he had been reduced to a ragged, gawping, dishevelled wreck! Weak character of me, I know, but I admit to experiencing a momentary surge of triumph, to see him reduced to this beaten bewildered scarecrow.

But as I turned further, I could see several more of the pathetic soul. In fact, there were hordes of him in every direction . . .

'We're in a Mirror Maze,' Gemma noted, somewhat deflating my cruel delight.

Reflections of ourselves stretched out wherever we looked, mimicking our movements in unison like some crazy dance troupe. It was almost impossible to see where, if anywhere, was the path forwards. I made to take an exploratory hop . . .

'Nobody move!' Gemma ordered. 'There's some sort of inscription etched on this mirror here.' She used the sleeve of her cardigan to wipe the mirror closest to her, where a patch of condensation had misted its surface, revealing various pictoglyphs.

'Why do all aliens seem to use hieroglyphics?' I wondered aloud.

'Everything's a hieroglyphic if you don't understand the language,' Gemma explained. 'Guuuurk?'

'Why always ask me?' he complained. 'Haven't a clue.'

Gemma scrutinised the etching carefully. 'Well, this is clearly a lightning bolt.'

'Oh,' Guuuurk smiled sarcastically, 'that sounds inviting.'

'And below it, here . . . this looks like a route through the

Mirror Maze. We have to head forwards and take the first right—'

And *ZZZKKKKOWWWWCRK*!

A jagged blue bolt of lightning sliced through the air without warning.

Gemma, Troy and I quite easily rocked out of its path, but poor old Guuuurk barely escaped being sliced in half!

'Sorry, what did you say?' Troy asked Gemma. 'I was distracted by that indoor lightning bolt.'

'Oh, you mean the one that nearly bisected me?' Guuuurk raised himself from the floor.

'What was that you said about the route through?' I asked Gemma.

'She said,' Guuuurk condescended, 'head forwards and take the first right—'

ZZZKKKKOWWWWCRK!

Another bolt ricocheted around the mirrors, leaving Guuuurk's hair smouldering slightly.

'Wow!' Troy enthused. 'I thought it never struck in the same place twice.'

'Wait! Nobody say anything else!' Guuuurk dabbed at his singed hair with his hand. 'It seems to have some sort of verbal trigger.'

'So,' Troy mused, 'you're saying that a special *word* makes it happen. Right?'

ZZZKKKKOWWWWCRK!

Guuuurk nodded. 'Right.'

ZZZKKKKOWWWWCRK!

This last bolt actually sliced the end off the cigarette in Guuuurk's holder. He narrowed half his eyes and motioned for us to be quiet. 'Shut up! *Shut up!* Yes. I see it now. Troy, you understand what word you mustn't say?'

'No.'

'Well, obviously I can't *say* the word, or I'll set it off again.'

'Oh yeah, you're right.'

ZZZKKKKOWWWWCRK!

Gemma and I had resignedly ducked before the bolt had issued this time.

'Ow!' Guuuurk yelled, beating out the flames on his blue spotted silk pocket handkerchief. 'How does it know where I *am*?'

I decided to bring some sanity to the proceedings. 'Troy – as long as nobody says it again, we'll be all—'

'Ah-ah!' Gemma warned. 'Careful.'

'Sorry!'

Troy was still baffled. 'So – *what's* this word we mustn't we say?'

'The word,' Guuuurk said carefully, 'is R-I-G-H-T.'

ZZZKKKKOWWWWCRK!

'For the love of sand!' Guuuurk frantically doused the collar of his protective suit. 'The wretched thing can *spell*!'

'But I can't,' Troy pointed out. 'I still don't know the word.'

Guuuurk pulled out a scrap of paper. 'Anybody got a pencil?'

I gave him mine.

'What are you doing?' Troy asked.

'I would have thought it was obvious even to someone of your level of cognitive inanity,' he drawled. 'Since I can't *say* it, I'm going to write—'

ZZZKKKKOWWWWCRK!

'*Ow!* That's not even spelled the same!' He scribbled frantically before the flaming pencil burnt away completely, and handed the note to Troy. 'There! This is it – see now?'

Troy studied the scrap of paper for some considerable time,

concentrating as hard as I'd ever seen him. 'Yes,' he nodded. 'Yes. Yes.'

'You see what the word is?' Guuuurk twinkled.

'Not really. It's very long.' His lips tried to form the letters one by one. 'Rrrigggiitee? Rrrrigghuhurtt? Arruggitta?'

'It's *Right!* The word is *Right! Right! Right! Right!*'

ZZZKKKKOWWWWCRK!

ZZZKKKKOWWWWCRK!

ZZZKKKKOWWWWCRK!

ZZZKKKKOWWWWCRK!

ZZZKKKKOWWWWCRK!

Multiple bolts forked around the chamber like flights of deadly flaming arrows. They ricocheted back and forth through the gallery of mirrors, blasting them into clouds of glittering shards.

When we picked ourselves up off the floor and pulled out the tiny slivers of glass from our clothing, only one mirror was still standing intact.

'Well, my brilliant ploy worked rather superbly,' Guuuurk crowed. 'Now we can see our way clear to the exit.'

'Your . . . foot's actually burning like a log fire', I pointed out.

'Yes, I meant it to do that,' he lied casually, trying to pretend it wasn't hurting quite a lot.

'Here,' Troy offered, 'let me stamp you out.'

'Thank you very much!' Guuuurk winced, pretending it wasn't hurting even more as a size 14 boot smashed his toes repeatedly.

'We've wasted too much time already,' I warned. 'We need to move now.'

Guuuurk began limping towards the exit, Troy followed, and I hopped after them, realising after a moment that Gemma wasn't with us. I turned round to see where she was.

She was rooted to the spot, staring into the single remaining mirror.

Her ear was rotating . . .

Chapter Ten

So that's what I looked like.

And that's why I'd banished all mirrors from my bedroom.

I'd thought, at the time, it was merely to avoid vanity, which is a foolish waste of effort and energy. But the truth was I had simply been avoiding looking at myself. Because I didn't like seeing what I saw. It made me anxious, inadequate – unhappy, even. And feelings like that are best locked away, safe inside where they can be ignored. As long as I was fully wound, they'd stay there, and I'd be safe.

And yet, hadn't Brian said he thought I was beautiful? Of course the lovestruck always think the object of their desires is beautiful. Beautiful I wasn't! There, I'd finally acknowledged those feelings, and now that I had – somehow I realised they were completely irrational.

I looked over my features again, but more calmly this time. True, I wouldn't win the Miss World Contest – and frankly who would want to? – but the inventory wasn't too depressing.

My hair was thick and healthy enough. Eyes were a warm hazel colour and rather clear. Skin fairly free of blemishes.

Lips not exactly Rita Hayworth, but not Boris Karloff, either. I wasn't fat or thin, just normal really. Actually, I quite liked how I looked.

Of course the worries of inadequacy hadn't gone away, but they had been tempered by fact. I was, in truth, quite presentable. And that was good enough for me.

And if Brian wanted to say I'm beautiful to him – who was I to stop him?

I though he was rather handsome too, between you and me, *when* he stood up properly and stopped wittering on and forced a smile . . . There he was behind me now, with that lost puppy dog expression. What a useless lump! But quite a cutie, though, if you ignored the—

'Gemma! Please – come on!' he was urging.

'Good grief! We need to go!' I wound up my ear in a flash, grabbed his hand and we scooted off. In spite of the urgency and the peril we were in, just for a moment it felt to me as if we were a couple of schoolchildren happily running the three-legged race.

Chapter Eleven

The Daybook of 'Jenkins' Jenkins, RQMS Royal Fusiliers (very confused), Sunday the 6th of January, 1952

We're shoring up the cellar, as per instructions. 'Course, I already knows the so-called 'intruder' was only Brother Nylon inspecting the cellar for ancillary site safety purposes and allied management misconducts, but I carries on the charade anyways.

I've just finished stacking the last of the slow-motion gas cylinders, taunting the attack penguin into a bloodlust frenzy, and replacing the ball bearings with exploding kumquats from the Farm.

This Prof's not too pleased to see what I'm doing when he comes back from looking through the other Prof's latest notebook.

'Slow-motion gas? Killer attack penguins?' He dodges its lunge and goes to pop a kumquat in his mouth, but I stops him in time. *'Weaponised fruit?* And as if *that* weren't enough,' he smacks the notebook with the back of his hand, 'now he's trying to gain access to dangerous alien technology to retrieve a hopeless situation, using experimentally modified human replicas like himself! Is there no *end* to his god delusion? Is there no end to

his hubris? Is there no end to . . . my nose?'

The nose does seem to be rather crumbly at the end, now I looks. It's sort of . . . caving in, like a sandcastle when the tide takes it.

He feels the tip of his conk with his fingers. It shatters like a biscuit. There's a whole lot of tiny granules down his shirt front now. He looks down at them, sprinkled all over the place, and groans quietly: 'Nooooooo!'

'Don't worry about your nose, sir. Just brush the crumbs to the floor and I'll fetch the Ewbank.'

What's left of his face is ashen. 'Jenkins, this is a bitter blow – my corporeal form is clearly unstable. You realise what this means?' he keens. A tiny bit of his earlobes falls off at the bottom.

'Yes, sir. It means you're falling to pieces.' I don't add, 'If you could crumble into a neat pile, that would be most helpful.' Though it's true.

'It means *I'm* the duplicate, not him! It means that unethical, mad iteration *is* the real Quanderhorn after all.'

I can't help feeling disappointed, on account of I quite liked this version. I sighs. 'Well, at least we know where we are now, duplicate sir. He's the top copy, you're the carbon.'

'I'm deteriorating rapidly,' he rasps as his little finger crumbles to the floor. 'Regrettably, the duplication process itself must be fatally flawed. We have to warn him: he can't rely on those facsimiles.'

'Bit late for that, sir. They're well inside that ziggurat by now.'

'Then we'll have to warn him *before* he sends them in. Yesterday.' He holds up the notebook again. 'Where's this so-called "Future Phone" I—' He checks himself. '*He* invented?'

'There's an extension over here, sir. But there was only enough tempor-what's-i-um for one call, and we used it yesterday.'

He snorts a *ha*! '*Think*, man: this will *be* yesterday's call.'

'You may be a crumbling wreck of a duplicate, sir, but you still outranks me in the brains division.' I hands him the receiver and dials in 'Yesterday'.

It starts ringing at the other end.

'Jenkins,' the crumbly Prof hisses, 'this is critical – I may need you to prompt me from time to time, so it's *exactly* the same as yesterday. Clear?'

This Future Phone business makes my head fair spin, it does. It's always trouble, if you asks me. I leans in close to listen.

'*Hello*,' I hears me yesterday self answer.

'Quanderhorn here. I need to speak to Quanderhorn.'

I thinks back, and whispers to the crumbly Prof: 'First, you've got to tell him about the ziggurat, sir.'

He covers up the mouthpiece. 'That makes no sense. Why don't I go straight to the warning?'

'Dunno,' I shrugs, 'but that's what you did.'

And we both hear the Yesterday-Prof says to Yesterday-me: '*Tell him I'm out.*'

The carbon Prof yells: 'And I know he isn't out. I'm in the future, dammit!' He covers the mouthpiece again and turns to me. 'You're *sure* the dire warning didn't go first?'

'Definitely not, sir'

'*I'd better not be wasting my own time*,' comes from the other end. '*Hello?*'

'Listen, Quanderhorn, there isn't much time. The advanced technology in that Mercurian vessel has stirred a powerful alien artefact, a giant ziggurat, slumbering these many millennia under Piccadilly Circus.'

'*Oh, really?*'

'Anyone who penetrates the heart of its structure will

discover astonishing secrets beyond human understanding.'

'*I see. And why are you bothering to tell me this?*'

'To be honest, I don't have the faintest idea. I need to get to the point.'

'*Well, get to the point, then.*'

'Well, if you'd just stop interrupting me, I *would* get to the point—'

'*You're interrupting me!*'

'No – you're interrupting *me*. Just listen: I must give you this dire warning . . . whatever you do, don't . . .'

And that operator's voice. '*To continue this call, please deposit more temporium.*'

'. . . rely on the duplicate crew, because they're going to crumble . . . Hello?'

But the line's gone dead.

'Dammit!' He slams the phone down in such a fury, his hand snaps off with it.

We both stare at the hand on the floor as it trickles away like the grains in an hourglass.

'I've had it, Jenkins', he says quietly and he begins to sink slowly to knee height into a growing pile of dust. 'I don't have long now . . .'

I unfolds a sheet of newspaper and lays it on the ground. 'If you wouldn't mind just aiming yourself onto this, sir, it would make my job so much easier.'

But he's staring into the distance. 'It was all going to be so wonderful. Virginia and I had such plans. We would cure the sick, feed the starving . . . Where is she, by the way?'

'Um – Dr Whyte? She's, er . . . not been quite herself just recently . . .' is the best I can come up with. 'Rotting in a putrefying mass on the compost heap' seems too cruel.

He's down to the waist now. 'Sixty-six years in a cupboard,

403

and then this!' he manages to croak, as his torso collapses.

'I must say, sir, it's been a real pleasure working with you.' And it's true, even though he's ruining my newly swept floor. 'Sorry you have to leave us.'

Then, with just his head remaining atop a pyramid of flakes, he barely murmurs: 'I'm sorry, too, Jenkins – only the real Quanderhorn can save you all now . . .'

And he's gone.

Chapter Twelve

Mission log. Flight number 001, Advanced
Laboratory-Blasting Squadron ('The Lab Busters') Wing
Commander William 'Wee Willy Winkie' Watkins, Office
Commanding. Dateline: Sunday the 6th of January, 1952
02.03 hours

I've been *awfully* patient with the Scotsmen, but I'm afraid I finally snapped.

'Good God in *Heaven*! Can't you kilted bastards play anything else?'

There was the hideous baby-strangling strains of the bags deflating, followed by an ominous silence. Then the chief Jock stood up, took several steps towards me, creased his brow and rumbled: 'We *could* do a selection from *Showboat,* but Angus here's a wee bit iffy on "Can't Help Lovin' Dat Man".'

A bagpipe was hurled to the deck at the back, and an even deeper voice boomed: 'Only on the middle eight! D'ya want to *mak* somethin' of it?'

'It's no' a criticism, Angus,' the pipe major rationalised. 'It's down to the tonal range o' th' instrument—'

'Could we just calm down a bit,' I intervened, 'and perhaps you'd enjoy a little rest for a moment or two?'

But the piper wouldn't leave it. 'Are you sayin' ma "tonal range" is inadequate?' he challenged, real menace in the voice.

The pipe major squared up to him. 'Are *you* sayin' ma tessitural knowledge is inaccurate?'

'Aye, I'm sayin' it. Ye dinna ken wha' the deil ye's talkin' 'bout!'

'I'm takkin off m' pipe major hat, now this is jus' between us, mon tae mon.' He put up his fists. 'What's keepin' ye, Shirley Temple?'

'I'll no' sully m' knuckles on a scabby scunner frae Aberdeen. It'd be like punchin' a wee blind kitten.'

'Oh – a kitten, is it? Well, even a kitten could beat a hackit jessie frae Inveraray wi' a face like a scrot—'

'Why don't we all sit back down,' I soothed, trying with my free hand to cram the feather bonnet back on the pipe major's bullet-like head, 'and just have a nice cup of char . . .?' I suddenly realised that the message light had been flashing urgently for some seconds. I yelled 'Quiet!' and flicked the switch.

'*Come in, Lab Busters . . .*' It was unmistakably Old Bulldog himself! I felt myself come to attention, even though I was sitting down.

'Yes, sir, Prime Minister, sir.'

'*The urgency of the situation demands I speak to you directly. Do you acknowledge my commands?*'

'Yes, sir. Of course, sir.'

'*Now listen carefully: I'm making an alteration to your orders*'

Much as I ached to obey my *de facto* Commander-in-Chief, there was a complication. 'Sir, your standing orders were to ignore any deviation from the mission, no matter what efforts were made to the contrary.'

'*And now I'm changing that standing order.*'

I took a deep breath. 'Sir, I'm most *terribly* sorry, but I cannot disobey the standing order without your giving me the top secret termination phrase.'

'*Yes, you're right, I remember now. I rather cleverly devised a phrase that no one else would think to utter it in these circumstances.*'

'Understood, sir.'

'*Very well, open your sealed envelope now.*'

I nodded at the co-pilot and he dialled in the combination of the tactical security locker, and handed me the sealed envelope within.

I tore it open and scanned the code in dismay.

It read: 'Proceed with the bombing'.

'*Wing Commander, have you read it?*'

'Yes.'

'*I now say to you: Proceed with the bombing. Do you understand?*'

I didn't. 'Not entirely, sir.' I could feel my heart pounding under my shirt.

'*Proceed with the bombing. I couldn't be any clearer than that, could I?*'

My mouth was dry and I had difficulty speaking now. 'Are you saying "Proceed with the bombing," meaning I should proceed with the bombing? Or "Proceed with the bombing," meaning "don't proceed with the bombing"?'

'*I'm saying "Don't proceed with the bombing".*'

'But, sir – that's not the phrase.'

'*I know it's not the bloody phrase. The phrase is: Proceed with the bloody bombing.*'

'No, that's not the phrase, either, sir.'

'*All right, all right: Proceed with the bombing. Clear?*'

'I'm . . . sorry, sir. I'm still rather confused.'

'*I don't know how to make it clearer to you: Proceed with the bombing! Don't proceed with the bombing!*'

My head was spinning now. 'Sir, we're approaching the point of no recall. Bomber Command will automatically switch us to radio silence.'

'For the love of mercy, man, listen to what I'm saying: Proceed with the bombing! Proceed with the bombing! Proceed with the bombing!'

I gulped back the lump in my throat. The radio silence light above the cockpit blinked on. 'Acknowledged. Over and out, sir.'

I wasn't sure but I thought I caught the final faint words as the radio faded out. *'The idiots are proceeding with the bombing . . .'* But it was drowned out by the pipes striking up 'Old Man River'.

There was no turning back now.

I had my orders and, whatever my personal reservations, I intended to carry them out.

Chapter Thirteen

Outprint from Gargantua, the pocket Quanderdictoscribe.
Dateline: Sunday the 6th of January, 1952 02.12 hours

NEW BRIAN: We seem to have lost signal
for a few moments there.
To bring you up to date:
we negotiated the Riddling
Sphinx of the Living Flames
with consummate ease, and now
find ourselves in an immense,
echoing, airy chamber.
Clearly, this is the heart of
the ziggurat. The walls are
glowing with a gentle amber
phosphorescence of some kind
— it's magnificent! There are
fluted columns of gold and
other lustrous metals I've
never seen nor heard of, and
glimmering crystals embedded
in the vaulted ceiling—

NEW GEMMA: Look, Bri-Bri! Tell them about the—

NEW BRIAN: Yes, yes, I'm getting to it, darling. Please don't interrupt.

NEW GEMMA: Sorry, darling. Do forgive me.

NEW BRIAN: (CLEARS THROAT) As I was about to say: ahead of us is a wide flight of steps. We're mounting it now. It leads to an altar-like platform . . . Half a tick! The chamber's entrance is opening again behind us . . .

Chapter Fourteen

From the journal of Brian Nylon, 6th January, 1952 – [cont'd]

Bruised, singed, half-choked and exhausted, we staggered into the welcome coolness of a rather grand corridor with an enormous carved and gilded door at the far end.

Guuuurk was still moaning. 'Oh, the untrammelled ecstasy of answering riddles where flames shoot out of the floor every time you're wrong!'

'We weren't wrong *many* times,' Troy protested.

'We were wrong *all* the times! We didn't get one *right*!' Guuuurk exploded. 'Not even that one where it was *obviously* a penguin in a lift! Whatever possessed you to say *"a skunk on a trampoline"*? My co-respondent shoes are still smouldering!'

'Shall I stamp them out again?'

'*No!*' Guuuurk snapped. He was right at the end of his tether. We all were.

On the bright side, at least my trouser legs were no longer glued together. On the dark side, my trouser legs had been entirely burnt off. Along with my leg hair. Not to mention, the elastic in my pants had slightly melted. Gemma had offered me a safety pin, but it wasn't very effective in keeping them up.

I had to walk with my legs ludicrously far apart in order to maintain my dignity.

As we approached them, the palatial double doors swung open grandly, bathing us in a brilliant golden glow from the chamber beyond.

A thought suddenly struck me: could it be we were actually approaching the culmination of the quest? Did we dare to hope?

We stepped through the arch into an immense, echoing cathedral-like vault, and stood blinking in the unaccustomed light.

'Oh my goodness! We've made it! We've won!'

'Brian . . .' Gemma warned.

As my sight adjusted, I could see an immense staircase at the far end of the vault, and a group of figures just about to reach its top.

The duplicates had got here first!

'We've lost!' My face collapsed. 'They've beaten us fair and square.'

'There is no "fair and square".' Guuuurk shoved me aside roughly. 'Haven't I taught you shower *anything*? If we've lost fair and square, then we *cheat*!' And he and Troy raced off towards the prize.

I looked over to Gemma. She was following them. 'Well, what are you waiting for?' she barked over her shoulder. 'Pull up your knickers and run!'

Chapter Fifteen

NEW GEMMA: Brian! It's those dreadful
coarse people from outside!

NEW BRIAN: They'll never reach us in
time Just two more steps,
poppet . . .

[UNKNOWN SOUND]

NEW GEMMA: What's that peculiar ethereal
music? Where's it coming
from?

NEW BRIAN: Good heavens! An
astonishingly bright light
has just fired up right
above us, illuminating an
intricately carved plinth,
which is rising from the floor
. . . and displayed on top of
it is—

NEW TROY: *A dirty old bucket?*

413

Chapter Sixteen

From the journal of Brian Nylon, 6th January, 1952 – [cont'd]

Guuuurk and Troy had reached the steps, but my splay-footed jogging had left me seriously behind Gemma, who stopped and turned to urge me onwards. 'I think they've found it, whatever it is!'

'Why are we doing this?' I panted, 'We're honour-bound to enter the Obliteration Chamber.'

'No,' Gemma insisted. 'Pure rationality: who doesn't get the *relic* gets obliterated, and it isn't in their hands yet.'

We started up the vertiginous steps.

Guuuurk, already halfway up, yelled: 'No! Wait! Stop! Don't touch it!'

'Too late!' My *doppelgänger* (excuse the German!) did that annoying Robin Hood laugh again and nudged his Gemma. 'Look at them: the Losers' 800 yard relay! Truly pathetic. And why is the other me waddling like a *platypus*?'

'He isn't wearing any trousers!' she squealed, staring incredulously.

'The man's a downright pervert! Don't look at him, darling.'

'I can't help it! His legs are smoother than *mine*! He looks like Betty Grable—'

Guuuurk, almost at the top now, shrieked breathlessly: 'Keep your filthy hands off that bucket!'

'And what if I don't?' My duplicate reached out, hand teasingly hovering over the relic, but not quite touching it.

Guuuurk cried, rather desperately I thought, 'You realise it could be dangerous!'

Guuuurk's other shook his head. 'That's a scurrilous lie. As usual.'

The smile died on my other self's face and he drew back his hand. 'Actually, he could be right.'

Troy stepped up to the platform. 'But it's only a bucket!'

I still had at least twenty steps to go, and my calf muscles were cramping up like billy-o.

The other me smiled patronisingly at Troy. 'Only a bucket? Look at the symbols running round the dais: they can only mean one thing . . .'

'What's that, Brian?' his Gemma simpered.

Meanwhile, my Gemma had reached the others at the top and was peering intently at the inscriptions. 'It can't be! I've heard tales of it, but I never dreamt it was *real*.' She straightened, her eyes wide. 'It's the *Gaulus Tempus*.'

New Gemma looked at her with faux innocence. 'Which, translated for all us Latin duffers, means . . .?'

'Oh, for pity's sake,' Gemma snorted, 'you're *me*! You have a double first from Oxford!'

The other Gemma smiled with a superior air. 'There's nothing worse than a self-important clever clogs, is there, though?'

'Well, let me see . . . There's a self-denigrating, simpering man-worshipper?'

'I'm sure I don't know what you mean.'

'And I'm absolutely certain you do.'

I reached the platform, wheezing and holding up my pants.

My namesake ended the incipient catfight. 'It's the legendary *Gaulus Tempus*. Literally translated: the Bucket of . . . Chicken.'

We all stared at him.

'Chicken?' I echoed.

'Bucket of *Time*!' He was suddenly sweating a little. ' What did I say? I seem to be feeling rather peculiar—'

'We came through all that for a *bucket*?' girly Gemma pouted. 'Why?'

The other me seemed to have recovered somewhat. 'You scatterbrained lovely! It's no ordinary bucket: It holds time, and it's bottomless.'

Troy's duplicate frowned. 'But if there's no bottom, won't the time all fall out though it?

'Ha!' our Troy laughed. 'You're so stupid!'

'No, *you* are!'

'No, *you* are!'

'No, *you* are!'

'No, *you* are!'

'No, *you* are!'

'No, *you* are!'

'No, *you* are!'

Sensing victory, our Troy announced triumphantly: 'No, *you* really really really are!'

'I'm not.'

Troy was crestfallen. 'He's done it again!' he yelped. His brow creased. 'But he *is* right: if there's no bottom, the time *would* fall out through it.'

My duplicate explained: 'Not *literally* bottomless, Troy, *figuratively* barnacles.' He blinked and shook his head to clear it. '*Bottomless*. I'm getting a little confused.'

Both he and the *ersatz* Gemma were indeed looking distinctly peaky. 'I'm feeling a bit queer myself, darling,' she trilled, wiping her brow, 'but at least the *Gaulus Tempus* is ours.'

True enough. In a moment, the Bucket would be in their hands, and it would all be over for us.

Amazingly, inspiration struck.

I turned to our Guuuurk and raised my eyebrow meaningfully. 'Guuuurk, old chap,' I crooned, casually, 'this may be the time for you to show us all that delightful childhood game from your homeland . . .'

He looked baffled. 'What? Pin the Tendrils on the Blubber Beast?'

'No!' I smiled. 'The *other* game.' I squinted with one eye and pointed to it inconspicuously. Everyone stared at me strangely for some reason.

'What?' Guuuurk frowned. 'Hop Round the Snakes? 1-2-3 Stab?'

'No!'

'Children Skittles?'

'No, I mean . . .' and I hummed through my teeth, 'Mnnhun clurzee urszey.'

'*Martian Closey-eyesy*? Oh, no. Martian Closey-eyesy would be totally inappropriate at this moment.' A thought appeared to strike him. 'Just a minute, though – how foolish of us!' He peered at the relic. 'It's the final trap! Obviously this rusty old bucket isn't the true *Gaulus Tempus* at all. Clearly, it's that splendid golden thing right over there in the other direction!' He pointed to the far end of the chamber, and naturally we all turned to look, before we realised we'd been had!

We heard an odd clicking sound and all turned back to see Guuuurk with his hands in the air, frozen in the act of reaching for the relic.

Slowly, he stepped back, revealing his counterpart brandishing a rather fearsome-looking Ray Gun.

'Hands up, everybody, and keep absolutely still,' Copy-Brian warned, arms akimbo.

There was a blinding green flash and a deafening *zap*!

My duplicate's recording device was blasted off his shoulder, leaving only smouldering wires and a metallic stench.

'As your pathetic Earth "hero" says,' the alternate Guuuurk snarled, 'put your hands up.' He carefully edged his way over to the bucket, keeping his weapon trained on us. 'With this relic, the Glorious Martian Attack Force can turn the clock back to the last invasion – only *this* time, victory will be ours!'

'Great plan, Martian brother!' Guuuurk stepped forward again with seemingly genuine enthusiasm. 'I say, is that the Blast-O-Matic E-Z Kill DeLuxe? That's my favourite Ray Gun!'

'Get back in line, you nauseating *spuuung-deng-bankkerrtt*!'

I've no idea what it meant, but Guuuurk visibly stiffened and stepped back immediately.*

'Brian – do something!' replacement Gemma pleaded.

'Do what, darling?' other me replied. 'The Martian devil's beaten us fair and squirrel. *Square!*'

Out of the corner of my eye, I spotted Gemma surreptitiously sliding her hand towards the clasp of her duplicate's handbag, in which there would certainly be a compact mirror . . .

As I made to step forward to distract the mad Martian, there was another blast and the handbag blew to bits with a shriek from substitute Gemma, and a resigned sigh from the proper

---

* It means literally 'mushroom in the sandwich', a reference to a particularly virulent fungus which disguises itself as one of its more delicious and rather less deadly cousins. Once consumed, it immediately spores voluminously, causing its unfortunate host to expand rapidly and explode, usually before pudding is served. Besides spoiling many dinner parties, the fungus was also reputedly the method by which the legendary Empress Bazzzogg the Fairly Unpleasant secured so many successful 'divorce' settlements.

one. I noticed, with some horror, that the blast had scorched her hand. I began to feel real hatred for this ignoble alien fascist.

'It would be a serious mistake to think me a foolish posing popinjay, like that ridiculous purple quisling.' The rogue Guuuurk nodded towards his counterpart. 'Now – all of you get back down the steps,' he rasped, 'except, of course, for Imperial Spy X-One-Zero.'

Chapter Seventeen

Private Diary of Winston Leonard Spencer Churchill:
Sunday the 6th of January, 1952

Having explored every possible recourse with the Air Chief Marshal himself, I was compelled to conclude there was no earthly way to recall those deadly bombers.

I hastened back to the platform to find Quanderhorn cursing his stenographic machine, which seemed to have seized up like a motor car engine on a frosty morning.

'Dammit — they're not transmitting!' the reprobate spat. 'Something's gone terribly wrong in there. And now there's no way of finding out what.'

'I care little to what desperate reckless shenanigans you refer, Quanderhorn. The darkest hour is now irrevocably upon us.'

'What? You can't even reverse your own bombers, you septuagenarian incompetent?'

'Rant and rave as you wish, it will avail you nothing. I now have the solemn and unenviable duty to inform Her Majesty the Queen that, regrettably, the entire fabric of existence is about to come to an end in a little under seven minutes. And, for all it matters, Her Royal Highness the Princess Margaret might just as well go and marry Group Captain Townsend. Or, for that matter, Admiral Nelson, General Custer or Colonel bloody Mustard in the library with a candlestick, should she so desire!'

'It still may not come to that.'

'If by some fantastic contrivance it does not, and we somehow survive, be warned.' I fixed him with my fiercest stare. 'I intend to put an end to your infernal "Xperimentations" once and for all!' I slammed my Homburg onto my head and turned. 'I bid you farewell, Qu*wwaaaaaa*nderhorn!'

I left the scoundrel to his own devilish machinations, much good would they do him.

Much good would they do anyone, now.

Chapter Eighteen

The Rational Scientific Journal of Dr. Gemini Janussen,
Sunday 6th January 1952 (Again)

The evil Martian was looking directly at Brian, who seemed utterly poleaxed by the suggestion.

'I-I'm a spy for *Mars*?'

'Yes,' Guuuurk nodded with considerable enthusiasm. 'You're an honorary Martian, Brian.'

Brian's shoulders sank. 'I am? I . . . That can't be . . .'

'I recruited you, remember. I gave you the discounted membership rate of three shillings and sevenpence ha'penny . . .'

The other Guuuurk looked at him askance.

'Purely to cover administrative expenses . . . It's non-returnable, unfortunately.'

'That's simply not possible,' Brian protested. It couldn't be true, could it?

'Surely you remember the initiation ceremony?' Guuuurk insisted.

The other Martian took it up: 'You swore allegiance to the Sacred Bag of Dust, and we hung you up by hooks through your cheeks for forty-eight hours.'

'But I don't have any scars on my cheeks.'

Our Guuuurk raised all his eyebrows. 'Not *those* cheeks, I'm afraid.'

'I'm fairly sure I'd have remembered dangling from hooks skewering my buttocks for two whole days,' Brian protested with genuine indignation.

'Well, *I* remember it,' his duplicate raged. 'I still make a whistling sound when I sit down! What is *wrong* with you? You'll agree to do almost anything just to avoid making others feel uncomfortable, won't you?'

Well, that was Brian, all right! But would he really take it to such an extreme he'd betray his own *planet*?

'Right.' The bad Guuuurk waved the gun. 'Stay next to me, Agent X-One-Zero—'

Brian bunched his fists unconsciously by his side. '*Please* don't call me that,' he cautioned, coldly. I'd never seen him in such an icy fury.

The Martian was oblivious. 'The rest of you line up over there. I'm taking the bucket now. Agent X-One-Zero . . .'

Brian's knuckles turned white.

'. . . pick it up!'

Poor old Brian was clearly suffering. There was a battle raging inside him. A civil war between the man he was now, and the man he'd once been.

I suddenly felt such a pang of sympathy for him, I could scarcely breathe. I ached to tell him he didn't have to *be* that man any more. The past meant nothing. The things he'd done – they're not what Brian was any more. He was his own man now. A good man. Kind. And faithful. And a jolly decent sort. 'Don't be the man you *were*!' I wanted to shout. 'Be the man you're *becoming*!'

'X-One-Zero! I *said* pick that up!'

Brian thrust out his chest. '*No*,' he insisted firmly.

'No?' Bad Guuuurk repeated, incredulous.

'No.' Brian was quite calm and steady now. 'I'm not going to do it.'

'Then,' the Martian said, quite matter-of-factly, 'I shall have no option but to kill you.'

Brian met his gaze. 'There are worse things than death.'

The Martian levelled his gun.

Brian folded his arms. 'You can shoot me if you want, but I've had it up to the eyeballs with being special agent Cheaty Liar for every Tom, Dick or Bastard who asks me.'

His ersatz counterpart chided: 'Old chap, this isn't the moment.'

Brian stood firm. 'It's *never* the moment. There's never any time to explain. There's never any time to *think*. Enough's enough—'

I wanted to hug him so very much right then.

'I'm drawing a line in the sand,' he went on, and then his eyes caught something on the floor. He frowned. 'Actually – what *is* this sand? Where's it all come from?'

There were, indeed, loose crystals of what looked like silicon drifting over our feet.

'I don't want to make a fuss,' my floozy counterpart stammered, 'but my legs seem to be crumbling . . .' And they were!

'Darling.' The other Brian looked on, aghast. 'It's all right – take my . . .' He peered down his empty sleeve. 'Hang on a second: where *is* my hand?'

'Hey, look.' Duplicate Troy's voice came from ground level. 'I can play football with my head!' He started playing keepy-uppy with his own cranium, yelling, 'One – *ow*! Two – *ow*! Thr—' His head fragmented into a cloud of dust, followed momentarily by the rest of him.

'Wow!' Troy said. 'I wish I could do that.' He tried to bicycle kick his own head and fell over heavily, scattering the mound of his duplicate's remains.

The Ray Gun clattered to the floor next to him.

We all turned to the rogue Martian, or rather, what was left of him. He was already up to his waist in a pile of himself and dwindling rapidly.

'Yes!' he cried. 'I'm going! I'm going to Bzingador!' He gazed in wonder at a vision none of us could share. 'Ahhh! I am at the Great Black Door. It opens! Yes! I see the twelve-breasted serving wenches awaiting my commands. Lord Phobos himself is gliding forth to greet me – I see the bounteous tables of cream horns and mountainous pink blancmange glimmering in the firelight . . .' His eyes widened and his mouth sagged. 'What? No! They're scorning me! Something's opening beneath my feet! It's the Pit! It's the Pit! They're saying I'm a snivelling coward and repulsive turncoat!'

'Oh, hard *cheese*!' Guuuurk grimaced unconvincingly. 'They must have muddled you up with *me*!'

'I'm descending! I'm descending to the fiery pits of *Croydon*! Aarrrrghhhfgh!'

Then there was nothing left of him but a mound of grit, an empty safety suit and a pair of jackboots.

I found it surprisingly distressing to see my namesake and her paramour also sinking into heaps of their own detritus. Though it was rather touching that, even at this grimmest of moments, they had eyes only for each other.

'I loved you, Bri-Bri,' she whispered.

'And I you, Gem-Gem . . .' But she had wafted away.

To my surprise, at this terrible moment, he turned his decaying head to Brian. 'You! Come closer,' he rasped.

Brian looked at me, shrugged, then knelt beside his

dwindling form. 'What is it, old chap?'

'Closer still,' the moribund duplicate croaked.

Brian put his ear to the remains of the ruined mouth. The duplicate whispered something into it, which I couldn't hear, then he, too, was gone.

Brian was very still for a moment or two. Then he slowly stood.

'What did he tell you, Brian?'

But Brian said nothing, just shook his head.

Guuuurk broke the spell. 'Now, are we going to take this bucket, or are we going to stand around all day knee-deep in piles of old eczema?'

I reached up and grasped the relic's handle. It seemed to be slightly embedded in the stone plinth. 'I think I'm going to need some help!' I called. Then all of a sudden, it seemed to free itself. There was an ominous click.

'Gemma!' Brian yelled. 'You've triggered something.'

It *was* a trap after all!

I froze, unsure whether to move or stay where I was. There was a swishing noise, and too late I saw the arrow heading straight for me.

And then the world was upside down.

I hit the floor, and simultaneously heard the terrible thwack of the shaft embedding itself in flesh.

I looked up to see Brian swaying with the arrowhead buried deep in his chest.

Chapter Nineteen

The Daybook of 'Jenkins' Jenkins, RQMS Royal Fusiliers (forcibly retired), Sunday the 6th of January, 1952

Obviously, that fake Prof ain't going to shovel himself up, is he? I might eventually use him to grit the front steps – I reckon it's what he would have wanted. But first things first: I has to call the real Professor and warn him about this disintegrating duplicates business.

Just as I'm reaching for it, the walkie buzzes of its own accord, and it's Himself.

'Interesting development, Jenkins,' he says. Well, any conversation what starts off with *that* usually entails disinfectant and a mop. *'That Neanderthal Churchill has launched a squadron of lab-busting bombers, and they're headed your way.'*

Beggar me, that's going to need more than a mop, I thinks to myself.

And right on cue, the tocsin starts up, and that flippin' woman announces: *'Lab-Busting bomber squadron six minutes away.'*

'But what about your Alien Arctic Cat of Immense Power, sir? Have you got it yet?'

'I'm afraid we've completely lost communications with the

427

ziggurat. *But I have every confidence those excellent improved duplicates will get it to us in time.*'

'Ah. That's what I was wanting to tell you, sir,' I says. 'There ma-a-a-ay be a problem in that department.'

'*What sort of problem, man?*'

I looks at the sack of dust beside me. 'How can I put this, sir?'

'*We don't have time for you to search through your colourful but limited selection of similes, Jenkins. Put the other me on.*'

'That's just it, sir. He's crumbled.'

'*Crumbled?*'

'He's basically Harpic now.'

There's a long pause. '*I see.*'

'Chin up, sir. There's still the Originals to rely on!'

Even saying it, my heart sinks. Poor comrade Brother Nylon. Nice enough bloke, but he stands about as much chance as Rin Tin Tin in a Korean restaurant.

Chapter Twenty

The Rational Scientific Journal of Dr. Gemini Janussen,
Sunday 6th January 1952 (Again) – [cont'd]

Brian stared at the arrow buried in his chest in what looked like amused disbelief, then suddenly toppled onto his back, his shirt drenched in blood.

I scrambled over to him. 'Brian!' I cradled his head in my arms. 'Don't worry – you're going to be all right.'

'Of *course* he's not going to be all right' Troy exclaimed. 'He's got a dirty, great arrow in his chest, and he's gushing blood all over the— *Owwwwww*.' I horse-kicked him in the shins to shut him up.

Brian moaned and his eyelids fluttered.

'Can you hear me?' I coaxed. 'Stay with us.'

Troy whispered loudly: 'Nobody tell him he's dying.' He knelt down tenderly next to Brian, put a hand encouragingly on his shoulder and said: 'Brian, you're dying. *Damn*!'

'He's right, Gemma.' Brian smiled sadly, looking down at the awful wound. 'I'm afraid there's no happy ending to this one.'

I blinked back a tear. What good would lachrymosity do?

He met my eyes. 'Gemma, I have to know . . . If I'd ever mustered enough courage to ask . . . would you have married me?'

I smiled. 'In a heartbeat, my darling.'

Brian's voice was getting weaker. 'I can't feel my chest any more . . .'

'Well,' Guuuurk crooned, 'just a theory, but that *may* be because it's now crawling across the floor, spluttering . . .'

I glanced over. It was, indeed.

Of course – it was the bra!

Guuuurk peered warily at the stricken creature. 'The arrow's finally made it lose its grip! Look, there's not even a mark on your *actual* chest.'

Brian sat up groggily and looked down. 'The Living Bra! I'd forgotten I still had it on – it was so *comfortable*.'

'The poor thing's cowering behind the plinth, coughing up blood,' Guuuurk announced, tugging on the jackboots. 'I'll put it out of its misery.'

He chased over to it and started trying to stamp it to death. It snarled and snapped back at him in wounded fury.

'It's a resilient little devil! Naaaaaaaaaah! It's crawling up my leg!'

We ignored him. Brian struggled to his feet. 'Uhm, about that getting married business . . .'

'Ye-e-sss, well, of course I thought—'

'Yes. So did I.'

'It's not that—'

'No, no, no. Of course not.'

'It's worse than the duck! It's worse than the duck!'

'But under the circum—'

'Yes, yes, yes. You don't have to say anything.'

We both looked at each other. Had we meant it?

I smiled at him gently. 'We'll talk about it when we get out of here. We'll have all the time in the world.'

'It's on my *face*! Mah muhn mah fuuuumn!'

There was a tremendous clang as Troy hit Guuuurk in the face with a shovel. The bra fell off, stone dead.

Guuuurk was clutching his bloodied nose. 'You absolute *stinker*!' he snarled.

'You're welcome.' Troy picked up the bucket. 'Hadn't we better get this to Pops?'

As he raised the relic into the light, it seemed to glow, and that strange, ethereal polyphony resounded again.

The floor beneath us began to rumble and shake.

We staggered against each other. 'Hang on, everybody!' Brian yelled.

The plinth slid down into the staircase, and then the staircase rumbled and began to concertina and descend into itself.

When it came to rest, we found ourselves at ground level of the chamber, facing two great golden doors, hitherto obscured.

'It's the final test.' I fought not to show my frustration. 'We had better choose wisely.'

Chapter Twenty-One

From the journal of Brian Nylon, 6th January, 1952 – [cont'd]

'For the love of sand!' Guuuurk railed, dabbing his nose with his 'E. S.' monogrammed handkerchief. 'We're *never* going to get out of this hellhole!'

'Nonsense,' Gemma countered. 'All it takes is a little intelligence.'

'For the love of sand!' Guuuurk repeated. 'We're *never* going to get out of this hellhole!'

Suddenly, there was an ominous sequence of sounds – hatches opening – and all around the chamber great sluices started pouring forth tons of coal-black sand.

'I didn't mean I *literally* loved sand,' Guuuurk whined. 'If I'd said "I like peanuts" would we all now be inundated in a cascade of salty legumes?'

We studied the doors hurriedly. They seemed infuriatingly identical.

As we watched, there was a sizzling noise, and a white-hot arc carved symbols into each of them.

When the smoke cleared we could make out on the left a horizontal crescent, and on the right, a circle. 'The Moon and the Sun?' I offered.

'We have to choose quickly,' Gemma urged. 'Which of them is the way out?'

'Careful,' Guuuurk cautioned. 'I've heard a lot about these types of devilish two-door conundra. The wrong one probably leads to certain death.'

The sand was ankle-high now. This was the moment for leadership. I didn't hesitate. 'The Sun,' I said, stepping forward with calm conviction, 'obviously means "outside".'

I wrenched the great door open.

Giant towers of crockery crashed to the floor, in what was becoming a rather familiar motif. The tumbling and smashing went on for several minutes.

'That's not a sun, it's a plate!' Troy pointed out rather unnecessarily.

I looked at the others and simply screamed 'Why!'

'Because,' Guuuurk said, 'you're a confirmed nemesis to all baked earthenware?'

'And the other one's not a moon!' Gemma cried. 'It's a smiling mouth.' She pushed the door lightly with her finger, and it slid silently open.

There, grimly smiling before us on the Tube platform, was Professor Darius Quanderhorn.

Chapter Twenty-Two

From the journal of Brian Nylon, 6th January, 1952 –[cont'd]

Troy held up the relic. 'We got it, Pops! We got it!'

'Excellent. Don't concern yourselves with the idiot original crew. They'll doubtless be dead by now.'

'Actually,' I said, 'we *are* the idiot original crew. The duplicates have crumbled to dust.'

'As I said,' he went on without pause, 'don't concern yourselves with the idiot duplicate crew. They've probably crumbled to dust by now. We have to get that bucket to the lab immediately.' He busied himself wiring up a strange-looking heavily modified telephone booth.

'First, there are a few things we need to clear up—'

'There's no time to explain right now.'

I wasn't falling for that old chestnut this time. 'You already knew the Time Bucket was in the ziggurat, didn't you, Professor?'

'Yes, yes. If you *must* know.' He fired up his soldering iron. 'Six months ago, I located it using Gargantua, the subterranean X-ray surveying mole and potato planter. I realised it might be our only hope for the future if things went wrong. Now, why don't—'

I wasn't letting him off the hook. I held firm. 'But the problem was – how to trigger the ziggurat?'

'Yes!' he snapped, irritably. 'I realised only the presence of superior technology that doesn't currently exist on Earth would do it. Can't we do this later?'

Gemma stepped forward. 'Are you saying . . . you deliberately rigged the lift to send us to the Moon, and marooned us there, so we'd pilot the Mercurian vessel back to Earth?'

'Of course I did. No choice. Not even *Nylon* would have volunteered for that! And it worked! Well done everybody, but mostly—'

'Soooooooo—' Guuuurk menacingly selected a teal Sobranie from his musical cigarette case and screwed it violently into his holder. '—why did you try and blast us out of existence with the Giant Space Laser?'

A look I've never seen flitted across the Professor's face. Was it . . . could it be . . . *shame*? Confusion? Despair? It was impossible to read.

'There seriously is not time to explain right now,' he recovered. 'That maniac *Cheeuuuurchill* has launched a bomber squadron to take out the laboratory. We needn't go into detail, but if that cellar takes a bomb . . .'

Oh my Lord – the *cellar*? If those tanks down there were to suffer a hit – it didn't bear thinking about. 'The lab? But we'll never get anywhere near there in time.'

'Wrong.' The Professor smiled grimly. 'There is just one way . . .' He tapped the phone booth with his soldering iron.

Guuuurk dragged his hand across his face. 'No, Professor! Please tell me that thing isn't your notorious Not Entirely Tested Matter Transfuser Booth!'

Chapter Twenty-Three

The Daybook of 'Jenkins' Jenkins, RQMS Royal Fusiliers (don't care any more), Sunday the 6th of January, 1952

That tocsin's still blaring away. I don't even bother to switch it off.

I've jemmied open the Prof's locked desk drawer and liberated his bottle of twenty-year-old Napoleon Brandy. I must say it's pretty good stuff for a shortarse Frog to have knocked up. Slips down the gullet like wax off a floozy's hairpin. I'm all comfortable now, boots off, feet up on the radiator, third tumblerful to hand and a well-filled roll-up going – no point saving any snout for later now, is there?

I'm just getting all relaxed and totally plastered-like, when that tinny voice comes over the tannoy: '*Lab-Busting bomber squadron five minutes away.*'

I leans over to the speaker behind me and has a word. 'Don't take this the wrong way, sweet lips,' I breathes, all polite, 'but I always wondered what a striking woman like yourself – I assume you're striking, by your voice – statue-*esque*, I mean. That's what I've always pictured – classy, but with a generous chestillage. I always wondered what you *get* out of a job that's so bleeeeeding *depressing*? I mean – "Two minutes to the end of

436

the world" – "Five minutes to the bombing" – "Atomic blast in ten seconds" – don't you ever feel the urge to announce something – well, a bit more *cheerful*?'

She don't answer me, of course. Never does. I takes another long swig of the old Dutch courage. Dutch? Don't like 'em. Too much like the Belgians. Don't like 'em either . . . and don't start me off on the Luxemburgians . . .

Where was I?

Oh yes. 'I don't suppose,' I says to the loudspeaker, 'now that we *do* only have five – well, less than five minutes now – I don't suppose you'd consider – not a *complete* cod supper – but a short romantic interlude with a extinguished decorated war hero, such as oneself – who has the greatest of respect for ladies with enormous—'

'*Lab-Busting bomber squadron four minutes away,*' she cuts in.

'No? No, I *thought* not. No harm in asking, though.' I adds another dribble to the tumbler, looks at it, fills it up to the top. 'I bet if you *could* answer, though,' I says, 'you wouldn't turn me down, *would* you, luv?'

There's a crackle from the speaker.

'*Don't kid yourself, Jenkins, you unctuous little powder-monkey.*'

Blimey! Who rattled her cage?

'*Lab-Busting bomber squadron three minutes, forty-five seconds away,*' she says, and sarkily throws in: '*But on the bright side, the weather for it's looking marvellous!*'

Then, blow my pipes, if there isn't *another* alarum. This time it's that Not Entirely Tested Matter Transfusification Booth thingumabob in the corner. Ain't used that in a while, and with good reason. Last time it went off, I had to spend the whole day cleaning up an inside-out monkey.

Chapter Twenty-Four

Mission log. Flight number 001, Advanced Laboratory-Blasting Squadron ('The Lab Busters') Wing Commander William 'Wee Willy Winkie' Watkins, Officer Commanding. Dateline: Sunday the 6th of January, 1952 02.58 hours

It's a grim business. And I don't just mean bombing your own. I mean the pipers, currently murdering the score of *Show Boat*. That infernal instrument can only play nine notes, and none of them appeared to be in 'Only Make Believe'. Or, as they insisted on caterwauling, 'Ownlah Mak' Bellee'.

Suddenly, the target approach light flicked on, and I was finally able to yell: 'Shut up that filthy racket! We have visual on the Quanderhorn Lab.' I twisted to look through the canopy glass either side and hoisted my thumb to signal to the rest of the Wing.

One by one they peeled off into attack formation, opening the bomb bay doors as they slipped aside.

I sighed a fathomless sigh. No escaping it now: orders are orders. With my guts knotted like an amnesiac's handkerchief, I called out: 'All right, pipers, this is it: let's have the Wagner!'

I waited. There was only silence from the back of the plane.

I craned round.

The pipe major, despite having lost a tooth and gained a black eye, was looking rather coy. 'If it's all the same to you, sir, we'd prefer to segue into "Life Upon the Wicked Stage". Only, Angus here has been practising his fingerwork and—'

'This isn't a matinée at the [PROFANITY EXPUNGED] Victoria Palace! You'll do as you're ordered, you check-skirted drunkards! And while I'm at it, can one of you, just *one* of you, for once in your life introduce yourself to a pair of [PROFANITY EXPUNGED] *underpants*?'

There was a brooding silence behind me. I thought for one dreadful moment that I'd gone too far, and I'd wind up with an angry Scotsman's dirk in my back.

Then, mercifully, the pipes started up, and the strains of the 'Valkyries' swelled through the cabin.

I began the final descent . . .

Chapter Twenty-Five

From Troy's Big Bumper Drawing Book

[PICTURE OF A STICK MAN BEING SENT ALONG A PHONE
WIRE, LABELLED 'ME!']

Its grAte! IM beeing senDiD DoWn A Fone Winr. Its
DAngerus, pops sez. Hee Went lArst. Gerk Went Firs. He
sMells. He shoutiD O No no no no no no no no no no no
no no no no. I Don think he wontiD to go Firs. I wontiD
to go. Its grAte. Wil I bee verry long An thin When I gett
two the uther enD? I hop so. I CuD go up ChiMernees lik
fArther crisMus. Only bAkwooDs

Chapter Twenty-Six

Mooday the rth of Phobos, Martian Year 5972 Pink

*Secret Report to Martian Command, by Guuuurk 'the Valiant',
also called: 'Guuuurk the Dauntless' and 'Guuuurk the Dread-
naught'. Holder of the Imperial Star (23rd Class), the Imperial
Leaf (honorary only), and the Grand Jewel-Encrusted Imperial
Gold Wedge (temporarily in pawn shop) (all rescinded by Emper-
or pending embezzlement investigations).*

When the Professor explained exactly what was in the cellar,
you can imagine how overjoyed and delighted I was to discover we were on our way to the Most Dangerous Place in the
Universe.

In the unlikely event we were to succeed in preventing the
destruction of the entire fabric of reality, we would merely be
blown to pieces by vast barrages of enormous bombs.

A glorious death, in any eventuality.

Eager to seize the honour of this hideous fate for the glory
of Mars, I insisted, nay, *insisted*, on entering the Not Entirely
tested Matter Transfuser ahead of all the Terraneans, despite
their desperate pleading with me not to do so. Anyone who
knows me well would confirm that I laugh at Danger, and

guffaw at Death! I also chortle at Horror, chuckle at Torment and grin wryly at Hideous Dismemberment.

I stepped jauntily into the booth, and saluted jovially. 'Toodle pip!' I chirped. 'I'll see you all in Bzingador.'

Bzingador! The poor saps! Every Martian knows the sign on the Great Black Door reads: 'No Blubber Beasts, Scum Slugs or Earthlings'.

Still, I didn't mention that.

You have to keep the troops' spirits up, don't you?

Chapter Twenty-Seven

From the journal of Brian Nylon, 6th January, 1952 – [cont'd]

To decide who went through the machine first, Guuuurk insisted upon the Martian game of 'ABC – That's Definitely Not Me', but we had no time for his monkey business, and despite his ferocious remonstrations – or to be more accurate pathetic begging – we bundled him straight in.

I elected to go next.

This time, I found being disintegrated into my component atoms not quite so pleasant an experience. Rather like having every single bone in your body simultaneously smashed with a toffee hammer, then being shoved into a toothpaste tube which someone then stamps on with enormous hobnail boots.

I arrived in the assembling booth feeling nauseous and giddy, but I did at least seem to be in one piece.

I pushed the glass door to step out and nearly fell over Guuuurk, who, apparently unaware he'd already been transferred, was still protesting. 'No! No! I absolutely refuse to travel in this thing! You can't send a living person through a copper wire!'

Jenkins turned from concealing what looked like an empty bottle amongst the straw lining an empty rat's cage.

He over-enunciated, in that way dipsomaniacs do: 'Ah! Mr. Guuuurk! Are you all right?'

'*All right?* Look at *this*!' He swept his hand in the direction of his legs.

Jenkins blinked at them. 'Never fear, sir, we can soon put your trousers back on the right way.'

'It's not my trousers!' Guuuurk slapped his groin. 'Those are my *buttocks*! My entire lower half is on backwards!'

There was a sort of fizzing, popping sound, and Gemma arrived in the booth behind me.

'Are you all there?' I asked.

She patted herself down. 'I think so. That was . . . disturbing.'

'Get out of my way!' Guuuurk waved his hands wildly. 'I'm going back through that thing until my feet point the right way! How on earth can I tie my shoelaces when they're round the back? I shall have to wear my boudoir slip-ons *outside*, like a louche Italian roué!'

He marched off resolutely in completely the opposite direction, the back of his head hitting the wall with some force. 'Hang it all!' he wailed, rubbing his pate.

Troy popped into view, holding the bucket.

'Wow!' he grinned, wide-eyed.

'Don't tell me,' Gemma interjected. 'That was great.'

'Wasn't it, though?' Troy looked down at his body and frowned. 'Aww! I'm still exactly the same!'

'Oh, rub it in, why don't you?' Guuuurk staggered backwards and forwards, like a remote-controlled toy robot being operated by a small, tired child on Christmas morning after an accidental box of chocolate liqueurs. 'Blast! I'll *never* get the hang of this.'

'Shall I hit you in the face with a shovel again?' Troy offered with genuine concern.

'No! How is that supposed to help, for Phobos' *sake*?'

We were all silenced by the arrival of Quanderhorn himself, who was in no mood for levity.

'Jenkins, put your boots on, you idle man, and hand out the black goggles and sound-deadening helmets.'

'Sound-deadening helmets?' Gemma glanced at me.

'There may be . . .' Perhaps the others didn't notice Quanderhorn's almost imperceptible hesitation, but I did. '. . . temporal hallucinations down there, and we can't risk them disorienting you. Not at this critical moment.'

Temporal hallucinations indeed! He knew jolly well what *was* down there, and he knew jolly well they were real.

He slickly moved on: 'Troy, bring the *Gallus Tempus*. We have to get to the cellar and start bailing as soon as humanly possible. The rest of you will need to take over in turns. This way.'

He raised a section of carpet in the corner, wrenched open the trapdoor concealed beneath, and disappeared down some rough wooden steps, followed by Troy tugging a wildly tottering Guuuurk. 'How am I supposed to run down stairs when I can only see where I've *been*?' he wailed.

I made to follow, but Gemma caught my arm and in a confidential tone asked: 'You never said – what *was* it your duplicate told you back there?'

Now it was my turn to hesitate.

'He told me,' I replied honestly, but not quite fully, 'where I could find all the answers I sought. The answers to everything.'

'*Lab-Busting bomber squadron ninety seconds away.*'

'Not that it will matter if we all get blown to smithereens first.'

There was a scream and a clattering noise below us, and Guuuurk yelled: 'Who left that *beastly* invisible shield there?'

445

We descended breathlessly through the gloom towards the faint blue glow from the cavern at the base.

By the time we arrived in the cellar, a begoggled Troy was already jamming the helmet and specs onto the protesting Martian. I gratefully accepted my own from Jenkins – I had no desire to repeat the mind-warping experience that close proximity to the time tanks had induced the last time I'd been in there.

'*Bombers three minutes away.*' The metallic voice paused, and in a new tone announced: '*You're not getting out of this one, Professor. I'm handing in my resignation and leaving the building.*'

'You can't leave the building, Delores!' Quanderhorn yelled as we all lurched into the frightful chamber itself. 'You're completely synthetic.'

There was a horrible, crackling pause. '*Now you tell me!*'

The goggles didn't exactly black everything out – I could easily perceive the others and the outlines of the vast storage tanks. In the helmet there was mercifully no sound from those dread phantasms, but Quanderhorn's voice came over loud and clear.

'Troy, take the bucket over to that tank, and up the access ladder.' I made out the blurred outline of the Professor as he grabbed a sturdy lever. 'When I open it up, you'll have to start bailing the time into the bucket for all you're worth.'

'Do you know?' Guuuurk was staring down at his front. 'I'd never realised my bottom was so extraordinarily dashed attractive! It's usually round the back, you see.'

'I'm on it, Pops!' Troy shouted, shimmying lithely up the ladder.

He reached the top with astonishing speed, and I began to believe there could really be a chance we might, just *might* survive this.

Then the first bomb struck.

Although we didn't technically *hear* it, it felt like we did, and the ground shook mightily under our feet.

'Well, I'm luckier than you chaps!' Guuuurk announced rather bitterly. 'If I bend forward, I can now literally kiss my arse goodbye.'

A second, stronger tremor.

Cracks networked across the ceiling, and chunks of limestone and chalk dust started showering down on us.

Gemma slipped her hand into mine. Even though the circumstances were dire, I still felt that amazing electric *frisson* at the touch of it. I squeezed it back gently.

Then another, more violent blast.

Then another.

They were coming every few seconds now. Each one closer than the last, each one bringing bigger chunks crashing all around.

Troy yelled: 'Pops! What are you waiting for? Pull the switch!'

The Professor's hand was frozen on the lever. His whole body was shaking, shucking off clouds of chalk dust. Was I going insane, or was he actually laughing?

'*What the devil is so funny, Quanderhorn?*' I screamed over the deafening avalanche.

'To think, that I, of all people,' he grinned bizarrely, 'should finally run out of . . .

7

Time

Everything is determined, the beginning as well as the end, by forces over which we have no control. It is determined for the insect, as well as for the star. Human beings, vegetables, or cosmic dust, we all dance to a mysterious tune, intoned in the distance by an invisible piper.

Seneca, *Natural Questions*

Chapter One

Note from Dr. Virginia Whyte to Brian. December 31st, 1952 — Iteration 65

Dearest B,

I know this may sound the most appalling cliché, but these really will be the last words I shall ever write.

Last night, I finally worked up the gumption to visit the cellar. As you know, Darius guards the access like Cerberus himself, but after some surreptitious nocturnal snooping, I found there is, indeed, a secret entrance.

No. I shan't tell you how to find it — you must never, ever go down there.

You would never be the same again.

Can Q'horn have any notion what he's done? The casual, unspeakable horror of it?

The lives unlived! The destinies unfulfilled!

I cannot stand by and let this continue. What I must do to myself is abominable. But I fear it's the only way I can make myself strong enough to literally beat the clock. To stop the man I was meant to love.

This ends tonight.

To slay a monster I must, myself, become a monster.

Forgive me, Brian. If you could have seen them, you'd understand.

The children.

The poor, beautiful children I was meant to have with Darius. Who never got to be. In that life we should have had together.

Your dear friend,

V.

Appendix One

Transcription of transmission from Advanced Lunar Station Q, translated by Gargantua: the Linguaphonic Quanderlator (Estimated Earth date: Saturday 5th January, 1952 – iteration 66)

```
TEE-POL:  Hello? Hello? Is there any
          [PROFANITY EXPUNGED]there?
POL-TEE:  This place is a [PROFANITY
          EXPUNGED] hole. Can only have
          been built by those Tellurian
          bastards.
TEE-POL:  Shut your fetid crackhole!
          I'm trying to send a message,
          here!
POL-TEE:  400 years we spent repairing
          that bastard ship! Finally
          get it working, go out
          for ten minutes to forage
          supplies, some [PARTICULARLY
          LARGE SEXUAL ORGAN]'s nicked
          it!*
```

* Presumably, this is Mercurian years, which would be approximately 70 Earth years.

TEE-POL: I said I'm *trying* to send a
distress message. To *save*
our *lives*. If that's all
[PROFANITY EXPUNGED] right
with you, your 'majesty'.

POL-TEE: [PROFANITY EXPUNGED] you and
[PROFANITY EXPUNGED] your
[PROFANITY EXPUNGED] message

TEE-POL: Do you want to do it? Do you
want to send the [PROFANITY
EXPUNGED] message?

POL-TEE: What am I? Head of
Interplanetary Diplomacy all
of a sudden?

TEE-POL: Well, not 'all of a sudden'
exactly, sputum brain —
it's the third badge on
your [PROFANITY EXPUNGED]
sleeve. Look, it says right
there: 'Mercurian [PROFANITY
EXPUNGED] Diplomatic Corps.'

[SILENCE]

POL-TEE: Well they'd never let *you*
in, would they? You've got
no [PROFANITY EXPUNGED]
diplomacy at all.

TEE-POL: I can be [PROFANITY EXPUNGED]
diplomatic. Ask any
[PROFANITY EXPUNGED] alien
bastard.

POL-TEE: What a load of [REPRODUCTIVE BODY PARTS]! Remember your interview? You shat in the face of the Venusian ambassador.

TEE-POL: For the [PROFANITY EXPUNGED] thousandth time - I thought that was the official *greeting*!

POL-TEE: Oh, just forget this. The Tellurians aren't going to rescue us. Let's just grab supplies and find another ship to fix.

TEE-POL: Yes, then after we've spent another 400 years repairing it, you can forget to lock that one, too!

POL-TEE: Oh, I'm in charge of locking the [PROFANITY EXPUNGED] ship now, am I?

TEE-POL: What d'you think *that* badge is for? A rocket ship with a lock next to it - Put a Chain Round My [ERECT MALE SEXUAL ORGAN]?

POL-TEE: Well, you do *have* a . . .

TEE-POL: That's nothing to [PROFANITY EXPUNGED] do with it! Just snag what you can and let's get out of here.

POL-TEE: Hang on, there's a bath here. I haven't had a bath in centuries.

TEE-POL: Really? That's not a big secret to me. Or anyone within nasal range.

[SOUND OF RUNNING WATER]

TEE-POL: What the [PROFANITY EXPUNGED] are you *doing*?

POL-TEE: Have they got any soap, the dirty mother-[PROFANITY EXPUNGED]? Here — this packet's got a picture of a bath on it. Must be bubble bath?

TEE-POL: Seriously? You're seriously going to have a bath?

[RIPPING OPEN PACKET]

POL-TEE: Oh. They look like bath bombs. [SNIFF] Smell a bit [PROFANITY EXPUNGED] porky.

TEE-POL: Just [PROFANITY EXPUNGED] get on with it. [SPLASH] [PAUSE]

[MUCH GRUNTING, SNORTING AND SPLASHING]

POL-TEE: Oh crap.

TEE-POL: What the [PROFANITY EXPUNGED] have you done now?

> POL-TEE: There's hundreds of the
> bastards! They're stampeding.

> TEE-POL: What *are* they? What *are* they?

> POL-TEE: It's a [PROFANITY EXPUNGED]
> Tellurian trap, the evil
> scum! I told you we should
> have blasted the planet to
> smithereens.

[LASER FIRE. HIDEOUS SQUEALING AND BLOOD-SPLATTERING
BLAST]

> TEE-POL: Stop shooting you dozy
> [PROFANITY EXPUNGED]! You'll
> breach the airlo—

[METAL BLASTED. SLOW SOUND OF AIR ESCAPING]

> POL-TEE: Look out — it's going to bl—

> TEE-POL: [PROFANITY EXPUNGED]

[GARAGE DOOR EXPLODES, DEBRIS SUCKED OUT ONTO VOID]

> TEE-POL/POL-TEE: Oh, fuuuuuuuuuuu—!!!

[RECORDING ENDS]

Appendix Two

Typewritten note. Author: Unknown. Date: Unknown, but almost certainly from this iteration of 1952

```
MY dear professor QuandherhOrn,
just a kind note, to give you ample warning: I'm
freee, and Im coming for you . Vengeance will
indeed be midne. Not just for me, but for all of
us. Put your affairs in order and prepare to die,
your Friend,
```

And in a scrawled, almost illegible hand:

Edmond Dantès